THE OATHBEARER
A PROPHECY OF FLAME

20250823

ISBN: 978-1-0696985-1-3

www.harwoodjones.com

Contents

CHAPTER I: STONE AND SEA

Once, I fought for the king.

Mstislav, his black beard streaked with salt, his eyes sharp and cold as an axe edge. A king not by birthright, nor by the love of his people, but because no man stood long against him. You did not follow Mstislav out of love. You followed because you had sworn, because an oath bound tighter than chains, and because breaking it meant death — and shame deeper than death could ever reach.

They called him the Grey Hand, for behind him lay ash and ruin. They said it as they spat, as they cursed him, as they died. Mstislav conquered the broken isles as the sea conquers the shore — by hunger, by patience, by never turning back. And when hunger failed, he brought fire; when patience wore thin, he let the cold of indifference do its work; when men thought the wind might bring rescue, it carried betrayal instead.

I was no lord's son. I came from Stone Bay, a small town on High Mound in the Outer Isles — a cold, harsh place of stone and salt. Mstislav came from the sea like a storm — with men, with fire, with ruin — and no one stood against him. He killed my father and my uncle for refusing to kneel. I bowed. I had nothing but my blade, my back, and a name no one had yet heard. I gave them to Mstislav, and he used them well. I was a stone in his wall, a plank in his ship. I learned to kill, and I killed clean.

Our ships went where he pointed. Low in the water, black-sailed, heavy with oars and men who had nothing left but their lives. The sea lashed our faces, the spray like cold needles. The straits were narrow and dark. We came with fire and steel, and left silence behind. I heard the cries, the cracking of beams, the hush that falls when there is nothing left to burn.

The clans — proud, stubborn, each man a king of his own blackened hall, each thinking himself safe behind rotted walls and broken pacts. But Mstislav saw what they did not: the cracks. And he waited for them to widen. He made his wars as the wind makes the dunes shift — slow at first, then sudden, then ruin.

One by one the chieftains fell. Their warriors fought, bled; the earth drank deep. And we fought, bled, and died as well. But in the end, the isles were taken. Mstislav killed those who would not kneel, and some who did. He took not just to conquer, but to keep. We salted their fields, pulled down their stones, and left only ruin where defiance had stood.

At last, after twenty years of bloodshed, there was only Sava Mirov — lord of the jagged isle they called Wreck Rock, where the sea breaks ships as easy as twigs. A crown of cliffs rising from a sea that hated all men. The gates were of iron and stone, cold as the hearts within. His kin matched him in stubbornness — men and women who fought storm, sword, and hunger itself, who chose death over shame. When our black sails came, oars beating the sea to foam, they threw us back with fire and stone.

Twice Mstislav tried to land; twice the sea ran red and we fell back broken. He offered single combat to spare the blood, and Sava gave him only silence. So Mstislav sealed the isle tight. Six months we watched, as hunger turned flesh to bone, thirst turned hope to dust. No parley. No mercy. I saw their women raise driftwood crosses to Saint Yevstafiy of the Deep, their last hope that the sea might take them before we did.

Sava died hollowed out, with defiance still in his gaze. When they raised his corpse upon the wall, his wife Yelena threw it down and begged Mstislav to end it. She knelt, proud even in her ruin, and Mstislav beheaded her where she knelt.

Her blood was warm on my hands. I held her head a moment longer than I should have, and its weight seemed more than bone and flesh. She had been queen of a people, a mother, a daughter of these cliffs. And now — nothing. I cast her to the sea — not in hatred, but so the waves might take what the crows would have claimed. I whispered Yevstafiy's name as I did — a poor prayer that the deep would grant her peace. The sea swallowed her as it had swallowed all else.

We stood upon the rock, Rybach burning behind, smoke clawing at the sky like the fingers of the dead. Mstislav beside me — salt-crusted, blood-caked, hollow-eyed. For a moment, the sea seemed still, black and endless, as if it weighed our deeds. Mstislav set his hand on my shoulder. Heavy. Cold. His eyes met mine and saw the hunger in me — not for more conquest, but for an end to it. He said nothing. Turned away.

Then came the crowning.

The Torc of the Broken Isles, broken no longer. A twisted band of blackened iron and silver, forged in blood, heavy with the price paid. They swore their oaths by God, yes — but more by Danilo Iron-Brow, by Stepan the Endurer, by the stones and saints who had seen their fathers fall. Set at last upon Mstislav's neck in the hall at Velgrad, before all the chieftains — one kingdom, born of ruin, bound by sorrow.

The queen was there. Vezhena. Tall, proud, her hair bound in silver. Her eyes grey as the storm-lit sea, sharp as flint. She raised her cup to me. The look she gave was a blade in velvet — respect, perhaps, or pity, or both.

Prince Illarion beside her — young, bright-eyed, his smile sweet. But the hunger beneath it was plain as a wound: not yet sharpened, but already there.

The hall was full of faces — red with drink. Pale with memory. Mstislav sat high, shoulders heavy beneath the weight of what he had won. He called me forth.

"You have done all I asked of you, Yaroslav," he said, voice raw from command. "More than I had right to ask. Speak your wish, and it will be yours."

I knelt. My knees struck the stone, and for a breath I felt the weight of the dead upon me — those I'd killed, those I'd failed, those who watched now in whatever halls the sea and saints keep. "Let me put down the sword. Give me a rock no lord will want, no king will miss. Let me live, and die, and be forgotten."

Illarion looked at me as the young look at a man who turns from power — a riddle beneath notice.

Mstislav was silent a long time. The sea beyond the walls spoke in his stead.

At last: "Yaroslav Krovin — hear my word, as all here bear witness. You are free of it. My word upon it, before God, before the sea that remembers all, before the stones that drank our blood. No man shall call you to war again while I wear this twisted strand. Go now. Build the peace men dream of but seldom find."

His blessing was heavy. As heavy as the crown they set on him, when the isles bent the knee at last. As heavy as the oaths sworn beneath the black spiral banner, the mark of the sea's hunger.

The feasting was long. We drank as all men drink: to live, to feel their blood burn, and to forget. But I tasted only ash —

and knew, as I sat among them, that there are victories so great
they leave a man emptier than any defeat.

CHAPTER II: SKELD

I had earned peace.

I sailed to Skeld, a day's hard rowing northwest of High Mound, where I was born. I'd known of it since boyhood — a place the old fishermen spoke of with rough affection, a place the maps forgot. Hard, forested, cold — but with mornings when the light caught the birch bark and made it gleam like silver, and evenings when the sea lay soft as a child's breath. A place where the winds speak louder than men, but not always in anger.

The sea batters it on all sides. The trees cling to black rock as if they fear the sky's weight. In winter, storms grind ice against the cliffs. In summer, the gnats rise thick from the marshes. No lord claimed it. No raider troubled it. It was enough.

Enough — a small word. A man spends his life chasing it. I found it here, for a time. And that is all a man can hope. But in finding it, I learned: peace is not the absence of storm, but the knowing that you can weather it, and still find joy in the morning's light.

I had thirteen winters when I knelt and swore to Mstislav — a boy grown thin on hunger and fear, old enough to know what it meant to live, too young to know what it meant to serve.

Twenty winters I bore Mstislav's flag — the white hand on a black field, the mark that froze even the strongest hearts, the sign that death had come riding the sea. Twenty years of salt spray and smoke, of steel drawn for the crown. Twenty years of oaths held fast, of duty done without pause — because duty is the chain a man hammers for himself.

At thirty-three, I laid down the sword. I had borne my weight as long as I could without shame. Mstislav granted it — his word upon it, before God, before the sea, before the stones that drank our blood.

Seven winters since I left the wars behind. Seven years since I came to Skeld — a place no banner flies, where no raider comes. Seven years of peace, and each one dearer than gold. In all my years of blood and storm, I never found better than this.

The mornings come cold and slow. But sometimes the sun breaks the clouds, and the sea catches its fire, and for a breath the world seems made new. Pale light, the colour of old bone, creeps over the sea's edge on most days — but not all.

The tide leaves its gifts on the black stones — ropes of bladderwrack knotted by waves, gull feathers clotted with rot, bones of some small thing broken by sea or beak. The air smells of salt and iron, where the rocks bleed rust into the surf. My boots slip on the slick stones as I cross the shore, steadying myself on driftwood washed up in the night. The wind is sharp. It keeps a man honest.

The storm tore shingles from the roof. I see where rain came through — boards split, thatch scattered like straw in a yard. I gather what can be saved. I wedge my knife between cracked planks, prize them free, fit new wood tight, lash it down with rope where nails have failed, smear the seams with pitch that reeks of smoke and pine. I muttered Saint Stepan's name as I worked, as my father did, not for miracles — only for the strength to see the task through. When the wind comes again, the roof will hold — for a time. That is all a man can ask.

The traps are next. The tide is low, the rocks slick with weed. I pick my way down, boots finding the holds I know by feel. A few fish caught — small, silver-backed, stiff in the morning chill. I smile despite myself — they are enough, and their scales gleam like coin in the rising sun. I clean them on the stones, gulls watching from a safe distance. The guts go to the sea. The fish I take. I stake the traps deep so the tide won't steal them. The sea owes me nothing. Still, I cross myself after setting the last — old habit from the days I sailed under oaths. Not for mercy, only for what a man might win with honest work. Whatever you do, do it well. Even setting a trap. Even gutting a fish. That is the measure of a man.

The garden lies above the cove, a thin strip where rock breaks enough for soil to gather. There is a kind of tenderness in it — the way the barley bends to the breeze, the way the skirret's pale flowers cling to the edge of the plot. I work it not only for need, but because it reminds me that even here, life takes root. I work it with a short-handled hoe, blade worn down to a curve, handle smooth with use. The ground is stingy. Barley, skirret, turnip — they fight for life here, as I do. I tear out weeds, pile stones at the edge to hold what soil I can. The wind dries the sweat on my back before it can chill me.

I gather driftwood where it lies, drag it up the slope, split it with the strength of my back and the cut of my axe. The wood yields with a clean crack that pleases the hand. The scent of salt and resin rises, sharp and good. These small things — they gladden a man, if he lets them. No more cutting flesh or bone — only honest labour, freely offered. I stack it high against the hall wall. The storms will come again, as they always do. The wood will burn fast and hot, and be gone — in the way of all things.

I built this hall myself, on the high shoulder of the hill where the birches bend like men in prayer. No shrine here, no saint's stone — but I touch the threshold each night as I enter, as if Saint Vira herself might guard it. The walls of pine and stone drink the salt air; the roof, battered and sagging, still holds.

Each night, when the wind howls through the chinks, I feel the timbers shudder like a man in his last fever. And still I mend it, plank by plank, as if hands alone could hold off time. Not to win — no man wins against time — but because the labour itself is worth the doing.

Before the light fades, I walk the cliff's edge. The sea below is dark, restless. But sometimes the last light catches its back, and it shines like hammered bronze. The wind cuts over it in low, hard gusts, but tonight it carries the scent of heather, sweet and faint. I watch. I listen. Not for ships. Not for men. Just for the sea itself — and the promise, perhaps, that it might let me be a little longer. And for a breath, I feel at peace — not for what I have, nor for what I have built, but for what I can still see, hear, and hold in my hand.

CHAPTER III: THE STONES THAT REMAIN

I took a wife, Anya, whose hair smelled of smoke and wild fennel, whose hands could coax warmth from wood, from stone, from my scarred flesh — and who laughed, soft and low, as if she did not fear the world.

There is no beauty in me. There never was. A face like old stone — flattened nose, brow like a cliff-line, jaw heavy enough to break teeth rather than show them. The kind of face that closes doors before words are spoken. One ear's notched like a butcher's tally. I've seen prettier men break under the lash, under the weight. Me, I was made for bearing.

Anya never lied to me. She said I looked like the hills above the sea — battered, plain, and still standing. I believed her.

We were wed in Fish Shore — a lean village where the huts huddle close to the sea's edge, as if seeking its mercy. I met her there first, trading for salt fish, onions, and barley. She was mending a net with hands quick and sure, the wind lifting the hair from her brow. She looked up at me, not with fear, nor with the hunger or guile I'd come to expect. Only calm, as if she weighed my soul and found it wanting nothing — and in that look, I felt, for the first time in years, that I might be a man again, not only a sword.

Our marriage was simple, as was fitting for such a place. No priest came. No need. The sea bore witness, and the wind carried our vows. The old folk spoke Saint Yarila's name, as is the custom, that no soul be lost between shore and tide. The village headman bound our hands with a strip of linen — frayed and clean — the kind used to swaddle babes or shroud the dead. Anya set a bowl of water between us, and together we washed the salt from our hands, that we might begin clean.

There was no feast, only bread broken and shared, a cup of weak ale passed between us. But there was joy, quiet and sure as the tide.

She gave me a son. Little Semyon, who laughed like the brook above the marshes when it runs swift with spring's melt.

For five winters, I knew joy. The kind that comes quiet, without herald or feast — the joy of a child's hand in yours, of a woman's voice singing low as she bends to the hearth. That is more than most men can claim. More than I ever thought to ask. More than I ever thought a man like me would be granted.

Peace is a shape the sea does not know. The sea gives, and the sea takes. But in those years, it gave me more than I had any right to hope for.

There is a rise beyond the garden, where the birch trees thin and the stones lie flat beneath the sky. I go there when the work is done. Two graves. No cross. No words. Just great stones I raised with my back, the lever's marks still plain, the scars of my labour deep. Names fade. Faces fade. Even love fades, when no voice speaks it. But stone endures. Perhaps that is why we mark the dead with it — so that something remembers, even when we do not. The sea can see them. The wind can touch them. It is the best I could offer.

I remember the cough that hollowed her. The way it bent her over the hearth as if the fire's warmth could save her. How her hands shook, how she pressed a cloth to her mouth and thought I did not see the stain it bore. Red, like the rowan berries in autumn. Red on the cloth, red on her lips. The cough came with the cold months, when the wind found every crack in our walls and the damp crept under the door.

And the boy — the fever took him first. It burned so fierce I thought it would scorch the breath from his small chest. His hair clung to his brow, slick with sweat. His skin burned under my hand. I fetched snow in my palms, laid it on him, watched it melt as if the heat of him could drink the whole winter dry. Then the fever broke, and the chills came. His teeth chattered like pebbles in a stream. And then, like his mother, the cough. At night, when the storm howled beyond the shutters, I heard that thin, raking sound.

I went to the wise woman at Fish Shore. Old as the rocks, her hands knotted like roots that claw the shore. She came when I called, silent as the tide. She fed them broth, wiped their lips, listened to the broken air rasping in their chests. Her face was like driftwood — bleached, hollow-eyed — as she spoke the words no man wishes to hear. Lung rot, she called it. The wasting cough. No cure. No hope. Only what comfort I could give, and for as long as I could give it.

I prayed. I cursed Him. I bargained — as if a man like me had any coin to trade with God. And still, in the dark, I thanked Him for what I had been given, even as I begged Him not to take it. But He does not listen to the cries of men. No more than we listen to the cries of gulls wheeling over the dead.

When Semyon would take no more than milk — thin, weak, his lips too dry to close around the cup — Anya turned her eyes to me. Eyes once bright as a storm-lit sea, now dull, dark with fear.

"Go for the priest," she begged. We had not baptised him, foolish with dreaming of better days, of time. But time was a thief, and it had taken nearly all.

"Bring him," she said, her voice a thread near breaking, *"if you love us. Let our boy's soul be safe, if his body cannot be."*

I did not want to leave. My heart beat so loud I feared I would not hear their last breath if it came. I feared I would return to cold flesh and silence. But she would not let me stay.

"Go," she said. *"I will see that he lives until you return. God does not hate us so much that He will not allow our son to enter His gates. There may be mercy yet."*

The sea was cold and mean. The spray froze to glass on the gunwales. The waves broke over me; I thought I would not see land again. Seven days to reach Black Bridge. Seven days of rowing, bailing, praying — and cursing into the wind.

The priest I found was a man of few words, his hands smelling of tar and old spirits. His knives were his trade as much as his rites. His poultices were black as pitch. He cost me near all I had: coin, gear, promises made. And seven more days to bring him back, thin and hollow-eyed, wrapped in a cloak that stank of fish oil and failure.

They lived to see me return. But no more than that.

The priest came to Semyon's side as the boy's breath thinned. He spoke the words, made the sign with his black-stained hands, and blessed him as best he could. Semyon went in his sleep, as the snow fell soft against the shutters. His small hand still clutched the scrap of cloth I had given him. Anya held him close, rocking him as if that could call him back. Her tears wet his hair. She would not let him go, not even when his face turned cold beneath her hand.

She lingered till the next night. I stayed beside her, felt her grip on my hand, saw the strength leave her with each breath. At the end, she said nothing. But her lips moved — words I could not hear, or that were meant for God, or the boy, or me. I will never know. And then the storm eased, and she was gone.

I hated God that night. But even then, in my heart, I knew He had already given me more than I deserved. And even now, with all I have lost, I know I would not trade these years for any crown or glory.

The ground was hard — stone and root bound tight beneath the thin skin of soil. Each stroke of the spade jarred my bones. Each root I hacked through fought me, as if the land itself would not yield them a resting place. My back burned. My hands bled. And I welcomed it. I could not weep; the tears were long spent. But the pain — the pain was honest. The pain was something. Pain reminds us we are not yet gone. And through it, I remembered not only their dying, but their living — the weight of Semyon asleep against my shoulder, the warmth of Anya's cheek when she kissed me at dawn. A man who feels nothing is already half-dead. Let my back break, my hands bleed — better that than softness. Better that than forgetting.

I buried them. I raised their stones. I spoke no prayers — what saint would heed a man like me? But the stones stand, and that is my oath to them, and it is not done until I join them.

I rise, stiff, the cold in my bones now as familiar as breath. The cold has worked its way through wool and hide, and still I linger — as if their stones might speak. But there is only the wind's moan, and the hiss of the tide at the wrack.

I climb slowly, frost treacherous beneath my boots. My breath comes hard, salt and iron on my tongue. Each step sends a pebble skittering to the waiting waves.

The hall waits — the axe, the fire, the long day of work that is the shape of my penance. The sea's gaze presses at my back. The weight of what I've done, what I've lost. One day it will come for me, as it came for them.

It greets me like a friend who bears no love, only shelter. The heavy door groans as I shoulder it open, the latch stiff with salt. The air inside is warmer, but it is the warmth of a place long empty of voices. The timbers creak overhead, like a man in troubled sleep. The hearth smoulders. I feed it scraps of pine, splinters of birch. I sit where the fire's warmth can find me. The smoke stings my eyes. I taste the bitter memory of mornings when the hall rang with their voices, with the crackle of greenwood. I add another branch. The warmth creeps outward, slow as a promise half-kept.

And I think: this is what remains — stone, sea, and the silence between them. And the memory of voices I loved, carried in that silence like a song half-lost to the wind. And peace, hard-earned, bought with blood, yet dearer than gold.

CHAPTER IV: THE BLACK SAIL

The sea was flat as iron. Cold as a grave. The swell rose and fell, slow and heavy, like some beast too tired to rage. No wind. No gulls. No sound but the hush of water against stone.

I sat at the threshold, mending a net. My hands worked by memory. My eyes stayed on the place where sea meets sky.

That's where I saw it.

A speck at first. So small I might have thought it a flaw in the eye. But it grew. Darkened. Took shape. I studied its lines — too small for a storm-runner, too blunt for a teeth-ship, too heavy in the water for any honest ash boat. The hand-ships of kings rode deeper, broader, iron-bound — this was none of those. Just a hull that looked cobbled together, patched and tarred like a wound that wouldn't heal.

No gulls behind it — no catch aboard. No colour on the sail, no sign of trade or faith. Just a scrap of cloth hanging limp on a mast that seemed ashamed to stand. A nameless kind, the sort that bears men who come to take and leave no witness behind.

The weight settled in my gut. A ship like that comes for no good. But what good does the sea ever bring? The sea gives only to take. And when it takes, it leaves you hollow, and calls that mercy.

I set the net aside. Stood. Wiped my hands, though they were clean of all but salt. Reached for the axe. Not the sword. That I had sworn not to lift again. A sword is for men who believe in cause and glory. The axe — the axe is for honest work. And for honest killing, if it comes to that. A man swings an axe and owes no forgiveness for it.

The ship crept on, slow as rot. Even the sea seemed ashamed to bear it. The oars worked steady — too steady for hunger to have weakened them. Men who had planned this coming, not men driven by storm. The rigging frayed, the hull scarred but not broken. Not wrecked. Dangerous.

And silent. No hail, no call.

I could hear the oars now — the wet slap of them in the water. The soft groan of wood. The hush between their breaths as they drew near. Even the stones seemed to shrink from their step, as if the land itself would be rid of them.

When they reached the shore, they came like wolves. Two stayed with the boat. Six climbed the stones to my house where I waited, axe in hand.

They were hard men, lean as famine, hollow-eyed. Faces lined like cracked stone, some scarred, some burned, none soft. Salt-stiff tunics, cloaks of ragged wool or sea-worn fur, boots hacked from seal hide — or none at all. Each moved as if nothing was left to him but the steel he carried. Blades worn smooth by years, pommels dark with sweat and sea air. No ornament — if ever there had been any.

Not comrades. Not brothers. A pack, aye — but one that might tear its own if hunger took it.

Within them, a man in a brown cloak. No clasp, no helm, no badge of rank. Plain wool, hem frayed by hard miles. The hood hung low, shadowing his face. Skin weathered like old oak bark. Not young, not yet old — pared down by the years to what mattered. His cloak hung heavy on one side — a blade but hidden, not revealed. One hand, I saw as he moved, was scarred where two fingers ended at the knuckle. Frost, or steel, or both — the kind of loss that makes a man step with care.

He moved like a man who knew the ground owed him nothing, and so he took what footing he could. Light, but not soft. Careful, but not slow. A man who'd learned, one fall at a time, that the world gives no mercy. His eyes, when I caught them beneath the hood, were dark, quick — and empty of warmth.

Around him, the men kept their space, as they do when they sense the one among them more dangerous than all the rest.

He stopped short of my door. His hands empty. His voice low, rough, sure.

"By the old laws, we claim the right. The sea's too long behind us. The night's too cold ahead."

The old laws. A man may run from his king. He may turn his back on his God. But no man runs from the old laws. They follow like the tide. The old laws mean food, shelter, and no blood spilled where the hearth's warmth reaches. A hard law. But a true one — or so we tell ourselves. I have known it betrayed. And yet still, we keep it. Because without it, we are no better than the wolves. And when a man breaks the old laws, even Saint Kosma turns his face away.

I could have turned them away. Could have shut the door and lived with the shame. But the old laws are not meant for ease — only for men who remember what it means to be one.

I let the words hang. Let the sea speak in the hush between us. The men behind him shifted, waiting. Not yet reaching for steel — but ready, if it came to that.

"At my hearth," I said, "you'll have what I can give."

CHAPTER V: THE QUEEN'S GIFT

They ate my bread — hard as stone, baked days before. They took my fish — dried and salted, meant for my own supper. They drank just enough to take the edge off the cold, not enough to dull their wits. By that, the bond was made. Food given, shelter offered — and so the old laws bound us. But I knew better than to think it shield enough. I have seen what men will do when hunger, fear, or greed gnaw deeper than any law. A man with a soul worth saving keeps his word. The rest? The rest serve only their need.

But watched and I saw, sure as I saw the axe by my side: they didn't come to kill me. Not unless they had to. Not unless the word was given. If it was, they'd do it. Not with rage, not with hate. Just as a man guts a fish or splits kindling. Without a breath between order and deed. But they'd prefer to eat and live.

When they had done, I asked the Brown Cloak, "And where is it you sail, when you leave this shore?"

He met my gaze. No flicker, no flinch. "North to Black Bridge. Then a trader's cove beyond — there's whale oil and timber to be had."

A lie. A good one. Close enough to truth that a man could believe it. But I knew the sea, and I knew the kind of ship he sailed. That cove would never see his keel. And his men — they heard the answer meant for them, and no more.

He spoke low to the ship's master — a scarred man with one ear. The captain's mouth twisted, as if to say the men wouldn't like it. But whatever thought he had died behind his teeth. He gave the word, and the crew rose. They took what gear they had and went to make camp down by the shore. Not in my hall, not under my roof. Near enough to watch me. Near enough to come swift, if called.

The Brown Cloak stayed.

I watched the swords leave with mixed feeling. They were the simple threat, and I was glad enough to see them go. But what remained — his purpose unknown — was likely worse than being killed in my sleep.

"One more glass," he said.

Not a question.

I poured what was left of the mead — not much, but enough for two. We sat across from each other at the rough table, the fire low between us. His eyes were dark and still, and I felt them take my measure. Not what I did. Not what I said. What I was.

His gaze stalked my hall the way a warrior throws testing strikes. Worn boards. Smoke-dark beams. Nets mended and waiting. He measured these things, but that was not where the blow would land.

The weight of the moment pressed like the hush before a storm.

"You live far," he said. "Far from hall and kin."

"I earned that distance."

"Any sort of danger could arrive at your shore. As those men have today." He gestured beyond my door to where the sellswords kept their silent watch.

"My home is not on any war routes, or trade routes. There is nothing here worth taking."

"Do you not fear death?"

"There's no benefit in fear. If death comes, I'll take my price and die. The sea takes what it will. A man's part is to stand, and meet it clean."

At last, his eyes rested on the sword. The one that hung above the door, where I had put it that first day — and tried, ever since, to forget. Wrapped still, in the cloth I'd bound it with: old linen, stained with smoke, salt, and time. The hilt showed through where the cloth had worn thin — dark with age and sea air, the grip's leather cracked, the iron pommel dulled with use. No shine left. No glory. Just weight.

"A fine gift," he said, nodding toward it.

And so he named himself. For he could not have known it was a gift but that he already knew.

I took a slow breath. My hand gripped the cup, though I had no thirst. "A gift I never asked for."

I had not wanted it. God knows I had not.

I had asked only for my release. My piece of rock at the sea's edge. To be forgotten. And Mstislav, to his credit, had granted it. But she — Vezhena — had followed me out, after the feasting was done. The moon low, the tide high. She brought the sword then. One of Mstislav's own. *Greyfang*, it was called. Forged by Sava the Red-Handed. A blade too fine for a man like me.

It was not his finest — no gem-studded relic, no gift for an heir. But good steel, honest steel. Broad and straight, with fuller deep and clean along the length. The edge still keen as frost, though it had seen battle. The hilt plain: iron crossguard blackened by salt and time, grip bound in dark leather, worn smooth where the king's hand had held it. The pommel heavy, rounded, marked with a simple cross incised shallow — no gold, no silver. A sword for a king who ruled by strength, not finery.

My hand had drawn back from the blade she offered. Not because it was too good — though it was. Because I knew no gift comes free. And I saw it in her eyes, what price she meant me to pay.

She smiled then, as only she could smile. "Take it, Yaroslav," she said. Soft as the sea at dusk. "You have earned it. And more." And I knew better than to refuse her.

So I had taken it. And when my home was built, I had hung it above the door, where I would see it each day. Partly I was proud of the work I'd done, and of the gift itself — a king's gift is no small thing. Partly I wanted it close, where my hand could find it if need arose. Partly it stood like a gargoyle, guarding what was mine. But mostly, I kept it there so I would not forget. Not the oath. Not the duty. The cost of blood and honour.

Now, as the dawn bled cold through the cracks in the door, I looked at it again. The cloth seemed thinner. The sword heavier. And the price — the price always comes due.

"Even so, perhaps you remain worthy of it."

I drank, weighing his words. Every word of his had two meanings, at least. He saw the strength in my arm, the fire not yet gone from my eye. He meant to claim. I did not want to be claimed, so I spoke the truth.

"I was never worthy of it."

He nodded — not in agreement, but as if tucking the words away.

"In my experience, those who claim worth rarely have it. And those who deny it — they often do."

My answer had not turned him aside. It had only given him more to work with. That is how men like him move — they twist what you give until it binds you tighter. I knew him then for what he was. Not of my kind. Men who speak with swords and blood — they are simple, clean in their way. He was the other kind of power. Hers.

"Who do you serve?" I knew, but I wanted him to say it.

He did not.

"You do not travel to Black Bridge," I pressed.

He met my gaze, steady as stone. "I may yet. It depends."

I felt anger stir — not the hot rage of battle, but that cold, bitter kind that comes when a man is cornered by words instead of steel. "I do not have the tongue of a liar," I said. "Say what you've come to say, and be done."

His gaze moved through the hall, taking in what was left of my quiet life.

"I see the marks of other lives here — the child's carving on the post, the loom set aside, the small boots by the hearth. But you are alone. Have you hidden your family?"

"What I had is gone."

He nodded, slow. As if weighing what that meant. What it cost. What it bought him.

"You mend your nets," he said. "Cut your wood. Stand your own watch."

"I have no one else to do it," I answered, flat, and without apology.

"A hard life. A lonely one."

I heard the invitation in it — almost gentle. Perhaps he hoped I was weary of loss, of labour, of silence. That I longed to be useful again. But I am no young man dreaming of glory. I'm not sure I ever was.

"It suits me."

I met his eye then, and let him see the price he was asking, and the wrong of it.

He allowed silence then, to see what I'd do with it. I left it where it lay. A crack of wind snapped open the door. The fire hissed and blew sideways.

I rose and stepped out to end out meeting and be away from him. The cold bit deep. The wind carried the sea's breath, salt and raw. Below, on the shore, the men's fire glowed faint. Figures moved by it, small against the night.

I felt him come to stand at my shoulder.

"A man alone," he said at last, "has no ties to hold him when need arises."

The wind stirred, faint and cold. A taste of the storm that would come. Storms always come. The only question is when, and whether a man will still be standing when they pass.

"I earned my peace," I said. A reminder. And a plea.

His face stayed in shadow when he answered.

"Peace is for the dead."

He thanked me, as the old ways required, and took his leave. But though he spoke the old words, I heard the double meaning.

"You have given what was owed," he said. "We thank you."

His voice was even. No warmth in it, no scorn. Just duty, done clean, in the way of knives and shadows. And beneath it, like silk under a knife, I heard her voice plain:

Come, or die in the night.

And so I answered, "We all must do our duty."

I thought on it: Mstislav's betrayal. Before all, he had offered me peace. A small thing to him, perhaps, but to me it was everything.

Or was it betrayal at all? The queen — she was the sharper half of why he was the Grey King. She had withdrawn his gift, as the sea withdraws the tide, leaving a man stranded. Maybe the king had meant his word when he gave it. Maybe he still did. But in courts, meaning little matters less. The king's word may be his bond, but a bond is only as strong as the hand that guards it — and the queen's hand is the one that grips the hilt. That is the way of power. Kings speak of oaths. Queens see them kept — or broken. The court shapes its truth as a smith shapes iron: for its own use.

I shifted, the cold stiff in my knees. A man like me is a tool easily taken down from the wall, no matter how long left to rust.

That night, beneath a sky black as coal, I went to the graves. The wind scoured my face. Two stones, plain, marked by nothing but wind and rain. I knelt, laid my hand on the earth, and let the cold rise through my palm. I spoke no saint's name. What could Saint Stepan offer now?

I said nothing. The wind spoke better than I could.

I thought of Anya's face in firelight, her brow furrowed over some small worry — the bread, the weather, the child's cough before it turned cruel. The way she hummed as she spun flax — a tune from childhood, forgotten even by her, I think. I thought of Semyon's small hands, sticky with honey, reaching for mine. His eyes wide at the wonder of a world I no longer saw.

Maybe soon, I thought.

But not yet. The dead ask nothing of us. The living — they ask more than we have to give. And still, we give it.

Then I came back to the hall and stood beneath the sword. That gift. That burden. I did not take it down. Not yet. But I stood a long while, feeling its weight without touching it. A man can lay down a sword. But he can't lay down what the sword made him.

Dawn came cold — the kind of cold that lingers when winter's hand loosens but will not yet let go. I stepped from my hall, the ground soft with thaw, patches of frost clinging where the sun had not yet touched. The air cut through wool and hide, sharp as a blade drawn slow along the skin.

The boat waited at the shore — broad of beam, low in the water, the sail furled, the lines dark with wet. The Brown Cloak stood like a stone, his men hunched at their oars, silent as the sea itself. I crossed myself — fingers to lips, heart, sword, shield — not for blessing, only for strength. Then I climbed in, felt the cold of the wood beneath me, the weight of what I left behind — the hall, the graves, the nets strung as if I might yet return to mend them. With each pull of the oars, Skeld fell behind. Smaller. Distant. Until rock and memory were one.

The sea was steel beneath a sky the colour of old bone. And the cold — the cold went deeper than bone, a cold no sun could thaw.

CHAPTER VI: SALT AND STORM

Mstislav's kingdom is no gentle land, no soft green crown upon the sea. It is a scatter of stone and storm, islands flung like a net across cold waters that hunger always for ships, for men, for hope itself. The sea rules here as much as any king — and perhaps more.

The Outer Isles stand as the kingdom's ragged edge, where the world ends in cliff and moor. Grey Isle rises bleak, its western cliffs gnawed by waves that have no master. There, Boyar Vezemir the Grey Boar keeps his hall lashed to the stone above Black Bridge, a man as stubborn as the rock beneath him. South lies the Isle of High Mound, low and windswept, where the ancient barrow broods beneath withered grass. Thane Oleg Barrow-Keeper keeps his watch there, though what he guards, and why, no man speaks of. And to the west: Stormgrave Isle, high and broken, lashed day and night by rain and wind, ruled from its stronghold by Boyarina Salava, Widow of the South — a woman said to know the taste of poison as well as wine.

The Central Isles are Mstislav's heart. Morskoygrad Isle — the Sea Fort Isle — is the greatest of these, where Velgrad rises behind its driftwood walls, and the king's bone-throned hall looks down upon all who come by sea. Here the land softens: hills and forests, flax fields and barley where the rivers cut through. The king's banners snap above pine and alder, and his hand — the White Hand — holds tight. Nearby, the broken isles: Strayhorn, craggy and forested, with reefs that tear the hulls of the unwary; Stonehook, broad and rugged, its streams edged in birch; Blackreef, marsh-wolf's ground, where the land is more water than earth; Splitfang, where the rocks rise like a beast's jaws from the sea.

And beyond — the Inner Isles, where the kingdom frays at its edges. Sealwatch Isle, long and narrow, where Thane Moroz hunts and guards the king's straits. Wreck Rock, a crown of ruin, where no lord rules — the stronghold shattered, the cliffs bare, left empty by Mstislav's wrath, a lesson carved in stone.

And further still, where no true crown holds sway: the land men call Shadow's Heart. Cold, vast, and filled with dark woods and broken hills, it broods at the edge of the maps. Monsters, clans, outlaw chiefs — all find shelter there, and none bear the king's mark save where the brave or the foolish raise his banner for a time.

Mstislav's kingdom is a kingdom of salt and storm, of stone and oath. All the lords of the isles bow to him — Mstislav, High King and Lord of the Isles — not by love of crown or coin, but by the weight of blood given and blood taken, by the oaths they swore and the strength of those who keep them. It is not held by parchment, nor by silver, but by the hard bond of word and steel.

The ship was the *White Gull*, a broad-bellied seal-barge, heavy in the bow and slow to answer the helm — but stout enough for the open sea's hunger. The captain was a broad-shouldered man called Torsten Seal-born, with a voice like a cracked bell and a scar that puckered the skin from brow to cheek. He was lean and leathery, his eyes pale as sea-foam, and he watched the horizon as if it might grow teeth.

It's a day's hard row to Fish Shore, but the *White Gull* rode the swell as the captain guided her true, and we made it there in half that. The Isle of High Mound rose from the mist ahead, low and brooding, its slopes bald as a skull where the sea's endless pull had chewed the earth down to bone. Patches of withered grass clung to the thin soil, and here and there the black stumps of trees long dead stood like broken teeth. At its heart, the barrow swelled from the earth, older than kings, older than prayers — a mound that watched us pass, a buried eye beneath the turf. The sea foamed at the island's feet, always gnawing, always taking.

We reached Fish Shore by mid-afternoon — a clutch of turf-roofed huts crouched at the water's edge, as if the land itself had tried to swallow them for shelter against the wind. The folk watched us come as though we were ghosts borne in on the tide. They spoke little but traded fair: smoked eel, onions, a pair of scrawny hens, two small casks of weak ale, in exchange for salt fish, barley bread, and cheese hard as oak. The captain — Torsten, though the men called him Stone-Eye behind his back — saw to it we took on extra rope and tar. And when he took stores enough for eight days, I knew what I had already guessed: we were not bound for Black Bridge.

There are two sea roads from High Mound, around Fort Sea Isle, and on to Velgrad. North: the faster way, but it risks the Howling Sea — strong currents, gale winds, waves high enough to break a man's hope along with his ship. Or south, through the Wolf's Mouth, then up along the northern straits — a place thick with the bones of ships, the wrecks of men who thought to cheat the sea. The channels shift with every storm. A man can think himself safe, and find his keel staved in an eyeblink — or worse, find the Tonezhiv rising from the depths, drawn to the living as if they remember how they died, and will not rest till they pull another soul down into the dark.

As evening fell, we set out again, sailing north out of Fish Shore. The cold bit deep. The sea's breath lay thick on the air, and the sky lowered with the promise of what was to come. The sail strained as the wind freshened, and the sea beneath us ran dark and heavy, as if it too knew the road we had chosen.

The brown cloak called himself Beran. No more name did he give, no less. A quiet man, eyes downcast, voice soft as the wind before a squall. He kept to his place, and I kept to mine. He did not sail, nor work the lines or the oar; he was no seaman, and made no pretence of being one. He kept out of the way, watched more than he spoke, and let others labour while he guarded whatever purpose he carried.

I could not sit idle. The benches mocked me, the dark below deck smothered me. So I took the oar when hands wearied, hauled the lines when Torsten barked the word, bailed when the sea came in as if it owned the deck. The crew watched, at first with suspicion, then with quiet approval. I asked no man's share, spoke little, and kept my back to the work.

We hugged the coast, the sky low and bruised, the wind rising as we rounded the north of High Mound — the place the fishers call Barrow Point, where the slope falls sheer to the sea and no tree dares grow. The sea grew choppier, the waves shouldering the hull like giants testing our strength. Then the current seized us — strong and sudden, as if some great leviathan beneath the strait had taken hold. The wind came down from the northeast, sharp and cold, driving at our backs, and between wind and water it felt as if the sea meant to drag us where it would. The sail filled, full-bellied and sure, and we flew through Barrow Strait, the dark water narrowing between High Mound and Grey Isle — the last great isle of the kingdom, beyond whose northern cliffs lies nothing but open sea and the emptiness men call the World's Edge.

Night fell like a lid slammed over the world. The sky vanished into black, the stars hid behind clouds torn ragged by the wind. The sea kept its grip, the current running strong beneath us, dragging at the keel, as if that same leviathan still had us in its jaws. The cold deepened, and the wet found its way through every seam. We took turns at the tiller, shoulders aching, hands raw from rope and salt. The *White Gull* leapt and plunged, the sail straining, the timbers creaking like a man under too great a load. Sleep was a thing no one dared for long — not with the wind's cry in the rigging and the sea's teeth close about us.

The day that followed was hard and grey. The wind kept to our backs, sharp as a blade's edge, and the sky stayed low, as if the weight of it might press us into the sea. The waves ran steep and close, shouldering the hull so that every man braced without thinking, knees bent, hands tight on rail or line. Spray flew up, cold as ice, and left salt crust on beard and brow. We chewed salt-hard bread and fish cold as the sea — and drank what we must to keep the chill from our bones. No man spoke more than needful. The sea roared in our ears, and the boat groaned with each blow of wave and wind.

That second night in the strait was no kinder: the wind held steady, the current still dragged at the keel, and the dark pressed close about us, heavy with salt and cold.

Dawn came slow and bruised, the light mean and thin, showing the sea black and heaving beneath a sky of iron. Grey Isle loomed to starboard on the third day — a grim wall of moor and cliff, where the pines clung like lost souls to the wind-scoured rock. The cliffs below the Grey Boar's hall were sheer and cruel; the sea smashed itself to froth there, as if enraged at the land's defiance. Black Bridge was hidden from view. We did not turn north to its harbour, but instead kept west. Storm petrels skimmed the waves, and once we saw the black back of a whale as it rose and vanished again, leaving only a slick of foam and a great breath of mist.

That evening, as the wind still favoured us, we came to the end of Grey Isle. The cliffs there fell away in great steps of black rock, as if the land itself had tried to hold the sea at bay and failed. The pines thinned to nothing, and the moor gave out to bare stone and heather burnt brown by salt and storm.

The Howling Sea opened before us — vast, grey-black, endless. The waves there ran higher, the swell deeper, the water darker, as if all the world's sorrow had drained into it. The horizon was no longer land and sea, but sea and sky alone, a meeting of grey upon grey where no man's hand or hall had claim.

The wind thrust at our backs, eager, cold, smelling of ice and iron. The sail strained full, the lines hummed like harp strings stretched too tight, and the boat leapt forward as if the sea itself meant to fling us into its heart.

Behind us, Grey Isle shrank with each breath, each pull of the sea. The last of its cliffs became a dark tooth against the sky, the gulls a scatter of white in the distance, the land no more than memory and shadow on the water. The sound of it — the crying wind through the stones, the crash of waves at the cliff's foot — faded until only the voice of the Howling Sea remained: a low roar that filled the world.

No man spoke. There was nothing to say. We were in it now — the open sea, where the land's shelter and the gods' mercy both seemed far behind. The saints too — for the Howling Sea has no ear for prayer. The salt was thick on my lips. The cold bit deep, and still the wind drove us on.

This was the heart of it. The Howling Sea earned its name well. The wind screamed through the rigging day and night. Waves heaved us high, then hurled us down into valleys of water where the sky vanished and only the hiss of foam and the creak of timbers remained. We reefed the sail down to almost nothing. Men took turns at the tiller, backs aching, hands raw, fighting the sea's will. Torsten barked orders in a voice hoarse from salt.

Spray soaked us through, our clothes stiff with salt, our beards crusted white. The cold gnawed the bone. We ate little — hard bread, salted fish — and drank sparingly from the ale, though the sea stole as much from our casks as we managed ourselves. When I offered my hands to the lines, Torsten looked me up and down and spat over the side, but he let me work. He saw, as all seamen do, that a man who helps is worth more than one who prays.

I have loved the sea all my life. We come from it, we are taught by it, and in the end we return to it. Water is life: a drop on the tongue, a stream at the roots of the barley "A drop is gentle, tame, a servant. But the sea is made of countless drops, and in that number their frailty becomes the strongest thing on earth. The sea makes no oaths but one — that it will claim you in the end. But there is truth in that, and I have never hated the truth. The sea does not dissemble. It does not pretend to be what it is not. Men do. The sea is cruel, and honest, and I prefer it.

Once, on the fifth day, the mast shuddered as a squall struck us broadside. We lost a yard of the yardarm, snapped like kindling. Torsten spent his breath on curses — upon the sea, upon God, upon the ghost of his father — but the sea did not care, and we lashed what we could.

The storm eased by dawn, and with it the sea grew calmer — though still a heaving thing, like a world not yet done with its rage. By midday we sighted the north cliffs of Sea Fort Isle: dark rock streaked with white where birds nested, above forested slopes and green valleys beyond. We stayed north of Coldreach, the wind now a kinder thing, though wary — the Howling Sea is never tamed, only suffered.

Sea Fort Isle. Greatest of the isles, and Mstislav's stronghold. At the heart of the isle, at the heart of the kingdom, stand Mstislav and Vezhena — king and queen, will and mind, the storm's hand and the eye within it. I thought of the king's hall far beyond those hills — Velgrad, with its driftwood and bone — and of the oaths I had sworn there. The man who rules, the woman who watches — both as much a part of that place as stone and sea. I felt the pull of the sea, the last freedom slipping from my grasp as the land drew near. The deck no longer pitched as wildly; my legs braced for storms that had passed. My hands clenched the rail without knowing why.

The coast softened as we sailed east, the cliffs softened to pine woods and shingle beaches. The sky cleared for a time, stars bright as spear points at night. The cold remained, but now it was the clean cold of the north, not the salt rot of storm spray. We saw seals basking on rocks and once a great sea eagle wheeling above.

Owl's Haven came into sight at dusk on the eighth day: a cluster of halls and sheds along a sheltered bay, the air thick with the stink of whale oil and smoke.

Eight days it took from Skeld — thrown through Barrow Strait, then across the Howling Sea where the winds have no master — to Owl's Haven at last. Eight days of hard water, salt spray, and a sky that closed over us like iron. The ship groaned, the timbers crying out when the sea struck her sides, but the *White Gull* bore us true. Torsten steered us in, and as we made fast the lines. I felt the sea's grip loosen — but only a little. The Howling Sea does not let go easily. And in truth, I was not sure I wanted it to.

CHAPTER VII: ASH AND OIL

We anchored as the last of the light drained from the sky.

Beran paid the captain — a leather bag passed hand to hand, quick and quiet beneath the lantern's sway. The crew watched the coin, their weariness held back by the promise of silver. When Torsten gave the word, they went ashore. No cheer. Just men who had outrun the sea's teeth this time.

Torsten stayed. His hand, rough with salt and rope, found my arm. "You've a strong back," he said, low so the others would not hear. "Strong hands. But mind the man in the brown cloak. He let others row and bail while he kept his boots dry. The sea shows a man plain." He spat, as if to be rid of the words, and went to his ship.

"I know what he is," I said. Nothing more was needed.

Owl's Haven stank of smoke and whale oil. The cold air carried it thick, bitter. The wharf was broad, timber grey with salt, scarred deep by rope and boot. Sheds, smokehouses, and workshops crouched along the shore, walls dark with soot. The town counted near three hundred souls. Big enough for need, small enough for hunger. Whalers, fishers, herders, and those who fed them — smiths, shipwrights, butchers. Two inns near the dock: one for traders with coin, one for men like us. The sea slapped at the pilings, patient as the grave.

Beran walked ahead, boots near silent on the boards, his cloak tight against the wind. I followed. The stink of fish and tallow filled my mouth. No voices called greeting. No dog barked. The town watched behind shutters and cracked doors, measuring what the sea had spat up.

We turned in at a low inn by the water's edge. No sign above the door, only a carved post, split and salt-worn — once a whale, perhaps, now nothing but a shape the sea had nearly taken back. Inside: dark, warmer. The air thick with smoke, the smell of stale ale and damp wood. The walls and beams were of heavy timber, blackened by soot, the weight of years plain upon them. The floor was gritty underfoot. The tables bore the scars of knives and spilled drink. A few men hunched over their mugs, faces lost in shadow.

The innkeeper stood behind the counter, thin, grey at the temples, his eyes tired in the way of a man who has watched too many nights pass without profit or peace. His wife moved among the tables — broad-shouldered, loud, quick to laugh, the kind of woman who kept a house standing when the roof sagged and the men drank too deep.

A barmaid worked the room as well — a girl near twenty winters, fair enough, hair pulled back in a braid, bodice laced tight to draw the eye. She cast a glance at us as we entered. A practiced look, meant to weigh purse and temper both, meant to offer a smile that might soften a man's mood or open his coin-hand. But one look at Beran's face, at mine, at the dust and salt on our cloaks, and she turned back to her work without word or smile. We were not the kind to pay for flattery, nor to welcome it. The barmaid kept to the other tables, where her charms might still buy an extra coin or two.

It was the innkeeper's wife who came to us, wiping her hands on her stained apron, her voice carrying across the room. "Sit, sit. I'll have something hot for you." She pointed toward a table near the hearth — low fire, more smoke than heat.

Beran gave her no heed. He led us instead to a table in the back, where the hearth's light failed, where the smoke hung heavy, where the walls were black with soot and the corners kept their shadows. A place for men who wished to be unseen. He lowered himself slow, like a man whose bones remembered too much winter. The bench creaked under him. I took the seat opposite.

The woman came after us, her steps firm, her breath loud with the work of the place. She stood, waiting. Beran did not look up. "Stew," he said, as if it were his right to order what was already given. "And beer."

She did not answer him. Her mouth tightened, but she turned her gaze to me. There was no smile, but her look softened, as if she saw a man who asked little and would cause no trouble. "It'll be stew, and beer if you want it," she said. I nodded once. That was enough for her. She turned, calling toward the kitchen as she went.

Beran sat silent, hands on the table, waiting.

"Seven years," he said at last, his voice low. "I assume you've lost the taste for news?"

I leaned back, stretching out the muscles in my back. "Never had use for it. My work was with the wars, not courts or gossip. Where I live, kings and councils are words on the wind."

The stew came — thick, more grease than meat. Bread hard as stone. "Eat it hot," she said, and was gone again.

Beran spoke low. "Mstislav has aged."

"All men do."

"True. But the men of the isles — they bow still, they come still, but slower. Their hearts itch for rebellion. Their mouths speak of a new king."

I broke the bread, dipped it in the broth. "And his son?"

"Too young to hold what his father took. What you helped him take."

"Illarion has twenty winters now. Old enough to shed blood. Old enough to make men kneel. His father's blood is in him."

"Still," Beran said. Just that. The word hung heavy.

I drank. The ale was bitter as his news. "And the queen?"

"She watches. She bargains. She holds peace where she can. But the seams fray. It will not last."

"Nothing does," I said. "Still, what does this have to do with me? I've no army or warchest."

Beran's eyes searched mine. "The crown will speak its need. It's not for me to say."

At these words, the door groaned on its hinges, worn by years of salt wind and poor repair. Cold came in at once, raw and bitter, the smell of the salt sea carried with it. The smoke from the hearth, sluggish until then, stirred and coiled above our heads like a thing that had no peace.

The man who entered moved light, cat-quiet, as if he had crossed thresholds all his life — not with boldness, but with an eye to what waited on the other side. He let the door fall shut behind him without haste, without apology. He shook the wet from his cloak, the silver clasp plain, the hem patched where wear had won against care. His boots, soft leather, well-patched, soles made for silent steps, shamed the greasy floor by their neatness. His face was narrow, sharp at the jaw and cheekbones. His eyes flicked from table to door, from hand to face, never still, never trusting. His mouth grinned, thin-lipped, the grin of a man who has talked his way free where steel would fail. And I thought: here is a man who measures every room for its exits before its company.

He saw us at once. Or he had seen us before he touched the latch. His eyes — grey, quick, weighing us as a butcher weighs flesh — passed from Beran to me. He came straight to the bench, weaving through the tables like a man threading a net, and sat beside Beran as if the place had been marked for him.

"Evening, friends," he said. His voice was low, fast, words smooth as oil on water. "Thought I'd find you here. Two hard men in a dark corner, stew cooling, ale unfinished. Dragomir, you might have waited."

Beran paused, shifted — as if the name had rubbed him raw — and let it pass.

"This is Yaroslav Krovin, who men once called Volkodlak."

Volkodlak. The wolf-made-man. A name still spat by those who remembered.

The man's grin turned to me, but not his eyes. Those sharpened — weighing, measuring. "So it is. Markov, they call me. I'm to see you safe to Velgrad, if God wills. In pieces, if not. God won't mind the difference."

He laughed at his own jest. I saw no jest in it.

I looked to Beran, and in that moment preferred his silence and danger to this fool's grin.

Without more, Markov tore my bread and ate as if he had earned it. He caught the glance and answered it. "You'll find me worth keeping. My trade is locks and lies — one I open, the other I tell. I know the men who can be trusted, and those who'd drink their own spit if left to it."

Seeing that Beran had not touched his drink, he took it, raised it to me, and drank.

"Bitter," he said, wiping his lips with the back of his hand. "It will serve."

I watched him as a man watches a blade — not for its shine, but for its edge, for how and when it turns. I saw the quickness of his hands, the glibness of his mouth, the hunger in his eyes. A man of shadows, made for them. A man who would speak where I kept silence. A man who would grin where I weighed my words. Such a man brings death or buys life. No middle path.

Beran rose then. No word but one, no hand offered, no farewell. His voice was low, meant more for the fire than for my ears. "Listen to him. He'll guide you." And he went, leaving his ale in Markov's hand, and me in Markov's company.

The morning broke in rain — cold, steady, the kind that soaks through cloak and patience both. The sea mist clung low, blurring the line where water met sky. Owl's Haven crouched beneath it, the smoke of its hearths and workshops smothered by the wet air. The streets ran with mud and ash, and the wharf shone slick as a butcher's block.

Markov and I walked the dockside, boots heavy with clinging filth, rain dripping from hood and beard. Markov's mood, like the weather, was thin-lipped and sharp. He moved quick, eyes everywhere, weighing ships, men, coin-purse, and opportunity in the same glance. I followed — slower, watchful. The rain had eased the stink of whale oil little; it ran in dark streaks from the sheds and smokehouses, mingling with the tide's rot.

We passed a score of craft — ash boats low in the water, knarrs heavy with timber and salt fish, a widowmaker tied up awkward at the end of the quay like a forgotten tool. Markov paused at each with the eye of a man who means to bargain, but shook his head each time. Too slow, too proud, too nosy, too soft. Then we saw her: *The Tusk.*

A converted storm-runner, broad of beam, high-sided, her sail patched where storm or claw had torn it, the prow carved plain but strong — no figurehead, no vanity. The hull was dark with old tar, the deck marked by years of hard work and harder weather. Lines coiled neat. Nets hung to dry in the rain's drip. The smell of oil and brine clung to her timbers like a second skin. She was right for this: fast, quiet, built to run hard seas and carry hard men.

Her master stood on deck, overseeing a load of barrels: oil, by the smell; heavy, slow work in the wet. A big man, stooped at the shoulder, his hands broad and scarred, his hair gone at the crown but hanging in greasy ropes at the sides. One eye milky, the other sharp as a hooked blade. His coat was seal-hide, patched and black with age. Around his neck hung a string of teeth — whale, shark, and something larger, yellower, that I did not wish to name. A man who'd sailed where others drowned, and brought his ship home by luck or stubbornness or both.

Markov smiled — the kind of smile that promised nothing and everything. "This one," he said. And I knew why. A man with debts, a ship with scars, and a route that could hide our going in plain sight.

We climbed the gangplank before the captain could wave us off. His good eye narrowed. "If you're selling, I'm buying nothing. If you're begging, I've no coin. If you're looking to crew, I've men enough."

Markov didn't so much as blink. His grin grew easy, warm beneath the rain. "Radomir One-Eye, isn't it?" He said it like the name was carved in saga stone, like the man was a hero sung of in halls. "They said you sailed where no sane man would, and came back with your ship beneath you and silver in your hold. That's the captain I seek."

Radomir spat — not in anger, but perhaps to hide the flicker of pride that straightened his back a little. "Name's mine. But I'm no man's road to fortune. If you're after safe passage, you'll find softer hands down the quay."

Markov lifted a small purse — not too fat, not too lean — and let it chink just loud enough against his palm. "Passage to Ironmark. No trouble. No baggage but what we wear. And silver for the taking, clean and fair."

Radomir spat into the rain. "No passengers. I carry oil and meat, not soft hands and city mouths."

Markov's voice went smooth as oil on wet stone. "Not soft, nor city. This one —" he nodded to me — "pulls oar and line better than ten men. And me, I'm worth a place at table for the talk alone."

Radomir snorted. "I need coin, not talk."

Markov let the purse dance in his fingers. "You'll have both. And more at Ironmark — I know the buyers, know where the price is best. I can ease your way. Whale oil sells there if a man knows who to see."

Radomir's eye sharpened. "Saltbay's closer. Easier sold there."

Markov's grin widened. "But poorer sold. And you've debts that Saltbay won't cover, if the talk is true. I offer silver now, and a better price at Ironmark. And hands that won't sit idle while you sail."

Radomir hesitated. Pride fought with need. The rain drummed on the deck. The crew watched from under their hoods, waiting.

Markov leaned in, voice low, the edge of steel beneath the honey. "You can say no. And still need coin when Saltbay's price cheats you. Or you can take our silver, sail for Ironmark, and come home whole."

Radomir scratched at the string of teeth, spat again, and glared at the sky — as if weighing whether to trust God's counsel, or the older powers that rule the deep. His boots shifted on the rain-slick boards. The weight of the choice bent his shoulders lower than the years had done. He touched one of the yellowed fangs at his throat, muttered words too low for Christian ears, and spat once more to seal it. "You're trouble.

But less than the debt-collector. Aboard then — but you work, or you swim."

Markov clapped him on the arm, as if they'd been friends all their lives. "Done and done. May God see us safe."

And so we boarded *The Tusk*. I felt the rain soak to the bone, felt the sea's breath in my lungs, and thought: the sea will take its price, as it always does. Saint Yevstafiy, guard our course. We have just bought our place at its table.

CHAPTER IX: GHOSTWATER

The Tusk began her life as a storm-runner — a ship made for speed, for hard weather, for running the open sea where other hulls cracked or foundered. But time, and what the sea does to all things, changed her. Trade, hunger, and debt shaped her anew. Now she is no ship of glory. She is a survivor — scarred, patched, built for endurance, not beauty.

Sixty feet stem to stern, broad of beam to ride out the heavy swell, shallow of draft to nose into coastal waters, yet steady enough to bear the sea's long hunger. Her hull, once pale, shows dark now with tar, brine, and toil's stain. Clinker-built — you can trace the lines where plank overlaps plank, the pattern of men's labour. The tar that seals her seams smells sharp even now, under the salt stink of the decks.

On her partial deck, the marks of knives and boots tell their own story. Cuts deep from flensing. Stains of old brine, of oil. The work of whalemen does not wash clean. Her lines and gear are kept neat, for slovenly work costs lives. The block and tackle are salt-rusted but sound; the casks and barrels lashed tight against the rail or stowed below, holding oil, brine, or the greasy fruit of the kill. Nets hang patched and drying where they can.

Amidships, the flensing space lies clear. The grooves where spades and mincing knives worked show in the deck, worn deep by the labour of cutting a giant to pieces. Chains and heavy lines lie coiled, ready to secure carcass or part. Two small whale boats ride lashed ready — each the length of two men lying head to foot, scarred by ice and beast.

No cabins grace *The Tusk*. The crew sleeps rough — beneath tarps, beneath makeshift lean-tos of plank and sailcloth, or on deck beside their gear. Only beneath the raised stern deck is there any shelter, a crude space where Radomir keeps his few private things and takes refuge when the weather drives even him below.

The tools of their trade are plain and brutal: hand-thrown harpoons, cutting spades, flensing knives, blubber hooks, mincing knives. The sea offers no mercy, and so the gear is built to match.

And the men, like *The Tusk* herself, what you would expect of such a ship: scarred, enduring, plain. No part of her built for show. No man aboard her given to vanity. All shaped by storm, by salt, by the hard years of a life at sea where no man can lie to himself, not for long. She is no ship of heroes. She is a ship that survives — and that, in the end, is what the sea teaches.

The first day dawned without colour, without sound. The sea lay grey and still as a dead man's eye, the mist hanging low over it like a shroud. There was no wind to rouse the water. No ripple, no gleam. Only that dark skin of the sea, smooth as hammered iron, and the slow, steady drip of mist from yard and line. Cold crept through cloak and wool, boot-leather and bone. The kind that does not sting but seeps — a thief that takes its time.

The Tusk drifted on iron water, her patched sail slack, her men silent. The crew watched the sea's face as men watch a grave mound, waiting for some hand to stir the earth. But no whale came.

Radomir One-Eye stood at the bow, his weight heavy on the rail. The swell, small though it was, rocked the ship under him, but he stood as if planted. His good eye swept the water, slow, patient, as if he meant to stare the beast up from the deep by will alone. The other eye — the blind one, the one the sea had taken — stared white and empty into the mist. The string of teeth at his throat shifted as the ship moved, as if the dead things he'd killed whispered at his throat.

Petar Brinehand came down the deck then, slow, steady. His narrow face was set, the lines of weather and salt carved deep, his mouth a straight hard line. He spoke little — only what needed saying — and now he said it plain enough.

"Yaroslav." His voice was low, meant for my ear alone. "You've the back and the hands. Take the larboard gear with Nik Vran'sson. He'll show you what's wanted."

I nodded. There was no need for more. Nik was already waiting, leaning against the rail where the coiled lines hung. Big, dark-bearded, his arms thick as oar shafts, his face slow to smile. He watched me come with eyes steady, measuring, but not unfriendly. A man of strength where it counted, loyal to Radomir without words or show.

Together we checked the lines, the harpoon shafts, the tackle that would bear the weight if the sea chose to give up one of its giants. The work was slow, methodical — as it must be. A rotten line, a slip of knot, a careless coil — any of these could mean a man overboard, or worse, a whale lost after the strike. Nik worked without waste, without talk. I matched his pace, and in the quiet of our labour, I felt the day settle over me: the cold mist on my neck, the reek of old oil in the wood, the waiting.

Petar, meanwhile, set Markov to the starboard rigging with Danko Knotfinger. I saw the shape of it at once — let the quick-tongued man keep company with the one who cursed knots to the depths. Danko, small and lean, fingers scarred from rope-burn, worked fast and sure despite his muttered oaths. Markov dabbled at it, fingers quick where they needed to be, but quicker still with words. He spoke low, light, weaving small jests and tales of men and ports, enough to draw a grin even from Danko between curses. Enough that the crew — silent watchers all — listened without seeming to, and the weight of the still day lightened a little.

Radomir heard, I know. But he said nothing. So long as the work was done, so long as the lines were true and ready, he minded no man's voice. The sea was silent enough for all of us.

And so the day passed — grey, still, waiting. No wind to lift the sail. No whale to break the sea's black skin. Only the slow drift, the quiet work, the breath of men and ship mingled with the mist. The kind of day that teaches patience, or breaks it.

Night came the same way — slow, heavy, without a sound but the soft slap of water on plank. We set the watch and lay where we could, beneath tarps or open to the mist. And I thought, as I closed my eyes, that the sea that day had shown us its face — not its hunger, not its fury, but its endless, waiting emptiness. And that is its own kind of danger.

The sea woke bitter on the second day. The wind came out of the south — cold, heavy with the salt of distant ice — and with it the waves. No swell, no easy rise and fall. These were sharp waves, short, steep, with white at their crests, eager to break and take what they could. *The Tusk* groaned in her seams, and the men moved with care, boots set wide, hands ready.

The rigging sang in the wind's grip, the sail straining where it had been patched. Spray flew cold as sleet across the deck, stinging face and hand. The sea was black now, deep oil streaked with white where wave met wind, where wave met ship.

It was in that rising storm that a whale showed itself — just for a breath, just long enough for us to see the roll of its back, the great scarred curve of it, the spout torn away by the wind. A shape too large for the sea that held it. And then it was gone, swallowed by the waves and the mist. No man spoke of chasing it. Not in that sea. *The Tusk* had all she could do to ride the storm, and we had all we could do to hold her true.

At the helm stood Stavko Driftwood. Broad, slow-moving, he looked carved from the same dark wood as the tiller he held. The sea broke over the stern, spray and rain lashing him, but he never flinched, never bent. His deep-set eyes missed nothing — the lift of the wave ahead, the sag of the sail, the strain on the lines. When *The Tusk* rode high on a breaking sea, it was Stavko's hands that held her steady; when she dropped into the hollow behind, it was Stavko who kept her from broaching, from turning broadside to the sea's anger. He did not curse or pray. He worked, as if he and the ship were one, the storm a thing to be endured.

The riggers lived in the ropes that day. Danko Knotfinger — small, lean, fingers scarred and red — worked the lines with curses soft as the wind's own voice. Every knot that slipped, every coil that fouled, he damned to the depths where no man could follow. Juro Hailmark climbed where needed, frostbit face set like stone, humming low as he went — a sound that might have been for comfort or for memory, I could not tell. Sava Gullsigh, lame in one leg, moved sure with his hands, sharp with his eye — a man who saw the danger before it came, who called out when a line threatened to part, when a block strained too near to breaking. They kept *The Tusk* answering to the helm, to the sea's test, to the storm's hunger.

Below the poor shelter of the raised stern deck, Miro Saltgut did what he could. The galley was no more than a tarpaulin strung over a box of coals, but still he kept the pot from spilling, the stores from shifting. I saw him once, crouched over his gear, the bone charm at his neck swinging with the ship's lurch, his face set with a grim patience. It was no easy thing to eat in such weather. The bread was wet with spray, the fish too cold to comfort. We held it in our hands, swallowing what we could, chewing as the deck heaved beneath us, as the sea's voice rose and the wind tore at our cloaks. Miro kept the casks tight, portioned the stores with a miser's eye. He knew how much of the best was gone, how long the worst must serve.

And I — I worked, I ate, I watched the sea. And I thought, as a wave broke high and cold over us, as the ship trembled in the wind's grip, that this summons I followed — this call from the king — might be cut short not by blade or order, but by the sea's will. I wondered if it would matter — to me, to God — where and how the end came. A clean death, I told myself, is no less clean for salt water in the lungs. But still, I felt the weight of it. The cold, the depth, the endless dark, and I did not wish for that end.

Night came with the storm unbroken. We took what shelter we could. And *The Tusk* kept on, groaning, shuddering, but unbroken, like her men.

On the third day, the storm's back broke. The wind shifted with the dawn, sharp from the north, cold and clean after the storm's roar. The sea ran high still, but no longer wild — long black swells under a pale sky streaked with racing cloud. Radomir One-Eye gave the order: "Come about." His voice was raw from the gale, but steady. His good eye swept the water as Stavko took the helm and turned *The Tusk* south, where the deep channels ran and the whales were more likely to roam.

Full sail we carried. The patched square of it strained at the yard, the lines thrumming with the wind's strength. *The Tusk* ran fast, too fast at times. We had to ease the sheets, spill wind, trim to keep her from outrunning herself. Radomir knew these waters. Knew when speed was a gift and when it was a danger.

And with Radomir at the bow stood Urek Ashhook, harpoon in hand, the sea's wind in his blonde hair, his long frame balanced as if born to the deck's roll. Urek stood bare to the cold, the ink of the Voryani dark against his pale skin: spirals, hooks, beast-shapes, the black coil of the Ashhook name. His arms, his chest, his back — all marked by the sea's rites and his own wild will. The harpoon rose in his hand, and in that moment, he looked less man than storm-made thing, called up from the deep to strike at its own kin.

The others gave him space — not for fear, not quite, but as men leave space for fire. He was Voryani — Strayhorn Isle blood, the kind that sings to storms and laughs in the face of a beast's charge. Tall like the mast he leaned against, narrow as a spear, the scars of war and sea upon his face, his hands, his back. His eyes — blue as dawn in frost, restless, alight with that hunger that no peace can fill.

They say the Shadow's Heart beats in him. The old name for doom — or for men too wild for the land to hold. I did not doubt it. I had seen such men before. They live too hard, too bright — and the world snuffs them out before their time, or so the tales go. But Urek? He seemed a man who might snuff the world out first, if it came to that.

He stood bare-armed in the cold, the wave-tattoo on his shoulder black against the pale of his skin, the leather cord at his throat hung with tooth and bent nail and sea glass. The harpoon rested easy in his grip, but I saw how the fingers flexed, as if eager for the cast. He grinned once — quick, raw — as the whale's shadow broke the water ahead. A grin like a dagger's flash, joy and danger tangled. And then he was still, the harpoon rising, his whole frame set like a drawn bow.

It was late in the day when we saw it — another whale. A great shadow beneath the waves, the roll of its back broad as a field, the spout torn white by the wind. The cry went up — not loud, not wild, but sharp and certain. The Tusk gave chase under full sail, her bow driving through the swell, the spray flying cold across the deck. No call for boats — not yet. We were closing, or so it seemed. The harpooners stood ready at the rail, irons in hand, lines coiled, eyes on the whale's trail.

It was long work, hard work. The helm fought Stavko's hands at every crest, but he held her straight. The riggers lived in the lines that day, keeping us on the whale's track.

Markov filled the chase with his tongue, easing the waiting with jest and tale.

We ran hard. The Tusk held the whale's trail as long as we could. But as the sun sank low, casting its last light in long gold streaks across the sea, the whale was gone. No sign of it. No spout, no roll of back, no shadow beneath the waves. The sea had taken it, as it takes all things.

That night, Radomir called us to his table — a plank over casks beneath the crude stern shelter, the lanthorn swinging with the ship's slow roll. We ate salt pork, hard bread, thin stew tasting of sea and smoke, the deck creaking beneath us, the sea speaking beyond the rail.

Radomir listened as we spoke — or rather, as Markov spoke for us. When Radomir asked our stories, Markov spun them out: Yaroslav, he said, was a prince's bastard turned monk turned outlaw, who had killed a king's man in a duel of honour and fled to sea. And Markov himself — a noble's son, cast out for a woman, a smuggler of relics, a man who had tasted the dungeons of Velgrad and lived to mock the jailers. He left our names true, for those were known. But he wrapped them in finer cloth, and the man drank it in like a warm draught on a cold night.

When the talk ran out, Radomir told us why these waters were called Ghostwater. How ships had vanished here, without wreckage, without cry. How the dead could be heard on certain nights — oars creaking, nets splashing, voices calling across the black. And how even the whales here seemed to slip away more often, as if the sea kept its secrets closer.

We sat long, listening to wind and wave and the dark beyond the light. And I thought of what it would mean to vanish thus — not by blade, not by betrayal, but by the sea's will, without mark or memory. I thought of it, and I knew: not yet.

By the fourth day, Markov's tongue had slowed. The wind was sharp and fair, the sea steel-grey beneath a high sky, and still we had nothing to show for our chase. Markov stood at the rail that morning, silent for once, his grin thinned out, as if he too felt the long weight of the empty days. When he spoke, it was low, for my ear only.

"We could be at this for weeks," he said, his breath steaming in the cold. "Weeks at sea, Yaro — for Radomir's casks to fill, and our bones to rot of scurvy? Is that the trade we've made?"

I said nothing. What was there to say? The sea takes the time it takes.

But then — as if the sea heard him — the call went up. Not wild, not frantic, but sharp and certain.

"Whale!"

It was close. We saw the roll of its back, the long dark gleam of it in the morning light, the spout high and white against the cold air. A bull, and not small. *The Tusk* came alive at once. Radomir's voice cut through the wind. Stavko brought her round. The sail strained full, the riggers at their work, lines creaking, canvas tight. The ship bore down, the whale ahead of us, close enough now that we could see the scars on its hide, the curve of its flukes as it sounded, the broad V of its wake.

The boats were lowered — swift, sure, clean into the sea, no time wasted. I took my place at oar, the salt spray cold on my face. Urek stood at the bow of my boat, his long form swaying with the rise and fall of the swell, the harpoon poised. He did not speak — not then. The Voryani tongue is for song, for curse, for prayer. But Urek's silence spoke sharper than any word. His laugh — that came when death was near. Not before.

As we closed the distance, oars biting deep, Urek's eyes never left the whale. I saw then what men meant by the Shadow's Heart: the look of him in that moment, wild, fearless, as if no sea could drown him, no beast could crush him, no end could claim him. And for a heartbeat, I believed it.

There is a madness in that moment, when the oars bite the water and the boat surges, every man pulling as if to tear the sea apart. The breath tears the throat, the salt stings — but all you see is the quarry ahead, vast, alive, terrible in its grace. The world narrows to the swing of the oar, the rush of the boat, the voice of the sea and the beat of your own heart.

Urek stood at the bow, the harpoon raised, the ink on his skin black with spray. He was silent — not the silence of fear or prayer, but the kind that steadies a hand and makes men believe death will come clean. His dark eyes tracked the whale's course, cold and certain, as if the sea itself had taught him when the moment would come. And when it did, he would strike — and if the sea swallowed him after, he would laugh as it took him.

We had not spoken, Urek and I. Not beyond the work — the coil of line, the weight of gear. But a man like that, you know him without words. The sea knows him. I watched him as we made ready, as the whale's trail showed itself, as the chase began. And I thought: here is a man the world will not break, not clean. He will shatter it, or be shattered by it, and laugh either way. A man like that — he draws death nearer, for himself, for all. But I was glad, in that moment, that he stood at our bow. If death came, better it found him first. And better still if he struck first, and death fled.

We closed. Oar after oar, pull after pull, the boats came alongside, the water breaking white at the bow, the whale's wake boiling ahead.

Then — the strike.

The iron flew, arcing clean, biting deep. A second, a third followed — no chances taken. The lines hissed out as the whale sounded, the boat jerking hard as the beast ran. The men sprang to the lines, to the drag-boards, to the irons, working as if born to it. The boat slewed and surged, hauled through the water behind the fleeing giant.

The kill is a long thing, and not easy. The whale runs, and the boats hold fast, letting it wear itself down against its own strength. When it surfaces, the lances come out — long, narrow blades for the soft parts, the lungs, the heart if you can reach. The sea runs red. The whale fights, but strength fails, breath fails, blood runs out, life ebbs. A lucky hunt, they say, ends with a kill within four days at sea. And so it was for us — four days of chase, of toil, of blood. Radomir called it a godsend. I thought it the sea's weariness of us.

When the flukes at last stilled, when the sea grew quiet around the carcass, Radomir pounded Markov on the back, near enough to break him in two. His good eye shone like a man with a king's ransom in sight. The men cheered in their way — low, rough, weary, but glad.

Then came the butchering. The boats worked close, the carcass chained fast alongside. The flensing spades came out, long-handled, sharp as sin, biting deep into the blubber. The men worked in shifts, stripping skin and fat in great white ribbons, hauling it aboard with block and tackle, slicing it down on the deck where the marks of old kills showed. The blood ran black in the scuppers, oil slicked every plank and hand. The smell — thick, hot, cloying — mingled with salt and tar, a stench no wind could carry off. Blubber hooks caught the strips, mincing knives cut them for the casks. The meat, what could be used, went to salt. The rest, what the sea would take, went over the side — sharks already circling, gulls screaming, the water boiling with the feeding.

Long, filthy work. The kind that sets in the bone and mind alike. But it was done, at last.

Radomir grinned through the blood and oil, his teeth white in the mess of it, his eye bright. The casks were full, or near enough. The ship heavy with her prize.

And I — I thought of luck. Radomir called it good luck to kill in four days. The men called it Markov's charm, his way with God, or with the sea, or with the beast itself. But I thought: I have no luck. Perhaps it goes with the talking.

CHAPTER X: IRONMARK

Ironmark rose from the sea like a beast with a broken back — all jagged lines, smoke, and ruin, yet hungry still. The first sight of it struck me like the crack of an axe on bone. Seven years gone — seven years of exile, of stone and sea for my only company — and yet the weight of men's work, men's hunger, men's filth pressed down on me as if I'd never left.

A city of smoke. Of salt. Of sweat. Of voices — loud, bitter, bartering, cursing, pleading. No two alike, yet all bound by the same hunger. I had thought myself hardened to it. I had thought the sea had scoured that part of me clean. But Ironmark reminded me: the world of men leaves no man clean.

Ships packed the harbour so tight the sea itself seemed choked. Fat cogs, their sides heavy with trade's burden; storm-runners lean and scarred from outrunning death; whalers black with toil and old blood; a siege barge squatting low in the water like a bloated wolf. The piers crowded thick with sheds thrown up in haste, boards already warped, roofs already bowed — as if the city knew it would fall before it ever rose.

The stink of it reached us before the lines were cast. Tar. Brine. Oil gone rancid. Fish too long dead. The breath of men packed too close, living too hard. The Tusk came to berth slow, as if she too mistrusted what waited ashore. Radomir One-Eye stood at the tiller, his good eye sharp on the ropes, the blind one staring past Ironmark, past the sea, past the world.

Markov was over the side before the line bit the cleat. His boots touched the quay soft, sure. His grin flashed — all teeth, no promise. I saw silver pass to Radomir's palm, saw him lean close — a whisper meant for no ears but ours.

"Those two," Markov said, pointing with fingers quick and certain to two crooked shopfronts, "they'll cheat you no worse than their neighbours. Cross yourself to Saint Kosma before you deal — might earn you a fair weight. That's the best I can give."

Radomir's laugh came low — like stone scraping stone. His fingers closed on the coin. His eye gleamed. "Your tongue's worth more than silver, little fox," he said.

I turned to Nik Vran'sson. I had pulled the oar with him, shared the sea's salt with him. We had needed no more than the sea's language. But I would not go without word. I took his arm.

"Good hunting to you," I said.

Nik's grip met mine, firm, sure. His eyes said what words did not. "And to you."

Then Urek came — long and lean, his hair wild with the wind, his grin fierce as a shark's maw. His hand clapped down on my shoulder, near drove me to my knee.

"You've the makings of a whale-man, Yaroslav," he said. "The way you hauled at those oars — I thought you'd tear the sea in two or drag the beast to us by will alone. I'd ship with you again, and glad of it."

His eyes saw me plain. No jest in them. No lie.

"And I with you," I said. The words came of their own accord. That surprised me.

We went ashore.

Ironmark closed round us like the jaws of a trap. The press of men. The stink of fish guts, of oil gone sour, of piss and rain and rot. Green wood smoke clawed at the throat. The stones of the quay slick beneath our boots — with filth, with spilled ale, with the offal of trade. Voices came from all sides. Loud, shrill, pleading, mocking, bartering, cursing. A city grown rich — and grown rotten. A wound, not a tree.

Markov breathed deep, as if the stench were a balm. His shoulders eased. His step quickened. His eyes glimmered like a man come home.

"Ah, Yaro," he said. His grin widened, wolfish. "Here's where silver walks the streets looking for a hand bold enough to claim it. Here's where a man makes his fortune — or dies trying."

I watched the faces. The hands. The shadows. My own hand rested near the blade at my belt. I trusted no silver that walked here.

Markov's fingers brushed my arm — light, coaxing. "Come," he said. "I know a place where a man may drink and not pay for it with his throat. Not every night, at least."

And he was off — weaving through the crowd like a fish through reeds, the city seeming to part for him, as if it too knew its own.

Markov led me through Ironmark's veins — narrow streets choked with smoke, fish guts, and human waste. The sea's breath could not cut the stench; it only pressed it deeper into the stone. His pace was light, easy, as if he walked to a feast.

"This way," he called over his shoulder. "Best food in the city."

My boots struck the wet stone. The filth splashed up the hem of my cloak. Markov moved like a man at ease among his kind, a man who belonged in the press and stink of human hunger. His step had the spring of one who knew his place in such a world. I felt the weight of the walls, the crush of lives packed close, clawing for breath, for coin, for warmth. Markov needed this — the noise, the nearness, the chance to measure a man by his grin or his purse. Like a gull, he thrived at the shore's edge, where the scraps are plenty and the wind brings scent of spoil and prize. I had always sought the open sea, the long hunger of the waves, where a man stands alone and the wind strips him bare. The deep teaches a man what he is. The shore teaches him what he can get.

Are men born for shore or sea? Or does the current shape us? Are fish formed by the waters they swim in, or do they find the waters that match the shape of their need? Does a gull choose the shore, or was it made for it?

Markov, the city's son, was made for this — or made by it. His tongue was his oar, his jest his sail. He rode these streets as I once rode the storm's edge, sure of his way. But I had lived too long with the sea's hunger to stomach the press of men. Still, I followed. Some currents drag a man whether he wills it or no.

We came to it: a house of dark timber, varnish dulled by salt air, lanterns burning steady against the dusk. The sign above showed a mermaid — paint cracked and weather-worn, her smile still leering down at all who passed.

Markov swept his arm wide, as if presenting a hall fit for kings. "Behold — the Siren's Mercy. The finest house in Ironmark. Where a man drowns happy, if he must drown at all."

And with that, he stepped through as if through his own door.

Inside, the warmth hit like a blow — thick with meat, wine, perfume, sweat.

Mother Sveda met us at the threshold — broad at shoulder, thick at hip, solid as a ship's rib. Her grey hair, coarse as rope, was braided tight and coiled at the nape, not a strand loose. She wore dark wool, plain but well-kept, the hem neat, the cloth heavy enough to outlast a dozen winters. A simple belt bound it close, from which hung a ring of iron keys — the weight of the house in her keeping. Her boots were sound and scuffed, made for hours on stone. Her eyes swept us once — dark, quick, cold — purse, boot, bearing, all taken in at a glance. A net cast and drawn tight in a breath.

"Markov," she said, as if expecting him. Perhaps she was. Her voice was deep, rough, and inviting.

Coin passed, easy as breath. Likely not his own, the way Markov spent it. But the weight was true.

She stepped aside.

A man stood at the stair's head — pale scars across his throat, a gold chain heavy at his neck. His gaze swept the room once, and the air changed. The laughter grew louder, brighter; the girls' smiles widened, their voices turned sweeter. His glance weighed their worth.

The house's true master. I marked him. The kind of man whose smile means nothing good.

Markov led me to a table near the hearth. Women drifted close — young, painted, bold-eyed. Their beauty sharpened to catch the unwary, their laughter the lure. They were beautiful the way calm water is beautiful — bright on the surface, hiding the pull that will drag a man down to the depths.

That thought shamed me. Once I'd called a woman beautiful for what she shaped of the world, not what the world shaped of her. Men's hungers spoke loud in places like this — the hunger for flesh, for touch, for warmth in the dark. I did not scorn it. A man's blood runs hot, and cold nights are long. But that hunger was not the same as what I'd known with Anya. With her, I had known a fullness no coin could buy, no painted smile could counterfeit. Her touch did not bind, but set me free.

And now? Now I sat among snares, watching them tighten, knowing I would not struggle in them, but neither would I seek their comfort.

The food was good. Better than I'd tasted in months. Roast lamb, bread soaked in the meat's juice, and sharp cheese. The whitefire was better still — clear as meltwater, sharp as a blade. Distilled from barley or skirret, strong enough to still your hands or strip the grief from your throat. A drink for oaths, pain, and nights you didn't want to remember.

Markov ate like a man starved, drank deep, laughed louder than needful — but I saw his eyes. They weighed the room, the door, the shadows at the edge of the firelight.

I ate sparingly. The weight of the place pressed down: the hunger in the walls, the barter behind each laugh. I thought of

Saint Dobrina, who gave comfort without price, and felt the shame of this house press deeper.

Then she came — Vesha.

She moved through the room like a snake through grass, all grace, all danger. Eyes grey as a gull's wing, sharp as the hook beneath the bait. She stopped at our table and let her hand trail along Markov's shoulder — slow, as if weighing the meat beneath. Her fingers traced the scar at his neck, the hollow at his throat, as if she might take his measure by touch alone.

"Markov," she said, voice soft as smoke, words shaped to wound. "What rock turned and let you crawl out tonight? Or have you come to sell the Queen's secrets to the lowest bidder?"

Her gaze passed over me once — a flick, a weighing. I saw the twitch at her mouth. Not scorn, not surprise. The flat bridge of my nose, broken more than once. The heavy brow, the squared jaw, the ear half-missing. And I've known what it is to be looked at that way — as if a dog had climbed aboard and learned to walk upright.

"There she is, the queen of thieves." Markov grinned, lifted his cup in salute.

She sat, draped herself on the bench as if it were a throne. "And you, king of fools."

"And here I thought I'd find kindness, Vesha. Mercy, even."

"Kindness?" Her laugh rang low and bitter. "From me? That's a poor man's hope."

Markov reached for her wrist, caught it light as if afraid she might vanish. "No need to beg if my purse is swollen enough to satisfy."

Her smile sharpened. "Your purse is full, but your goods are poor. You'll give me your coin, your pride, and your dignity — and you'll pay glad for the chance."

Their barbs flew, but the look between them was hunger made flesh. Her scorn cut him, but he leaned into the blade as if no sweeter pain could be had.

I drank, though I had no thirst.

Markov turned to me. "What do you need, my friend? Something soft, to thaw that heart?"

Vesha's eyes glinted. "Soft? No. Something sharp, to cut him free."

I felt the blood rise in my face and cursed it. Not for prudery — for memory. For the woman who had smelled of smoke and fennel, whose hands had shaped warmth from stone and scarred flesh.

"A man who loved true once has no taste for coin-bought smiles."

Vesha tilted her head, resting her chin on her hand, the picture of lazy interest. Her smile curved, sweet as bait. "And who was she, sailor? This beauty who taught you such fine sorrow? Tell me, so I may dream of her too."

I held her gaze, but said nothing. I had spoken too quick. One of the women drew her thin shawl close, as if to guard against the draft — or the house master's glance from the stair. Another's smile faltered when the laughter rose too sharp nearby. They worked, as I did, to keep ruin at bay.

And I saw it then — how she played the part, how the softness was as much craft as kindness, how even her interest was another net to draw a man closer. Not malice, not danger — just the trade. And I knew: this was not a battle worth joining.

A wise man knows when to strike, and when to steer clear of the reef.

I set my cup down. "When do we sail? What's the plan?"

Markov's grin stayed, but his eyes turned wary. "Not here," he said, voice low. "Not where ears are bought as easy as wine." As he slid coin across the table, the murmur of the room shifted — quieter, watchful. A man at a corner bench paused, his cup halfway to his lips, gaze lingering too long before turning aside.

Markov called for rooms. Gold made doors close, made tongues still — or so we hoped.

But the warmth of the brothel pressed too close. The air thickened, sweet with perfume, rank beneath. I left the fire's glow, stepped out into the night. The cold wind cut through the stink. The sea's voice rose faint beyond the city's din — raw, clean, honest. Saint Yarila's name passed my lips, not as prayer, but as a man's wish to be washed of the shore.

Better the sea's hunger than the comforts of this place.

Markov led me up the narrow stair, his boots light on the warped boards, the last of his bottle swinging loose in his hand. The air pressed close — smoke, old drink, bodies too many for the space. The hall above ran crooked beneath a low beam, doors set uneven, walls streaked with soot from years of lamp oil burned cheap. He paused at the first door and nudged it open with his heel.

"Mine," he said, the grin easy, the eyes sharp. "Come in. One more before bed — seems a shame to waste good whitefire."

I ducked beneath the lintel. His hand, quick as a gull's snatch, brought out two tin cups as if conjured. He poured — with a flourish, of course.

I watched the spirit catch the candlelight, pale and perfect, and considered my companion.

In the main room he'd played at half-drunk. Now, in the quiet of his chamber, his eyes were sharp again. The grin lingered, but the man behind it stood ready — weighing the night, the house, me.

Markov wore his jests the way I wear silence — shield, blade, bargain. His craft is words; mine is steel. But both are born of the same hunger: to measure the world's edge, to find where safety lies in a place where none is given.

What is a man if he lays aside the thing that shields him? Can he stand as he is, bare to the storm? Or is there nothing beneath the mask but wind and salt and ash? I have seen men cast off their shields, calling it courage, and fall to ruin. I have seen others cling so hard to the thing that guards them they shatter, and the pieces cut all those near. Perhaps that is all: to choose the mask that fits, and pray you die before it slips.

Markov's room was larger than I expected. The bed was broad, the mattress sagged where too many had left their shape. The bedding — coarse linen, clean enough, patched at the seams. A single candle guttered on a table scarred by knife and cup. A cracked basin crouched in the corner, water dull and still. A chair waited beneath the window — one leg loose, like the whole place might tumble if leaned on too hard.

Markov crossed to the window, threw the shutters open. The night air stirred the candle, brought the stink of the street: fish, piss, smoke. He stood a moment, as if taking the air, but his eyes were busy — mapping the alley, the roofs, the road that led out and away.

"Fit for a king," he said at last, mock-proud, turning back. "Or a prince of the gutter, at least."

He slouched against the wall, tipped his cup at me, offered the chair with a sweep of his hand. I stayed on my feet.

"You've questions," he said.

Too many. And none I could shape into words.

"When do we sail?"

"We don't." He drained his cup. "We ride."

"Tanglewood in the isle's belly? Not wise."

"There's a road." He smiled — but the edge of it had dulled.

"Two days by sail. Seal's Passage is kind in this season."

"Too many eyes at the port. Too many tongues that'd wag to see an old wolf shipped off on royal business."

I stared at him. "Why the secrecy? What's an old fighter to the crown?"

"Not just an old fighter," Markov said, voice lower now, the jest gone. "A man folk still remember — for doing what was asked, no matter how hard. The king's enemies, their kin — none were spared. That's the word."

"Bards' lies and soldiers' drink-tales," I said. "I did what was asked. I did what I swore. That is all — and more than I care to remember."

He shrugged, poured again. "Why you? I couldn't say. Dragomir's mouth said the words. Told me: wait at Owl's Haven. Bring a man without notice. Didn't even know it was you I was fetching till I walked into the hall and saw your face."

"He called himself Beran."

Markov laughed — low, quick, as if the truth tasted bitter on his tongue. "Of course he did. The queen's shadow's worn so many names he'd need a ledger to remember his own."

He fell quiet for a breath. His eyes dropped to his cup, but I saw the flicker of something behind them — memory, maybe. Or regret. Or hunger for a thing long out of reach. He didn't speak it. Just took a sip, wiped his mouth with the back of his hand, and let the moment pass.

"Orders are orders," he said at last, voice lighter than his eyes. "I was told: by land."

I felt the weight of that, though the words came light from his lips. The queen. Her spies, her whisperers, her knives in the dark. All at her call. And she calls *me*. I, who fought for Mstislav, not for her. It made no sense. Unless the world had turned more crooked than I feared.

"I never served the queen," I said, though the words felt thin between us.

"As if I didn't know that." His tone stayed easy, but his gaze sharpened — watching me, weighing what I'd do with the truth.

"Does the king know?"

He shrugged, as if the question were smoke in the wind. "I deliver you. I get paid. That's what I know." He drank again, slower this time, and set the cup down, his thumb tracing the rim.

A silence settled between us. He broke it first, his voice shifting like a man changing his grip on a blade. "Can you ride?"

"No."

"Horses, mules, ponies — all the same once you're on. You'll learn."

"I'd rather not meet what magic calls those woods home."

"There's a road," he said again — and this time his grin came full, bright with the promise of trouble. "It'll be fine."

I didn't believe it. Famous last words. The kind men carve on their own stones.

A knock broke the moment. Markov's face lit, all sharp edges smoothed away. "Ah. There's my prize."

He clapped my shoulder and crossed to the door. "Sure you don't want a taste of what's sweet?"

The door swung wide. She stood there — Vesha. The silk at her hips clung like seaweed to stone. The cloth at her breast no thicker than a net, and meant to catch as surely. Hair black as storm cloud, eyes grey as a wave's break. She knew what she was — and flaunted it.

"I'll take my leave."

I tried not to look where my gaze wanted to fall. I bowed without thinking. "Ma'am."

She laughed, full of delight and mockery. "He ma'am'd me! Like I'm some princess!"

Markov, grinning wicked, swept a low bow. "Your majesty."

"Down with you, serf! Grovel before me!" she commanded, sweeping past me, the scent of rose and wine trailing in her wake.

Their laughter followed me out. I shut my door on it.

My room was no more than a cell. A narrow bed, rough blanket of undyed wool thrown over sackcloth stuffed with straw and what little wool the owner could spare. No basin. No chair. Just a hook for my cloak, a battered chest for my pack. The boards creaked beneath me as I crossed.

I knelt, as I did in my hall, as I had on ships' decks in storm — no words, no saint's name, only the weight of my hands on my knees, the cold of the boards, the promise that I would stand again. Then I lay back, arms folded, staring at the cracked plaster where the ceiling sagged. The mattress yielded too soft beneath my weight, as if it meant to swallow me. I longed for the cold planks of my hut, the clean hardness of the earth. The blanket scratched at my throat.

And then the sounds came.

The creak of the bed next door. Slow at first, then faster. The rhythm sure, steady, like oars pulling through water. Her voice — soft at first, breath and sigh, then louder, a low moan that rose like the wind in rigging. The bed struck the wall in time with their joining. A laugh — his or hers — hard to tell.

I turned my face to the wall, but the sound filled the room, filled me. My blood stirred, the old hunger waking where I'd thought it starved quiet. I should have said yes. Should have taken the comfort offered. But pride cut deeper than need. And no gold in my purse to buy what I could not ask for. No words for it, even if I'd had the coin.

The bed kept its beat. Her voice, sweet and terrible, filled the night. And I lay there, listening, as the darkness stretched long.

CHAPTER XIII: TANGLEWOOD

The morning air was cool and damp as we left Ironmark, the sea's salt still clinging to our cloaks. The city's noise — the creak of ships, the calls of merchants, the distant clang of the shipwrights' hammers — faded behind us as we made our way inland. Despite Markov's claims, my attempt to ride ended as I knew it would: shame, laughter, and bruises for my pride. Markov rode ahead, urging his mule along the rising trail, while I walked behind, more comfortable on my own two feet than trusting the temperamental beast. He cursed my pace under his breath, but I heard him well enough.

We took the east road, what road there was: little more than rutted earth, the marks of old cartwheels softened by moss and the tread of time. As we climbed, the land changed. The low, rolling fields that stretched out from the city gave way to the thickening forest. Birch and pine crowded the path, their branches intertwining overhead to form a canopy that filtered the sunlight into dappled patterns on the ground. The further we went, the more the forest seemed to swallow the world behind us. The air grew cooler, the scent of the sea replaced by the earthy aroma of moss and damp leaves.

Tanglewood sprawls over the Greyspine Mountains, that great shadowed backbone that runs down the heart of Sea Fort Isle like a vast, knotted cord of stone and forest, full of dark secrets and terrors no man dares name aloud. The forest chokes hidden valleys where the sun rarely falls, and clings to cliffs shorn by ancient ice and storm. Rivers cut through it — whispering low in the autumn, racing wild in the spring — their voices lost beneath the sigh of the old, gnarled trees that hide their dead and worse. High above it all lies Lake Vorona, cold as iron, dark as old blood, where the water's depths hide cruel creatures that hunger for the flesh of the unwary. The men of Bryn's Hollow and Svetlow are few, but hard as the stones they farm and the nets they cast — folk who feel neither cold nor fear as other men do, and who, when roused, fight like the Chuchuna: wild, silent, unrelenting, until blood runs in the snow.

Markov had not truly explained our journey in full. Not as a man might who owed honesty. What he offered was the shape of a plan, smooth on the tongue, easy enough to swallow by the fire's light. He spoke of paths he had ridden as a courier — dark, narrow ways where no lord's banner flew and no tax was asked, but where quick feet and quicker wits meant more than sword or prayer. The main road from Ironmark to Velgrad, he said, wound through the mountain towns — a hard ten days of travel at best, with tolls at every bridge and no promise the roads would be clear. But he, Markov, knew a better way. A shorter way. A path that would cut the journey near in half if a man kept his head and his coin ready.

"So long as we pay Miro's toll, and slip past Sava's dogs, we'll be through before Velgrad's bakers have the next batch cooled," he'd said, with that grin of his that dared you to call him a liar.

Easy words. Easy enough to speak of paying Miro's toll, of slipping by Sava. Especially if you were a liar — or if you meant to seem a fool while keeping one eye always on the door. The reality was certain to be harder. I had walked long enough in such lands to know the price men like Miro and Sava set was not paid only in coin. But then, Markov did value his own skin, and likely mine as well, given what price he stood to earn for delivering me safe to Velgrad. And he had proven himself less of a fool than he pretended. The kind of man who wore his cleverness like a patched cloak — plain at first glance, but stitched with thread too fine for honest work.

He spoke lightly of dark woods, of hidden tracks, of the chance of danger — as if naming it robbed it of its fangs. But I had heard what fangs waited in such places, and no word ever dulled them.

As the sea disappeared from sight, I hesitated. The path bent and rose, and for a breath I stood still at the crown of the ridge. Below lay Ironmark, its crooked streets and smoke-stained walls pressed close to the grey curve of the harbour. Beyond that, the sea — a broad sheet of steel beneath a pale sky, restless even in peace. Its breath carried faint to me on the wind: salt, rot, the sharpness of old fish and old blood. A smell I had known all my life. A hunger I understood.

The sea is danger, yes. But danger a man can see, can measure — the set of the waves, the dark of the clouds, the cut of the wind. The sea gives a man warning, if he knows how to look. And I did. The forest ahead — that was another thing. No warning in it, no reason. Only shadow, and what waits in shadow.

Markov had ridden on, his mule picking its way down the slope. The trees gathered thick below — black-stemmed birch, alder twisted with age, pine dark as night. They seemed to lean together, closing the path, swallowing the last of the light. The first breath of the wood reached me then: damp earth, leaf mould, a coldness like water left too long in the dark. I felt it settle on my skin, on my heart.

It is a small thing, a single step. But the weight of it was not small. I turned from the sea — from the known, the bitter, the honest danger of it — and set my feet on the path that led into Tanglewood. The land took me in, and the trees closed behind.

Markov kept his mule to the path, the beast sure-footed where mine only sought the next patch of grass. His voice drifted back, easy as ever, as if the trees weren't closing in and the shadows didn't press so close you could feel their breath.

"Ironmark raised me," he said. "Fish guts and piss in the gutters, and me running between them. My mother sold scraps from a barrel. My father — he sold what little sense he had. Streets taught me faster than they taught most. No man's fool, no man's dog. First, I ran messages to the out-farms, then up to Bryn's Hollow. Even Mad King Voran, once or twice. You'd have liked him, Yaro. Wooden fort that leaned like a drunkard's grin. Five wives — no, six by the end — and enough brats to found a village of his own blood. Thought himself a king, and maybe he was. In his own eyes, at least."

My mule stopped again, head down, teeth tearing at a clump of grass as if the world had nothing more to offer. I yanked at the reins. The beast shifted, stubborn as stone. My pack dragged at my shoulders, my boots sank in the muck at the path's edge, and sweat stung my eyes.

"Move," I hissed. "Damn you."

Markov glanced back, grinning. "That mule has the right of it. Knows to eat while it can. Knows what's coming."

Then — a snap in the undergrowth. Sharp. Close. My heart rose. Greyfang was in my hand before I thought. Mstislav's blade — the linen wrap falling away as I drew. The steel caught what little light the forest spared, glistened like wet stone. The weight of it was right in my hand. The edge, bright as frost. A king's blade, meant for war, for the shaping and breaking of kingdoms.

The brush parted. A porcupine waddled out. Nose twitching, quills rattling, black eyes blind to threat. It sniffed, snorted, and trundled on, undaunted, leaving the path as it found it.

Markov all but fell from his saddle. "My God, Yaro! Look at it flee! Mstislav's own steel bared against the terror of needles! Let the bards sing it: the mighty sword, the beast of quills, the hero who saved the path from doom!"

His laughter rang long after the porcupine was gone. I sheathed the blade, my hand still tight on the hilt, my face hot with shame. I said nothing. The forest mocked me well enough without his help.

We rode on, the path narrowing, the hush of the trees closing round us again. After a time, Markov spoke — low, with that grin of his, the one that meant trouble or truth. "Quite the blade at your hip. I'm no expert in long steel, but even I'd say a man could trade that for a year's wine, or a wife — two, if he haggled."

"It was a gift," I said. "From the king." I was not eager to speak of it, and less to make light. "No bought woman, nor all a year's harvest, is worth what that blade cost."

Markov chuckled. "That's you all over, Yaro. Another man sees a king's gift and thinks of gold. You see it and count the graves behind it."

I said nothing. There was no jest in it, not for me.

We reached the fork by midday. The main road curved east, broad enough for carts, kings' taxes, and merchant trains. It climbed the valley's shoulder where trees thinned and the light grew clearer — but the way was longer. The southern path — Markov's shortcut — bent hard into the dark, narrower than a cart's axle, the trees crowding close, the ground uneven, the light already failing though the sun stood high.

Markov didn't hesitate. He turned his mule south, his voice light, as if he guided a friend to a tavern, not a grave. "Here's where we shave days from the journey, Yaro. You'll thank me when the ale's in your hand and Velgrad's gates at your back."

We pressed on. The trail dropped, steep toward the Mir. The river below was no longer broad or lazy. The floods had carved a gorge sheer and dark. Water churned through broken stone, loud enough to drown a man's shout. The gorge walls rose, the ledge narrowed, my mule's hooves slipped — and my stomach clenched at each misstep.

Then we came to the bridge.

If it could still be called that. The timbers were grey with age, some blackened where old lightning had found them. The handrails were gone. The planks bent under their own weight, bowed like the back of a beaten man. It spanned the gorge with the look of a thing forgotten by time, and too stubborn to fall.

I stopped. The mule stopped. Both of us stared at that ruin of wood and rope and old prayers.

To the east the road curved away, safe, easy, longer by days. South was the bridge — a promise of peril and of haste.

Markov turned in the saddle, his grin sharp as ever. "It's sturdy enough. I've crossed it a dozen times. It only looks like death."

My mule had more sense than I. It balked, snorting, ears flat, backing from the bridge's edge. I couldn't blame it. My own feet felt rooted. My heart beat hard, my hands were damp on the reins. The gorge yawned deeper, the water roared louder. The river's hunger called in its own voice.

Markov sighed. "Here. Give me the beast." He slid down, took the reins from my unresisting hands, and led the mule out onto the planks. The animal followed, unwilling but trusting him more than me, its hooves knocking hollow on the old wood.

I stood alone, watching, feeling the shame burn hot under my skin. A king's sword at my hip, fear in my bones. Markov's voice came light across the gap: "Come on, Yaro. The bridge doesn't eat men — only their pride."

The wind caught at me, cold as a thief's hand. My knees knocked. I kept my eyes ahead, though the black water called. I whispered prayers — to God, to the saints, to the sea itself. Each step betrayed sense. But shame carried me where courage failed.

On the far side, Markov handed back the mule's reins with a wink. "See? Easy as a tavern floor. You even managed to keep your boots dry."

I said nothing. The wood creaked behind us, the river roared below, and the forest waited ahead.

The trees closed in above us, their branches knitting together so tight that what light the day had left seemed to die at their edges. The trail — if trail it could still be called — wound through the dark like a forgotten scar. The wind shifted, but down here it did not stir the air; it felt dead, heavy with damp and rot.

At times I could not tell if we followed a path or the bed of an old stream long dry. Stones jutted from the earth at odd angles, moss-eaten and black with age. The ground rose and fell without sense, and more than once Markov stopped, swore low, and led us back the way we'd come, searching for some mark — a blazed tree, a pile of stones, a notch in a fallen trunk — that would swear we hadn't wandered into a hunter's forgotten ground or worse.

The forest watched. I felt it as sure as I felt the weight of Greyfang at my hip. The trees leaned inward, their limbs twisted like the limbs of old men crippled with age and malice. The stones seemed to lean too, hunched shapes in the gloom, as if they'd crept close when we weren't looking.

I thought of the stories told at hearths and in the barracks — and of Olek, the scout, who boasted he could not be lost, and whose bones we found a season later, stripped clean, the path twisted round his grave. There were those who said the forest fed travelers to the leshyi — creatures of hunger and spite, like trolls in the old tales, half beast, half man, who stole children, twisted the limbs of trees to mark their dominion, and boiled the bones of those they caught in their cauldrons of tar and blood.

The stories were for children. But the trees did not know that. And neither did I, as the dark gathered close and the path ahead grew harder to see.

By the time we reached the ruined fort, the sun was dipping low, casting long shadows across the crumbling stones. The fort had once stood as a sentinel at the edge of what men dared to claim, but now it was little more than a marker — the place where the king's law ended and Miro's began. Moss and ivy clung to what was left of the walls, the stones black with damp. The air was heavy with the scent of rot and wet earth. It felt as though the forest itself watched us, silent and patient.

We made camp within the shelter of the fort's broken heart, under what remained of its roofless hall. On the stones by the old gate I saw what the forest had not yet claimed: the faint cross-scratch of men's knives, the soot-mark of a vigil lamp long cold — signs left for Saint Kosma, perhaps, or Saint Mikula, where the king's law failed and only oaths and saints kept the dark at bay.

The night crept in fast. The fire Markov kindled threw thin light, no match for the dark that crowded close. I could not shake the sense that eyes were on us already — Miro's, or worse. The forest seemed to whisper as it breathed, a reminder that this was no man's land.

Markov, as ever, was untroubled. He set to the fire and the meal with the ease of a man born to it, handing me a strip of dried meat as he settled himself on a fallen stone.

"You worry too much," he said, chewing slow, his grin quick in the firelight. "Miro's just a man. And these woods are just trees. Keep your wits, and Velgrad will be at our backs before you've learned to like that mule of yours."

I said nothing. The weight of the fort's ruin, the press of the wood — they spoke louder than Markov's easy tongue.

After a time, he grew more serious. He leaned forward, voice low, the fire's light catching in his eyes. "You should know — they call him Miro the Good. Not for kindness. Because when he robs you, when he takes your coin, your horse, your last crust of bread — he does it with a smile. Because his kind of good means you walk away breathing, and not all men in these woods grant you that much. You understand?"

I nodded.

Markov continued. "So. When we meet him, I talk. You keep your mouth shut. Look dangerous — but not like a man spoiling for blood. We'll show just enough coin to be worth robbing, but not enough to make his boys think there's more hidden. And the king's sword — that stays hidden."

I frowned. "And how am I to look dangerous without it?"

Markov grinned, sharp and quick. "You've got the face for it, Yaro. A man wouldn't need steel to know you're trouble. And steel's no help if it makes Miro hungrier than we can afford."

I didn't argue. There was sense in it, bitter as it tasted.

He stretched, laid back against the stone, his voice softer now. "If he remembers me, it might get trickier. But I doubt he will. Been years. And I've kept my nose clean since. "Either way — we'll manage. Or at least I'll die trying to make it look like we did."

And with that, he closed his eyes and let the night take him, trusting the fire's thin light and my watch to keep the dark at bay.

The forest whispered on. We'd agreed to shifts, but I let him sleep. Someone had to keep the dark at bay.

CHAPTER XIV: MIRO THE GOOD

Morning broke thin and mean, grey and cold as steel left too long at sea's edge. The wind had shifted in the night — no longer soft from the south, but out of the east, raw, bitter, with the taste of stone and storm. We rose early, driven more by that cold, worming through our cloaks and into our bones, than by any wisdom in our plans.

The trail led us high. The forest fell behind us — the last stunted pines clinging to rock like dying men to prayer — and what had been a road, or the ghost of one, dwindled to a stony path no broader than a cart's axle. It clung to the mountain's shoulder, above a sheer fall into mist and ruin.

The mules bore it well. Their hooves found purchase where mine slipped, breath steaming, steady as the dawn. Markov, curse him, rode as if born to it, easy in the saddle, his grin sharp against the wind. I walked. I have never trusted any beast but the sea's own hunger. Better my own feet beneath me, though each step burned my legs and bent my back, and the wind cut me raw.

When at last the path eased, sloping down toward softer land, I dared to think we'd earned peace for a time. But peace is a thing men like me have no claim to.

They waited where the way widened — wolves in men's skins. Miro, and his pack. They lounged among the stones, spears and axes resting easy in their hands, their eyes sharp, hungry. The boulders framed them like a gate of the damned. The wind funneled through , cold as the sea's teeth.

Miro leaned on his spear, his smile all yellow teeth and mock welcome. "Well met," he called. His voice easy as a tollman's at his post. "A silver for safe passage, good sirs. A fair price, on a fair day."

Markov laughed, light as if the man's words were jest. He made a show of rummaging his pouch — slow, open, careless. He handed over what coin he'd let ride visible on his belt. Let the wolves take what they see, leave the rest. The oldest trick there is, but well played.

And for a moment, it seemed it would serve. Miro's eyes weighed the coin, not us. I felt the tightness in my chest ease. The toll paid. The wolves fed. Let us pass.

But men who talk too much are dangerous. And Miro liked to talk.

"You'll not be staying at Varon's Hollow, I hope?" he asked, easy as you please.

Markov, cursed be his silver tongue, answered with a lie so smooth it slid through the air like a knife through fat. "There's a cave beneath the Crowfall," he said, low and confiding. "Used to be a hermit's place. Dead these ten years. Safe spot — approach from the south. A ledge there, best shelter for miles."

The men nodded, satisfied, shifting easy on their feet. But Miro's head cocked, like a dog at a scent half-remembered. The wind stirred then, and I tasted the storm in it — the storm we'd walked into.

"A cave, you say?" Miro mused. "Quite a find. Tell me again where it lies?"

God help us. We had been through. The path had been clear. I could have wept for the waste of it. "We're for Varon's Hollow," I said, quiet but sure.

But the bit was in Miro's teeth. "Would there be rubies in this cave?"

Markov's grin stayed quick. "Rubies? No. Glowing mushrooms, perhaps. Touch one, you'll be chasing mountain goats — or each other — up and down the cliffs."

They laughed — all but the youngest, who flushed red beneath his hood.

"Bring me some," Miro said, "for young Janko here. He could use the seasoning."

The air tightened. The wolves shifted — subtle, slow — hands finding the balance of blade and haft.

"I like the way you talk," Miro said, his smile growing wider. "Reminds me of a lad once. Sweetest swindle I ever swallowed — tale of ten silver for two rubies. Told it so smooth, I near believed him myself."

Markov kept the grin. "Quite the trade."

"So it was — if it had been true."

My hand found the hilt beneath the saddlebag. Six men. Three I might take, before they cut me down. The rock walls pressed close. I named Saint Stepan then — not for mercy, only for strength, if steel must sing. The mist rose from the chasm like breath from a grave.

"What did you say your name was?"

Markov's voice stayed easy. "You didn't ask. Luka, simple courier. This is my oath-companion, Ivan."

Eyes turned to me. I had inched toward the mule, toward Greyfang. I stilled.

"A courier, was it?" Miro said. "Strange. Now I think of it, the boy who spun me that tale — he was a courier too. Carried silver, said it was from Gavrilo Redhand's own hand.

Promised two rubies for it, or the miser's hoard would be forfeit. So — where are my rubies?"

Markov laughed. "Miro, you know well the only rubies Varon ever owned were what the gulls left on his doorstep."

Miro's laughter boomed, loud enough to stir the crows from their ledges. A tear gleamed in his eye. "This is him!" he roared. "The sweetest rogue I ever met!"

And just like that, the storm broke. The danger bled out of the air, as tide from a bay. I felt the weight lift from my chest, my hand slip from the hilt. The wind eased. The rock let us breathe again.

"And how's Gavrilo these days?" Miro asked.

"Still as mean as the sea," Markov said. "And his girls still sweet."

Miro spat, for luck or for joy. "Off with you, then. And may the crows keep watch."

And just like that, we were let go — like old friends parting at a feast, with jests and blessings to see us on our way. Robbed all the same. Miro took no coin back, no toll repaid. Only the storm in the air had lifted — not the price of passing.

We found the Crowfall at dusk. The gorge split the rock like an old wound. The water spilled through it, black against the red bleeding from the sky, star-shaped where it burst from the cleft. The crows filled the ledges, their cries sharp, lost to the wind.

"You near got us killed," I said. My voice shook with what I would not name — fear, or fury, or both. My hand clenched, aching for the blade I'd not drawn. "If I had drawn — if steel had sung — we'd be feeding those crows now."

Markov said nothing, for once. He looked at the fall, but not as a man admiring the view. His face was pale in the dusk, his jaw set tight, his eyes dark with a weight I had not seen in him before.

And I saw it, then — the truth beneath his grin, beneath the easy tongue and quicker lies. He had been afraid. As afraid as I. But where I had reached for steel, he had reached for words. And perhaps we had both come close to dying for it.

His hand rose, slow, as if to wipe sweat from his brow, but it lingered at his mouth, covering what words might have come. When he spoke, at last, his voice was low, meant for me alone. "You think I liked it? Hearing Gavrilo's name in that bastard's mouth? God's truth, Yaro — I'd as soon walk naked into the sea than have it known whose coin I once carried."

I stared at him, the anger ebbing, the shame rising in its place. "You still carry it," I said. Not a question.

His mouth twisted — not a grin, but something bitter. "Maybe I do."

And there, for a breath, we were not rogue and soldier, not liar and fool. Just two men too long at the edge of ruin, too long at the mercy of their own choices.

I drew breath, slow, heavy. The wind off the fall carried the cold of the heights, the cold of the grave.

"God help me," I muttered. "A greater fool was I — following you. Trusting you."

But the words came without heat now. The crows cried above us. The water fell. The day ended.

CHAPTER XV: THE HOLLOW

We followed the river south. Its voice, strong with the melt, filled the valley with a cold that spoke of stone and bone rather than water. The trail clung to its edge, narrow, slick with moss where the sun reached, and where the shadows ruled, black mud sucked at our boots. The mountains leaned close on either side — as if the world wished to swallow the river and us with it.

By midday the clouds thickened, the light turned leaden. The first drops came — cold, hard, few. Then more, until the rain fell steady, washing the trail to slime, streaking our cloaks, soaking the mules to the skin. The wind woke with the storm, a mountain wind: bitter, swirling, tearing at our hoods, driving the rain into our faces no matter which way we turned. The river frothed and roared beside us, as if it laughed to see us struggle.

The mules fought us at every turn. Stubborn, cold, afraid of the wet stone underhoof. I cursed them softly — not in anger, but because a man's hands can only do so much. Markov fared no better. His voice, quick and coaxing, turned sharp. Once his mule nearly fell, scrabbling at a slick bend, and I saw him pale beneath the rain's filth.

By late light we found shelter. Not a house — no such thing in that wilderness — but a place where men, or beasts, had once raised rough walls against the storm. Three sides of split logs, a roof of branches and mud that let the rain through in thin threads, but still better than none. We lit a fire — the wood was wet, the smoke bitter, but it burned.

It was there Markov spoke, low as if the rain might carry the words to the wrong ears.

"Voran's a cruel bastard," he said. "Mean. Dangerous. Lives out here not just because he hates men, though he does. Because what he's done — what he's wanted — no village would have him. No hall would give him place. Miro and Sava both claimed him. Both said his hollow was theirs. And both took payment from him. With what? I don't know. Maybe coin hid from raiding days. Maybe daughters. The wild has its own ways."

He spat into the fire. "But he'll honour the old laws. I think."

The rain eased as night fell. We pressed on, with the dark close behind us, and came at last to Voran's Hollow. If it could be called that. A fort once — a ring of rotten timbers leaning like drunks, gaps wide enough to drive a cart through. Within, broken houses, their roofs half-fallen, walls sagging, black with wet and age. The smell of smoke, filth, and beasts lay heavy.

No choice. No other shelter for leagues. And the woods held worse than wet.

Voran came at Markov's call — not at once, nor as a man eager for company, but slow, as if from a den, as if drawn against his will. A great man, though man seemed too kind a word. Hair hung thick over his face and breast, dark and matted with old filth. His eyes, deep-set, small, glinted like wet stones under that shag. His hands were heavy, fingers thick as roots, nails black with earth. He stood with his shoulders rounded, his head thrust forward, as if his neck had grown too short to bear his weight. The rain clung to him, ran down his beard in streams.

No word. Just the stare of a beast that measures whether to suffer your presence or tear you down.

Markov spoke the rite, voice steady despite the stink of the place and the weight of those eyes.

"Bread and salt between us. Water given. Knives bound by the bond."

A woman came — thin, her hair lank, her mouth tight as if it had forgotten how to smile. She brought a clay cup, a crust of bread hard as horn. Watched as we ate, eyes sharp, waiting for the act to seal what the words had begun.

Voran grunted. A sound more fit for a boar. He raised a hand like a shovel and pointed to a space against the inside of the broken wall — boards leaned to make half a roof, mud-chinked in places, gaping in others.

"There." His voice was rough as bark. "Shit in the woods."

I gave the thanks owed, the words rough in my mouth. His eyes did not leave me. I could not read them — hunger, hate, envy, fear — only that they watched, and weighed.

We unpacked the mules, moved under the boards. The rain had eased to a spit, the wind a restless thing that found every crack. The night came down hard, the clouds thick, the hollow drowned in black. The fire we tried to build guttered low, the wood too wet, the flame too weak.

The place stank — of damp wood, of smoke, of beasts, of filth unburied. The wind brought other smells: rot, fur, the rank of old blood. From Voran's house no light showed. No sound. As if it, too, had gone to earth for the night, or waited.

The dark deepened. Rain hissed on the boards, spat at the fire, whispered through the timbers. The river's voice was far now, dull behind the wind's moan.

Then — the mule's scream. High, sharp, full of terror. The sound of hooves crashing through brush, the thud of panic.

Markov's face paled in the fire's weak glow. He grabbed two sticks from the flame's edge, shook them till they flared.

"Stay close," he breathed, though I already stood, Greyfang drawn, back to the boards.

Another scream — wet this time. Cut off. The sound of a thing dragged down.

Voran's house stayed dark. No door opened. No voice called. The silence of those within was its own kind of terror.

Markov moved quick, low, torch raised, along the broken wall, his shape flickering in the firelight. I went the other way, through the sagging houses, the torch's glow leaping from beam to beam, shadows writhing like things alive. The wind caught the flame, bent it, near tore it out. Smoke stung my eyes. The rain hissed at my feet.

The hollow felt wrong. Empty — and yet not. The kind of stillness that comes when a great beast waits to strike.

And then I saw it. A shape beyond the edge of the light — too big for a man, too low for a tree. The torch caught it as the wind eased, just for a breath. Fur black as tar. Eyes like coals in ash. Breath steaming white. Blood fresh on the muzzle. The mule lay beneath one broad paw — broken, still, its flank torn open.

It growled — a sound that seemed to shake the ground, as if stone ground on stone.

I did not speak. I stepped back slow, the torch low, the sword ready, though what blade could turn such a thing I did not know. Markov came from the dark, his torch near out. His breath caught when he saw.

"Back," I said. "Slow."

The thing watched. The rain fell. The hollow held its breath.

The torch flared as the wind died a breath, and I saw it plain. The shape no man could mistake, once seen. Black fur matted with mud and blood, shoulders broad as a door, claws like hooked iron. A muzzle split wide, teeth yellow as old bone, red with the mule's life. Eyes that burned — not the beast's eyes, but the eyes of a thing that remembers being man, and hates what it became.

The bauk. The word rose in me unbidden. The name from the old songs, the old prayers. The bear-thing that walks like a man, feeds like a beast, hungers like both. The shadow that haunts the hollows where no honest man will dwell.

It bent to its kill, tore flesh, fed as the dark hid it once more.

I stepped back slow. Markov beside me, his breath loud, his face pale.

"We can't fight that," he said. No shame in it. Only truth.

"No," I said. "We go back. Keep the fire, what little of it's left. Keep close. If it's fed, maybe that's enough."

"And if it's not?"

"Then we wait for dawn, and see."

We drew back, slow, torches shaking in the wind. The hollow seemed to close behind us — as if the dark itself wished to keep us there. We reached the lean-to. The mule stood near, trembling, eyes wide, the whites showing in the flicker of flame. We pulled it close, lashed it to what post we could find, though no rope could hold it if terror took it next.

I found the salt in my pack — a small bag, meant for the road's meat, for the sea's wear on boot and blade. I cast a line of it before the shelter, slow, deliberate, as if care might make it more than it was. *Saint Kosma guard this line*, I prayed — *where no king's law holds, let his justice stand instead*. The grains caught what little light the fire gave, like frost on black stone. I shaped the line as best I could with hands that shook.

And I spoke the prayer. Thrice over, low and sure, the words of the saints, shaped for the night's fear — not for mercy, only for strength to see the dawn. Markov said nothing. He only watched, and did not mock me.

The fire smoked, the rain hissed on it. The bauk fed in the dark. We heard the bones crack, the wet tear of flesh.

And we waited. For dawn, or for death.

CHAPTER XVI: THE CLEFT

The dawn came mean and thin, a light that did nothing to warm, nothing to drive back the night's weight. We had not slept. The fire died with the dark, the cold crept in, and the hollow kept its silence. The storm had passed, but left behind a world drained of colour — all grey, all wet, all still.

Voran's Hollow lay as the grave lies: waiting. No smoke from his house, no stir of life among the broken walls. Only the smell of mud, old blood, and ash, and beyond the gap in the timbers, the lake — still as glass, black as tar, where two mountain streams came together in a cleft of stone. It was beautiful, and that made it worse. A beauty that asked no witness, offered no comfort. A beauty fit for the dead.

We went to where the mule had fallen. The ground was torn — earth and moss flayed back, blood dark in the mud, black in the thin dawn. A trail led away, a smear of red and brown through a gap torn wider in the wall's rot. The carcass was gone, dragged into the trees. For later. For hunger that knew patience.

Markov said nothing. His face was drawn, pale under the filth, his eyes rimmed red with the night's watching.

We packed what we could. The rest we left — gear too heavy for what lay ahead, food we could not carry, tools I hated to part with but knew we must. Every weight mattered now. Every step would cost.

Voran's children watched as we left. I do not know how many. Eyes in the gaps of broken walls, shapes behind the timbers. No word. No farewell. No sign of Voran himself. As if the hollow had swallowed them whole in the night, or as if they watched to see if the dark would take us too.

The path led down, between peaks that loomed on either side like jaws. The light failed as we entered the cleft — not night, but something worse: a darkness that seemed to drink the day, to weigh on the skin, the breath, the heart. I crossed myself — *lips, heart, cross, shield*. We lit the torches. The flames hissed, bent low as if afraid of the place.

The walls closed in. Raw stone, wet with seep, slick where moss clung. In places the gap was so narrow we had to strip the mule of its packs, carry the burden ourselves while the beast squeezed through. The sound of water ran somewhere unseen — the streams we had crossed above now lost below our feet, whispering through rock.

And over that whisper rose another sound. A moan. Low at first, like wind in a hollow tree. Then rising, thin, sharp, until it seemed to scrape the bone. Then falling again to a whisper. Never still, never gone.

Markov's mouth was tight. His eyes searched the heights, the shadows, the gaps where nothing showed but the stone's black mouth.

I knew the name of that sound, though I had never thought to hear it. Viy's Daughters. The dead who died betrayed — women whose grief chained their souls to the dark places of the world. Pale as snow, their hair like riverweed, their eyes hollow as empty graves. Their voices could charm a man or break him. Some said they led travellers to ruin. Some said they wept for company, but killed all who came near. No blade could cut them. Only iron blessed at a saint's shrine might drive them off. I carried no such iron.

Above us, the cleft's roof vanished into dark. There, the torchlight showed strands that shone like wet rope — webs, but no spider spun so wide. The moan rose again. The mule balked, refused the path. We lashed it, coaxed it, begged it, then lashed it again. My arm burned with the effort. The beast shuddered but would not go. Only when Markov and I both set our backs to the load did it move, one step, then another, trembling as we pushed.

The moan became a wail. The wind rose, sudden, sharp — a breath from the throat of the stone. It blew out the torches. Left us in blackness thick as pitch.

Markov shouted. I did too. Saint Stepan's name burst from my lips. But his voice seemed to race away, as if the dark itself carried it down some hidden tunnel. My sword was in my right hand. The torch, dead stick now, in my left. I swung it wide, a blind man's blow — felt it strike something soft.

Then pain. A blow to the head. The world spun. I felt stone at my back, wet under my hands, then nothing.

I woke with the side of my face pressed into cold earth, stone biting at my cheek. The dark clung closer than sleep — a dark that weighed, that watched, that whispered I had not wakened at all. A moan rose above, soft at first, then swelling, until the stone itself seemed to keen, as if the mountain mourned its dead. I did not know what horror of the cleft had struck me, but I was alone.

Markov's voice echoed in memory — a shout, swallowed by the dark, the clatter of hooves like bones tumbling down a well. Then silence. My head throbbed, full of blood and sea. I raised a hand; it came away wet. Salt. Iron.

My fingers found Greyfang. The hilt was slick beneath my grip— blood, or water, or dream, I could not say. The torch lay cold beside me, useless as a prayer the gods no longer heard. With effort, I rose. Pain flared white, then dulled to a throb, a tide receding but leaving its wreckage behind. I leaned into the stone's wet face, as if it might grant strength — or mock me for needing it.

Time had no shape. Only my heartbeat, loud as surf. I did not know if I lived. Perhaps the cleft had swallowed me whole. Perhaps I walked in Nawia's cold halls, where the dead wait in endless night, no voice but wind, no hope but forgetting. The dark held me as the sea holds a drowned man — no past, no future, only the weight of now. The moan rose and fell — grief too old for comfort. I thought: so, this is death. No sea's embrace. No God's peace. No torment. Only endless dark, endless cold, endless wailing. As if I had fallen into a crack in the world, and the way forward led only to deeper night.

One hand to the wall, the sword's weight in the other. My boots dragged through water, or blood, or shadow — I could not tell. The cleft played its games: the clatter of unseen bones, the scrape of claw or stone, the brush of a rope at my feet. As if the rock birthed things that watched and waited. The air thickened with damp, rot, and something older that wished me gone.

I sat when my legs failed. Ate bread that tasted of dust. Drank water turned bitter. I doubted the world's truth. Perhaps I had never left Skeld. Perhaps I drowned long ago, and this was the dream that followed. I thought: this is the price for turning from the sea. I should have died there. I should have died with her.

If I was cursed to wander, why move at all? But I moved. Because a man cannot be still. We are not stone. Even the dead find no peace in stillness. We press against the world as blood presses against skin — seeking proof we are yet alive. I do not know why. Perhaps because we know we end. Or because no man can wholly surrender while breath remains.

At last the black softened. Grey seeped in like dawn through storm cloud. The walls showed their wet faces; the stream's trickle gleamed at my feet. I followed it, breath tight, hand to stone.

Voices. Faint. Then nearer. The world returned. And with it I learned: I could see from only one eye. The other was swollen shut, the flesh hot and tight. The dark was no longer complete — but broken.

I crept forward, good eye narrowed against the sudden grey. The stone's edge bit my palm as I leaned, slow, careful. Beyond it, the cleft widened — a clearing, if it could be called that. A bowl of torn grass and broken rock, hemmed close by dark pines, their trunks wet and black with seep. Markov stood at its heart, wrecked — his coat dark with blood, one leg dragged near useless, his face a ruin. Ringed by three shapes:

one thin and still, one broad and waiting, one loose-limbed with a bow half-raised. And beyond them, the trees closed like jaws.

The leader stood foremost — thin-faced, long-nosed, mouth hard as stone. No grin, no jest — only the cold look of a man who weighs lives and finds them light. His coat had once been fine, now worn thin, the colour of old blood. A stave in his hands, sword at his hip — the sort who lets others bleed first, but does not flinch from blood.

The archer — loose-limbed, yellow hair bound by a rag.

The axeman — thick, low-browed, a boar's face under a matted beard.

A fourth lay at Markov's feet, his throat a ruin. Markov's hand still gripped the dagger.

The leader's voice was low, flat, with no heat — as if he named what would be done, not what he wished.

"Maim him. Take the hand that held the knife. The tongue that mocked. Leave the rest for me."

Markov spat blood at his boots. His voice came thick, but steady. "All this because I shamed you, Sava? Then come take what's left yourself."

The archer gave a harsh bark of laughter — not joy, but the sound of a man relieved it was not him. The axeman shifted, eager, eyes on Sava's nod.

Sava's gaze stayed fixed on Markov — cold, measuring.

"You'll beg before the end. And I'll take my time."

The bow creaked. The arrow flew. Markov twisted — too slow. The shaft punched through his arm. His scream split the cleft like a bell of pain.

I moved. Not clean. Not fast. Just all I had left.

The archer tried to draw again. Greyfang found his throat. His blood came hot, fast, marking stone and skin.

The axeman turned, charged — quick for his bulk. His axe rose high, fell — a blow meant to break shield or skull. I gave ground. The blade bit earth, stone. He dragged it free, teeth bared.

I lunged — too eager. The point of my sword scraped his thigh — shallow, angering. He swung back, low. The edge kissed my ribs, tore cloth, drew a line of fire. Shallow. But pain enough to remind me I'd grown slow.

We circled, boots slipping in torn grass. His axe wove patterns, testing my reach. I kept Greyfang between us, two hands firm.

He feinted high, came low for my knee. I turned it aside, shock running up my arms. He pressed close, stinking of blood, sweat, old leather. He tried to shove me with the haft. I stepped in, shoulder to his chest. My pommel cracked his brow, opened skin. Blood in his eye. He shoved me off, but ragged now.

No words. Only breath. The thrum of blood.

He charged. I stepped inside his swing. The haft cracked my shoulder, dull pain deep. But I was in. Greyfang rose, edge took his ribs — deep. His axe scraped my back, but we were too close. His knee struck my thigh — numbed it near useless. I braced, lifted the blade, drove it up beneath his beard. Felt his breath, hot and wet. His hands faltered. His weight sagged. I let him down slow.

Sava ran. His boots slapped stone, curses flying. The forest swallowed him.

Markov fell. His breath ragged. "God," he said, wrecked mouth slurring. "Your face. That eye — can you see?"

"No."

He tried to grin, but pain dragged it crooked. "You always were ugly. Now you look like what the crows leave."

I broke the arrow shaft, drew it out. His cry rang to the stones.

"The mule?"

He raised a shaking hand. A shape — small, trembling — among the rocks.

I brought it close. Found the bandages. My hands shook as I worked, heavy with his blood. The wounds were bad — brow split, arrow through the arm, jaw and ribs bruised black, thigh gashed near bone, hands torn: But he'd live. If God was kind. I reached to Saint Dobrina as I bound him: *keep him from death's door.*

"There's a lot of blood," I said.

"Not all mine," he gasped. His grin thinned, near to death. He tipped his head to the forest. "He'll be back. And not alone."

CHAPTER XVIII: THE FOXWATER

Markov said it was two more days to Bors Mill — one to the forest's edge, where Sava's reach might fail, and another beyond. But first we had to outlast the dark that hunted behind.

I heard the Foxwater before I saw it: swift, cold, full of hunger. Its voice rose through the trees, a voice that never tires, never yields. I left the path, led the mule down a steep bank where the river cut stone and root like a blade. The water ran shallow, but fast — white with foam where it broke on rock.

We were out of sight. Safer, perhaps. The path behind twisted through the Tanglewood, every hollow and stone known to Sava's dogs. But the river, I thought, might shield us, if only for a time.

The mule balked. It stood trembling, snorting, eyes wide and rolling at the rush of water. Deaf to reason. Deaf to the hunger that truly followed us. I spoke soft, tugged the lead — useless. Markov could not help; he could barely stand.

In the end, I took what I could — food, rope, flint — and struck the mule hard across the haunch. It bolted, clattering up toward the path, hooves loud as a drumbeat. Perhaps Sava's men would hear, give chase. Perhaps. I had no faith in luck.

We made slow work along the river's edge. Markov's breath rasped; his strength failed him often. His blood ran thin as water, his face pale beneath the bruises. I tried once to carry him, but the ground betrayed me — slick with moss, treacherous with stone. The current ran faster than it looked. My bad eye turned the world strange; each step risked a fall.

The cold bit like iron.

A branch cracked behind us. Nothing — only the forest settling, I told myself. But I turned all the same, hand to hilt. The world seemed to hold its breath.

The river carved its own road, away from the path. The trees thickened. The world closed in, dark and close. A thorn tore at my sleeve. The sound was loud as a cry. Each branch seemed a bow drawn back, each stone a crouched shape waiting. I cursed myself for turning from the path. The river whispered — not of shelter, but of lies, of death in cold water.

Evening fell. Red and gold bled across the water's skin, as if the river carried our wounds with it. When the light failed, I found a hollow behind fallen trunks, broke branches to mask us. Markov slept before I was done, his breath shallow but steady. I watched him. I watched the dark. And at last, sleep took me too. The forest kept its secrets.

The next day rose cold and clear. The forest changed. The trees no longer pressed so close; the pines thinned. Where the sun reached, undergrowth gave way to stone and coarse grass. The peaks stood near now — high, harsh, their crowns white with snow, their flanks scarred where ice and storm had gnawed them bare. They watched us, unmoved, as if we were nothing to their long memory.

"Pretty, aren't they?" Markov said. His voice was thin, but he tried for lightness. "Maybe I'll take up painting. Sit here, bleed into the grass, sketch the view."

I looked at him, marveling that he could still jest. "Paint with what? Your own blood?"

He managed a grin — a poor thing, wan and worn. "Better be a small mountain, then. I left most of my paint back at Sava's ambush."

The Foxwater kept pace beside us, swift and sure. Its voice rang bright with the melt, as if the cold itself sang through the stones. Where yesterday it had whispered of hunger, now it rushed with purpose — silver-bright in the sun's pale fire, leaping over rock.

The wind off the heights scoured clean. It stripped the rot of the woods from the air. For a breath, the world opened wide, terrible in its beauty. The ridges beyond the river's bend stood stark against the pale sky; the gorge yawned deep, carved by old water's hunger. I felt small, yes — but no longer hunted.

Markov leaned heavier on me as we went, though he tried to hide it. His breath burned, his coat damp with fever's sweat. His face had gone the grey of old ash.

"Not so bad, this road of yours," he rasped. "Could have led us to worse."

"You're eager to test that, are you?"

He stumbled, and I caught him. His grin flickered, thinned, but held a heartbeat longer. "See? You doubted my sense of direction. And here we are — nowhere near dead."

"Yet." The word tasted like stone on my tongue.

The trail rose and fell with the river's curve. At times, the spray touched our boots. At times, the stone lifted us high above the rush. The sun shone, but its warmth did not reach us. In the gorge's shadows, ice clung still. The rock's wet faces gleamed like bone left long to the weather.

Once Markov slipped on moss-slick stone and fell hard. I hauled him up. His laugh was thin as the wind. "You'd think with all this water I'd be cleaner by now."

"Your mouth moves steadier than your feet."

"One's had more practice staying out of trouble."

"Not so sure about that. Your feet don't tend to run toward trouble."

For a while, his jesting held. But as the day wore on, his voice failed him. The banter thinned. The silence grew. The world pressed in — wind's bite, river's endless voice, the drag of his weight.

At midday we rested on sun-warmed stone. I gave thanks in silence for what little we had — as my mother taught, and her mother before, *in Saint Dobroslav's name*. We ate what was left — salt fish, a scrap of oat bread, a withered apple. The warmth eased our backs, but not our hunger.

Markov lay back, eyes half-shut. After a time, his voice came low. "Thought I'd lost you in the cleft. Thought I'd lost myself. Once you run, you forget how to stop. Your mind fills with madness, with flight."

He lifted a strip of fish, a ghost of his old jest. "You do that to your face, running into a rock?"

I was silent a long while. Then I spoke, because there was no use in lies. "The torches blew out. I swung in the dark. Hit something — then something hit harder." My hand found the bruise, the ache beneath. "Then dark."

His laugh turned to cough. "Your mule."

The shame of it settled like cold ash. The beast had trusted me, and I had answered that trust with a blow. A man who keeps oath or herd or comrade must strike true, even in darkness. I had failed that measure.

"One day," Markov wheezed, "you'll laugh about it."

I wasn't laughing. "You make it to Bors Mill, I'll listen to all the fool's talk you can spill."

"Promise? Because I've years of it saved up."

By afternoon, his wit guttered like a dying lamp. His weight dragged at me. I let him rest when I could, though every pause cost us. The ground betrayed us — moss-slick, stone-broken, sharp with frost. My bad eye turned the world strange. I slipped near as often as he.

At last the forest fell behind. The land opened wide — steppe silvered with frost, empty under a sky pale as milk. The air was lighter. The wind cut still, but clean, honest. A hawk wheeled above, its cry sharp against the hush.

Far ahead, thin smoke rose. Crooked roofs, dark walls — a village's stubborn mark on the land. I gave thanks — to God, to Saint Vira, that the walls might hold and the hearths be kind. For the first time in many days, I let my breath out slow. The land no longer hunted us. Not here. Not yet.

"Some shortcut," I said, voice low — for Markov's ear, though his head lolled, and he had no answer. For once I had the last word, though I did not like it. I raised a silent plea to Saint Dobrina, that Markov's breath might last, that his wounds might find healing.

CHAPTER XIX: BARS MILL

The land opened its hand to us. The trees fell away, the undergrowth thinned, and the ground softened — a patchwork of pasture and frost-scabbed field where the thaw had chewed the furrows raw. Ahead, smoke rose in threads from low houses, dark against a sky heavy with cloud. The mill stood at the stream's bend, its wheel turning slow, green with moss, as if stubbornness alone kept it from collapse.

Ivan came first into view — a thin man atop a tired horse, his face lined deep as bark, beard patchy as winter's last grass. The beast's hooves made no music on the thaw-soft earth, only a dull, sodden beat. Beside him, on a flat-bed cart drawn by that same sad creature, sat a small woman. Magda, I would learn. A patched shawl cloaked her narrow shoulders; bright eyes watched us from a face the wind had worn hard.

They turned at the sound of our coming, saw the ruin we were, and drew rein. Ivan dismounted, slow but sure. His boots sank in the soft ground. He raised a hand, palm open — a gesture plain as the wind: no threat, only offer.

"You're in a bad way, strangers," he said. His voice was low, steady. "What's your need?"

I watched him a long breath, but the strength for pride had left me. "If you have a healer, point the way. I have no coin. Only work, if that will pay."

Ivan glanced once at Magda — a look that passed like speech between them. "Aye," he said at last. "We have a healer. Mavra — old, sharp in tongue, but her hands know their work. We'll take you to her."

He gestured me forward. I followed. We lifted Markov to the cart. The boards creaked under our weight and the wheels groaned in their ruts. The horse stood patient, head low, ribs showing under a coat matted with old mud. The kind of beast that lasts because it learns not to hope.

Ivan walked beside me, quiet. I felt his eyes, but he did not press with words. It was Magda, as was right, who broke the silence.

"You're not of these parts," she said. "A sailor?"

I nodded.

"No place to stay, then."

There was no point denying. I nodded again.

She laid a hand light on my arm. "Then you'll come in. Ivan will fetch Mavra. The wind's turning — better under a roof than out in this." Her voice had the weight of a woman used to being heard.

And so, we came to their home — low-built, of stone and timber, thatch patched with sod, with hope, with whatever they'd had to hand. The hearth smoked; the air stank of damp wool and turnip broth. Above the hearth, an ashwood cross blackened with soot watched us enter.

They pressed me to sit. I did. Ivan brought water in a cracked jug. I drank — the water was cold, tasted of clay. We laid Markov on a straw pallet. His boots clung with mud and blood; I worked them free, slow, so as not to wake him. Something heavy thudded to the floor — a coin, gold, dulled with sweat but gold still. I froze. Magda saw, drew in a breath — but her face showed no greed. Only surprise.

"There may be more," I said. My voice was low, as if the gold itself might judge me.

Together we searched him. Silver, gold, blades — more than a man should carry, hidden where fear makes a man hide it. His shirt hid a vest of hardened leather, thin as cloth to the eye but thick enough to turn a blade. Markov, who moved like wind might carry him off, dressed as a man who feared ambush at every turn.

I set the gold aside, near his pack. His coin, I told myself. No man will say I took a kopeck.

Mavra came at dusk — small, bent, hair like smoke, hands stained with ash and fennel. She looked at me once, at Markov longer, then said nothing. Her touch was sure; she cleaned his wounds, bound my face where the mule had marked me. Her draughts were bitter, her silence sure. Each day she came. On the fourth, she spoke: "He will live." Her eyes flicked to me as I pressed silver into her hand.

"It was his," I said. "No debt should follow us."

She nodded. No more was needed.

When I could stand without sway, I worked. Hauled wood from the stream where the thaw had left it half-sunk. Mended fence where storm or rot had broken it. Patched the sod roof where the wind had torn it. Ivan tried to stop me. I would not be stopped. Work binds a man to the world in a way oaths do not.

And as I worked, the thoughts came. As they always do. I had burned homes like this. Killed men like Ivan. Not for hate, not for gain. Only because a lord's quarrel made it so. The world of men is wrong. Strength rules, and the just mend what the strong break. But I mended. It was not enough. Could never be enough.

Markov woke. His eyes went first to his boots, his cloak, the gold. I gave it back — all but what had paid for roof, for food, for care. He stared at it, then at me. Shrugged. The grin came after — crooked, thin, more shield than jest. But his eyes met mine steady, as if to say: it was well the gold was hidden, and well it served.

When he could stand, the road called. The queen's summons waited. The last leg waited.

"I can go on alone," I said one evening, as the sun bled low behind the hills. The words tasted bitter.

Markov snorted. "And let you have the last word? Don't be a fool, Yarik." The name was a barb — mocking the peasant kindness that had sheltered us — but under the barb was heart. I took it as such.

When we left, I pressed coin into Ivan's hand — honest pay for honest care. Markov gave little at first. My look stopped him. He gave more, and meant it.

The mill's wheel creaked behind us as we turned to the road. The wind rose, cold and clean. The world, for a little while, had shown its better face.

CHAPTER XX: VELGRAD

From Bars Hill, the King's Road ran south, following the Vorya's winding course. Broad enough for ten men abreast, its ruts hardened by cart and hoof, it bore us down like a river bears driftwood — carried not by will, but by weariness, hunger, and the faint promise of an end. The land opened: low hills blurred by mist, fields stripped bare by winter's hand, air thick with thawed earth and old smoke.

Night neared when Velgrad rose before us. The last of the light clung low, iron-grey and ash smeared across the west. Lamps kindled along the walls, embers stubborn against the dark. Smoke from a thousand hearths drifted — bitter with tar, fish, and damp wood. I had thought memory would dull the strangeness. But the city met me as the sea meets a man: vast, cold, more than I could hold.

There it stood — the Sea-Fort city — where Vorya and Grey Pilgrim joined strength to pour into the Seal's Passage. The walls rose thick as ten men, scarred where storm or siege had gnawed, patched with timber hoardings leaning like broken teeth. The west watchtower marked our coming, squat and black against the dying light. Above all flew the king's flag: white hand on black field, stark as bone against night.

Markov had made us draw our hoods low. "No need to stir the fish before the net drops," he said. I let him have his way. The city's weight pressed close as we neared the gate.

The portcullis hung like a jaw half-shut, iron teeth dark with salt and rust. Murder holes gaped above. But no oil poured, no arrow flew. The guards lounged, breath white in the dusk, eyes empty of care. No challenge. No question. The gate stood open — as if Velgrad no longer feared the road.

It had been twenty-seven winters since I first saw this place. Then, before Mstislav's hand closed on the isles, it was smaller: low walls, timber halls, the river's mouth crowded with fishing cogs and traders' knarrs. The Sea-Fort was a lord's hall, not a king's seat. I remembered tar on the wind, the gulls' cry, the hammer's ring. Even in the seven years since exile, the city had grown fat on war, heavy with rule.

The king's fleet lay at anchor like wolves in a pack — lean, grim warships with figureheads scarred by storm. *The Grey Hand* ruled them: broadest, blackest, its hull pitted by sea and battle. Lanterns glimmered along its rails, casting pale gold across black water. The docks still bustled, sailors' voices sharp, barrels rolling, nets mended by lamplight.

Markov led us through streets thick with folk — traders, beggars, soldiers, whores. Oil lamps burned at doorways, glow catching wet stone, smoke drift. The city stank of salt, sweat, dung, and fish. I kept to his heels as he wound round the Sea-Fort's bulk to a door small and thick as a ship's hatch. A door for men not meant to be seen.

He knocked, spoke low words. We waited. No sound but water slapping piers, rope creaking, a gull's cry lost in dark. Then the scrape of a bolt. The door groaned open. A hooded face, shadowed. A hand lifted: in.

We passed within. Cloaks drawn back, we followed narrow, damp ways. The Sea-Fort had grown like a tree warped by storm — new walls on old, halls added as power demanded, corridors twisting like a rat's burrow. At one turn, I passed a saint's face carved in oak, worn hollow by years of hands seeking grace. I touched it, as any man would, and the wood was cold. The air stank of cold ash, damp stone, old sweat. The walls pressed close: no clean cold, but the cold of stone that holds men's secrets.

We came to a bare chamber: table, bench, brazier's dying coals. Markov shifted, fingers drumming the table. I sat still. The dark pressed close.

He spoke at last, low, hopeful. "Perhaps this is the moment. They'll see sense. I could be done with Gavrilo's leash. Serve clean, for once."

"Perhaps." I said it, but I did not believe. I wanted to give him hope. But the world is not kind. His hope clung thin as spider's silk. I feared it would break by dawn.

As for me, I thought on what had drawn me from exile. What secret needed such shadowed hands. I was no spy. No sneak. If I was brought for an impossible task, I was a tool set for breaking. No point wrestling fate when the axe is raised.

The bolt scraped. He stepped in — no longer the Brown Cloak of the sea, but dressed in dark wool of fine weave, silver clasps at throat, boots polished though travel-worn. A man of the king's counsel, the queen's shadow. Dangerous, and now he looked it. The air shifted, cold as a door opened on winter.

Markov stepped forward, eager, voice smooth. "Dragomir. An honour. We've come far for the queen's will. I trust I may be of further service?"

He barely glanced at Markov. Set a purse on the table, coin's weight soft in the hush. "Well enough. Your part's done." His voice: sand on stone.

Markov hesitated. Took the coin, slow. His eyes met mine — one last jest rising, but swallowed like bile.

"He served well," I said.

Dragomir's shrug was a blade sheathed. "If we need him again, we'll find him."

Markov turned. At the door, a glance — nothing spoken. Then gone.

The door shut like surf over stone.

Shadows slip away.

Dragomir spoke no further word. He turned, and I followed, my boots loud against stone worn hollow by years of men's passing. The Sea-Fort's innards twisted like a ship's hold: low beams, narrow stairs, stone damp to the touch, rank with old smoke and sweat. Yet even here — the back ways — wealth whispered from the weight of wood, the set of stone. The doors, though plain, were thick, well-hung, iron-banded. The floors: clean-swept flagstone, no grime beneath my feet. I glimpsed kitchens through an archway — bright with hearthlight, copper gleaming on racks, cooks moving swift and sure, knives flashing, voices low but sharp with purpose. A hall of labour, not filth.

We climbed. I counted my breath, the steps, the beats of my heart. Upward through corridors lined with dark wood polished by generations of sleeves and hands. Tapestries hung where damp could not touch — not crude weavings, but fine work: hunts, saints, the sea's fury tamed beneath a king's hand. No laughter. No idle song. The hush of duty cloaked all.

Dragomir halted before a plain door, fitted so close no light leaked at its seams. No carving, no mark. I felt its silence before I touched it.

Two guards flanked it — men I did not know. No badge marked them, but the set of their shoulders, the hard stillness of their eyes, spoke service deeper than livery. They stepped aside at Dragomir's glance, no word given.

The door opened on a breath of incense — sweet, heavy, holy.

I stepped within. A chapel, small, perfect. The walls: dark wood worked smooth as wave-worn stone, polished to a soft gleam. The floor: flagstone scattered with rushes, fresh-laid. Above the altar, stained glass glowed with a saint's tale — not the bold reds of battle, but soft blues, golds, sea-green: the light of dawn on water. Tapestries cloaked the walls, worked so fine I could see each thread's sheen. The air hung thick with frankincense, and something older — a weight I could not name, but felt in my bones.

She stood before the altar.

Vezhena.

Tall still, though age had thinned her — not with weakness, but with the leanness of a blade honed too long on stone. Her hair, once dark as wet rock, now streaked with frost, drawn back in a plait that fell between her shoulders. A circlet of blackened silver bound her brow, plain save for a single shard of jet at its heart — dark as sorrow, sharp as judgement. Her face: once men called it beautiful, and they had not lied. But now the beauty had hardened. Eyes grey as storm sea, lips set, brow carved by years that spared no kindness. The queen who had given joy to duty — and found it gone.

Her gown was black wool, heavy, plain, save where dark thread traced knotwork so fine it seemed shadow rather than stitch. At her throat hung a simple cross of bone, bound by leather cord. No jewel. No gold. Only faith worn thin by care.

Dragomir waited. I felt the pull of Greyfang at my side, a burden I could not shed, even here where steel had no place. I stepped forward, slow. My knees bent to stone. The incense stung my throat.

"My queen."

She turned — slow, as if time itself had to bow. Her eyes met mine, cold as the sea's heart, hard as ice on stone. For a breath, she did not speak. Only looked — and in that look, I felt myself weighed, measured, found wanting or fit. No warmth lived in her gaze. Only command.

"Yaroslav." The name fell like a stone dropped from a height. A test, a summons, a blade.

The hush deepened. The incense's ghost wrapped us close. She let silence stretch until it burned.

Then, voice low but sharp as drawn steel: "The sea shapes a man. What has it made of you, I wonder?"

I met her gaze. "It has made me what I must be."

Her eyes narrowed. "And when you look at the sea — when you hear the storm, or see the king's banner rise — whose hand do you see in these things?"

"The Lord's," I said. "As it was. As it will be."

Again, the silence. Again, the weighing. Then, harder: "You left the king's side. Seven years. When a man walks so long alone, what binds his heart?"

"Oath. Faith. That which no storm can wash away."

Her voice cut like wind off the ice. "Once you were called Mstislav's Volkodlak. His wolf-skin. But seven years is long. A man's arm may keep its strength — but here" — she touched her heart — "here is where steel lies. Has that steel rusted, Yaroslav? Or does it wait?"

The name struck like old iron — not sharp, but cold, stained deep. I had borne it once as a badge. Now I did not know if it had been a mask, or if the beast it named had always lived beneath my skin. Perhaps both. Perhaps that was the trick — to forget which was the hiding.

"It waits." My voice was steady. "Unbroken, as long as breath remains."

She stepped once toward me. The storm of her will filled the space. "And death? What price is too high?"

"There is no price too high," I said. "If it be the king's need. Or God's will."

Her gaze pinned me as a hawk pins prey. "And if you are called to give all — with no reason given, or none you can grasp — will you give it still?"

"I will." The truth. No more, no less.

The hush held. Then at last — slow, as dawn breaks stone — the edge softened. The storm within her stilled. What remained was the woman beneath the crown: weary, worn, but human. For a breath, she let herself be so.

She turned, and knelt at the altar. The stained glass above caught the low light, threads of blue and gold across her shoulders and the stone at her knees.

"Come," she said. Not command. Not plea. A simple word, heavy with what had passed between us. "Pray with me."

I rose, stepped to her side, and knelt. The stone was cold through cloth. The hush thickened, as if even the sea held its breath. The weight of the Lord's hand was heavy here — not comfort, but reckoning.

We knelt long, or so it seemed. The incense burned low. The glass above caught no dawn, but held its promise all the same.

At last she spoke, voice low as waves beneath a storm. "Thank you. For coming."

"Of course, milady. I am yours, and the king's. Always."

Her breath caught — a sound like a latch lifting, then still. "Just Vezhena. As we once were."

But the word she wanted from me would not come. The hush swallowed it.

She sighed. The sound of a door shut on some hope. The pause that followed was heavy as stone.

Then, quiet, as if the saying shamed her: "I have envied you."

I blinked. The words struck harder than any blow. I could not answer.

"You escaped the crown. You were lucky."

"For a time."

Her hands clenched, then stilled. "Ruling is not like conquering. Conquering is a storm. Ruling — cold waves eating at stone. Slow. Without end."

"I do not know the ways of ruling."

She laughed, but there was no joy in it. Only bitterness old as salt. She spoke then of what shaped her.

"Before Mstislav, there was no kingdom. Only a dozen kings, each calling himself lord of his rock. War without end. Blood on every stone, the kind that soaks through boot leather and stains a man's soul. I was young. They said I was beautiful — hair like night's sea, skin pale as shorebone. It was no blessing. Beauty was a banner men would cut each other to seize. Igor came then — a bastard son of no one, carving his name with axe and fire. My father spurned him. I was betrothed — to a kind man, soft, good, who smelled of cedar and spoke as if words might heal. Igor slew them both. Took me. Claimed me. As a dog claims a bone, rough, snarling, without grace. There was no law, no mercy, no God then. Only what men could take. The nights smelled of smoke and blood, and no prayer rose loud enough to reach heaven. I was not alone in my sorrow. The isles were full of women like me — no roof safe, no shrine sacred, no dawn unshadowed."

Her voice hardened, iron beneath ash. "Then came Mstislav. God's own hand. The first breath of salt air after a storm. He took what was his by right. Those who bent the knee lived, under one king, one banner, one law. Those who would not — the sea took them, or the sword. You saw it, Yaroslav. You saw what he built. Peace that stung because it came too late for some. Safety that ached because it asked a price. A land where the strong no longer fed on the weak."

She fell silent. The weight of memory pressed close, and for a breath she seemed lost to it, her gaze on some place far beyond the chapel walls. The air thickened with the ache of what had been. When at last her eyes returned to the present, they were sharpened by that old sorrow, and the cold steel of her understanding.

"Men will not obey unless they fear," she said, voice low but sure. "I have seen what they are — hungry, always hungry, for power, for coin, for safety. And they will take, and kill, and ruin to fill that hunger. A pack of dogs, and unless they feel the alpha's teeth at their throat, they will tear at each other until all lies in blood and ash. But when the alpha is strong, the pack thrives. A king must be that strength, or all is lost."

Then I saw it — the queen's sorrow set aside, the will beneath it rising like iron from the depths.

"But the Grey Hand weakens."

The words left her as a breath torn from the heart — low, but it filled the chapel.

I spoke, low but sure. "Age comes for all, my queen. Even kings, even stone. The sea takes, the storm weathers, and no man's hand can turn it aside forever. That is no shame, no failure. It is the way of things, as God set them. The strong must rule while they can, and when the storm claims them, others must stand. This is the order of the world, harsh but true. We are not called to fight the tide, only to stand firm in it until our hour ends."

She turned on me, eyes bright with pain. "The cost is too high. I will not pay it."

I drew breath. "Illarion is his blood, and his heir. He must be shaped now, made ready."

I did not know what might live beneath the boy's skin. But I knew how to make men fear. If the prince could not rule by strength, he could rule by the shadow of mine.

Her face changed — a flash of anger, then something deeper: sorrow so great it stole her voice. "Illarion…" she began. But the word died. She could not bring herself to name what I saw plain: that Illarion had failed her, and all she had given her life to build stood on sand. The burden of it crushed the air between us, bowed her — but her head stayed high.

"There is time," I said. "The Broken Isles remain unbroken."

"The kingdom stands," she said, voice low. "But it is hollowed. Hollowed by the sea's hunger."

I waited, empty-handed. There was nothing more I could say.

And then I understood. She had summoned me for what I had been — the Volkodlak. To stand at Illarion's side. To shape the boy into something that might pass for a king. Or at least the shadow of one, while she held the leash. To bare my teeth so the lords would kneel. To make terror serve where strength could not. And if that were her will, I would give it. To my last breath.

She drew a breath — long, slow, as if it cost her all that remained. For a moment, I saw it: the burden she bore, carried too long, too far. Then she straightened. The queen again.

"You must find the scattered remains of Saint Ilyin the Flame-Bound."

The words struck like ash in the lungs. She asked me to gather fire that once judged kings.

I drew breath, slow. Saint Ilyin. The Flame-Bound. The judgement given flesh. A man once called prophet, then heretic. Who condemned a lord as a liar and was burned for it — lashed to a stake with gospel in his mouth. But the fire did not end him. They buried his bones, but he rose all the same, an ash-crowned skeleton, eyes alight. Faced with death's judgement, the lord confessed, but still was dragged screaming into flame. After that, no one dared call him martyr. Only saint — in whispers, and with salt on the tongue.

But he had risen from the stake not radiant, but wrathful. Fire took the guilty — the lord who condemned him, the soldiers who bound him — but it did not stop. Priests burned without charges. Shrines kindled of their own accord.

The bishops said his resurrection had drawn fire too deep — that hell had clung to him in the rising. That even holy vengeance, left unchecked, rots into ruin.

They could not burn the bones. Could not break them. So they did the only thing left. They divided him. The torso, sealed in a blessed crypt beneath his shrine in Velgrad. Five other fragments they scattered to the far isles. Each sealed in a reliquary of ashwood, bound in iron, lined in black stone. They packed the bones in sacred ash, scattered salt like a warding, and carved the signs of silence into wood and band alike. Not relics to be venerated — but wards, set in place to keep the world safe.

"Milady… it is a tale. A myth."

"No." Her voice sharpened. "Our priest — **Bogdan** — says it is truth. That if we gather his bones, the fire may yet burn away all that is broken. That it might restore the king's strength."

"Bogdan?"

"You do not know him. You will. He sees beyond what we see. He walks close to God."

The incense was gone, but the hush pressed close.

"You will travel the isles," she said. "Bogdan will guide you. Dragomir will tell you what the lords must hear. What oaths must be won or broken. You will find the relics. All of them."

I stared at her. At last, words came. "This is no task for a man. This is a task for a saint."

"You will not fail. You must not falter. Mstislav's life, the kingdom's life — both hang on you now."

I hesitated. "I…"

She would not hear it. "Your training begins now. We will waste no more time."

Her head bowed. I did the same, though my heart was heavy as stone. The light cast the chapel in dappled lines. The hush closed round us like stone above a man not yet dead.

CHAPTER XXI: THE MAD QUEEN'S CHARGE

"She's mad, Yaro. Mad as the sea is deep. You know it."

Markov's voice cut through the stink of rot, smoke, and damp wool. His cup struck the table — pewter on wood — sloshing cheap whitefire, sharp with the scent of burnt skirret and spoiled barley mash. He held to it like wreckage in a storm — knuckles white, eyes sunk deep, as if the sea had already claimed him and forgot to finish the job.

"Saint Ilyin's bones!" he spat. "The queen's sent you chasing brimstone. Bones scattered for a reason. She'd have you drag them from ash and grave so some priest can light them like a torch and call it healing. Madness. A death quest dressed in relics."

I let him speak. Words poured from him like rain off a roof, and I needed the storm. No one had stopped me leaving the Sea-Fort. I hadn't asked leave, and none was given. The room they offered — a bed soft as sin, tapestries thick enough to muffle a scream, polished silver laid beside the basin — smothered me. I needed smoke, filth, and a man too far into his cups to notice the cracks in my silence.

The Drowned Lantern was a pit. A place forgotten by light, favoured by rats. The walls ran with damp, the rushes on the floor long since trampled to mulch. Smoke clung to everything. A dog slept near the hearth, ribs showing, one ear torn to a nub. The fire gave no heat.

Markov hunched like a man grown used to being struck. His eyes still burned sharp, though the whitefire dulled their edge.

"You know what I think?" he said, jabbing a finger. "They're all mad. The queen most of all. And you, you poor bastard, snared in your own honour. You should've told her no."

"Perhaps I should," I said.

"You won't."

I said nothing.

He snorted, bitter. "Always her way. Uses a man until the bones show, then casts him off. Ask me about Dragomir. No, don't. I'll tell you anyway."

He was off again — a flood of curses, names, and threats of violence best left to tide and night. I let it come. Somewhere beneath it lay a truth, if I could stand the noise.

"That snake," he growled. "I'll gut him, Yaro. I swear. One day."

"You should drink slower. Or curse softer."

He laughed, once, sharp. "This from the man who let himself be summoned like a dog."

"You dragged me from exile."

"To save you!" His eyes were wide. "Or try. Owl's Haven, whaling, the Tanglewood — I nearly died, Yaro."

"So did I. And yet here we are. The sea chooses."

He slammed his cup down. "We got used. Then tossed. Dragomir gives me coin like a dog gets scraps. I'm done."

"You took the coin."

"And now she sends you to fetch bones from the edge of hell? Saint Ilyin?" He spat again. "Aye, I believe in saints. I believe he's dead! That's the point."

"Men still pray at the shrine in Velgrad," I said. "Some say the fire blesses. Some say it judges."

"Judges, aye. Like a knife judges a throat. That saint didn't leave blessings — he left warnings."

I drank. The whitefire was foul, but it burned clean. "The sea takes and gives. The saints intercede. The queen believes."

"She believes in fire. And sends you to cradle it."

"You asked what I believe?" I set the cup down. "That some work is given, whether I understand it or not. And that I must do it well."

He wiped his mouth, his sleeve stained dark. "Still you bend your back. Like a beast worked to death, proud it pulls straight."

I shrugged.

He leaned in. "And what of the kingdom, Yarik? It seems fine to me. The roads don't run red. The ports are open. The fields get tilled."

"For now."

"There's peace. Why would anyone throw it away?"

"Because peace bound to one man's strength ends when that strength fails. And Mstislav's hand is failing."

Markov waved it off. "Talk. Rumours."

"If you've heard them, the blood's already in the water. And Illarion's not ready. Might never be."

A pause. The hearth hissed. The shutters groaned.

"Illarion?" Markov's mouth twisted. "I heard jests at the Siren's Mercy — says he struts like a cockerel but hides his spurs. Keeps to shadows. Wears gloves even in heat. Folk whisper there's something wrong with his face. They laugh, but never close. No fear, no love — and that's the worst sort."

I said nothing. The flame in the lamp had shrunk to a blue tongue.

"So what will you do?" he asked.

"What I must."

He sighed and leaned back, that old grin tugging at his mouth like a man remembering pain fondly. "You're a fool, then. But I'll watch. Maybe dance on your grave when it's done."

There was silence after that — not peace, just space. Smoke rose between us. The fire in the hearth had gone to coals, and the dog was snoring now, ribs rising slow.

"And you?" I asked at last. "Back to Ironmark?"

He tilted his head, bird-like. Wicked gleam in his eyes.

"Oh no. I'm coming with you."

I turned to look at him, slow. "You just said I was a fool."

"Aye. But a lucky one. And you'll need luck." He tapped the side of his nose. "You've got the stink of story on you, Yarik. That fetches coin. And fear. And women, if you're not too picky."

I didn't answer.

He leaned forward, elbows on the table, voice low.

"What's waiting for me back there?" he said. "Gavrilo's gutter? A knife in the dark because someone else blinked too slow? No thanks. If I'm going to get killed, I'd rather it be chasing saint-bones and storm-visions than bleeding out in a rat-hole over a missed debt."

He shrugged. "Besides. If you die, someone's got to sing it well. Might as well be me."

"There will be danger," I said. "Storms not spent."

Markov raised his cup in mock salute. "Good. I'd rather drown in deep water than rot in the shallows."

"If we fail, the queen will not forgive. Her grief may kill more than hope."

"Then we don't fail," he said, with a shrug like it cost him nothing. "Or we fail well. Loudly. Gloriously. With saints and storms and Dragomir gutted on a cairn stone."

"We don't even know where the bones are."

"Then we find them. Or we don't. Doesn't matter. The tale's good either way. The queen wants a legend — I say we sell her one. And make it cost her."

I looked at him. "I don't think coin was promised."

"Then she'll owe us. And I'll collect."

He raised his cup again. "Come, Yarik. Drink. Tomorrow, we chase ghosts. Tonight, we drink like men they'll remember."

I drank with him. The whitefire still burned. But it warmed, too.

Saints keep us, I thought. *For we do not keep ourselves.*

CHAPTER XXII:　　　THE WEIGHT OF INK

I woke with cold in my bones and Dragomir's shadow over me.

The stink of piss, rot, and sour ale clawed at my throat before my eyes even opened. Stone pressed hard beneath me, slick with night rain. My cloak was half-spread beneath me, soaked through. Something gnawed at the wall above — a rat, or a demon in rat shape. My head throbbed with each heartbeat.

"Up," said the shadow.

Water dripped from the bucket in his hand. My cloak was wet. His was dry. The man was a ghost or a bastard, and I knew which I preferred.

"You stink," he said. "Get up."

I sat up, slow. The inn loomed behind me: shutters sagged, the piss-trough overflowed, a few embers still whispered in the ash-pan. No Markov. Just me and the city's filth, and the man who never seemed surprised to find me neck-deep in it.

"Where is he?" I asked.

Dragomir didn't answer. Just turned and walked.

But he'd found me. Sprawled in muck outside the worst inn in Velgrad, guttered and forgotten. That wasn't luck. Either I'd been followed, or he had a net of eyes in every alley and ash-heap of the capital. A man like him did not trust chance.

I followed.

Velgrad in morning had a different face. Ash smoke rose straight in the still air, thin and blue. Market wagons creaked on stone. Gulls shrieked over the river mouth. I passed a boy carrying dead eels in a sack that dripped blood, and two women elbow-deep in a dye-vat the colour of dried heart. Tanners were already stomping hides in piss. Steam rose from cookpots; the stench of boiled barley and cabbage caught in my throat.

Children ran barefoot through the alleys, shrieking. A one-eyed dog followed them, tail low, ears flattened. He looked better fed than I was.

The Sea-Fort brooded above it all, hunched like a waiting fist. But its shadow had breath — smoke, sweat, the scrape of iron. Even here, even now, the kingdom lived.

I said nothing as we walked. Neither did Dragomir.

We passed through a side gate I did not know. The guards nodded. One had a fresh wound on his jaw, stitched clumsily. His eyes slid past me and fixed on Dragomir with something close to fear.

Inside, the Sea-Fort's heart beat harder: kitchens, smiths, pages with scrolls, couriers with wax-sealed dispatches. I smelled blood and mint — the surgeon's rooms. Bells rang somewhere deeper, but not in joy. Just order.

I broke the silence. "Will I see the king?"

"No."

No apology. No explanation.

He led me to a side-building grown from the citadel's stone like a wart. The base was old — blackened stone, fitted without mortar, older than memory. But above: fresh oak, tar-sealed beams, narrow slitted windows high under the eaves. This had not stood here when I last walked these halls.

"New?" I asked.

"New enough."

"For what?"

Dragomir didn't answer. He opened the door.

Not a monk's library. No gilded saints, no cloister hush. But shelves, thick and groaning. Skins scraped flat and marked in fading ink. Bone tablets. Rolled vellum. Carved slips. Wax boards stacked beside pins of fire-hardened ash. Boxes of tally sticks, labelled in shorthand I could not read.

I stood in it as a butcher stands in a scholar's dream.

On the far wall, above a cracked window shutter, hung a portrait — the king and queen, painted in the early years of rule. He looked younger than I remembered, though no less grim; she looked unchanged. Her eyes followed the room like knives held at rest. Between them, a black-bannered ship — *The Grey Hand* — rode a stylized sea. The paint was cracked, the faces worn smooth with smoke and years, but even so, the presence lingered. Not watching. Judging.

I turned away. Better to face the maps.

Dragomir lit a lamp and set it beside a long, scarred table.

"You know what this is?"

I shook my head.

"The mind of a kingdom. Or close enough. What men saw, thought, bought, took, traded, swore. Every deal, every oath, every error. Some written by men who could not write — dictated in gutter dialects by men with blood still under their nails. Others sent from lord's halls in the far isles, or copied from records older than the king's crown. All here."

He ran a finger down the side of a curled hide-map bound in twine.

"You can't read," he said.

"No."

"Good. You won't overthink." He smiled, thin as a whetted blade. "You've bled far. But war is not knowing. War is *remembering*. This—" he swept his hand to the shelves "—is pattern. Shape. Wind and root and coin. Even saints burn differently in different hands. Remember that, when they send you chasing bones."

He unrolled a chart that stank of mildew and salt. Ink lines spidered across rough hide, coastlines sketched like wounds. Dots marked ports I'd never heard of. One was shaped like a curled dog. Another had been burned through — a hole where meaning once lived.

"We start here," he said.

I touched the edge of the map. It was the same hide as any war-banner. But this one bore no king's mark — only scratchings made by men who thought they could outwit tide and time.

"I know these names mean something to you," I said. "They mean nothing to me."

"They will."

"What if they don't?"

He looked at me for the first time in an hour. His eyes were dark and flat.

"Then you'll die. Or worse — you'll fail, and someone else will die in your place."

That landed. He saw it. He nodded.

"Don't mistake ink for safety," he said. "Words can kill as clean as knives. I've seen cities burn from one misplaced mark."

He moved to a side-table, sorting slips.

"There are men who think knowledge is power," he said. "They're wrong. *Memory* is power. Because history outlives blade and crown. The man who knows what happened — truly knows — owns every man who forgot."

He handed me a slate scratched with shapes I couldn't parse.

"Start learning," he said.

I stared at it. "This isn't what I was made for."

"She doesn't care," he said, nodding to a portrait of the queen. "So I don't either."

I took a slow breath. "Alright. I'm ready."

I wasn't.

CHAPTER XXIII: A BAG OF KNIVES

My second education came not by books, but by the blunt instrument of Dragomir's voice — and the weight of the kingdom poured into my skull like cold brine down the throat of a drowned man. What I thought would be a briefing lasted weeks. We began at dawn, and ended only when Dragomir's ruined hand wearied of pointing. One day it was maps, the next histories. Then books of saints, ink-smudged and brittle with age, each name a thread in the knot of the Isles. Then came the relics — not trinkets, but things feared and hidden: sketches of fire-blackened bones, symbols etched in salt and blood, fragments sealed in ash. Saint Ilyin's name recurred — always whispered, always warded. The fire-saint. The unbroken. His relics were not mapped as prizes, but contained like storms.

After that, pronunciation. Greetings. Ritual forms.

"You call a Fangborn lord 'your highness,'" Dragomir growled once, "they'll cut your tongue for mockery."

He did not so much hide me away as ensure there was no time for my discovery. The odd shadow reported in — some quiet knock, some slip of parchment — and the lesson would pause while Dragomir read or nodded or muttered a brief curse. But otherwise, his full effort, and all my waking hours, were turned toward reshaping a killer into a diplomat. He did not enjoy it. More than once he called me thick-skulled or salt-dulled, and once — only once — he stopped mid-lesson, sighed, and looked near to saying that the Queen's quest was madness. The words never left his lips, but I heard them in the silence.

I had thought it was one kingdom. Seven isles under a single banner. Simple enough. But as Dragomir peeled back each name, each custom, each long-tended feud, the truth emerged: the Isles had bent the knee, yes — but kept their hands in the water of their own ways. Some lords had been placed by Mstislav, and held power with grace, trade, and quiet fear. Others had to fight revolt after revolt, never ruling more than a league beyond their hall.

"A crown from Velgrad means less than a shrine-stone," Dragomir said. "Forget that, and you'll find your throat opened in a saint's name."

He left me to practice during the evening meals. That was when the lords and envoys gathered in the grand hall — daily feasts dressed as councils. The Queen presided, calm and watchful. The prince was always there, his pride stoked by the flattery of lesser men. The King, I was told, rarely appeared.

Dragomir sneered at them all. "They feed like dogs under a butcher's table, and think themselves kings."

I was not permitted to join. I ate alone, in my room, under guard.

The lords were not born to crowns. They were raised from the mud like me — men of the shield-wall, blooded in the king's wars, handed scraps of the kingdom to hold in Mstislav's name. Some earned their lands by siege, others by slaughter. A few, like me, had refused reward and walked away. The rest stayed, swore again, and learned to rule.

The queen had a hand in their choosing — that much was clear even then. She did not favour old blood or bold claims. She chose men who owed everything to the crown, and could be broken by it if they forgot. Oath, coin, threat — always one, often two.

I remembered them not as boyars, but as brothers.

Boarcliff Hold came first — a wind-blasted stretch of grey moor and cliffside halls, where the sea never stopped speaking and the land gave little but heather and stone. Vezemir ruled there now. Vezemir the Grey Boar, they called him, though I remembered when he was just Vesko, a blunt-voiced killer from the siege lines, who sharpened his axe with saltwater and swore louder than he prayed.

He had a taste for punishment, even then — not cruelty, but pressure, the slow grind that wore a man down. When the Grimfolk of Boarcliff refused the crown, it was Vezemir who was sent to take the hold. Not with fire — with famine. His ships ringed the isle for a winter and a spring, and when the grain rotted and the sheep turned on each other, they bent the knee. He never let them forget it.

Now he wears furs stitched with boar-bristle and sits a throne of stormwood, but his eyes are the same — small, dark, calculating. The folk beneath him still name Mstislav *shield-king* and light driftwood lanterns for Saint Yarila the Ferryman when a boat goes down. But they fear Vezemir more than they hate the crown, and that was the bargain.

"Saint Yarila," I repeated once, misplacing the stress. Dragomir corrected me without looking up.

"YAR-ila, not ya-RI-la. And don't cross yourself before the driftwood burns. It offends the rite."

Then came Stormward — silk, salt, and poison. Boyarina Salava ruled from Stormhold, where the wind never ceased and neither did the games of knives and veils. I had never met her. That was the point. Her face was painted in stories, not memory — one tale claimed she'd drowned her first husband in a ritual for Saint Stepan the Endurer; another, that she'd kept his tongue in a shrine box to remind herself what loyalty sounded like.

What I knew for certain was this: she owed her rise to the queen. No battle banners, no siege won, no brotherhood in the blood-soaked mud of the old wars. Salava came up by whispers and wine cups — and by binding herself to Vezhena with a blood oath too old to break. The queen called her loyal. Dragomir called her dangerous.

"Give them honesty," he muttered once, "and they'll test it on your skin."

Stormhold itself perched high above black reefs, its causeway slick with spray and fish-guts, guarded not by soldiers but by saints and secrets. Pilgrims came there to bleed — truly bleed — into the tide pools beneath the shrine of Saint Stepan the Endurer, hoping the sea would take pain in place of flesh. Some returned pale-eyed and shivering. Some didn't return.

I grimaced when her name crossed the map.

There are places in this kingdom where steel holds sway, and others where song and symbol rule. Stormward was neither. It was something worse — a place where truth drowned and only those who floated learned how to smile while they slit your throat.

Evenings brought one small mercy. Markov slipped in, grinning like a man who had outwitted fate itself.

"I've charmed the guard," he whispered once. "They don't see me."

He was wrong. Dragomir knew, I was sure of it. He let him in. Perhaps he understood that I needed Markov's voice, his jests, his irreverence. Perhaps he knew that a man who has no human tether cannot be controlled. If I ever cared for Markov — and maybe I did — Dragomir would not hesitate to use it. Nothing happened by chance with the Brown Cloak.

"You poor bastard," Markov said one night, picking a fishbone from my plate. "You thought this was a kingdom. It's a bag of knives, tied at the top."

The Hornlands were worse. There was no single lord, only the rotating Clan Pact — tattooed Voryani who took oaths before broken fetters and vanished garrisons into forest shadows. Their saints judged by ordeal. Their shrines lay hidden, their law older than any seal from Velgrad.

Mstislav had placed a lord there, of course — Ilian, of all men. I remembered him from the siege of Kravosk: a nervous wreck who dropped his sword more than once and wept when the wounded screamed too loud. He'd clung to orders like a drowning man to driftwood, and followed me like a dog. I thought him harmless then, maybe even pitiable. That he had risen to rule anything — even in name — was beyond belief.

The Voryani called him *the Tethered One*, and treated him like a scarecrow nailed to the edge of their woods — a warning more than a presence. He held court from a timber stockade and read the king's edicts aloud to trees. But the true rule still rotated — blood to blood, pact to pact, judged beneath the oaks, not beneath the crown.

"Trust no smile there," Dragomir said. "But speak truth, and they'll hear it in your blood."

"That's the third time you've said that," I snapped once. "Truth in blood. Which part of me are they supposed to bleed to check?"

Dragomir didn't answer. Just turned another page.

Krogmarsh was stone and ship-keel — a land of quarried strength and salt-soaked craft, where hands shaped what mouths did not boast. The roads were paved with trade, not conquest, and their banners bore neither beast nor blade, but a stylised keel set over rising stone. I remembered Borin well. Not Thane Borin, as they named him now — just Borin the Steady, broad-shouldered and dark-eyed, the kind of man who said little and struck true. We fought together in the southern marshlands, when the leech-kin of Ironmark still called their oaths into question. He was the one who carried me half a league through water thick as blood when my knee gave out.

Mstislav gave him Krogmarsh not for blood spilled, but for coin earned — Borin had ties to the old salt-traders, and knew how to keep peace between knife-wielders and ledger-men. He took the fief like a mason takes a plumb line — no ceremony, no triumph, just measured work. He ruled the way he had fought: with few words and good stone beneath his feet.

Their rites were simple, open. Hymns for Saint Dobrina of the Cross-Roads, herbs steeped in oil and fire, healing shared from palm to palm. Krogmarsh was known for its midwives and its songs — not the kind sung for kings, but for birth, burial, and bread. They marked their dead with carved stone and wild rosemary.

But even there, Dragomir had muttered, obligation could sour.

"They remember who gave what," he said once, "and how well it held."

Trust runs deep in places like Krogmarsh. But when it cracks, the break echoes like a snapped keel — clean, sudden, final.

The Mirefast was harder. Even Dragomir admitted that.

The land itself was half-drowned — black reeds, stinking shallows, water that whispered where no wind blew. The Brackfolk lived on rafts and stilts, their homes rising from muck like bone from a grave. They obeyed no banners. They heeded signs. Priests and dreamers ruled more than thanes, and their shrines reeked of fish oil, rot, and incense made from things that never grew on dry land.

Their lantern rites honoured Saint Vira — not in stone, but in driftlight. On holy nights they set tiny oil-lamps afloat, a thousand flickering lights drifting through the bog like lost souls. It was meant to guide the drowned home.

"They speak in rot-songs," Dragomir told me, tapping the bog on the map. "They give visions, not oaths. Don't lie to them. They'll already know."

And over that sodden maze ruled Ivan. Ivan the Broad, once.

I remembered him from the marsh battles in the south. Broad chest, heavier laugh, a spear that never missed. He'd carried a pouch of salt for luck, swore by Saint Stepan, and used to say a man should fight like a butcher and pray like a widow. I liked him. Most did. He made fear feel smaller.

I had not seen him in years. I only knew what Dragomir said now — that Ivan had taken the title Thane of Mirefast, though no one called him that but the crown. That he wore driftwood and bone for show, spoke through intermediaries, and had begun quoting visions instead of laws. That no courier stayed long in his hall. That his wife had vanished. That the Brackfolk listened more to the bog than to their lord.

Dragomir called it dangerous. I wasn't sure what to call it. A brother half-swallowed by a land that never truly let anything go.

Klykograd was sharp rock and sharper pride — a jagged wound carved into the coastal cliffs where salt sprayed upward like breath from a dying beast. The land offered nothing gently. Even the goats there were mean.

House Dravik ruled now. Not because they were trusted, but because their children were kept in Velgrad under royal watch. Their banner bore a split fang on black — crude, unmistakable — and their saints were fire-marked, cloaked in ash and old fury. Dragomir tapped the mark on the map with a blunt nail.

"You'll find obedience there," he said. "But only because they haven't yet decided which knife to draw."

The man who ruled was Ogrin Dravik — once called Ogrin the Stringman in the camps. An archer, a torturer, a man who sang while others screamed. We fought on the same side, but never together. Even Mstislav kept him at a distance. The kind of killer you only loose when you want a message written in blood.

I remembered one winter skirmish — a village taken back from rebels. I was burying the children. He was at the hearth, something steaming in the pot — and men said it was tongues.

How he was given land, I understood. It was not mistake but message. The crown wanted terror there — a cruelty to match the cliffs. A man too dangerous to leave untethered, but too useful to discard. And so they gave him Klykograd, then took his sons as collateral.

Dragomir said the hold had quieted. I believed that as much as I believed meat stays fresh when the maggots sleep.

I would find pain there — not open war, perhaps, but memory left to fester. Rebellion not yet cold. And a man who never knew the weight of mercy.

And finally, the Straitsward.

A salt-worn strip stretched along the Sealwatch coast, where wrecks lay rotting like old prayers and the sea whispered its own dominion. There, the Straitborn trusted the tides more than any king. Their speech was sparse, their gaze long. They watched the water, not the road. And they buried their dead not in earth, but in drift and ash — saltwood crosses set afloat from the black rock at the point, drifting out beneath the gaze of Saint Yevstafiy the Drowned.

The lord there was Kolgrim — once *Kolgrim the Red-Sailed*, a raider of seal-cloaked hulls, who'd made his living on shipwrecks and war-tax long before the crown made him a thane. I'd fought beside him once — briefly, at the mouth of the Grey Pilgrim, when the river tribes tried to seize the sandbar fort. He killed with precision, not rage — no shouts, no boasts. Just the quiet rhythm of a man who'd seen men drown too many times to think it worth remark.

He was no friend. But he was never a fool.

But this fief was no gift. It was a tether. Mstislav gave him Sealwatch not as reward, but as anchor — to guard a wound that must never be allowed to heal.

Wreck Rock lay just beyond his watch — black cliffs rising like a blade from the sea, where Sava died and his wife Yelena's blood stained my hands. I still remembered the taste of that siege — ash, rot, salt, and the long silence of a people who chose death over surrender. We made that place a tomb. The king made Kolgrim swear — before altar, before men — that no hall would rise on Wreck Rock. No seed sown. No grave dug. Nothing. Only watchfires. Only warning. The rock was to remain dead, as it was made.

And yet Dragomir suspected otherwise. "There are men on that rock," he said, low and bitter. "Not ghosts. Not saints. Men. That is Kolgrim's failing. And his charge to correct."

I did not know what I would find there — loyalty, perhaps. Or only the sea, remembering what we did and asking, as it always does: what comes of such silence?

By the end of the third week, I could barely remember what day it was. The fiefdoms blurred together — salt, blood, driftwood, iron. I dreamt in sigils, woke with saint-names on my tongue. My throat hurt from speaking in strange dialects, my eyes from reading by lamp-smoke, my patience from holding down what I did not know. Yet Dragomir pressed on, voice low, insistent: "Know this: oaths matter more than titles. A man's saint is closer than his king. Forget that, and you'll lose the relics — or your life."

And despite the passage of days, no summons came. Not from the Queen, and not from the King.

"Does the King even know that I'm here?" I asked once.

His maimed hand twitched, then stilled. A refusal without sound.

"I don't understand. Why are you keeping me from him?"

"You'll see the King," he said, "if the Queen sees fit for that to happen. Now study."

I guessed then what had only lurked in hints before: that the Queen ruled in all but name. That every movement, every gate, every guest, was hers to permit or deny. Even me — a man summoned, and yet held apart.

My heart ached for Mstislav. I remembered him not as this hushed absence, but as he was: tall as a pine under storm, voice like a warhorn, eyes rimmed red from smoke and cold and years of battle but clear as winter sky. I had seen him cleave a charging horse in two. I had heard him pray before the axe fell. His fury in the field had been holy. He did not ask men to die. He showed them how.

If the king was dying, his people should have been told — so they could grieve, and name their loss before silence took him. If he was mad, his madness should have been recognised — not feared, but named, witnessed, and borne. Even embraced for its wildness, like a prize wrested from the edge of the world, earned by trials no man should have endured. Not hidden.

They made him smaller with their veils and courtiers' lies. He deserved more. It was his kingdom — taken by blood, held by sacrifice. And yet I understood why they hid him. Power cannot afford pity. Rule demands the illusion of strength, even when the bones beneath are rotting.

But I would see him — for what he was, not what they pretended. That I swore, even if I had to carve a path through Dragomir's shadows to reach the old king's door. And if I found only silence there — if the man I had followed into fire was already gone — then I would mourn him as he deserved. But not before I saw with my own eyes whether he still breathed, or if only the crown remained.

CHAPTER XXIV: BOGDAN

We were bent over the southern coast — Dragomir muttering dates and port names while the smoke of the oil lamp stung my eyes — when the door opened without knock or warning.

A gust of wet air slid in — cold, mineral-rich, laced with a strange sharpness, like iron before a lightning strike.

Dragomir froze. Not startled. Like a man who'd just stepped barefoot into blood.

Soft boots on stone. No clang, no scrape. Just presence.

I turned.

A tall figure stepped through the narrow door, backlit by the rain-laced light. For a moment I thought him cloaked in sea-mist — but it was only a mantle of rough grey wool, rain-dark at the shoulders, and edged with tiny bone charms that clicked as he moved. His beard was thick, wild, shot through with silver. His eyes were deep-set and bright, impossible to read. The kind of eyes that might weep, or laugh, or drag a man to judgement — all without blinking.

He carried no blade. Only a pilgrim's staff, and a wooden icon slung from his belt: Saint Vira, her key held high, carved with exquisite care. But beneath the icon, half-hidden in the folds of his robe, I caught a flash of darker wood — charred, blackened, bound with nail.

"Peace to this house," he said, voice smooth and warm as poured honey.

Dragomir did not rise. "It is not yours to bless."

Bogdan smiled.

"Nor yours to guard," he said gently, stepping inside. "Yet here we both are."

He crossed to the hearth — unlit that day — and knelt to draw a faint circle in the ash with the butt of his staff. Some old rite. His fingers made the sign of the cross, but not in any form I'd learned.

"Stand up," Dragomir snapped. "You're not a priest."

"No," said Bogdan, rising. "Only a servant of God. And of the queen, whose will you serve… imperfectly."

Dragomir's mouth tightened.

I said nothing.

Bogdan turned to me. And smiled.

It was a strange smile — kind, but not gentle. As if he pitied something in me I had not yet lost.

His eyes moved over my face. I saw no revulsion. Only recognition. Like a priest studying a cracked altar, and deciding it could still hold fire.

"So," he said, "this is the sword the queen sends into the fire."

I stood.

He stepped closer — not threatening, just near enough that I could smell salt, incense, and something scorched beneath it. His eyes flicked over me, sharp as any blade.

"You were a volkodlak once," he said. "Mstislav's breaker of shields. I remember your name from the chants. Yaroslav. Son of no prince, but death rode your back all the same."

I didn't answer.

He reached toward my chest — not quite touching — fingers outstretched as if to read the shape of my ribs through air alone.

"She thinks you are steady," he murmured. "Rooted. She thinks your grief makes you incorruptible. Perhaps."

He turned away before I could speak.

"To Dragomir, a man is a vessel: fill it with orders, plug it with secrets, and send it sailing. But men are not vessels. They are altars. Either something holy burns in them — or something foul."

He faced me again.

"Do you know what you carry, Yaroslav?"

"Relics," I said.

He smiled. "No. Fire."

Then, softly, as if quoting: *"The chaff He will burn with unquenchable flame."*

He waited. I did not complete the verse.

"You read scripture," he said.

"I listen," I said.

He nodded. "Good. You'll need ears for more than wind and waves, where you go. There are forces in the deep that answer to neither king nor cross. But the saints still walk beside us — when called by faithful hands. Especially those who burn."

At that, he turned back to Dragomir.

"You've taught him trade routes. Feasts. Dialects. But have you prepared his soul?"

"He's not yours to prepare," Dragomir said coldly.

"No," Bogdan said. "He is the queen's. As am I."

That silenced the room.

Bogdan looked to the portrait above the shutter — the king and queen in younger days. His gaze lingered not on Mstislav, but on her.

"She carries burdens you do not see," he said. "The prince's illness is only part. The kingdom leans, Dragomir. You shore it with threats. I offer flame. Judgement. Cleansing."

"No," Dragomir said, rising. "You offer riddles and fear. You offer a queen wrapped in visions and fire."

Bogdan's smile returned, faint now.

"And yet," he said, "she listens to me. Not you."

He looked back to me, as if to weigh something not yet spoken.

"This path is not just duty. It is sanctified. The sea will test you. So will what sleeps beneath it. But if you walk in reverence — truly — the fire will not consume you. It will reveal you."

He stepped back.

Then, very gently, he laid a hand on my shoulder.

"God keep you, Yaroslav," he said. "And may Saint Ilyin walk beside your keel."

And he was gone.

No footfall. No door-slam. Just absence, like a storm that passed without breaking.

Dragomir let out a breath through his nose, sharp as flint struck steel.

"He wants you marked," he said. "So if you break, it's his legend. And if you don't — it's his miracle."

I looked at the ash circle on the hearth.

I wasn't sure if I'd been blessed. Or branded.

CHAPTER XXV: WHEN THE SHIPS SLEEP

One morning Dragomir did not appear.

I came to the library as I had every day since the queen's summons — out of habit now, like returning to the sparring yard though no match had been called. But the room was empty. The stone felt colder without the whisper of his presence. No tap of his fingers on the rough table. No growled correction. Just the hush of a room too tall and too still, with the faint smell of wax and ink long dried.

I waited. Pacing between the shelves.

The place made little sense to me, even after weeks beneath its vaulted ribs. The walls were hung with scrolls, skins, flat-bound books — stiff-backed like old soldiers, lined up in rows too tight to breathe. I could not read them. Not more than a mark or two. Dragomir had begun the work — names, titles, saints — but the rest was still closed to me, like a sea-chart drawn in smoke.

Even so, I wandered.

One corner held maps, wide hides stretched flat with lead weights. I could make out the lines: mountains like knotted veins, rivers like cuts across a wrist, the islands drawn as if seen from above — every bay, every shoal inked with care. Names scrawled beside them in a hundred hands. I imagined the men who walked those lines first. Quiet men, maybe. Careful ones. Willing to die with cold in their boots and blisters on their heels just to mark where a cliff ended or a ford might cross.

They had no armies. No banners. But still they went.

For what? To name what others passed by? To be right, even if it killed them?

Another shelf held the kind of bound skins Dragomir used when he cursed genealogy — the deeds of kings, saints, lords whose bones had long since turned to dust. But not all the books were royal. I saw drawings of men I'd never heard of — not crowned, not sainted — just strong-chinned in their portraits, holding scrolls or swords or shepherd's crooks. Minor lords, perhaps. Men who once thought themselves important enough to be remembered.

And someone had believed them. Someone had inked out their wars and children and coin-giving with the patience of a monk. A life's work, maybe, for a man who lived in someone else's shadow. All of it pressed into this place like dried seaweed, brittle and brown, already halfway to being forgotten.

One table held darker things. Glass vials sealed with wax. A copper bowl burnt black on one side. Charts that looked like spells — circles, knives, symbols like antlers or ash marks. Alchemy, Dragomir called it. Men trying to force the world to speak its secrets. To turn stone into gold, blood into power. I traced the lines on one of the scrolls with my thumb. There were burn marks along the edge, and a dark stain that might've been blood or worse.

Did they hope to save someone? Or just prove they could tear apart what God had made?

I touched nothing else.

Still no Dragomir. No knock at the door. No shadow's whisper. Just quiet.

Only Markov.

He sauntered in with the air of a man forgiven for something he hadn't yet done. The door creaked shut behind him like a priest's sigh.

"You look disappointed," he said. "Were you expecting a lesson?"

I said nothing.

"Don't worry. You've still got time to become the worst diplomat this kingdom's ever seen. But not today. Today's a holiday."

I raised an eyebrow.

"Saw your gaunt tutor heading down to the docks," he said, jerking a thumb behind him. "Fast, too — for a man whose blood's mostly vinegar. Had two of his shadows in tow, tight as barnacles. I'd bet my last tooth news just came in. From Stormhold, by the look of the sailcloth."

I glanced toward the window. Clouded. Still grey with sea-mist.

"No one told me."

"No one tells me either," he grinned. "But I listen better. So — what do you say, Yarik? Free day, fate's gift, straight from the queen's tight-lipped pitbull. Let's go see if Velgrad's got any joy left in her."

I looked again at the chair Dragomir had not sat in. Then at the shelves — at all the forgotten names, broken ink, dried blood.

"All right," I said.

Markov beamed. "God's teeth. I think that's the first time you've agreed with me on anything."

Markov was already babbling like a brook as I let the library door close behind me.

The city met me in pieces. Cold light spilled down the corridors of the Sea-Fort like milk gone thin, and I followed it.

Past guards who didn't challenge me. Past lesser men in lesser cloaks, who lowered their voices when I passed. The queen's tailor had done his work well: the tunic fit close across my shoulders, the cloak fell neat to the heel, and the cloth, though plain, was of the kind that made folk hesitate. Not fine enough to mark me as a noble. Not crude enough to make me a soldier. A man with purpose, then. Or worse — a man with permission.

Outside, the wind caught me. Sharp, clean. Salt-wet.

Velgrad stretched below.

From the height of the fort, the city was a tangle of stone and thatch and slate. Smoke rose from chimneys like thin fingers — slow, steady — and gulls screamed overhead, though I saw no fish and no dead. The roads wound down the hills in crooked veins. Low walls and crooked fences marked the fields where barley would soon fight to rise from the thawed earth. Children ran barefoot through muck. A woman poured piss from a bucket onto the street and shouted after a boy. A dog limped past with a fish head in its jaws.

The fort's gate stood open. No challenge, no notice. Another kind of gate entirely: a wide arch of stone, ancient and pitted, carved faintly with saint-marks — the kind weather wears like old scars. I passed beneath without prayer.

The cliff path to the docks began just beyond.

A slope of slick stone, shaped more by traffic than intention. Steps worn to hollows. Rope handholds strung along the steeper places, thick with salt and moss. The sea's breath rose steadily, cold and wet, bringing with it the stench of fish-gut, pitch, and old rope. Here and there, workers hauled barrels with groaning pulleys, swearing at one another in three dialects and a fourth made of gestures. Wagons creaked down, heavier than the mules pulling them. Children ran errands with hands full of dock-marks. No one watched me closely.

The docks lay beyond the city's walls, half-refuge and half-threat — an expanse of wet boards and salt rot where order thinned. Taverns had sprouted like barnacles along the cliff edge, hunched low against the wind, roofs patched with sailcloth and old tar. No banners flew. Their signs were carved driftwood or scratched boards — a red hand, a hanged gull, a cup cracked in half — none of them welcoming.

The piers themselves jutted out like ribs from the corpse of some great sea-beast, timber bolted to stone, green with moss and salted time. Eight arms reached into the grey chop — two wide enough for a horse-cart, the rest narrow, slick with fish-guts and sea-mud.

Even in the raw light of morning, the taverns were loud. Laughter in one, shouting in another. I saw men from three isles at least — Grey Isle grimfaces, seal-blooded Stormgrave lads, and one group I took for Fangborn, judging by the scars and the way their knives never left their belts. Ale was cheap in those halls — cheaper still the price of insult. A man might raise a cup and catch a fist before it touched his lips.

Stormhold sails bobbed at the outer berth — dark wool, shark-tooth pennants. Smaller ships clustered like chicks around the king's warships, though the latter loomed like old bulls: wide, iron-riveted, their blackened sails furled and hoarse with rust. And there, at the end of the longest pier, lay *The Grey Hand* — the king's ship, the one I once knew as well as my own bones.

I moved toward it without meaning to.

It had changed. Not in shape — the long ribs, the broad flank, the black spiral carved into the prow still marked it as a vessel bound by blood-oath — but in posture. It sat too low in the water. Ropes hung slack. No crew ran the rigging. The brass was dull. Tar streaks marred the timbers like old blood not yet scrubbed away. A blade too long in its sheath. Forgotten. Maybe feared. Once, I had stood at the helm of that ship. Not to command — that was never my place — but as the king's volkodlak, iron-bound, bone-willing. Ready to fight whatever rose from sea or shore. Now it slept. And the kingdom slept with it.

I watched a gull land on the rail. It picked at something in the grain of the wood — a dried scrap, a flake of scale — and then flew off, unhurried. Nothing startled it. Not even the wind.

Peace, they called it. The end of war. No more raids, no more burning, no more kings drowned in their own blood. And yet the ships rotted at anchor, the forges cooled, the warriors softened or drank themselves dumb.

Can a kingdom live in peace? Or does it curdle, like milk left too long in the sun? The king was failing — they said it softly, but they said it. No one saw him anymore. No voice from the throne. No ruling hand, save hers. Maybe the sickness came from within. From stilled limbs, from dulled blades. A sword unused rusts. It grows brittle. And then, when called upon, it breaks — or turns in the hand. But how can a man long for war? Knowing what it takes? What it burns? What it leaves buried? That is the curse. Not war, but needing it to feel alive.

I felt him before I heard him — that shape beside me, solid as an oath and twice as dangerous.

"You've got a look," said the voice. "Like you're choosing between drowning yourself or marrying a gull."

I turned. Urek stood grinning, arms folded, tattoos crawling up to his jaw like frostbite. His beard was rougher than I remembered, more salt than hair. A fresh split marked one ear, still red. His coat stank of sea and blood and fish-oil. He hadn't washed — but then, neither had the sea.

"You're not aboard," I said.

"No," he agreed. "Which means something's gone wrong."

We stood a moment, watching the grey chop between ships.

"Drink?" he said.

"Absolutely."

He led us below the docks, to a place he called The Hook-Eye. No sign, just a torn scrap of sailcloth nailed above the door — faded red, stencilled with something that might've been a fish or a noose.

Inside, the place hit like a punch to the teeth. Tar smoke, old fights, and the sour tang of rot. Sailcloth roof, patched with hide. Floor of warped planks slick with fish guts. Lanterns swung low from iron chains, their glass long shattered, flame guttering naked. The noise was worse — laughter, argument, the crash of a stool, and somewhere behind a hanging curtain, moans that could've meant pleasure or pain.

We stepped in — and a voice rose from the shadows, sharp and rough in the tattooed dialect of the Voryani.

"Urek Hornspawn!" it called. "Come for your mother's debts or your father's ghost?"

I saw shapes shift — hard faces, glint of teeth, knives at belts. Markov stiffened. I didn't move.

Urek only grinned wider, like a man greeted by an old scar.

"Depends," he called back. "Is she still charging for both?"

A roar of laughter followed, but no one moved to hug him.

We found a table in the back. A corner that smelled less of piss than most. Markov fetched drinks — eyes flitting, weighing exits and weapons. Urek paced while we waited, like a wolf with too much leg for the cage. Even when he sat, he sprawled — one boot up, arms loose, jaw working as if itching for a brawl to chew.

"Velgrad," he said, eyeing the warped beam overhead. "Ugly as a rotted tooth. But at least it doesn't pretend to shine."

Markov set three mugs down, foam already vanishing.

"To ugly truths," he said.

Urek drained his in a single pull and slammed the cup down so hard a nearby man flinched.

"I need work," he said. "Anything. Smuggling. Ship-guard. Priest-killing. Don't care. If I haul one more net, I'll bite the next man who speaks of tides like they're gods."

"Captain still afloat?" I asked.

He snorted. "Radomir? Lost half his pay to cards and the other half chasing whores who wouldn't have him. When the debt-men came, he fled to sea."

He leaned back, half-smile twitching.

"Then it got worse. Side boat crushed by a mad whale — ten men lost. Bran's cousin, maybe. Radomir started praying out loud. Wouldn't sleep without a saint nailed to the mast. One night he vanished mid-watch. No scream. No splash. Just… gone."

"You think he jumped?" Markov asked, voice low.

"Maybe the sea came calling. He owed it enough."

Urek reached for Markov's untouched drink, took a slow swig this time.

"You afraid of that?" I asked.

"Rot's worse than drowning. At least the sea's honest."

Markov's grin curled like a fishhook.

"So," he said. "Still looking for something sharp? Something mad? Something that bites back?"

Urek's eyes flicked to him — sharp, curious. Dangerous.

"Absolutely."

I said nothing.

Markov leaned close, voice barely above breath.

"There's talk of relics."

Urek's smile didn't change, but he tilted his head. A beast scenting blood.

"Markov," I said, flat.

"What? It's not like I drew a map."

Somewhere near the back, a stool splintered, followed by a curse and the sound of fists on flesh.

Urek laughed — a single bark, then a second.

"Relics. Holy bones. Saints that never pissed saltwater or drew a blade. Sounds like a fine death to me."

"There's no pay," I said.

"No promise of survival," Markov added.

"No cause to speak of," I said again.

Urek raised both hands like a prayer, mocking solemnity.

"Then I'm sold. Best offers always come without promises."

He drained the rest of the mug, wiped his mouth with the back of his hand, and leaned in.

"Pour me another. I like to be drunk when the saints stop smiling."

CHAPTER XXVI: FIRE AND IRON

I woke to noise.

Not the quiet stir of the sea or the shifting of guards in the hall — but the sound of boots on stone, shouted orders, the heavy tread of purpose moving through the Sea-Fort's bones. It was still early, though I could not say the hour. The light that leaked past the shutters was weak and grey, like cold milk poured over ash.

I dressed quickly. The walls of my chamber were thick, cut from old stone and mortared with salt and soot, but even here the noise found me. I smelled torch smoke and wet wool, the stink of many men pressed too close together.

By the time I stepped into the corridor, I could feel the shift in the air — something sharp, expectant. No servant came to guide me. No Dragomir with his rasping bark. Just the growing swell of voices outside.

I made for the great steps that overlooked the Sea-Fort square. The stone beneath my boots was slick with sea damp and old lichen. The fortress loomed behind me, black with age, its walls hunched like the shoulders of an old warrior, scarred and watchful. The steps themselves were broad, worn by time and the weight of kings, and led down to a raised platform that overlooked the square — a place built not for comfort but for proclamations. And punishment.

The square was nearly full. Not packed — the Sea-Fort was never that kind of city — but thick with bodies all the same. Men, women, children. Traders with red noses and heavy cloaks. Scribes with ink-stained fingers tucked into sleeves. A few soldiers in boiled leather and fur, standing at ease but with hands near weapons. And nearer the centre, the hard-faced men of the king's justice, helmed and waiting, spears grounded.

The air smelled of iron. Not blood yet. But it was coming.

At the square's heart, four men knelt in the mud. Their hands were bound behind them, and their faces turned slightly down, but not bowed. I had known the type — and if I hadn't, the state of them would have told me. Three were sailors, or had been. Their cloaks were sea-worn, now torn and muddied. Salt stains on the hems. One wore the remnants of a captain's coat — blue wool gone grey with weather, slashed open at the collar, one gold button hanging like a tooth ready to fall. Bruises bloomed purple across his cheek and jaw. Blood crusted at one temple, dried into his beard. Another man's nose was broken, the swelling so bad one eye had vanished behind flesh. The third grinned — a mouth full of blood and teeth like driftwood — and rocked slightly on his knees as if listening to a sea no one else could hear.

The fourth man was not like them.

No sailor. His cloak was linen, trimmed in dark green, with embroidery at the hem — now caked with filth. His hands shook. His hair had been carefully combed once, but the sweat and dirt had undone it. I saw the mark of a seal-ring on his finger, though the ring itself was gone. His face was pale and slack with fear, as though someone had scooped the bones from behind his eyes and left only a hollow thing pretending at manhood.

From the crowd came no jeering. No shouts. This was not a hanging in a field, or a gutter justice meted in some alley. This was the king's square. The Sea-Fort. And the silence here had weight. Even the children were quiet.

At the foot of the steps stood Dragomir, his brown cloak pulled tight, eyes locked on the kneeling men. He did not acknowledge me. He didn't need to. I stood where I was meant to stand — at his shoulder, but above him, as the steps allowed. This was a place of hierarchy. Every stone knew its place.

A herald stepped forward. He wore black, save for a red sash knotted at his shoulder — the mark of the king's voice in matters of death. His face was smooth, unreadable, like something carved rather than born.

He unrolled a parchment with slow care. Then, his voice rising to fill the square:

"Let it be known and recorded in the sight of God, the saints, and this crown — that Stormward, by failure of tribute and defiance of summons, stands in violation of the king's law. That the ships named *Red Swan*, *Barrel's Grace*, and *White Gale* withheld their due and ignored lawful collection. That these men, captains and envoys of that rebellious hold, are found guilty of treason."

A ripple passed through the crowd — not speech, but breath, like the wind shifting through winter grass.

The envoy lifted his head. His voice cracked as he tried to stand. "Mercy," he said. "I was not told. A clerical delay — the sums were ready, I swear it. If given time —"

"You were given time," the herald said, flatly. "And warnings. The king does not send mercy in triplicate."

"I speak for Boyarina Salava herself!" he cried, voice rising to a near scream. "She swears fealty still. There has been a mistake —"

One of the sailors spat beside him. "You speak for no one but yourself," he said, and his voice was rough as rope. "Beg if you want. But don't pretend it means anything."

The other sailor — the one with the broken face — gave a bitter laugh, and looked to the herald. "I'll fight," he said. "One against one. For my crew, my ship. Let the king see if I'm worth keeping."

The herald ignored him.

Another man approached. Not hooded, not hidden — just a soldier in black leather, with a sword so clean it looked unused. But I saw the tension in his hands. The readiness. He had done this before.

"Sentence is death," the herald said. "By blade. The ships are forfeit. The names struck from the charter. Witness this, all of you — that the king's peace is not a begging bowl, but a law of iron."

He stepped back.

The man with the sword stepped forward. He was lean, his face wrapped in cloth, his grip steady on the long curved blade. Not ceremonial — working steel, nicked and re-sharpened. He said nothing. Made no sign.

He stopped behind the first man — the sailor with the split lip and the gold-thread coat. Two guards stepped in and gripped the prisoner's arms, forcing him forward over the block that had been set in the mud. A flat-topped stump, stained near-black.

The sailor did not flinch. He bared his teeth once more — defiant — and spat into the dirt.

The sword rose. Not high. Just enough.

The first blow struck the neck at an angle, biting deep into muscle and tendon, but not severing. The body jerked. A groan escaped — or a curse. Hard to say. The second blow finished it — hacking through the bone with a wet crack, followed by a thud that landed wrong, soft, and ugly.

Blood soaked the straw. Steam rose from the stump.

The second man tried to twist away. He shouted something — Saint's name, a plea — but the guards held him. He fought them. He was strong. It took three to bend him to the block. The sword came down in two quick hacks — not for show, but with the rhythm of a butcher at work.

The third went limp before they touched him. Whether from faith or terror, he offered nothing. His mouth moved in silence. He was the cleanest of the lot — the sword passed through in one stroke, helped by the stillness.

The envoy was last. He collapsed before he reached the block, blubbering, kicking, trying to crawl. One of the guards grabbed his hair and dragged him forward like a sack. Another pinned his arms.

He screamed — no words, just raw noise — and then the blade came down, too far forward. Caught the jaw. The second blow found the neck. The third sent the head rolling into the filth, eyes open.

The square remained still.

The gulls did not.

The grim work done, and the crowd already beginning to thin, Dragomir turned his head slightly and looked up at me. "Come," was all he said. Then he moved — cloak whispering behind him, boots crunching over grit at the base of the steps.

I followed.

Dragomir's steps were even, unhurried, each footfall a verdict on the worn black stone. The Sea-Fort breathed differently in its upper chambers — colder, quieter, cut off from the voices of the city. It was a place of chambers not halls, of thick doors and narrow windows, where words could be locked away like prisoners. The kind of place you built when you trusted no one.

The guards outside the prince's wing stood rigid, helms polished, broad-hafted spears grounded like warning posts grounded to the flagstones like grave markers. They didn't speak. They didn't nod. Just opened the doors for Dragomir.

Heat struck me first — thick as stew. Not just fire-warmth, but the stale closeness of a room long kept shut against the world. Incense hung in the air, sweet and cloying, mixed with sweat, old leather, and the faint tang of medicine. Somewhere beneath it all: rot.

The queen's voice rang out from within, sharp and furious. Not words — not yet — only the rhythm of fury: clipped, rising, falling, slicing through the muffled chamber like a blade scraping metal. I heard the echo of footsteps pacing and the thud of something knocked over. A cup. A chair.

Dragomir didn't flinch. He reached for the door ring and opened it wide.

The prince's chambers were the most lavish I had seen in the fortress, but nothing in them felt alive. A canopy bed stood against the far wall, draped in dark green velvet, its frame carved with saints and sea-beasts. Tapestries covered the stone — storm scenes, battles, a woman with a torch driving wolves into the sea — but the colours had dulled with age and smoke. The windows were shuttered, bolted from within. Lamps burned low in iron sconces, and the hearth flared red with pitchwood, but still the room seemed dark.

There were mirrors. Four, that I counted. Each placed at odd angles — not decorative, not polished. Watching.

I had not expected him to be strong.

Rumour painted him wasted — a prince rotting from the inside, wine-sick and pox-bitten, too weak to rule, too proud to fall. But Illarion stood shirtless at the centre of the room, breathing hard, and the strength was still there. Not just in his shoulders, broad and battle-born, or the long line of his spine, straight as an oath unbroken — but in the way he faced her. Bare. Braced. Refusing to bow.

A goblet lay on its side, rocking gently against the stone. Dark liquid trailed from it — not wine alone. His trousers were fur-lined, black, fine. But they hung wrong — rumpled at the waist, wet at one knee. His left hand gripped the table's edge. The fingers curled inward, stiff and slow, like the leg of a bird caught by frost. The strength was there — but bent.

His right hand clutched a cloth, stained dark, slick in the lamplight. It shook.

The room stank of sweat and wine and something sweet beneath it — the sick-sweet smell of spoiled meat. I'd smelled it in camps. On men who would not live the week.

He was taller than I remembered. The bones of a prince had not left him. His chest still held the old strength: trained muscle, not yet turned to softness. But something in the skin betrayed him. Pale patches like candlewax marked his ribs and groin. A sheen clung to the belly. There were scars — some old and earned, others fresh and unclean. Not the cuts of war. The cuts of a man trying to feel something through the fog.

Near the bed lay a cloak and gloves — queen's colours, stitched silver, folded with care. He had not touched them. He stood as he was: not naked, but exposed. Facing the queen. Not flinching. Not hiding.

Whatever passed between them had burned through the mask. There was no velvet here. No prince. Only a son who refused to kneel, and a mother who would not look away.

His jaw was clenched. His left hand curled tighter. His right still shook.

He had his father's frame. His mother's cheekbones. But the face had changed. Subtly. Cruelly. The left side hung lower than the right. The eye blinked slow. The mouth curled wrong. Not enough to name — but enough to unsettle. Like a statue weathered by salt: the form still noble, but the corners blurred. The smile bent sideways.

As though part of him remembered what he was born to be. And part of him had already begun to rot.

He didn't flinch beneath our gaze. If he noticed us at all, he gave no sign.

He bared his teeth — not in defiance, not quite — but something nearer despair. Not a man resisting judgement, but one daring it to come.

"You humiliate me in my own rooms," he said. "And you expect loyalty in return?"

"I expect obedience," the queen snapped. "Not flattery. Not delay. Obedience."

She turned as we entered. Her face was pale, but her cheekbones flared with colour — not from shame, but from rage held hot too long. Her hair was pinned in iron thorns. One side of her cloak had come undone, slipping from her shoulder to expose the bone beneath — sharp, deliberate, like a blade drawn partway from its sheath.

Dragomir didn't flinch. He stepped in, cloak trailing across the stone, and said — quietly — "Enough."

The prince wheeled toward him, jaw tight.

"So this is it, then?" he snapped. "A prince — turned tax collector."

Dragomir stepped forward, slow and certain. "The king has rendered judgement on Stormward. The queen has sanctioned it. The boyarina is to be removed. Her ships are forfeit. Her line is broken. The lesson must be public."

"And I," Illarion said, straightening, "am to be the whip?"

"You are to be the heir."

That landed like iron on the floor.

The queen said nothing. She only watched her son — not with warmth, not with hate, but the way one watches a locked gate that has begun to groan under the strain.

Dragomir continued. "You will sail with one hundred men aboard four ships. You will land at Stormhold. You will take the hold, seize the records, execute those who resist, and ensure that the crown's authority is not mistaken for charity."

"You assume I've agreed."

"You do not have that luxury."

There was a silence after that. Illarion didn't move. But something in his jaw flexed. He picked up the cloth again and wiped his side — a smear of red trailed across his ribs.

"I see," he said.

Dragomir turned to me then, gesturing slightly. "This is Yaroslav."

The prince's gaze slid to me. Measured. Curious. I saw no fear in him. But I saw calculation.

"He will join your personal retinue. His task is his own — a matter between him, the queen, and the crown. But in all other things, you will heed him."

"That's a strange way to run a command," Illarion said. "What am I — a prince, or a puppet?"

"You are a symbol," Dragomir said. "And symbols are valuable only so long as they remain intact. This man will keep you intact."

I said nothing. The prince didn't look away.

"He comes and goes as he pleases," Dragomir said. "You do not question his movements. If he gives you a command, obey it. Or don't — but you may not get a second chance."

The queen stepped closer now, and placed her hand — gloved, pale — on her son's shoulder.

"You've asked to prove yourself," she said. "This is your chance."

She meant it. But I heard the fear under it.

And then — before the prince could reply, before Dragomir could assert the final word — the door opened.

It did not slam. It did not creak. It simply opened — as if the room had always been waiting.

A gust of cooler air followed, cutting through the incense-thick heat like a blade through wax. And with it came Bogdan.

He entered as though summoned, though no one had called. He wore the same grey mantle, now dry, the bone-charms at its hem clinking softly with each step — not whispering this time, but declaring. The robe hung neatly. His beard had been combed. The icon of Saint Vira still hung from his belt, but now a second symbol joined it — a shard of blackened wood bound in cord, too charred to name.

He stopped just inside the threshold, eyes passing from Dragomir to the queen, then resting on Illarion — and only there did he speak.

"Justice has been done," he said. "But more is required."

His voice was low, level — not the warmth of a priest offering comfort, but the gravity of a man delivering a verdict already written.

Illarion tilted his head. He didn't flinch, didn't sneer. But some corner of him — the proud, wounded boy behind the prince — straightened, listening.

Bogdan's eyes moved to the prince. He studied him for a breath — not the scars or the wounds, but the soul behind them. Then he looked at me. Just for a moment.

He smiled.

Then he turned back to the queen.

"The blade has spoken. But the sea has spoken also."

She tilted her head, wary. "What do you mean?"

"There was a dream," Bogdan said, as if it were enough. "There was a sign. A flame on water. A hand in the depths. A voice that named me."

"Named you?" Dragomir said, his voice iron again.

Bogdan did not turn to him.

"Yes. For this voyage. For this justice. The prince must sail — yes. But he must not go alone. Not in spirit. Not in grace. I am to go with him. I am needed."

His words were not loud. They didn't need to be. They hung in the room like incense — sweet and unclean.

"No," Dragomir said, but too slowly.

The queen turned to him.

"If Bogdan says he is needed, then he is."

There was no force in her voice. Only faith. Or the wreckage of it.

Dragomir said nothing. His face was stone. Not cold. Not angry. Just still. The stillness of a man standing where he must not flinch.

The prince stepped forward. "If he sails with me," he said, "then I'll go gladly."

I watched Dragomir's jaw tighten, but not clench. A single vein throbbed near his temple.

"He has no training," he said. "He is not of the guard, nor the fleet, nor the —"

"He is of God," the queen said. "And he is mine. That is enough."

Bogdan bowed.

"I will not hinder the command. I will not displace it. I am only to witness. To bless. To protect."

Illarion's eyes shone — not with joy, but vindication. He had won something. Or believed he had.

And in that flicker, I saw the flaw Dragomir feared.

Bogdan turned to me again. Not smiling now. Measuring.

"And you," he said, "are the blade at the prince's side."

I said nothing.

His eyes narrowed slightly, as if he'd hoped for something more.

Dragomir's cloak shifted as he stepped forward.

"Then it is done," he said. "We sail when the ships are ready. Yaroslav, with me."

He didn't wait for the queen's leave. He turned and strode to the door.

I followed.

Behind us, I heard the prince say something low to Bogdan. A question. A jest. Something about destiny. The priest laughed — softly, like someone closing a prayer book.

We walked in silence for some time.

Only when we reached the stair did Dragomir speak.

"Take what you need from the armoury," he said. "There'll be no time for fine fittings. You sail as soon as *The Grey Hand* is readied."

He paused a step above me.

"Speak."

Just that. As if he already knew. Perhaps he did.

"There are men I need. For the queen's charge."

"The braggart and the mad harpooner."

He didn't sneer. He didn't need to. He said it like naming symptoms of a sickness already spreading.

"They're mine," I said. "Or I don't go."

He stopped. Turned to face me fully.

"You're not a prince," he said. "You don't give ultimatums."

"I don't need permission."

Our eyes held. A long moment. Nothing moved.

Then he turned and kept walking.

No assent. No refusal.

Only the sound of his boots fading into the dark — and the sense that somewhere behind us, a hand of bone was writing all our names in salt and ash.

CHAPTER XXVII: THE WEIGHT OF IRON

We were to leave on the morrow. The queen had named the path. The oath had found its grip. Now came the matter of steel — to see what arms the crown still offered those it once cast aside.

The royal armoury lay buried in the Sea-Fort's belly, wedged between the cistern vaults and the old chapel. A place of iron and shadow, shaped not for beauty but for truth. There were no windows, no song. Just the slow drip of water from the stones, and the cloying, layered smell of whale oil, pitch, tallow, and old sweat — the scent of war long caked into mortar.

The stairs wound tight as a noose. Each step rang dull beneath my boots. At the threshold, I paused — not from fear, but recognition. I had come here once, long ago, with a broken spear in hand and a jaw clenched too tight to speak. I had bled for the king that week. He'd never asked. But the armourers had known.

Now they knew again.

The door creaked open to a room held low by arches and thick with breathless heat. Whale-oil lamps hung from rusted chains, their light thick with smoke, casting the vaults in a wavering gold that clung to the edges of helms, the curve of blade-spines, the folded weight of hauberks hung like sleeping men.

Two figures moved in the half-light. Old men, bent at the back but straight in their purpose — like hinges that never learned to fail. They did not wear livery. They wore soot, leather aprons, and the crusted ghosts of fifty campaigns.

One looked up.

"Yaroslav," he said, squinting as if the years between us were a trick of the light. His voice was a rasp dragged over gravel. "Saints take me — I thought you'd died in peace."

"Not yet," I said.

He spat, and the other gave a half-laugh, but the silence that followed was heavy. Not with suspicion, but memory.

They'd heard. The queen's seal had reached them before I did. No questions came — only the weight behind their eyes, the kind a man earns by walking through blood beside another and surviving.

"Coming back for war?"

I looked across the chamber. Racks of mail hung low, patched and sweat-darkened, their iron links still streaked with old tallow and red-brown crusts. The smell was thick with ghost-flesh.

"I hope not," I said.

We walked slow through the vault, as through a reliquary. That's what it was — not a storehouse, but a sanctum. Each dented helm bore a story. Each coat of mail had a name stitched in thread or bone, worn smooth by blood and time. I passed a scale shirt from the steppe — boiled leather gone black with oil, bronze plates bent and reforged. Another vest bore the spiral mark of Saint Olexa's banner, though its edge had been slashed clean through and mended with sinew. One helm was split at the crown — a killing blow survived, perhaps by miracle — and banded now with iron, etched at the brow with Saint Danilo's fetter. The rust around it was red, fresh as blood.

The weight of it all pressed inward — the steel, the smoke, the silence. Above us, somewhere beyond stone and soot, the chapel of Saint Vira kept her vigil with her key of flame. Her shrine held peace. This place held what was left when peace failed.

"Choose," one said.

I passed over the proud pieces, the new-polished ones kept for parades and young men eager to be noticed. I found a hauberk patched at the left shoulder — a thick mend done in square rings, not to hide the wound but hold it fast. Its weight was neither light nor cruel. It remembered the shape of a man.

I took it.

The helm I chose was plainer still — a spangenhelm with a nasal bar, reforged at the brow where some past bearer had taken a hammer-blow. The dent was still visible beneath the new steel. I touched it, and my thumb came away faintly red with rust.

A shield waited near the rack — round, bossed with iron, its rim rawhide-wrapped and worn to the grain. The sort of shield that had no name, but had been held against arrows, fire, and fear.

They fitted me without ceremony. The mail rasped down over my tunic. I shifted my arms, felt the pull of weight under each breath. The helm settled like memory on my brow — heavier than I recalled, but true. Straps pulled tight under my arms. I said nothing. They said nothing. Only the sound of leather creaking, buckles catching, the faint hiss of oilcloth drawn from blade.

One of them stepped back.

"Well," he said, eyeing the shape I'd become. "You look like Mstislav's wolf-skin, back from the grave."

I did not smile.

Then: boots, slow and careless, on the stone beyond. No knock. The door opened.

Prince Illarion entered, cloaked in wine and sweat. Not drunk — not yet — but close enough to see it from where he stood. The bottle swung from his hand like a censer.

The old men stiffened. Bowed, just enough. He didn't see them.

"My best three sets — they're loaded?"

"Aye, Highness," one said. "We packed them ourselves."

"Good." He shrugged out of his cloak, then his tunic, arms bared in a single motion — quick, angry, practiced. His chest was still thick with muscle, and his arms roped with sinew. But the skin betrayed him: waxy patches along the flank, a sheen not born of effort, and the scars — some shallow, some deep, some that looked like mouths just shy of speech. His left hand curled inward at the knuckles. When the strap caught wrong, he swore.

As they worked the belts, he looked at me — truly looked.

"I remember you now," he said. His gaze slid over the mail, the helm, the shield. "Shevrin's gate. That was you. The old lord — what was his name? Doesn't matter. He was half-buried under corpses. Shield shattered, leg twisted like rope. Bleeding from the eyes. His kin watched from the tower window. He begged. Not for his life — for them. Not to see it. You said nothing. Just knelt on his chest and brought the rock down again. And again. Until his skull wasn't a skull anymore."

I said nothing.

He drank, wiped his mouth with the back of his hand, and smiled.

"I liked that."

There was no triumph in it. Just the flat note of a man who had seen too much to know what decency costs.

Then, just as fast, the grin dropped.

"But you asked for exile. Coward's end. If I'd been king, I'd have given it to you — sword through the throat, clean and done."

"I would've taken it," I said.

He stared. Then offered the bottle. His hand trembled — not wildly, but enough to see.

I drank. Salted metal on the rim. Bitter wine. I handed it back without word.

He nodded, once. "Most who stayed are dead now."

"That is the way of such things."

He barked a laugh — more bark than breath. When the old men reached to strap his sword belts, he slapped their hands away.

"I'll do it."

He took his time. One long blade, one short — both clean at the edge, worn at the grip. The edges were clean, the scabbards worn. Not decoration. These were tools kept sharp.

"Trained by a master from Klykograd," he said. "You wouldn't know the style."

I did. And its weakness. But pride is louder than wisdom, and youth speaks where it should listen.

He turned toward me, wine in one hand, blades at his side.

"What else has my mother asked you to do?" he said. "Mark my steps? Watch my dreams? Count how often I piss the bed, then whisper your tally back to her across the sea?"

His voice stayed level, but the wine sloshed with each word.

"No," he said, quieter. "You're here to decide. To watch for the crack. To see whether the rot's only skin, or if the marrow's turned. If I can still wear steel. Or if it's time I be buried in it."

He stepped back, arms wide — offering himself, or mocking the gesture.

"This rebellion's a goat's cough. I'll snuff it in a fortnight. Then they'll fear me. Maybe I'll salt the fields. Burn the goddamn crops. Teach them what inheritance costs."

He stepped closer. The wine between us now. His voice dropped.

"They've sent you to guard me. Nursemaid. That's what you are."

"I will do my best for you," I said.

He looked at me, gloves in hand. Drew them on slow, fingers curling like claws into leather.

Then he smiled again — crooked, wet-lipped, teeth too bright in the oillight.

"We should fight. Then you'd see I don't need guarding."

I said nothing.

That silence stung him. I saw it.

At the wall, the old men stood still as icons, but I saw the tension in their hands — how they cinched straps a little too hard. How they did not meet his eyes.

He was strong. Still. And sharp. And cunning. But something inside was bent. Like a helm reforged with the wrong hammer. Like a prince who knew he was cracked — and dared the world to wear him anyway.

The weight came off slow.

I unbuckled the mail myself. It rasped down my arms, dragging sweat and memory with it. The hauberk hit the table with the sound of chains dropped into a grave.

The old men watched, but did not offer help. They knew better. Some burdens a man must lay down himself.

Illarion let them strip him bare. He raised his arms like a statue carved for war, unmoving as the clasps came undone. The oil-dark padding peeled from his skin — damp, reeking. Beneath it, his sickness bloomed: pale sheen, old scars, new tremors.

He said nothing. Neither did they.

When the fitting was done, we handed back the armour — sweat-wet mail, stiff leathers, cloaks still rank with pitch — each piece folded into oiled canvas, tied off, and marked by name. The bundles would not go to the ships. They'd wait below, in the barracks chamber under the Sea-Fort — guarded, kept dry, ready for morning. At dawn, we would dress again. For war, and for show. Illarion would need help — the clasps, the weight — but the rest of us would buckle our own. No servants. No soft hands.

The old men hauled the bundles away.

Then I turned to the prince. He stood bare-chested, sweat streaking his ribs, one hand gripping the neck of the wine bottle like it might answer him. This was the moment. There would be no better.

I cleared my throat. Not from fear — but to be heard.

"I served the king for twenty years," I said.

He didn't look at me.

"Dragomir has kept me from him."

That caught something. His head tilted. His eye twitched.

"I wish to pay my respects."

I let the silence stretch — one more breath, no more.

"Could you take me to him?"

He looked at me then. Really looked. Not as a prince weighs a subject, but as a wolf considers the thing in the dark that hasn't yet flinched.

"No," he said. Simply. "What makes you think I would?"

I met his gaze. Held it.

"You remember Shevrin," I said. "Then you know I'm a man who served his king no matter the price."

"I remember a man who killed without blinking. That doesn't make him worthy."

"I'm not asking for favour."

He smirked. "Then you're asking for pity."

"I'm asking to see my king."

At that, he laughed. One sharp breath. No humour in it.

"You're not owed anything."

"I didn't say I was."

He turned away, ran a hand through his damp hair. Then stilled.

Something shifted behind his eyes — that gleam of cunning, of sickness made sharp. He turned back slow, like a man rehearsing a story before the fire.

"Take you to him," he said. "Break Dragomir's circle. Let you into the room they've sealed for months. That's no small thing."

"I know."

"And what would I gain? Gratitude?" He spat. "I've had enough of that from priests and whores. Both wear thin."

He stepped close, close enough that I could smell the sour on his breath, the fever in his skin.

"Swear something, Volkodlak."

I said nothing.

His voice dropped. Cold. Precise.

"If the rot takes me — truly takes me — and I can't hold a sword or a thought, if I speak in tongues or strike at ghosts… if my mother keeps me breathing past the use of it—"

He leaned in.

"You'll kill me. Clean. Without asking. Without warning. Before they put me in chains. Or robes."

I didn't answer.

His eyes glittered like wet stone.

"Swear it."

The silence between us turned thick. Not just with wine and sweat and fear — but with what it meant. To say yes.

I looked down. Saw his hand, curled like a claw. Saw my own, broad, calloused, still steady.

Then I said it.

"I swear."

His face softened. Not with peace. With something else. Triumph, maybe. Or relief that looked like hate.

"Good," he said. "Then let's go see the old man."

CHAPTER XXVIII: THE HEART OF THE FIRE

The king's chambers crowned the Sea-Fort like rot beneath a circlet — high, shut, near holy in the way old wounds are. The stone stair twisted up through the tower's ribs, steep as penance, until we came to the doors: two slabs of alder-black wood bound with iron studs and ringed with carvings worn down to stumps of saints and beasts.

The guards did not move.

Illarion strode ahead. He wore his fine cloak too tightly fastened, and the torchlight caught the sheen of sweat at his temple.

"Move," he snapped.

They looked — not at him, but at me.

"He's with me."

That was enough. The doors groaned inward. The stink spilled first: old fire, old wine, the yellow tang of sickness turned sweet. Then came the heat — not warmth, but the cloying press of a hearth too long lit in a room too long closed.

Inside, silence ruled like a second king.

It was too large a chamber for one man. The rafters vanished in gloom above. Crimson hangings bled down the walls. The stone pillars — six in all — had been worked with spirals of ash and gold, as if fire itself had once risen here and left its trace in metal.

The hearth was wide as a barge and flanked with bears, their carved maws open in a roar no man heard now. Flame leapt high, but its light crawled instead of shone. It did not warm. It *watched*.

And in that fire-glow sat Mstislav.

He was draped in a bear pelt, its head sagging like a shadow over one shoulder. His frame, once great as a siege ram, had thinned. The furs swallowed him now. One arm lay limp across the chair, heavy with rings. The other rested on his thigh, fingers curled as if remembering war.

He did not speak.

Illarion halted just inside the threshold. I saw it in his stance — the stiffness at the neck, the weight he shifted to one foot then the other. He would not come closer. He had before. And been struck for it.

So I stepped forward.

The hush did not break. It bent.

I knelt, because I had once knelt in blood and oath before this man, and some things are not unlearned.

"My king," I said.

The old head turned. Not quickly. Not with recognition. The eyes were pale, milked, but not blind — worse. Seeing something else.

Slowly he rose, like a sail unfurling on a windless morning — stiff, half-rotted, yet still bound to rise by the habit of command. His joints cracked like old timber. His fingers gripped the arm of the chair as if it might bite.

He stared at me, through me, beyond me. When he spoke, it was to the stone, or to ghosts.

"Come."

I rose. Moved slowly, as one does when nearing a beast that might yet kill.

His jeweled hand found my shoulder. The grip was stronger than I expected.

"My son," he said.

My breath stopped. Somewhere behind me, Illarion shifted — a sound like a blade sheathing.

"I'm here, father," the prince said.

Mstislav scowled. Waved his hand toward the voice like at a buzzing gnat.

"No," I answered, soft but clear. "My lord. It's Yaroslav. Your sworn man. Still."

The king blinked. Turned his face toward me. His thick fingers brushed my cheek — not gently.

"The Volkodlak," he muttered. "Yes. I remember. Have you come to kill me?"

"No, my lord."

The hand came fast. The slap rang like a struck shield.

"Then why?" he bellowed. "Let it come! Let the wind tear down this tower! Let the sea climb the walls and swallow us whole! I'll stand in the rain with my arms out and dare the sky to split me! I named myself master of storms — now let the storm prove it! Burn my banners! Strip the roof! I was born screaming in salt — I'll die the same!"

The furs fell from his shoulders like snow off a shaken bough. His chest heaved. His beard dripped with spittle.

I did not speak. Not yet. There was no gap wide enough for reason to cross.

"I stink. I know it. I wake to my own piss and the reek of fevered skin. The servants light herbs, burn orange peel, smear balm under their nostrils. Like sweet scents can drown out the truth. But no perfume hides rot for long. Not in a man. Not in a throne. I drink to remember, but the drink forgets."

Suddenly, he turned on Illarion. "Bring me the bottle, you coward bastard!"

Illarion obeyed. His hands shook. His face did not. He fetched a bottle of pale gold glass. Three cups. Poured.

Father and son drank like men stabbing their own throats.

I did not join them.

The scent was sharp — pepper, wormwood, something honeyed and wrong beneath.

Mstislav laughed.

"You raise a boy, feed him from your hand, shield him from knives, and he grows teeth for your throat. That's the truth of heirs. Better to sire wolves — at least they don't weep when they eat you. My son speaks sweetly and watches like a butcher choosing which limb to take first."

Only then did his eyes seem to clear.

"I thought you were dead," he said. His eyes seems to delve into mine. His hand grabbed me again, but this time as if I were a ghost, and might slip away. "And now… now you stand here with me again. Where have you been?"

"You let me go," I answered. "To find peace."

His brow furrowed. Something behind the eyes stuttered and dimmed.

"Did I?"

He looked at his empty glass. Hurled it into the fire. It burst in a flash, and for a moment the flames seemed to snarl.

A guard opened the door. Cautious.

"My liege—"

"GET OUT!"

The voice was iron again. The door slammed. The guard was gone.

The king sagged.

Illarion made no move to steady him. He turned his face instead, blank as stone.

Mstislav leaned on me.

"They obey the collar, not the man. Dress a dog in velvet and he'll have men bowing to his bark. I've seen fools lifted high for knowing how to nod. I've seen killers crowned. You think rule means wisdom? No. It means timing. Blood. And luck. And knowing when to bite."

He was heavy. Too close. His breath stank of salt, rot, old milk. His words came low, thick, like mud whispered into a grave.

"Do you remember, Yaroslav? When I found you? Not born of me. But mine. You were ten, maybe. Caked in blood."

I remembered.

The battlefield had steamed with gore. The ash-pines had burned, their smoke sour with sap and blood. My father lay cut open at my feet, my uncle beside him, throat slit for standing proud. My hands clenched a broken blade until the skin split. I did not cry. I did not run. Mstislav stood above me in mail streaked black with soot and viscera. He looked once, and said, "This one's mine."

I closed my eyes.

"I built a kingdom," he said. "With you. And then you left. You broke me. I feel it. The bloat. The pus beneath the skin. My blood's gone wrong. My body rebels like a betrayed wife. I once broke men with this hand — now it trembles lifting a spoon. I am become my own punishment. No blade could hurt me like my own flesh does. You let her chain me with silence. Look at me."

His eyes filled — not tears, but something colder. Grief held too long to weep.

"I pray to the saints," he whispered. "But the Devil has me by the cloak. I've lost the thread. Names, faces — they blur. Maybe I said things. Maybe I wronged you. I don't remember. But I know I'm old. I know I was a fool, thinking time could be ruled like a fief. So — forgive me, if you can. Forget me, if you must."

I had no prayer to offer. No lie he'd believe.

Then he turned — sudden again — and stared at the hearth.

"What do you see in the fire, wolf-skin?"

Only flame. And a throne decaying in its own light.

"Only flame, my lord."

"I see fire-devils," he said. "Little ones. They whisper. They ask me to step into the fire. I like them."

His gaze did not leave the flames. I followed it. Saw only crackling logs — and in them, the shape of a crown melting. I felt the old dread rise, the kind that lived in men who'd burned towns and heard children scream. The Devil does not always lie. Sometimes he tells the truth too plainly.

"Don't listen, my lord," I said. "Even truth in his mouth turns to poison."

He nodded, but his mind had already wandered. Slowly, he sank back into the chair.

Illarion had stepped into shadow. He did not speak, but his face was pale — mouth set tight, eyes too wide. His father had not called him son. Not once. Not even in madness. That silence would grow teeth.

"Not madness, please. Not all the way. Let me keep a corner of myself, some ember of who I was. Don't let me howl like a beast and forget why. Take my strength. Take my pride. But leave me my mind, God — or what's left of it."

I straightened. I did not know if it was loyalty, or mercy, or cowardice that made me speak.

"I swear it, my lord. The Devil will not take you. I will drive him back — or fall trying. Either way — we'll die as men should."

He only stared at the flames.

Then, almost gently, he smiled.

"There. There you are. I thought you were gone. My wolf-skin. My sword. My — yes. Yes. My son."

CHAPTER XXIX: THE SHIPS BENEATH US

Morning broke gold across Velgrad.

The light came low and clean across the rooftops, gilding the tower stones, flashing off spearheads and the steel threadwork of banners rippling in the river wind. A city roused for glory. From the Sea-Fort's high halls to the taverns and fish-halls along the muddy quay, the people had gathered — hundreds, then thousands, some packed shoulder-deep, others lining balconies or crouched on tiled rooftops. They had come to witness something worth remembering.

A prince's send-off. A holy charge. A page torn from saga and pinned to the mast.

I walked near the front, just behind Illarion's personal guard, dressed again in war-coat and mail. The King's Road, cut with gravel and swept clean. The crowds spilled at the edges, pressing like surf against stone. Children shouted. Old men crossed themselves. Women flung heather and dry skirret stalks under the horses' hooves. I saw one girl kneel, pressing a candle to the ground in prayer as we passed. For us, or for the dead we'd soon become — I could not tell.

Illarion looked every inch a prince. His cloak was sky-dyed wool, pinned with a brooch of whalebone and gold. His helm had been polished bright; the bear crest glinted like sunlit ice. Whatever sickness ran under his skin had been masked by powder, balm, and faith. His horse — a tall roan, braided mane, barded in stamped leather — moved with the grace of pageant and training both. Today he rode straight. Today he smiled. He was a man anointed.

Bogdan rode behind him, and to his right. The people saw him and bowed without knowing why. His grey mantle hung still despite the wind. The bone charms at his collar lay quiet. The icon of Saint Vira gleamed with a fresh blessing. His presence was a flame held behind glass — all felt it, none touched.

Behind and to the left, the Queen. She rode down from the Sea-Fort astride a white mare, its mane combed to silk, hooves lacquered with ash. Her veil streamed behind her like sea-mist in wind. No crown. No jewels. Only pale hands, and a face still as carved bone. The people gazed on her as they might a vision — holy, unbidden, and not entirely safe. I heard a woman whisper, "She gives him to the sea herself." Another answered, "He goes by her will."

At the landing above the docks, she stopped. So did the priests, gold-robed and smoke-smeared, holding ash staves and reliquaries. And beside them, though easy to overlook in the morning shadow, stood Dragomir. He looked not at the prince, but at me.

We descended and reached the lower pier.

The smell of tar and salt struck hard. The crowd thinned here, held back by spear-wielding wardens in grey. Just us, now. Just those who would go — and the ships waiting to take us.

Three vessels, lined side by side, lashed to the long pier like horses before a charge.

The Grey Hand stood tallest. Her ribs had been scrubbed and tarred; the black pine shone like oiled armour. The prow bore no beast, only the white open hand — re-carved deep and chalk-whitened — palm forward, judgement held. The iron rivets along her flanks caught the sun like stars. Her deck was swept bare and braced for war. From her mast flew the black pennant of the crown, stitched with a white hand — fingers spread, palm raised. The king's banner — though the king himself was not aboard. I saw Markov crouched by the forward shield-rack, tying new leather to his sword-belt. His coat had been brushed, but the sleeves still bore wine-stains. He looked up, winked, said something to Urek, who leaned on the rail with the ease of a man born to wave and plank. The tattooed harpooner spat into the sea and grinned.

Beside her, *The Sea's Teeth* crouched lower — sleeker, faster. She bore a hunter's trim: long lines, shallow hull, a sail dyed the grey-blue of stormclouds. Her rail bore old gouges — patched, but not hidden. Her figurehead was a leaping wolf, jaws wide, poised mid-air. From her mast, too, flew the white hand on black.

Last was *The Pilgrim's Cross* — a broad-bellied cog, no beauty in her lines. A relic-bearer once, now turned to men. Her sail showed a faded saint's cross, over-stitched with a fresh red X — not a denial, but a doubling: martyr and sword made one. She rode heavy already, her deck packed with spears. The hand flew above her too — stitched smaller, but no less sharp.

Only two dozen of us remained on the stones — the prince's guard, the shipmasters, and a few chosen like me. The rest had boarded. Shields were stacked by the gangways. Oars lashed. Lines drawn taut. The pier creaked under boots and silence.

From the high platform above the pier, the queen stepped forward. She wore no crown — only the long black cloak of her station, lined in fox-fur and saltwind. Her hair was bound high. Her hands were bare. She raised one — and the square fell still. Men straightened. A gull cried once, and was gone. Only the banners moved, white hands caught in the wind.

She stood above the ships, and began to speak — to send her son, and her men, to war.

"People of the Broken Isles," she said, her voice high and clear, without tremor, "hear me now.

"There has been defiance. Stormward — once loyal, now lost — has withheld what is owed: not just silver, but obedience. The law of tribute has been broken. The word of the crown has been denied.

"But the kingdom will not fracture. We are not seven lords shouting across the sea. We are one land beneath God. One law. One peace — hard-earned and holy.

"My son rides not for conquest, but for justice. He carries no hatred, only the will of the crown and the blessing of the saints. Saint Mikula, who kept peace among kin. Saint Olexa, who bore the banner upright through fire. Saint Kosma, who judged rightly though kin stood against him.

"These ships — three in number — sail as saints themselves: sword, banner, and judgement. As three angels once came to Abraham, so these descend now with purpose. As three crosses once bore the weight of justice and grace, so too do these decks bear men who carry the law of the realm.

"Let there be no doubt. The insult done to the crown shall not be forgiven. Stormward will be brought to heel — not for vengeance, but for unity. Like an unruly child, it will be rebuked. Like a wayward brother, it will be returned.

"Let their walls be broken if they must. Let their fire be quenched. And if any raise arms against this charge, let them be scorched — as by angels of the Lord.

"But to those who yield — to those who remember their oaths — mercy shall remain.

"Go now, my son, with fire and with justice. Bring the kingdom home."

Bogdan dismounted without word or aid. His horse stood still — dark-eyed, rain-dappled — beside Illarion's tall roan. The prophet moved forward alone.

He had not been called.

Slowly, Bogdan's gaze passed over hushed crowds, then the assembled priests and the Queen above. He lifted his staff. His voice did not rise — but all of Velgrad heard him.

"There is no king without judgement," he said. "And no voyage without witness to its end."

He lifted the staff higher. The bone charms stirred in the sea wind.

"I name no lords. I name no crown. I name the saints, who see what men forget."

His eyes swept the gathered crowd — then the grey sky beyond it.

"I call Saint Kosma — who judged rightly, though he stood alone.

"I call Saint Yarila the Ferryman — who rowed through flame and flood, and did not ask the names of the damned.

And I call Saint Vira of the Hearthstone — whose key opens what must be opened, and seals what must not be loosed."

With each name, the hush deepened. The wind stilled.

Then he turned to the queen.

"You have given your son to the sea," he said, "not to lose him, but to test him. Let the storm shape what the cradle could not. Let the salt burn clean what gold could only gild. You have done what is hard. May God remember it."

She did not answer.

Then he turned and stepped toward Illarion.

The prince dismounted, slowly. He did not speak.

Bogdan looked him full in the face — not gently, not cruelly, but as one weighing iron on a scale.

"Do you go of your own will?"

"I do," said the prince.

"To punish the proud, and spare the penitent?"

"I do."

"To walk in fire, and not flinch?"

"I do."

"Then kneel."

Illarion did.

Bogdan drew a small vial from beneath his mantle. Not gold. Clay, stoppered with wax. He broke it with his thumb and dipped two fingers into the oil within.

"In the name of Kosma, who guards justice. In the name of Yarila, who bears the lost. In the name of Vira, who unlocks and seals. And in the name of the Lord, who sees even kings undone. Go now — as sharpened iron. As judgement wrapped in flesh."

With each benediction, he anointed the prince's brow.

The priests stood frozen, their ash staves still unlifted — upstaged, undone, as if the rite had passed them by.

The crowd did not cheer. They only watched.

When all the men were boarded on the ships, Bogdan, standing just behind the prince, bowed his head to the queen. The prince stood tall.

The queen raised her hand. A breath passed.

Then the bell rang.

The lines were cast. Oars dipped. Sails loosened. The three ships moved. Not in haste, but with the gravity of a stone dropped into sacred water.

The crowd roared. Flowers fell from high balconies. Someone beat a drum.

And still I looked for him.

The king.

He did not come.

I searched the towers, the walls, the high windows of the Sea-Fort. Nothing. No grey beard. No broad shape. No eyes to bless or bind or damn us.

He had let us go without farewell.

I stood at the prow of *The Grey Hand* as the docks slid away. Wind caught the sail above me. The river pulled us down toward the Seal's Passage, toward the open sea. Toward Stormhold, bloodshed, and the end of a rebellion.

I wore my armour still. A fool's choice, at sea — to wear weight where a fall meant drowning. But I had not cast it off. Not yet. The steel itched against my shoulders. It pulled at the small of my back. I could feel every buckle, every seam — as if the mail felt wounds I had not yet taken.

It was all shine, for show — like the sendoff itself. Oil-polished shields. Fine words. Saints named like banners. But the truth of the king, and the rot in the kingdom, would drag us down like any iron burden, if the sea chose to take us.

I did not raise a hand. I did not look back.

Only forward. Only down the river. Only toward what waited — in storm, in ash, in fire.

CHAPTER XXX: THE WEIGHT OF WATER

So we began.

The prince in his pride — a campaign for loyalty, for legacy, for Stormward's submission. The prophet beside him, eyes fixed on a fire only he could see. The men in their motion. And me, among them, but not of them.

We sailed to punish traitors. To settle a matter of tax, fealty, and pride. But beneath it ran another current — silent, hidden, and mine to bear. I had been given the true charge. Not Illarion. Not the crown prince anointed with oil before the crowds. The burden had fallen to me: to find the relics of a saint so feared they sealed his bones in ash and silence. To return with the fire that once judged a lord — and all who had sin upon them. To save a dying realm by risking what little soul I had left.

I was no priest. No noble. I had no crown, no vision, no blessing.
Only a name spoken by a queen stripped down to a desperate faith — and a task that felt more curse than command.

By the third bell, we passed the tide-beacon of Saint Yevstafiy — a driftwood cross lashed to a sea-rock, gull skulls tied at the peak with tarred cord. Salt crusted the wood like frost. The bones swung in the wind, a slow clatter. They said an oathsman drowned there with his master's name on his tongue. I did not know the tale. But I believed it.

We had shipped the oars. The last strokes left a ripple trailing like a cut across glass. Now the wind had us.

The black wool sail caught full. The mast groaned once, like an old man rising, then held. *The Grey Hand* leaned into her run, slow at first, then steady. She was a high-rider, broad in the waist, slow to heel but heavy through the shoulder. Her deck pitched down from the aftcastle like a blade toward the sea. The sail rose square and clean, stitched with the white hand. Her pennant snapped high above. And behind us, Velgrad vanished.

The wind came firm out of the southeast, driving us west-by-southwest through the Seal's Passage with barely a quarrel. The sail filled clean. The hull sang. It was good water.

Illarion stood at the rail. One gloved hand gripping brass, the other raising a silver cup rimmed with frost. Whitefire, kept full since cast-off. A pearl spilled as the ship rocked.

"To glory!" he cried.

Some answered — his guards mostly, twenty men hard-armed and sharp-bearded. Most wore only their tunics and belts for now. The rest of their war-gear was stowed below — hauberks hung on hooks beneath the aftdeck, helms wrapped in tar-cloth, the weight kept dry and ready.

The sailors did not cheer. They worked. The helmsman, brow split by old iron, shouted trim orders. Sail-handlers hauled lines. Boots thudded, rope hissed, cleats groaned.

Markov muttered about the draft and leaned into the wind like it might change for him. Urek was already climbing. No shrouds here — just laddered ratlines steep and fraying. He reached the yard, clung like a gull to the spar, hair streaming, grinning into the wind.

Below, the middeck was a sprawl of motion. Crates lashed, tarp bundles tied, a brazier still cold. Soldiers diced on benches. One was sick already, much to the delight of the others. Markov drifted among them, never still, sharp-tongued and watchful. He kept them laughing, but never led. When he caught my eye, he winked like we shared a joke neither of us had told.

I stayed near the prow. Not for duty. Not yet. Just habit. The sea feels cleanest there. The wind uncut. The lies fewer. The ropes pulled taut as oaths. The spray salted my beard and the boards slicked beneath my boots.

We passed the coast slow and close. Cliffs salt-scoured and streaked white. Birch groves shivering under the thaw-wind. Villages crouched like barnacles in clefts of stone, smoke rising thin and grey.

I heard the steps before I saw him. Soft-soled. Not a sailor's tread.

Bogdan.

Clove oil. Old wool. He passed behind me without word. Too close. His robe brushed the rail. The air colder after.

He climbed the quarterdeck in silence. The crew quieted. Illarion said no more.

The prince lingered an hour. He barked questions, demanded answers he didn't understand. The navigator — wrist-marked and fish-eyed — pointed to soot-marks on hide. Illarion frowned. Nodded. Called for more drink.

Bogdan brought it. He brought honey too. And incense. He rubbed oil into Illarion's brow while whispering in the old tongue. Whether for health or sway, I could not tell.

By noon, the prince was below, tucked in his aftcastle — a birch-paneled den with brass hinges, a saint's icon, and a brazier that he said loudly was never warmed enough.

The sea held calm. Long swells rolled beneath us, not high, not slow. The sky stayed pale. The wind steadied out of the south. The wake streamed behind us white and curling. The gulls circled low and silent.

By midmorning, we passed Brinehook — a black cleft that stank of blood. Nets like flayed skin hung from timber struts. A man gutted fish with a blade in his teeth. A boy on the rise above half-lifted a hand. Not a wave. Not a curse. Just a look.

Then Morye's Gate. A chapel ruin without bell or roof. Saint Yevstafiy's mark scratched deep into the lintel. Men hauled silverfish from the shallows, bare-legged and silent. One looked up. Spat. Turned away.

Then the children. Barefoot. Shrill. One dropped his breeches.

Markov bowed low. "A cultured people," he said.

Urek barked laughter from the mast.

That evening, we anchored in Lantern's Hollow — a black-toothed inlet beneath Koryana's Reach. They said a shrine once burned there, lit with whale-fat to guide the drowned. Now only mist, stone, and a bent iron hook remained, rusted into the cliffside like an old wound.

The ships rocked slow on the pull. The wind held steady. The stars came out, wide and low.

Urek had drawn the prince's eye earlier in the day — not by design, but by being the kind of man no crown-born could ignore. He had climbed the rigging like it was a cliff he meant to conquer, barefoot, laughing, hair wild in the wind. The Voryani were rare outside of the Hornlands. Strange, tattooed men with ash-ringed eyes and too many gods. Even now, many captains wouldn't trust one on their deck. They remembered the wolf-banners, the raider blood, the bone-painted hulls. Dragomir had warned me once: *They serve now, but not from love. Their oaths are cold, and they watch for storms with the patience of reef-stones.*

I watched from the prow as the prince sent for him. No fanfare — just a sharp word to his steward and a glance aft. A few minutes later, Urek stood beside Illarion beneath the lantern-strung canopy, the deckhouse behind them shuttered and dark.

I couldn't see their faces. Just one shadow leaning back. Another crouched low. Fur and dark hair and silence between them.

Then the prince's voice — too loud, too easy. "I've never met one of your kind," he said. "They say you bind your dead in fishbone and whisper to trees. Is it true?"

Urek laughed. Not loud. Not soft. Just enough to show teeth. "Some of us. Depends on the tree. And the dead."

"You don't fear them?"

"Only the ones who died quiet."

A pause. A creak of rope above us.

Then Illarion again: "Do you believe in fate, Ashhook?"

"Not mine."

Another laugh. Sharper now.

"Good. I need men who believe in me instead."

Some men follow orders. Some follow storms. The sea would sort which kind we had, soon enough.

Day two brought fog thick as wool. It curled over the deck rails and climbed the rigging, made the sail a grey ghost and the mast a gallows pole. Damp coiled in the ropes. Wet hair clung to cheeks. The helmsman barked every few strokes, but no one saw more than a ship-length ahead.

We muffled the lines and shipped the oars. Rowed slow, blind, and careful. The Grey Hand creaked with every lean. Salt pooled on the boards. Boots thudded soft. Somewhere to port, a gull screamed and was gone. Markov claimed it was a sign and spat. No one laughed.

Midmorning, one of *The Sea's Teeth* outriders struck a stone. A low tooth of reef, hidden under weed and tide. The shout came sharp, then the crack — splinter, not hull — and the cutter drifted, wounded but afloat. They threw a line and limped under tow. Not dead. Just pride bruised.

Urek watched from the tiller lashings and grinned.

Raskin's Teeth rose out of the mist not long after — black stone spires that cut up from the sea like the backs of sharks. Kelp slithered between them. Old bones, some said. A place where ships died before Velgrad was born.

I watched the cliffs as we passed, the way they chewed the fog like slow jaws. Something in me stirred at the sight — memory, maybe, or dread dressed as memory. The sea does that. Carries more than salt.

The prince hadn't spoken to me since Velgrad. Not after the Sea-Fort. Not after the king.

When the fog came, he vanished into the aftcastle. His guards stood watch, still as mastheads, but no orders passed. An hour slid by. Then another. Near noon, he emerged — shoulders hunched in that proud, broken way only the drunk can manage. He came to the starboard rail. Not quite beside me. Not quite apart.

"Thick as a beggar's breath," he muttered, loud enough to carry. "God's piss."

I kept my gaze on the mist. "The sea gives. The sea takes. No point cursing it."

He turned, just enough to catch my eye.

"Think you're better than me."

I said nothing.

"You're the dog my father wished he'd sired. Loyal. Grim. Obedient."

The rail creaked between us.

I could've lied. Said he was drunk. Said he was wrong. But lies don't float far at sea.

So I held my tongue.

He leaned closer. Not swaying. Not smiling.

"You'll die on this mission," he said. "If God doesn't take you, I will."

By midday, the fog lifted like a veil. The wind shifted faintly east, cold on the cheek. Spray turned sharp again. Pines rose sheer from the rock above, wet with mist and light. A bell rang faint and clear across the water — one chime, then none. On the ridge above, the bluff-top chapel of Saint Dobrina stood pale and sharp against the cliff. Someone waved. A child, I think. A smudge in the light. Markov waved back with both arms and made some crude gesture that earned a laugh from the crew. One of the sailors crossed himself anyway. Dobrina sees healers and fools alike.

That night, we slept in a hollow called Splitfish Haven. Narrow cove. Pebbled shore. The tide thrashed at the stones like something hungry. Salt-eels coiled in the shallows, white-bellied and quick. Urek caught one bare-handed, bit the head off in front of the garrison lads, and offered the twitching tail to the prince. Illarion took it, laughed, called him a wild bastard, and chewed like it was honeyed meat. The men roared. For a moment he seemed every inch their captain — laughing, strong, without fear.

A spit of grey beach ran beneath the cliff — seal-trampled, wind-scoured, strewn with driftwood and old kelp. The men stretched their legs, lit fires, pissed in the surf. A few sparred with staves, half-hearted. I watched from the shallows, boots wet. My ribs remembered the Tanglewood: the axeman's hook, the pain where I'd failed to turn in time. Too long since I'd bled proper.

Urek saw it.

"Yaroslav," he called. "Your spine stiff yet, or do you still bend?"

He carried no blade — just a long staff of birch, smooth and sun-worn. Someone had knotted a length of cord at one end, for grip or spite. He twirled it once, light as air.

Markov looked up from a ring of sailors rolling bones.

"Now this," he said, standing. "This is the kind of heresy I'd tithe for. Two coppers on Ashhook! Five if Yaroslav's back still cracks when he kneels!"

The men gathered quick. They always do when there's blood to guess at.

One of them tossed me a practice blade — wood, dulled at the edge. I tested the grip. Solid. Weighted right.

"Three touches," Urek said. "Fast or slow, clean or cruel. First to three."

I nodded. Pulled off my coat. My breath steamed in the air. Cold bit the scars down my side. Good. Let it bite.

They made a ring of boots and driftwood. Markov raised his arm.

Urek came in fast — staff low, a feint left, real strike high. I caught it on the flat of the blade, stepped back, angled off. The sand shifted beneath my heels.

He grinned.

I stepped in. A test — low slash toward the knee.

He knocked it away, spun, thrust for the ribs.

I turned with him, blade high, then low.

He parried again.

Quick hands. Loose shoulders. That seal-hunter balance — hips moving as if on tide-swells, always slipping just where you thought to hold him. He moved like the deck still rocked underfoot.

I dropped my weight, lunged, hooked behind his ankle with my heel — and drove forward. The flat of the blade kissed his side.

"One!" Markov shouted.

Urek backed off, laughing. "Fair."

Again.

This time he pressed harder — a snap strike to the thigh, then a twist of the staff up toward my throat. I caught the first. Missed the second. Wood thudded against my collarbone. A jolt down the spine.

"One!" Markov called again.

We circled.

Sand stuck to sweat. My breath came slower now — not winded, but measured.

He overreached.

I stepped inside, caught his wrist, pivoted, and dragged the blade across his flank — just hard enough to count.

"Two!"

He spat. "Clever."

One more. I saw his rhythm — the beat before the lunge, the half-pause before he spun. I baited it. Let him think I stumbled. He went for the high line.

I ducked, twisted the blade around, and tapped the hollow of his back. Not hard. Not soft. But clean.

"Three!" Markov roared.

Urek dropped to one knee, breathing hard, staff buried in the sand beside him. "Saints piss," he said. "Still got teeth."

I offered a hand. He took it. We clasped wrists. No shame in his grip — just fire.

That's when the prince called out.

"I'll take a turn."

He stepped into the ring. Head high. A smile on his lips, but not in his eyes.

I knew it for trouble.

I tried to demur. "Your Highness. We're only sparring. A poor man's sport."

"Afraid, wolf-cub?" he said. "Is my reputation so fearsome already?"

The men laughed. Rough, hungry laughter — not mockery, but hope. They wanted their prince fierce. They wanted blood without cost.

He turned to them, arms wide, basking in their noise.

I could not win this fight even if I won.

"I'm sure it is," I said.

But the men had seen the challenge. They clamoured now, clapped backs, shouted wagers.

Markov didn't miss a beat. "Two coppers on the prince! Four on the wolf — if he wakes up in time!"

Illarion stripped his shirt and tossed it aside.

He was still strong. Broad across the chest, light on his feet. The strength of youth had not yet rotted — but it was softening, and the rot was there beneath. His left hand curled wrong on the hilt, fingers clawed. A tremor ghosted his cheek. And in his eyes: that whitefire gleam — the kind that burns through bone before it reaches light.

I raised my blade. There was no escaping.

He came fast.

Two swords — one gripped true, one crooked. Quick-footed. Overbold.

I gave ground. Sand under my heels. Wind sharp off the water.

He pressed — a feint high, then a hook low. I caught it, barely. Parried. Let him come again. Let him find his rhythm.

Then he struck — low and fast — and I misjudged the angle. The blade slapped my shoulder, flat but fierce.

"One!" Markov called.

Illarion grinned.

No words. Just the grin.

I circled. Feinted. Let him lunge. I turned the line and clipped his thigh on the draw-back.

"One."

He spat. Shifted stance. Raised both blades and came again.

Overhand slash, twist, side-cut. I blocked the first. The second caught my ribs — not deep, but it landed.

"Two."

He turned to the men, lifted both swords.

"Drink!" he shouted. A mug was tossed. He caught it, downed it with flourish, wiped his mouth with the back of his wrist.

I waited.

He came again — stronger, slower, drunker. I caught the clash, turned my blade sideways between his hilts, and forced them wide. His longer sword tumbled to the dirt.

The ring howled.

Illarion stood breathing hard, holding only the short blade. I nodded to the one he'd dropped.

He stooped. Retrieved it. His hand shook.

When he came again, it was fury.

No form, no guard. Just rage.

I stepped aside.

He turned and lunged again. I twisted, and he sliced a cut across one of the onlookers' sleeves — drew blood.

The ring went quiet.

No laughter now. Only breath and wind.

He came again. Wild. Desperate.

I parried. Once. Twice. Let him tire.

Two openings came. Then three.

I could have ended it.

But I saw the hunger in his eyes. Not for glory. For proof. For worth.

I slowed. Gave him the line. Let it bite.

"Three!" Markov called, voice bright with relief.

Illarion raised both arms, laughing. His face flushed. His chest heaved.

"Old dog's gone soft," he said.

Then, quieter, to no one: "Tame."

I bowed. Said nothing.

Sometimes mercy costs more than pride. Sometimes, it's all you can give.

That night, I climbed the rise above the cove. Alone. The beach lay quiet below — only the sound of stones dragged by tide, foam and ash drawn back into blackness. The wind came hard from the sea, cold in the mouth. Salt stung my eyes.

I faced north.

Toward Velgrad. Toward the Sea-Fort. Toward the high chamber where the king sat dying, alone in a room too large for breath.

The stars were sharp above — not kind, not distant, but fixed and watching. Nails in a coffin lid.

Bogdan found me there.

I didn't hear him approach. Only the soft tap of his staff, once, against stone. No flame. Just grey — cloak, hair, voice.

"You let him win," he said.

I said nothing.

"He needed it," Bogdan continued. "And the men — they need a prince who leads."

We stood in silence. Wind tugged his mantle. Somewhere below, a gull cried once, then stopped.

"He's young," I said at last.

Bogdan nodded. "There is power in him still. But power twists, without guidance."

I turned to him. "Is that your role?"

He didn't smile. "I am only a vessel. As you are. God gives, and God takes."

He had not been there when I'd spoken those words. Still, I answered, finishing the line: "No point in cursing."

He left without another word.

I stayed. Watched the dark water. Thought of the king's white eyes and ruined mind. Of bones that still burned. And of mercy, sharp as steel, that left no wound a man could show.

CHAPTER XXXII:　　THE BLACK SISTER FEAST

The days blurred, salt-laced and grey. We hugged the coast as it fell southward — cliffs rising high to our starboard, stone shoulders veiled in mist. Salt-twisted pine clung to the ledges like penance. No hearth-smoke. No flags. Just gulls, and the long lean reach of land that had never been ruled.

Dolphins kept with us a while — three, maybe four. Shadows in the swell, surfacing, vanishing. Markov leaned over the rail, gaping like a boy.

"God's beasts," he said. "Come to show us how it's done."

The crew took it for a sign. Some touched their knives. Some prayed. Urek only spat into the wind.

We passed a ruined watchtower — fire-blackened, long blind. Moss grew where once the signal smoke rose. Another link broken. The Sea-Fort's edge frays in silence.

That night, we anchored behind Black Sister Isle — a fang of stone hunched against the waves. Seabirds screamed themselves hoarse on the rocks. Markov called it music. Urek said they were naming the dead.

We sparred on the flat stones, just above the tideline. Urek came barefoot with his birch staff, lean as ever, wild-eyed from stillness. I met him with a practice blade — wood, but heavy.

Markov served as judge, scribe, and gambler. He shifted odds with every blow.

"You call that a feint?" he called, when I took one to the ribs.

"It was a distraction," I muttered.

"From what? Winning?"

Urek laughed. The strike hadn't been light.

Later, walking the shore, I found carvings. Just above the wrack-line — spiral cuts, knot-marks, a hook drawn backwards. Sea-washed and half-lost to barnacle.

"Voryani?" I asked, when Markov came beside me.

He squinted. "Sea-witch signs. You find those near drowned places. They say it keeps the ghosts from walking back."

Urek joined us, skin still wet from the spray.

"Not ours," he said after a long look. "Could be old clan marks. But not the way I was taught."

"So whose, then?"

He shrugged. "Dead ones. Or ones who should be."

The tide came up and touched the stone. I did not touch it back.

The wind turned. Eastward now. The tiller groaned. The sail strained and twisted. We kept tight to the shore, sliding past Netwood Bay — a waterlogged bend of reeds and skiffs. Fishers raised their oars in silence. The air thickened. Brine and rot and marsh rot. The crew cursed the smell. Urek smiled.

That night, Illarion ordered the ships drawn close.

Three hulls tethered mid-sea, plank-bridged like a floating village. Lanterns swung from masts and ropes. A fiddle struck up somewhere in the dark.

"A feast," the prince declared, standing tall on the gunwale. "For no reason but the sea!"

Barrels cracked. Fish grilled on iron. Whitefire passed hand to hand in wooden mugs. I stood at the rail, arms crossed, waiting for sense. It didn't come.

Markov juggled stones.

Urek turned the planks to a stage. He danced barefoot — hips loose, shoulders rolling, hands like blades. The men roared.

Markov followed, mimicking the dance with lewd gestures and wobbling knees. He turned a stumble into a backflip and landed sprawled, shirtless. The roar turned to thunder.

Then came the knives.

A barrel-top game, quick hands and laughter. One man lost a finger. Another kissed the deck. Blood slicked the boards. They washed it with whitefire. Called it holy.

The prince sat with Bogdan — a fur thrown over his shoulders, two cups between them, and a crescent of crouched and lounging men around. Sailors, garrison, some with shark teeth on cords. The prophet spoke low, and the circle leaned close.

He spoke not of tales, but of fire.

"Where the old saints walked, the sea remembers," Bogdan said. "And for those who believe with both hands, their flame burns still. You need only bleed true."

A man called, grinning, "Prophet! Can you see the future?"

Bogdan didn't blink. "The future bends. It weaves like a river."

Illarion raised his cup. "What's that river like, when it runs through Stormhold?"

Bogdan met his gaze.

"Red," he said.

The men heard. And they cheered — not in fear, but hunger. Blood meant battle. Battle meant purpose.

***

Day five brought stormlight.

Cape Dobrina rose from the sea like a blade's hilt — white cairns marking its spine. Shrines to the lost. The wind had gone west, and we turned with it, rounding the horn toward Mirefast coast.

The current fought us. The sail shuddered. Oars went in. One of *The Sea's Teeth* turned nearly beam to the swell.

"Voryani wind," someone muttered.

Urek stiffened. "It's just weather."

But his eyes were wrong.

Illarion heard it. His voice came sharp: "It's just the wind."

I wanted to believe it.

At the Tide-Gate Wrecks, the sea bore crosses — bark-carved, drift-bound. Nails hammered into the arms. Charms of the drowned.

We threw bread in. The tide took it. Swallowed it.

By dusk, the roofs of Greyharrow rose ahead — low and lichen-dark. A watchfire burned behind the quay.

The oars took us in.

CHAPTER XXXIII: GREYHARROW

We came ashore in the grey light before dusk, dropped from the longboats into a town that smelled of woodsmoke, iron, and wet barley. The sea lapped at the quay like it meant to take it back. Behind us, *The Grey Hand* rode at anchor in Ashfern Bay, sail furled, black hull low in the swell — a hound waiting to be loosed.

Greyharrow stood where the River Vorya emptied into the bay. A wall of pale stone ringed the port — moss-flecked, low-built, its towers more for pride than war. Inside: a muddle of pitched roofs, shuttered workshops, muddy lanes. Beyond: farmland. Rich lowland soil. You could smell it. Green and good, thick with rot and promise.

The men scattered the moment boots touched dirt. Five days at sea had stripped them bare of patience. They fled for warmth, for women, for anything not salted or nailed down. Markov vanished with a wink and a promise. Urek strode off laughing, boots still wet.

Illarion remained aboard.

"He won't come," one of the rowers muttered. "Not unless there's a throne in it."

But Bogdan waited. He said nothing — just stood in the shallows, staff planted firm, grey cloak stirring like smoke in the river wind. The prince lingered at the gunwale, gloved hands tight, eyes distant. Then, with a sigh too soft for drama, he descended. Duty moved him where pride would not.

Lord Oles Borodin met us at the gate — wide, sun-burnt, and breathless, dressed in fox-trimmed wool and pride.

"Welcome, Your Highness," he wheezed, bowing deep. "My house is yours. My hall, my hearth, my kin. We've had the

Church light every lamp. The cooks have slaughtered three calves! Come, come."

Greyharrow's hall stood at the town's crown — a broad-shouldered house of stone and timber, two storeys tall, its frame built from blackened pine and river-cut granite. A long roof of red tile sloped low against the wind. The upper floor jutted slightly forward, supported by heavy beams carved with fish, sun-runes, and wheat. Nets crusted in old salt hung from the eaves. A balcony overlooked the bay.

Inside: smoke and firelight. Boots stomped. Men laughed. Roasted meat glistened on iron spits. Two hearths burned hot in the long chamber — wide-throated, ash-caked, fed with driftwood and old beams. The air was thick with tallow, pine pitch, and spilled ale. Garlands of last year's harvest — grain, garlic, berries gone to brown — still hung above the lintels, half-forgotten or half-feared.

A place meant to hold joy. Or at least, noise.

Lord Oles Borodin led us in with pomp and sweat. "Make way for His Highness!" he boomed, one hand on his belly, the other waving men aside. "He comes not as burden but as blessing. Let the lamps be lit and the whitefire poured! Tonight, Greyharrow sings!"

And so the rite began.

A silver basin was brought — old, dented, rimmed in stag's antlers. Into it, they poured the whitefire: a searing clear spirit brewed from barley mash and gods-know-what else, cut sharp with salt and something sweet-smelling, maybe birch sap. It was heated near to boiling, and the steam curled upward in pale threads, stinging the eyes. One of Borodin's sons carried it through the hall, both hands wrapped in cloth, face tight against the fumes. Each man dipped his cup — no sniffing, no dainty measures. A full pour, then down in one. Fire on the tongue. Salt in the blood. A bitter clarity.

Only when the prince drank could the feast begin.

Illarion lifted his cup with grace, though his hand trembled slightly as he set it down. He wore fox-trimmed wool, light gloves, and a smile that didn't reach the eyes. He gave a short speech — words of thanks, praise for Greyharrow's loyalty, remembrance of Saint Mikula and the unbroken oaths of the lowlands. He spoke clean and without stumble. Then he drank.

The hall roared. The feast began.

First came bread, black-crusted and hot, with bowls of whipped lard and green onion. Then pickled river-fish in clay trays, sharp as knives on the tongue. Boiled barley, thick with fat. Roasted swan basted with ashberry syrup. And finally, calf shanks — whole — set in their own juice with a ring of salted root. Borodin had spent freely, or meant to impress.

The ale was thick, half-sour. The whitefire kept coming. By the third course, the prince was flushed and upright. By the fifth, he was smiling — truly smiling — and had begun to charm the table. He complimented the cook. Thanked the widow who poured his cup. Asked after the names of Borodin's daughters.

There were five of them. The eldest was seventeen, dark-eyed and grave. The second was a smirking thing — too clever by half, already whispering to a courtier's son. The younger three were giggles and ribbons. Illarion bowed to each with careful form. When one kissed his glove, he laughed.

It was performance, but a good one.

When the last bowls were cleared and the bones tossed to the dogs, the tables were dragged aside and the piper mounted the stairs. He played a rough-tuned reel in the lowland style — all heel-stomps and handclaps, the kind danced at harvest feasts and river weddings — and the villagers took to it gladly. Borodin's youngest daughters danced in a ring. Two of the guards took hands with flax-haired girls who knew every turn.

The prince sat through it smiling, but he never rose.

Folk dancing was not to his liking. Nor mine.

I left. No one stopped me.

The balcony above the bay was half-crumbled, ringed in rusted iron. I leaned on it, listening to the tide gnaw the stone below. The moon hung low — a dull silver coin tossed careless into the dark. Beyond the harbour, the shoreline sprawled in silence: trees like teeth, marshes waiting. The lowlands spread rich and wide behind us, but I felt the sea's pull more than the land's welcome.

A boat slipped from the quay below. Small. No lantern. The oars dipped soft as breath. It turned north, hugging the coast like a shadow with somewhere to be and no wish to be seen.

I watched.

"There are always boats like that," came a voice behind me.

I hadn't heard him approach. One moment I was alone. The next, Bogdan was there — as if the dark had shaped him out of salt and wind. His staff tapped once on the stone. The bone charms clicked — quiet, sharp — like teeth settling in a jaw.

"Spies?" I asked.

He didn't answer at once. Just stood beside me, grey cloak stirring faintly in the breeze, eyes on the water.

"Maybe," he said at last. "Or pilgrims. Or sinners fleeing the saints."

He never answered straight. That was his way — to circle truth like a gull above wreckage, never landing, never touching blood.

"You're not worried."

"Should I be?"

I didn't reply. The boat was already gone — swallowed by the fold between water and sky. And still I stared, as if the sea might give it back.

I was no spy. Never learned the weight of whispers, the crooked craft of half-truths. My trade had been iron — open, honest in its own way. You entered the fray with the strength God gave, and met what came with blade and shield. No cloak. No poison. No lie whispered sweet behind a cup.

The common man lives without masks. His lies fail him fast. The court plays in shadows, but the peasant bleeds in light.

And this journey — slow, ceremonial, watched — gave the shadows time to crawl. Our ships moved in daylight, our sails known by crest and colour. If word had gone ahead to Stormhold — and why wouldn't it? — then some broken lord might already be stirring men from sleep, sharpening pikes, waiting. Not to face us fairly, but to wound us in the dark, before land was even touched.

Mstislav would never have allowed it.

He believed in speed, in surprise. In letting the enemy dream of safety right until the blade kissed throat.

Once — I was only fourteen — we rowed through the night on broken oars, sails patched with wool and hide. Mstislav pulled beside us, bare to the waist, hair dripping with sea mist. No heralds. No signal fires. We made land at grey-light south of Black Bridge's halls. Varin the Black, the self-styled king of the north, a petty butcher who'd called himself crowned.

They never saw us coming.

We hit them while they still slept in their furs. The dogs died first. Then the men. Then the women. Children too. Not out of fury — but so no kin remained to avenge.

One woman we caught running. A serving girl, not yet grown. Mstislav watched as I held the blade to her throat. He didn't order it. He didn't stop it. He only watched.

So I did it.

Her throat was warm. That I remember. Warm and slow, like the inside of a lamb, and she looked at me the whole time. Her eyes kept trying to speak, even after the breath was gone.

We left Black Bridge burning. No prisoners. No grave markers. Only ash.

That was how peace was made. A lesson in blood, taught without words. Mstislav never praised me. Never named the deed. But after that night, I rode with the captains, not the squires.

The sea pulled at the stone below, as if to remind me that nothing built on blood ever truly holds.

Bogdan hadn't moved. Only now did he turn, his face still half-shadowed.

"You know where to begin?"

I drew breath. "Dragomir said the shrine of Saint Kosma. There may be records. A monk who remembers."

Bogdan smiled. A curl of lip, not warmth.

"Forget Dragomir. His world is ink and iron keys. Saint Ilyin was not a ledger."

I looked at him. "Then what was he?"

"Fire."

The wind caught his cloak. He didn't notice.

"Vengeance. Justice. That is the trail. Not scrolls. Not seals. Vengeance first. Then justice. Then — if you still breathe — God may give you truth."

I watched the last of the moonlight vanish into the sea.

"I'm not planning to fight in the Stormgrave Isles. That's the prince's mission. The queen sent him to break Boyarina Salava — not me. I'm to find the relics. That's all."

Bogdan's head tilted slightly, as if listening to something far off. Then: "Fire doesn't ask what it's for. It burns what it touches." He tapped his staff once, just loud enough to mark the words. "You were anointed in blood, Yaroslav. Long ago. That's why it will find you. Whether you seek it or not."

He said no more. Just stood there, watching the tide with me — as if it, too, had secrets to whisper. As if the sea and the fire were not so different, in the end.

Below, the hall roared with laughter.

I looked down. Markov had arrived with half the city's brothels in tow. A dozen girls in borrowed silks and ribbons. He bowed as if to queens, led them inside like a conquering saint. Urek threw back his head and howled.

I stayed where I was, watching the moon. The night was cold. The tide kept pulling. It always did.

CHAPTER XXXIV: THREE DAYS BEFORE THE DROWNING

What should have been one, became three days in Greyharrow.

The first morning after our landing, the prince was still golden in the hall's memory — fresh from his charm, his rites, the laughter he'd kindled like a torch in a windless room. Men drank to him; women lingered where he had stood. Borodin smiled then, thinking himself host to glory. By the third night, he was wringing his hands.

Illarion had taken the lord's high rooms, but they became a den. Not of lions — jackals. Women came and went, sometimes paid, sometimes not. The red of whitefire grew deeper in the prince's eyes, and he laughed more loudly, more cruelly. Markov was often at his side. I saw him once slip a coin to a man at the gate and whisper something, and not long after, two flax-haired girls were shown inside.

I kept away. There was no use speaking. No use standing in the doorway like a priest or jailor.

Instead, I rose early, found the sparring yard, and let the rhythm return. My limbs remembered. The ache in my left shoulder dulled; my back stiffened less each morning. By the second day, a few of the Greyharrow garrison joined me. We did not speak much, but blades have a language. There was a wiry sergeant with a harelip — Danel — who circled well and struck like a hammer. We traded blows until the sun climbed high, then drank bitter tea and salted bread beneath the thatched awning.

He asked no questions. I gave no answers.

Borodin began to sweat. The sort of sweat that came not from heat but accounts. I heard him once mutter to his steward about barley stores, the ale-casks, the fresh meat. Each evening, he offered polite words about the sea, about saints waiting at the cape. Illarion batted them aside. He was the son of kings, and Borodin — for all his titles — was no more than a landlord with a low stone wall and daughters to marry.

Then came the fourth morning.

A commotion stirred the keep. Voices echoed down the stairwells — angry, hushed, quickly silenced. I heard boots strike the hall tiles in haste. By the time I reached the main chamber, Lord Borodin was already there, face red, hand clenched at his belt.

"She bears a mark," he said. "And says her honour is gone."

Illarion's jaw was tilted high, his good eye gleaming with insult, the bad one slow and unblinking. "She crept into my room like a cat," he said. "I never called her."

Borodin's fingers twitched. "She is sixteen. Your men saw her go in. She came out weeping."

"She came of her own will. What followed, or didn't, is hers to twist."

"She says—"

"She lies."

The room froze.

The hush was not silence but pressure — the weight before something breaks. Borodin's guards stiffened. My hand went to the edge of my tunic, where my belt-knife hung, though I did not draw it. Beside the hearth, Markov watched with arms folded, lips tight.

"We leave," said Illarion at last. "Today. Pack what we need."

Borodin's lips pressed thin, but he did not shout. Not in front of the prince's men. Not in his own hall. "The girl's honour is in question now," he said, careful with each word. "Some would say she cannot wed clean, without oath or dowry from the one who—"

Illarion raised a hand. "Get a priest, then. Let him look."

Borodin flinched — just slightly — but the gesture cut.

"If she is still whole, there is no scandal," the prince went on. "And if she is not—" He shrugged. "It was not my doing."

The silence that followed was not shocked, but sharpened — like the pause before a drawn knife is used.

Borodin looked at me. Just for a moment. As if I might speak sense into a prince, or shame into a stone.

I said nothing.

And that was the end of it.

No farewells. No parting gifts. Not even a saint's blessing on the quay. The girl was not there. But I saw Borodin standing in the wind, something pale in his hands — cloth, torn linen, I could not tell.

We marched down to the longboats in the chill before dawn. The wind had turned; it carried sea-rot and storm-thought with it. *The Grey Hand* loomed against the tide, still as stone, like she'd seen worse and would bear worse again.

I did not look back.

The sea met us harshly. By midday, we had passed the last of the fish-racks and tide-gates, the river's brown mouth bleeding out behind us. Ashfern Bay fell away slow on our stern quarter, and the sea began to breathe rougher. Not the wrath of a storm — not yet — but the long, steady churn of open water. The rhythm of something old waking.

We entered the Crosswind Gap on the second morning, sails reefed and men braced low.

To the east, the cliffs of Southfang Isle rose black and sheer — broken only by ledges sharp enough to flense a whale. On the west, Strayhorn loomed in silence: pale rock veined with old lava, streaked by the memory of fires. Between them lay the channel — narrow as a sword's groove, and twice as cruel.

The water here was not steady. It pulled and bucked like something chained. Currents spun from the south, twisted by the shoals near Fenmark, then struck the gap with sideways force. Beneath, there were tunnels — the old mouths of the sea — channels carved by ancient tides that had never forgotten how to hunger.

The captain of *The Grey Hand* — a man named Vasko, quiet and long-scarred — knew the route. He'd run it before, years ago, under fire. His voice never rose above a whisper, but his hands never shook. He marked the spines of black water where they rose, barked once to the tiller-men, and let the ship drift half-banked into the pull — trusting the slack to carry us clear of the crush.

The sea did not like that.

Spray struck the deck like thrown gravel. A sudden gust caught the main, and the mast groaned. The hull twisted with it — groaning as if it would split. One of *The Sea's Teeth* caught wrong on a wave-rip. I saw her yardarm snap in two and pitch sideways, the ship tilting south as her oars scrambled to steady.

Above us, the cliffs of Strayhorn waited — not passive, but watching. Close enough I could see the salt-lace at their base, the streaks where past wrecks had struck. The sea hissed there, as if angry to be defied.

We passed through.

But not clean. Not welcome.

The wind eased, but the water still roiled beneath us — as if it regretted letting us go.

That was when he told me.

"She wanted it," Markov said. "That's the thing. I saw her. She wanted to be seen, touched, claimed — maybe because he was a prince, maybe because she'd had too much to drink, or maybe because the room was already thick with sweat and moans."

I said nothing.

"She tore her own veil, Yarik. Slid into his lap like it was a throne. I'm not excusing what came after. Just—" He rubbed his face. "He tried. For a breath. Then he tore her shift, down the middle. She laughed — until she saw his face. Said, 'What's wrong with your eye?' That's when he slapped her. She stumbled back. Screamed. That was it."

I looked out to sea, letting the silence settle between us like a drawn blade. The horizon was a thin, grey line, wavering in the morning light.

"Why are you telling me this?" I finally asked.

"Because you'll judge him," Markov said. "And I'd rather you damn him for truth, not guesswork."

I watched the clouds then, low and moving fast, like bruises drifting across the sky. The silence that followed was not empty; it held the weight of unspoken oaths, the cost of loyalty, the burden of truth.

Beyond the Gap, the wind did not ease. It turned.

What met us along the Galehorn Coast was not storm — not yet — but the steady, punishing push of a sea that wanted us back. The cliffs there ran high and jagged, fluted like the horns of some giant beast. It was said the wind never stilled along that shore. I had not believed it until then.

It blew against us — hard and unyielding — a raw northwesterly that pressed like a wall. The ships had to tack, clawing the wind in long, dragging zigzags. Sails snapped taut and shuddered. Oars bit and backed again. We gained feet, lost them, gained again. Every mile toward Cape Yarila had to be won like a siege.

Beneath us, the water was no better. Currents still swirled, strange and contrary — spun by the reefs off Low Hook and some deeper force I could not name. One moment the prow would lift high and list left, the next it would twist beneath us like a live thing. Men staggered even when standing still. Rope-burns bloomed across the palms of the deckhands. Buckets were never empty long.

By the second day, more than one warrior turned green. A boy wept openly into the scuppers. An older soldier — I forget his name — vomited blood and kept rowing.

Urek laughed.

He stood bare-headed at the prow, arms wide to the wind, teeth bared like he meant to bite it.

"Come down and drown me, you bastard!" he roared. "Or stop licking my toes!"

Markov watched him from behind the shield-rack. "I think he's making it worse."

"He's making it honest," I said.

The sea was not honest. It lied with every calm wave, then bucked you from behind. But Urek did not bargain. He offered himself like bait.

Markov gripped the rail with white knuckles and did not move. I saw him once in the midwatch, whispering under his breath — to himself, to the mast, to Saint Yarila, I do not know. But his face was pale as salt, and his lips moved like a man counting backward from death.

"Stormgrave will be worse," I said.

He spat and wiped his mouth. "That's not comforting."

We rounded Cape Yarila at dusk — black stone like a buried sword-hilt, slick with spray and bird-filth. The air stank of kelp and iron. The wind sang high across the rocks. Some said you could hear Yarila's voice there, if you'd ever ferried the dead.

We did not stop to listen.

Beyond the cape lay the open water — the Wolf's Mouth. A vast black reach, bounded by clawed islands and cruel currents. The maps showed it as blank blue. Sailors knew better. They marked its edge with ash, salt, and oaths.

I had crossed it once, long ago, in war. I remembered little of the details. Just the sense of being watched — not by ship or man, but by the sea itself.

The Mouth was shaped like a maw, they said. Teeth all round: the cliffs of Strayhorn to the south, the reefs of Sea Fort Isle to the east, and Stormgrave to the west and north. Even in calm, the waters broke strange — a chaos of backwaves and churned tides.

But it was the centre men feared most.

The Drowned Holt.

A name spoken soft, if spoken at all. A place no chart claimed.

Once, they said, there had been an island there — tall, green, proud. Its people were witches, oath-breakers, worse. When their evil reached heaven, judgement came. Not fire. Not plague. But water. The sea rose like a hand and pulled the land down whole — forests, temples, towers, all dragged beneath. Every man, woman, and child drowned in a single night.

Some said you could still see it, if the sun hit right — streets ten feet below the wave, old stone steps worn smooth by kelp. Others swore there were roots there, black and still alive, reaching like fingers from the deep. Strongwater plants, thick as a man's arm, waiting to snare a rudder or ankle. A few swore they'd seen a roof rising just beneath the swell, barnacled and ancient. Always gone by morning.

No one went into the Holt. Not on purpose. Not twice.

The old hands said there was something at its heart — a whirlpool that never stopped, a storm that never moved. Sailors called it the Throat. A black spiral of current and wind, choked with bones. No ship had ever come out of it.

It pulled on the compass even now. You could feel it — not in steel, but in your bones. A dragging, a hunger. The oars needed more effort. The tiller fought you, just a little. The air tasted of rot and rust.

Vasko kept us to the east edge. Gave the centre a wide berth, though even that was not always enough. Currents bent toward it. Tides whispered.

I watched the sea.

It looked flat. Empty. But there were no gulls. No spray. No salt wind on the tongue. Only that stillness — the kind that comes before a scream. Then a smell came — not sea-rot, but something else. Like bruised fennel and burnt wool. Old, wrong. It passed quick, like breath stolen back.

We were inside the Mouth now. Past the teeth.

And the sea had not yet decided whether to spit us out, or swallow.

CHAPTER XXXV: THE DROWNED HOLT

To the east, the whitewater gnawed at the coastline — froth and crash against the fanged shoals they called the Wolf's Teeth. The sound of it never stopped: stone shearing spray, sea beating stone. We tacked hard to keep distance. The reef was not a place for men who wanted to live.

But to the west, the sea stretched wide and strangely calm.

Too calm.

The Holt lay in that direction — not marked by land, but by absence. No birds. No chop. Just a long grey stillness, low as breath, rimmed in green marks on the captain's map: The Snarls. He showed me once. "Here's where it begins," he said, tapping the parchment with a nail bitten to the quick. "Currents twist. Wind dies. Men hear voices."

So we pressed the edge.

The Grey Hand rocked in choppy water — not storm-tossed, but stubborn. Each wave struck crosswise. Every line had to be watched, every grip retied. *The Sea's Teeth* kept low to the reefline, hugging the froth like wolves circling ice. *The Pilgrim's Cross* wheeled wider still, her deeper draft dragging like guilt. And to the fore, Vasko called the bearing like a priest reading names of the dead.

Then Illarion came above deck.

He had not taken the air since the cape. The sea did not suit him. His skin was sallow, his cheeks drawn. He walked like a man half-hung — one hand gripping the rail, the other clutching a fur he hadn't bothered to fasten. The wind teased it open like a wound. His good eye searched the horizon. His bad one blinked slow and wrong.

"This way is wrong," he said.

Vasko didn't look up. "We're rounding. Safer water lies ahead."

"Safer water lies ahead if we are cowards," Illarion said. "Stormgrave is west. That way." He pointed toward the stillness — toward the Holt.

Vasko raised his head. Just slightly. "That is the Drowned Holt."

"A legend."

"It's no legend to the drowned. Or their widows."

"The sea is not a wall to fear," said Illarion. "It is a road. We take the straightest road. West — past the Howlstone."

Vasko turned. "That stone is no guide. It's a warning."

"A shape in the sea can't judge us," the prince muttered. "Only men and saints do that."

Vasko said nothing.

Illarion stepped forward, slow and unsteady, but his voice grew sharper. "You fear a sea ghost. A children's tale. We go west. Now."

A silence hung between them. Then the captain asked, flatly: "Do you give the order, my prince?"

"I do."

Vasko bowed — not low, not long. Just enough to be seen doing it.

"Ahead to west," he said to the tiller-men. "Full tack. Let the saints watch what we do."

The wheel turned. The sail strained. The prow shifted west — not by force, but by surrender. *The Sea's Teeth* hesitated, then followed. *The Pilgrim's Cross* dragged north behind.

And the calm sea opened before us.

It did not welcome.

It waited.

The sailors did not cheer the turn.

They watched the horizon with hard eyes, their knuckles white on the rails. A few spat. One man made the sign of Saint Yarila with a broken thumb, three times in quick succession. Another went below and did not return.

Urek laughed. "What, afraid of stories?" he called. "I thought this was a holy voyage."

No one answered.

We passed the last of the foam-slick waves and entered water that did not move. No chop. No sound. Just a glassy stillness, smeared grey beneath the failing sun. The ships slid forward without protest — not pulled, not pushed. Allowed.

The Sea's Teeth crept ahead of us. *The Pilgrim's Cross* lagged behind.

That night, we gathered near the aft rail — half a dozen men and no fire between us. The sea had gone still. You could hear the creak of every rope, the hush of every breath. Even Urek was quiet, for once — until one of the sailors muttered something about the Maw.

Urek turned, grinning. "There's no Maw."

Markov glanced over. "What, no whirlpool? I was counting on the whirlpool. At least that's a shape a man can drown in."

"It's not a hole in the sea," said Urek. "It's a mouth."

"A mouth," Markov said flatly.

"A jaw. Down deep. Wide enough to take a cutter whole. With teeth like bronze gaffs." His grin flashed again, too broad in the dark.

"You dream in teeth," said Markov.

"I dream true."

Another sailor stepped in. "My uncle swore he saw lights under the water. Said it was a city. Still down there. Streets, shrines, even bells that ring when no wind blows."

"There's no city," Urek said. "Not anymore. Just ruins. Roots. Things with gills that remember being men."

One of the older men spat. "They sank because they betrayed the saints. That's the tale. The Holt took them because the land wouldn't."

Markov shook his head, arms crossed. "So which is it? A ghost sea? A sunken shrine? A mouth? A curse?" He looked around, half-laughing. "Tell me how I'm meant to die, and I'll wear the right shirt."

A younger sailor crossed himself.

Then someone said: "And the Holt Devil? That real too?"

Silence. Even Urek stilled.

Then: "I don't disbelieve," he said. Quietly, this time.

No one laughed.

Markov looked at me, half a smile still on his lips. "And you, Yaroslav? You've seen the world crack open. What do you think waits out here?"

I watched the water. Black, flat, endless.

"If it's a devil," I said, "then it's an old one. And it's still hungry."

Evening settled like a hand. The wind died. Ropes went slack. Men stepped lighter, or not at all.

The sea no longer moved.

No gulls. No tide. No sound.

We slid through a silence so thick it pressed the ears like water.

There was no fog. No storm. Just dark — the kind that feels heavy on the skin. Some men lay down, but few slept. They watched the water, watched each other. One whispered a lullaby. Another tied a saint-knot into the hem of his tunic and kissed it.

We kept sailing. Slowly. Quietly. As if hiding from something that already saw us.

Someone lit a brazier near the mast. It guttered low — the flame clinging to the wick like a child to a drowning father.

Then, sometime in the middle watch, the sound began.

It was not a crash, nor a scream. Just a whisper. A pull on the edge of the air. Like wind in a skull's mouth. So faint at first that I thought it a dream.

But it grew.

The men heard it too. Eyes widened. Heads turned.

Markov stood frozen near the lantern-hooks. "Is that…?"

No one answered.

The whisper deepened. Became a rush. A howl. A wind not felt, but heard.

Then came the dead calm.

Not quiet. Not peace. Just stillness — so complete it crushed the ribs.

Someone cried, "Prophet!"

All eyes turned to Bogdan.

He stood near the prow, unflinching, his mantle loose in the rising dark. His staff hung from his wrist by a leather loop. In his other hand, he held a bag — old cloth, stitched with bone-thread.

"Salt," he said. "Kneel."

The men knelt. Even Urek.

Bogdan's voice rose.

"O Saints who see through sea and storm, mark this place. If one among us bears wrath, let it fall on him alone. If none do, then turn the evil back."

He reached into the bag and cast the salt wide.

"Saint Kosma, judge. Saint Vira, shelter. Saint Yarila, ferry us. Saint Ilyin, if you burn still — burn clear."

He lifted his hands.

"Let justice fall, or pass us by."

The sound grew louder — a wall of wind and voice and water. Like the Holt itself was waking.

Men prayed aloud. Some wept. Some kissed relics. Others just gripped wood.

Then we saw it.

A hill of water. Moving.

It arced toward us, grey and smooth, rising where no wave should rise.

"Oars," the captain said.

No one moved.

"Oars!" he roared. "Row, or drown!"

We grabbed them. The numbness was spreading — not cold, not pain, just wrong. Like we moved through someone else's dream.

The howl became a scream.

And then it rose.

A dark grey creature — just above the waterline — battering-ram head, eyes yellow as tallow. Spikes — or scars — or horns — jutted from its back. It watched us.

And moved.

A spurt. A surge. The water broke with it. Then we saw the mouth: huge, blunt, with a jaw like a war gate, ringed in teeth like harpoons.

"Pull!" someone shrieked. "Pull!"

We rowed like damned men.

Then — it dove. And struck. The ship shuddered. Wood cracked. A man screamed and vanished over the side. I had seen men fall in war. I had seen saints judged and martyrs burn. But this was something else. We rowed not from fear, but from something deeper. As if God had turned His face, and the sea had teeth in His stead.

The sea boiled behind us. The oars flailed. The shadow surged beneath.

Another strike. No impact — just pressure. Pushing us forward now, into unknown danger.

Then we saw it. The Howlstone.

Dark on the horizon. A split pillar of black rock, rising crooked from the sea's heart. At its centre, a hollow like a mouth. And from that hollow — the sound.

Not wind.

Not storm.

But a howl — long, rising, human and not — tearing the silence apart.

The men fell to the deck. Some praying. Some silent. One lay still, hand twitching.

"Row, you bastards!" Vasko bellowed. "Like hell itself's at your heels!"

And it was.

Then — wind.

Not much. Just a kiss.

But the sail took it.

We rose. The oars still moved. The ship groaned, then leapt. The sea hissed behind us.

I turned back.

Behind, the beast circled.

Not us.

The Pilgrim's Cross.

She turned slow in the water. Her deck crowded. Her mast gleamed with prayer-flame.

The devil swam beneath her, circling. Waiting.

Aboard her aft deck, I saw one man raise a torch — just a pinprick of flame against the dark. It flickered once, then vanished.

And we — windbound, wave-lifted — fled into the night.

"Pray for them," someone said.

I already was.

CHAPTER XXXVI: STORMGRAVE

We waited two days.

No mast. No smoke. No sound but the sea.

Only gulls wheeled above the waves — shrill and circling. They cried over what the Holt had claimed. No wreck drifted. No splintered oar. Just the emptiness. *The Pilgrim's Cross* did not come.

Men spoke little. They moved like ghosts, not from grief, but from the weight of knowing what must now be done with fewer hands. Thirty warriors gone — not scattered, not lost, but swallowed. With them, the strength meant for Stormhold's gate. We would be fewer, and the tide would be thicker with blood because of it.

Illarion paced the deck as if the boards offended him. His blades never left his hands. His armour hung from a railing like a dead thing — uncleaned, sweat-slick, forgotten. He did not wear it. He barely ate. Twice, I heard him whisper to himself, short bursts, like a man speaking to a saint or a fever. The crew gave him space. Even Urek kept distance.

Markov said nothing, but he no longer stood in light. He took to the leeward side, where shadows clung and sails muttered overhead. His fingers played at the hilt of his blade. Not drawing. Just touching. Like it might steady him.

Urek sat cross-legged near the foremast, sharpening his spear. His laughter had gone dry. When the whetstone slipped, he bled — and didn't seem to notice.

Then came the call.

"Ships! Portside!"

The shout struck like a slap. Every head turned.

"Five! Painted hulls! Coming fast!"

I crossed to the port rail.

Around the black shoulder of the cape they came — broad-prowed, low-slung, fast through the chop. Warships, but not like ours. Ochre and black, their hulls striped with storm-paint. Shields on the rails. Oars flashing. Twenty-five men each, at least. Shallow-keel cutters meant for harbour defense — not built to chase, but to close fast, strike hard, and spill blood in the surf.

Now they came not to block but to bite.

Illarion laughed — sharp, too sharp. The kind that cracked the silence in a way that didn't mend. He stepped forward, both blades high, sun catching on the edgework.

"At last," he said, loud enough for all to hear. "Let the saints see what is righteous."

Then he turned, quick and sudden, and pointed one blade at Bogdan. "Prophet. Call your fire. Show them God does not fear the tide."

Bogdan did not answer. But he moved — slow, assured — to stand among the archers at the aftcastle, his mantle catching the wind like a banner of ash. His staff rang twice against the deck. I saw no fear in him. But I saw no blessing either.

Illarion lifted both blades high. "*Grey Hand!*" he shouted. "*We charge! We do not break — we burn! Ready pitch! Ready bow!*"

And the ship came alive.

Archers — twenty of them — lined the rails, fingers at quivers, bows flexing in their hands. Tar-pots were uncovered, wicks soaked. Buckets passed hand to hand. The smell of pitch and salt and fear thickened.

Urek rose and twirled his spear once, slowly. Then again, faster. Then faster still — until it blurred. He grinned, lips split, blood on his knuckles. "Come on," he muttered. "Come on, then."

Five ships. That meant boarding — iron to iron, man to man. They'd swarm the deck like wolves into a fold, and if we didn't break them in the first moments, they'd break us by weight alone.

If I went overboard in mail, the sea would take me fast. But at least it would mean a clean fall. The hauberk waited where I'd left it — folded, still damp from the Holt crossing. The patch at the shoulder itched as I dragged it over my tunic. The mail rasped down my arms, heavier than I remembered. I cinched the belt. Fastened the ties. No time for the full set. Just the coat, helm, and shield.

And sword.

Greyfang waited in silence — no gleam, no cry, just steel darkened by age and oath. The leather wrap was worn to smoothness; the fuller still carried the ghost of salt. I drew her slow. The blade whispered as it came free — not sharp, but final. Old steel, oil-dark, etched faint at the base with the queen's seal and the mark of Saint Kosma — justice bound in fetter.

A blade not meant for parade. A blade meant for ending.

I felt the pull in my shoulder as I lifted it.

If I was to die, I would take some with me.

Let the deck run red.

Let the saints bear witness.

Illarion shouted again — *"Fire!"*

The pitch went first — great arcs of black flame hurled into the sky, trailing smoke. One landed true. The lead ship. A geyser of light. Flame raced up its prow, engulfed the foredeck. Men screamed. Some jumped. Some burned where they stood.

A second found a home — struck the midship of another, which twisted in panic, turning broadside.

Right into *The Sea's Teeth.*

I saw it happen — the crunch of hull against hull, the sudden flare, the roll of both ships locked in flame. No time for escape. No wind to save them.

They burned together.

The *Teeth* was gone.

Fifteen men flung into the sea, swimming or sinking. The rest — thirty souls — vanished beneath black flame and boiling plank.

Arrows sang from our rails. Sharp hisses in the saltwind. Ten more fell before the enemy ships reached us — some into water, some slumped across their own bowlines.

But the rest kept coming.

Three ships. Unbroken.

Hooks flew. Iron teeth seeking our bones.

Ropes thudded. Boards slammed.

"Archers!" came the cry behind — and ours answered.

A flight of arrows hissed overhead. Not at the ships — at the rails. At the men who reached too far.

One defender rushed the rail with a spear, leaned too far out to stab — and caught an arrow square in the face. His body twisted backward, arms splayed. He tumbled over the side without a sound. The others pulled back fast, shields lifted.

That bought seconds.

Then the boards struck true.

And the enemy climbed.

First one. Then three. Then more. They scrambled up the gangplanks with blades drawn, shields ready. But we were waiting.

They didn't come far.

Our front rank met them at the edge. Not in charge, not in chaos — just blunt refusal. We hacked at them as they came over the lip. Speared them before their feet could find balance. No wild swings. No ground given. The front line held tight to the rail, anchoring to the wood, careful not to overreach. To lean forward was to die.

Then they were on us.

Steel found wood. Blades found flesh.

The Grey Hand pitched, reeled, rocked with the weight of men and wrath.

Men shouted. Steel rang. Boots slid. Arrows stabbed from shadows.

Illarion fought at the fore like a man whose soul had slipped its tether — both blades spinning, reckless and precise at once. One man fell. Then another. But his guard was open. Too open. A short sword struck his ribs — he staggered but did not cry out. Another foe rose behind him, blade high.

I moved.

My shield slammed the man full in the gut, bone cracking. He doubled, pitched over the rail. The sea took him.

Markov crouched near the aft stairs, half-shielded by a fallen archer. The man bled from the thigh, still breathing. Markov had dragged him there — not to save him, but to stay low behind something solid. One hand clutched a knife, the other a short club slick with someone's blood. He didn't strike. Didn't charge. He watched, waited, ready to lash if cornered. Not fighting — surviving.

Urek laughed in the face of death.

His spear danced — tip flashing, shaft striking. He vaulted a crate, kicked a man square in the chest, turned without landing. His hook found a throat. Blood arced. He grinned like it was spring festival.

I held the centre.

Shield raised. Sword steady. Breath slow. I could hear them coming — not their voices, but the drum of boots on wet plank, the scrape of iron on rail. One of them snarled. Another gasped. Blood already thickened the boards beneath my boots. It mixed with tar and pitch — the smell sharp, metallic, bitter as rot in the mouth.

The first came with a hacking stroke, low and brutal, meant to split my thigh. I dropped my weight, caught it on the rim of the shield. Wood groaned. My shoulder shuddered. I stepped left as he stumbled from his own momentum, drove the boss of the shield into his jaw, then kicked low. His knee bent the wrong way. He screamed. I silenced it — steel down into the hollow of his collar, through muscle, into the lung.

The next was younger. Quicker. He came with both hands high, then twisted to stab low. I turned into the cut, caught the inside of his arm beneath the rim, locked it. He tried to wrench free. I stepped in close — close enough to smell his sweat, sour and sharp with fear — and twisted. Something tore. He cried out — not like a warrior, but like a boy. I let him.

Another. Taller. Axe in hand.

He didn't shout. He didn't feint. Just came on with the weight of someone who thought strength was all. I sidestepped. Brought my blade up under his wrist. The axe fell. He reached for my throat with the other hand, fingers wide. I drove the pommel into his temple. Bone cracked. He fell like a dropped sack.

I stepped back. Not far — just enough to see.

The deck was slick. Blood pooled in the seams. Somewhere a man was gurgling. Another was sobbing. The wood beneath my boots trembled with the clash of bodies. Arrows hissed above — one stuck quivering in the mast beside me.

Then another came — spearpoint first, not charging, testing.

Smart.

I didn't wait.

I threw my shield forward, caught his spear on the leather wrap, then stepped in close. Too close for a thrust. He tried to backpedal — too slow. My blade flashed once — shallow, across his thigh. Again, across the belly. Then the third time — the one that mattered — up through the ribs, angled cruel. His eyes found mine as he fell.

I let them close.

Blood soaked into my boots. It made a sucking sound when I moved.

Bogdan stood near the mainmast. Eyes closed. Hands raised. Lips moving. He was not fighting. He was not praying, either. Not truly. I saw no saint in him, only stillness.

A clang — not steel on steel, but iron biting wood. I turned — too slow. A man landed before I could lift my shield — shoulder-first, teeth bared. His weight hit like a battering ram. I staggered. Another leapt behind him — feet crashing down on my toes — and then a third, smaller, faster, blade already swinging.

I dropped to a knee. Shield up.

Too late.

The first blow struck the rim, then another — high, from the side — split the leather binding. A spear glanced off my mail, tore the skin just beneath my ribs. Hot. Shallow, but sharp. I grunted. Pushed upward. The shield cracked in my grip — not shattered, but broken across the grain. It flexed like wet bark.

I drove my shoulder forward, caught one in the gut. He folded. I hammered the hilt of my sword against his throat. Heard a click. He dropped.

But the others kept coming.

One grabbed at my collar — I felt fingers inside the mail, yanking — and I turned, elbowed hard. Something cracked beneath my strike, maybe nose, maybe cheek. He screamed, loud and wet. I pulled free, ducked under a blade. My own sword caught in the splinters of the deck for a breath too long.

Another strike came — edge down, fast. I raised the half-broken shield. It held. Barely. The blow numbed my left hand, shot fire down my wrist. My arm buckled. I turned into it — blade up now — swung short, tight. A cut across the thigh.

Another across the brow. Blood sprayed. The man fell back, shrieking.

I stood — panting.

The world shrank. Noise blurred. All I heard was breath and feet and the whisper of blades through air.

A fresh wave hit. I parried once. Twice. Then a spear-tip caught me just above the knee — not deep, but cruel. My leg faltered. I gritted my teeth and kicked low, felt the edge of my boot crush something soft.

Then I heard a cry — not mine.

"Back!" someone shouted. "Back to the stair!"

I turned — just in time to see Markov strike.

He rose from the shadows like smoke from wet coals — low, fast, knife in hand. A slash behind the knee dropped one. The man screamed, buckled. Markov didn't wait. He caught the rail with one hand, hauled the body sideways, and vanished with it down the aft stair.

A signal, not a cry.

He was opening the way — not fleeing, not calling for help, but clearing space. A retreat path. A death door. Something to fall back to if the deck turned red for good.

Above, Illarion cried out.

Not in pain — in fury.

A roar, more beast than prince. Steel rang in rhythm to his scream — one-two-one, the sound of twin blades dancing.

But I couldn't look.

The blood on my side had warmed my tunic. My arm throbbed. My breath came ragged.

Another was coming.

Then the wind turned.

A breath. A whisper. Then a cry:

"Pilgrim! To starboard!"

I looked.

She came out of the mist like a ghost with breath still in her lungs. *The Pilgrim's Cross* — broken-sailed, mast crooked, hull scorched. But afloat. Moving. Thirty men had died — but not all.

Figures scrambled at her rail. Ropes flew. Men in the water turned and swam. Fifteen reached her, or were dragged up. The rest drifted. Or drowned.

But the tide had shifted.

The enemy saw. And hesitated.

We did not.

We drove them back — inch by inch. No shouts now, only breath. Only steel. A man fell over the rail. Another clutched his stomach, dropped at my feet. Blood pooled, hissed on hot wood. One last boarder turned — and Urek met him, point first.

Then it was done.

Only the sea.

Only breath. And blood. And the sound of the water against the hull like the slow closing of a door.

The Sea's Teeth was gone. Nothing left but flame and foam.

Fifty dead.

Fifteen saved.

We lived.

And Stormhold still waited — high-walled, red-bannered, full of spears.

CHAPTER XXXVII: THE PYRE AT SEA

The deck was slick with blood.

It pooled where the pitch had split. Ran into the seams like ink. Some of the crew had taken brushes to the boards, working in silence, but the blood only spread — darkening with each stroke. Only a storm would wash it, and never clean. The air stank of iron and ash, salt, and voided bowels. Seagulls circled low, then lower still — not crying now, just watching.

We moved among the bodies.

A sailor with a broken spear half through his shoulder bit his tongue and nodded when I asked. I yanked it free and tossed it aside, then bound him with tar-stiff cloth. Another had his guts out — hands pressed over the mass like he meant to hold himself together. He said nothing. Markov held his shoulder. He died slow.

A boy lay twisted near the shield racks — not one of ours. Sixteen, maybe. His leg was nearly severed at the thigh, bone snapped, flesh flayed open, the last threads of skin stretched like sinew. He was clutching it with both hands, as if pressure alone could hold him together. Blood gushed beneath him — not in spurts now, just a slow, steady pour, like water from a split cask.

Markov looked once, then turned away.

I crouched beside him.

He saw me. Tried to speak. Only a breath came — not a word, just the ghost of one. His eyes were wide, not with fear, but with the dumb disbelief of pain too deep to understand.

A crewman from *The Pilgrim's Cross* knelt beside us. He didn't speak either. Just reached out with a thick hand, steadied the boy's jaw, and drew a short knife from his belt — curved, fish-handled, the kind meant for gutting in tight spaces.

The blade went in smooth, just beneath the jaw. The boy jerked once. Blood pulsed up in a bright arc, then dribbled down. He died looking at me.

The crewman wiped the blade on his sleeve and stood without a word. I crossed myself, and so did he. Then we moved on.

The Grey Hand's captain had been gutted. He lay on his back, guts spilled like a net of ruined rope, slick and glistening across the planks, eyes wide and unblinking at the sky — as if still trying to read the weather he would no longer sail beneath. His second — a broad-shouldered woman named Soroka with hair braided tight and bound in tarred cord — now gave orders. She did not raise her voice. Did not weep. She pointed, and the work continued.

By midday, the counting began.

The Grey Hand had been built for judgement. She had taken blows before — in sleet, in fire, in storms that snapped lesser ships in half — but she still held together. Scarred but unbroken. She had sailed with sixty-five souls. Forty-five warriors. Twenty crew. Now: ten crew. Thirty warriors who could still raise a shield. The rest lay wrapped or writhing. Fifteen too broken to fight — ribs crushed, arms split, bellies opened and sewn again. Of those, five would not see another sunrise. One was already praying. Another asked for his daughter's name. No one answered.

The Pilgrim's Cross still held the tide. Just. Her prow cracked and her hull opened forward like a torn seam. The ship moved like a man wounded in the spine: stiff, awkward, unwilling. The captain had lashed it with rope, caulking, and the name of Saint Vira — but I saw the slow leak staining the boards aft.

She carried thirty warriors. Fifteen crew. Some still able. Most shaken. They had barely made it through the Holt — harried by what moved beneath the black water. They spoke little now.

Of *The Sea's Teeth*, there was nothing. No sail. No timbers. No howl of her wild prow. She had gone down in fire and foam, and the sea had taken every splinter. It had carried forty-five — thirty-five warriors, ten crew. Thirty warriors has sunk into the deep. Five remained. One of them, a boy with a harpoon scar across his jaw, kept asking for orders. No one knew what to tell him.

Soroka scratched marks into a driftboard, counting with a carpenter's knife. Her eyes were pale, unreadable, like sky in morning frost. The knife moved steadily in her hand — thick-fingered, calloused, nicked from rope-burn and sail-work. She didn't flinch. Didn't pause. Just made lines. Each mark was shallow, firm, final — a tally of what the sea had taken.

We gathered our dead.

The enemy skiffs still remained hooked to us. We chose one and laid our fallen in rows: shoulder to shoulder, hand to wrist, no space between. Some we wrapped in wool. Others we could not touch without tearing. A few had no faces left.

The cleric from *The Pilgrim's Cross* stepped forward. His robe was stiff with salt, stained dark at the hem. A patch covered one eye; the other was bloodshot, rimmed with grief. His hands were red to the wrist — not his blood. He knelt beside the bier, head bowed, and made the sign of the cross three times, slow and exact. His voice, when it came, was rough but steady — like stone under water.

"Saint Vira, light the hearths to which these fallen do not return.

Saint Kosma, judge their death with clean scales.

Saint Mikula, keep them bound to peace — and us to their memory."

Then Bogdan stepped past him, slow, barefoot. His mantle was torn and ragged. A line of salt marked his brow. He raised his staff.

"Saint Ilyin of the Firebound," he intoned. "You who walked ash after wrath. You who bore flame through judgement. Take these."

From his belt he drew a pouch, black oilcloth bound with sinew. He opened it with care, as if unwrapping relics. Inside: coals, still faintly warm, and something black. A flicker. A whisper of smoke. Then flame — small at first, then leaping higher, bright against the dim sky.

He held the fire aloft in his hands, and intoned: "The blood of the judged is not ash. The fire remembers. The sea will carry. Let the flame rise. Let wrath rise. Let Your will be done."

The skiff burned bright. Then black. Fat popped in the heat. Smoke coiled skyward — thick as rope, foul as boiling skin. Men covered their faces. The gulls screamed and scattered.

Illarion stood at the stern. His mouth was tight. His hands did not stop shaking.

We met on the foredeck of *The Grey Hand* as the sun slid west, burnishing the sea with a dull copper sheen. The light had the look of blood over steel.

Soroka stood by the mast, arms crossed tight over her coat, face unreadable. Bogdan leaned against the rail, one boot braced on the curve of hull, the wind teasing the fringe of his mantle. Urek sat chewing something — root or sinew, I could not tell—and grinned like a man freshly woken from a good dream. Markov crouched beside a crate with his back to the rail, his blade across his lap, the whetstone scraping in slow strokes. His eyes flicked upward when the prince approached.

Sixty-five fit men. That was the whole of it.

Illarion stood unhelmed, the salt wind twisting his hair into points. His jaw was set. One eye still drooped from fever. But when he spoke, it was with fire.

"The Stormgrave Isles hold some two thousand mouths. That was our last count," he said. "Of fighters, perhaps two hundred, scattered across the isles. A hundred and twenty-five of those—and likely their best—lie in the sea. And not all the rest would have answered Salava's call. She's not loved."

No one answered. The wind clacked loose rigging. Far below, waves slapped the hull like a dog testing its leash.

"We still hold sixty-five fit men," Illarion went on. "Ten archers on each ship. Enough steel for two lines. Enough fire for one gate. If we strike before they regroup—"

Markov didn't look up. "Sixty-five against a city," he muttered. "Hope they like songs about beautiful failures."

Illarion's head snapped round. "I watched them burn," he said, voice sharp. "I counted the bodies. Thirty good men screaming as the sea closed over them. I won't let it be for nothing."

No reply to that. The scrape of Markov's stone stopped, but he did not meet the prince's eye.

I stepped forward. "Sixty-five against seventy-five behind walls is not good odds."

The words hung heavy.

Illarion turned on me. "You think I don't know the cost?" His voice cracked with heat. "I command this fleet. I stood at the prow while the *Teeth* burned. No man here holds the right to question my order."

Markov stood slowly. "And none of us means to," he said. His voice was quiet, careful. "But it may be we don't knock in the front door. We come at night. Fast. Quiet. Let them wonder if we're ghosts."

Illarion didn't even turn. "No." Then, sharply, "Bogdan. Do we have enough pitch to burn the city?"

The prophet shifted from the rail, his voice like worn bone on wood. "Not the city," he said. "But enough to burn the gate. Enough to seed chaos."

Illarion nodded. "Then we burn the gate. We storm the breach. They've just seen their best slaughtered in the bay. Let the fire remind them. They will break."

Urek spat into the wind and laughed. "Fire and blood," he said. "That's a song worth remembering."

No one else spoke.

The sun slipped lower. Shadows stretched across the deck. The prince turned without another word. I watched the burned boat drift further out — a black seam on the silver sea, staining the sea like ink from a split vein.

I had not meant to fight this battle. But fire does not ask. It comes. Finds what will burn. Leaves only ash.

Bogdan said I was anointed in blood.

He was right.

Since I was a boy, I've followed blood — not for coin, not for honour, but because I swore. And once a man swears in blood, he belongs to it. That's the part no one teaches: an oath is a chain, and every chain has its price.

For a moment, I thought this one might be different. The queen's charge — mad though it was — spoke of life. To find Saint Ilyin's relics. To save the king. To spare the kingdom from collapse. A quest of faith, not fire.

But somehow, blood found me still.

While I dreamed of bones in shrines and monks with keys, the warships came. The enemy climbed our rails like hounds to a scent. And again I was in it. Again I raised the blade. Again I added to the long tally that waits beneath my breath.

And there is the other oath. To the prince. That if the rot takes him — truly takes him — I must be the one to end him. Clean. Without asking. Without warning. That was the vow. I said it with my mouth. I carry it in my spine.

I studied him now. At his order, the ships turned toward Stormhold's docks. To break the city. And me with it.

He still walks. Still speaks. Still holds steel in both hands. But the signs are there. A tremble in the wrist. A smile that never warms. One eye that blinks too slow. And something else — not seen, but felt. Like the crack in a helm beneath fresh polish. He has not broken yet. But something has bent.

It is coming. Not today. But soon. And when it does, I will kill him. Not in anger. Not in hate. In duty. The king's son. The last hope of the crown. I will kill him like a horse put down before the limp sets in. And his name will join the rest. One more face. One more ghost.

I used to think there would be a reckoning. That one day I would sit with a priest, or a friend, or a fire — and weigh it all. The names. The faces. The blood. But no such day comes. Only the sea. Only more fire. Only more oaths.

Some men are made to build. Others are made to break. I do not know if God made me this way. Or if it was the sea, or Mstislav, or blood itself. All I know is steel. And the sound it makes when it splits bone.

We slid toward the docks — black sail low, the sea like silver drawn thin. Sixty-five men against stone walls and sharpened spears. A hopeless charge. Ordered by a prince who smiled too easily, and could not still his hand. And beneath us, the sea whispered of blood.

CHAPTER XXXVIII: THE GATE

The rain had begun to fall — not in drops, but in a soft cold mist that settled into cloth and hair and mail, seeping until you forgot it had ever been dry. The sea was quiet. The men were not. Murmured prayers. Buckles clicking. Oilcloth drawn off shield-bosses. Some tied saint-charms to their spears. Some wiped the heads with pitch.

I sat on a crate by the mast, arms bare, watching the horizon take in what was left of the sun.

Markov came with the hauberk folded over his arm. "Still not dressed?"

"I'll wear it soon enough."

He knelt and set the rings across my lap like a folded skin.

"Strange," he said, not looking at me. "How are you not hurt?"

I said nothing.

"I mean it. I watched five men die around you. Spears. Fire. That one with the axe? Missed your neck by half a breath."

I lifted the hauberk. The mail rasped as I set it over my shoulders. It settled like old memory — weighty, right.

"I am hurt," I said.

Markov stood. He blinked once.

"Wouldn't know it to look at you."

"I know."

Behind him, Urek slouched beneath the tiller ropes, running his spear's blade over a whetstone. "He's fire-born," he said, voice light. "Didn't you hear? Can't be killed. Comes out cleaner than he went in."

"No," I said, drawing the strap tight beneath my arm. "Not cleaner."

The helm was last. The brow still bore the dent where another war had struck it — perhaps a hammer-blow, years ago. The rust there was fresh again.

Stormhold crouched at the mouth of a large bay — low-walled, stone-built, old. I had seen it once before, in peacetime, from a ship's deck. Then, its towers had seemed modest. A fishing port with delusions of grandeur.

Now, with fires lit behind its battlements and black shadow between the stones, it looked larger.

Hungrier.

The quay ahead was empty.

No chains barred the inlet. No boats blocked the mouth. But the city gate stood sealed, and above it, the wall bristled with figures.

At first: twenty. Then forty. Then more. Spears, bows, the glint of helms catching flame. No voices. No calls. Just shapes — steady, unmoving, waiting.

The prince had said they had fifty defenders left.

He was wrong.

The Grey Hand and *The Pilgrim's Cross* came in slow — hulls scarred, sails slack, decks heavy with silence. No horns. No heralds. Just ropes tossed, planks dropped, boots striking wood.

Forty-five warriors stepped down in silence. Cloaks drawn, helms in hand, blades sheathed but near. Twenty archers followed, oilskin hoods pulled low, eyes fixed upward.

No voice gave command. None was needed.

The wind moved between us like breath through teeth.

Above, the city stood walled and waiting.

A brazier had been lit near the gangway. Ten pitch pots sat ready — squat, stoppered, fuming. The archers would step forward and fire when the word was given.

Illarion stood on the dock, watching the city, bound in plate. Unhelmed. Cloak loose. Swords at his hips. He had brought three suits of armour. I'd heard him say so back in Velgrad — loud, arrogant, insistent on bringing more than any man might need. Blacked plate with silver etching. It gleamed like wet slate, carved with vines that had no root in any forest I'd walked. Thin lines, fine inlay. Meant to catch torchlight, not steel.

Markov had helped him dress.

No squire would do. No soldier dared. The prince would not bear fumbling hands or downcast eyes. Markov, for all his wit, had quick fingers — and he did not flinch when cursed.

I'd heard them that morning. Everyone had.

"I said tighten it, not strangle me."

Markov muttered something low. I didn't catch it.

"Speak up," Illarion snapped. "Or have your balls gone soft with the rest of you?"

The vambrace clinked home. The prince flexed. Winced.

"Saints' tits — did the smith use pig iron? It *binds*."

"Because you've got arms now," Markov said, quiet. "Not just court wine and poetry."

Illarion didn't answer. Or didn't hear. He turned to the brazier, letting the fire reflect in the plates.

The breastplate sat high — chased in a pattern I didn't know, but someone had once called *princely*. A ring of white fox fur trimmed the gorget. His pauldrons bore the white hand, stitched in silver thread. The gauntlets had claws carved on the knuckles — a beast's, not a man's.

"Straps," he said. Markov fastened the last.

Then Illarion stepped back. Drew both blades.

The left rasped free — narrow, oiled, sharp. The right caught firelight — double-edged, Splitfang-forged, perhaps. He spun them once. Not to test weight. But as a man rehearses applause.

"Does it look right?" he asked.

Markov glanced up. "You'll sing in songs."

The prince gave a crooked smile.

But as he stood now, backlit by fire and sea mist, for all the steel and fitted joints, I saw the skin at his throat — pale, beaded, thin with sweat. He stared at the gate. His mouth was set. But his hands never stopped moving. I watched the twitch in his fingers. The way his thumb circled the pommel of his left blade.

Then, without turning, he spoke.

"Yaroslav."

He didn't even look at me. Just called the name — like a butcher names a blade.

I stepped forward. "Send someone else," I said. "I'm no speaker."

His head tilted. A smile curved just behind his lips — not a warm one.

"You'll do."

I held his gaze. For a moment, I thought he might add something. A reason. A caution. A second name to follow mine. But nothing came.

Only the wind.

And the gate, still shut.

At last I said, "I need the words."

Illarion's grin widened a hair. "You want instructions?"

I said nothing.

"Very well," he said, stepping closer. His breath reeked of whitefire — old and burned-down. "Tell her to surrender," he said. "And die."

I waited. That was not a message. That was the end of one.

"That's all?" I asked.

The smile widened again. "That's all."

I looked past him — to the archers behind, still watching, still waiting, their bows slack but hands ready.

No one spoke.

I turned toward the gate.

And walked.

The wind picked up — not strong, but enough to ripple the standard held by the boy at the dock. The white hand. Still clean.

I stepped off the dock.

Stone gave way to gravel. Gravel to packed dirt. The path to the gate rose in a slow curve — open ground, no cover. The kind meant to humble.

I walked alone.

Then behind me, boots scraped. Light. Careless. Not command.

Urek.

He caught up without asking, spear slung across his back, grin twitching at the edge of his mouth. I didn't turn.

"Bit quiet," he muttered. "Like a feast with no music."

We reached the place where arrows might reach — a far shot, but not impossible. The ground where a warning becomes a wound. Still no cry. No bowstring's snap.

I walked on. Ten paces. Then twenty. No arrows. No command. Only fire behind the walls, and the wind in the reeds.

I stopped. Planted my feet. And waited.

Ten minutes, perhaps. Though it felt longer.

Then — a dull thud. A groan, old and heavy, dragged from wood that had not moved in years.

The gate opened slow.

Rough timber — thick pine trunks blackened by sea wind, shaved flat on the inner face, left raw and barked on the outer. The tops were sharpened like stakes, not for show but for blood. Iron bands crossed them at intervals, cinched with heavy bolts the size of a child's fist. One had rusted through. Another wept pitch.

They swung outward, not wide — just enough to let the torchlight spill and the watchers see.

The city had teeth. And now it was baring them.

Defenders emerged— not charging, not cowering. Twenty men first. Then a dozen more. Shields raised, helms tight, swords bare. A column, not a horde. Behind them stood a figure I knew before her name was spoken.

Salava.

Boyarina of Stormward. Kin to none who ruled, bound by oath and blood to all who lived behind those walls. She wore scaled leather. Her cloak was damp but trimmed in gold-thread binding.

She stopped just past the gate.

My boots struck the stones loud in the stillness. I passed into bow range. No arrows loosed. My breath fogged once. Then again. I kept walking. Urek stayed behind. He did not follow. That was right.

When I stopped, Salava stepped forward the same distance.

We stood within a spear's reach of each other.

Salava stood just past the threshold — firelight behind her, thirty swords at her back. Her face was lean, fox-eyed, with hollows in the cheeks and a curve to the mouth that suggested charm, though none was offered now. The cloak hung damp from her shoulders, trimmed in thread meant to signal wealth or lineage, but dulled by sea air and time.

Her eyes moved over me — not with fear, but with calculation.

"You've brought fewer than I expected," she said. "No battering ram. No tower. Just two ships. Scarred ones."

I said nothing.

"I thought the queen sent a crusade," she went on. "Instead, I see a bruised dog with a burned tail and orders barked from across the sea."

Still, I said nothing. The wind touched my cloak. Far behind, I could feel the weight of eyes — archers, warriors, the prince.

At last, she frowned faintly. "Well? Have you come to speak, or just breathe salt in my face?"

"I've come to speak."

"Then speak."

"Surrender."

The word hung there — unadorned. It didn't echo. It didn't try to impress.

Just: *surrender.*

Her brows arched. "That's all?"

"That's all."

She waited. I didn't fill the silence.

"You don't speak like a court man."

"I'm not."

She stepped forward — slow, deliberate. Not quite threatening. Not quite safe.

"You know who I am?"

"Yes."

"And still you stand there, flat as a stone, telling me to hand over my city?"

"My orders are clear."

"Orders from a boy who shakes when he grips his blade."

I didn't answer.

She studied me, lips parting slightly — then shutting again. A shift in posture. A new tone.

"Tell your prince," she said, softer now, "that we want to speak. Not through arrows. Not through fire. Face to face. Before the blood spills."

I watched her.

It was not a bad offer. Not a true one, either. But well-phrased. In another world, a courtier might have answered with terms, with flattery, with the illusion of delay. But I was not made for that.

I nodded once. "I'll tell him."

I turned.

"Wait."

I stopped.

She was still thinking. Fast now — too fast. The bluff had cracked. The wall behind her stood firm, but she had begun to tilt.

"If we surrender," she asked, voice tighter now, "what happens?"

"You die," I said.

Her jaw tensed. "Just me?"

"Hopefully."

She did not speak for a breath. Then her voice came sharper, more controlled. A weapon, not a wound.

"Trial by battle, then."

"No."

"You can't refuse. That's the law. I have the right—"

"You don't," I said. "Trial by battle settles a man's claim against another. Not war."

Her mouth opened — shut — opened again. I saw the thoughts trying to line up. Her hands twitched at her sides.

"You're just a dog," she spat. "I order you to deliver my message. A champion's duel. If he wins, we die. If I win, you leave."

I considered.

There was no point in it. But no harm either. I'd been told to speak, not to argue. To listen, not to decide.

"I'll tell him."

I turned.

Again: "*Wait.*"

I stopped.

Her eyes flicked — not to me, not to the gate, but to the wall above. The girl with the braid was gone.

She opened her mouth. Whatever she meant to say didn't come.

I walked.

The wet stone whispered underfoot. Behind me, the gate stayed open — not as invitation, not as trap, but as a question waiting to be answered.

CHAPTER XXXIX: STORMHOLD

I walked back through the wet mist, boots whispering against the stone. The slope to the docks curved slow — wide enough to make a man feel smaller with each step. Behind me, no one followed.

At the quay, the firelight from the brazier guttered in the wind. The pitch pots steamed. The air smelled of salt, damp wool, and old fire.

Illarion hadn't moved. He stood at the dock's edge, cloak dragging, hands still now — as if they had remembered what they were for. Bogdan was near, but said nothing. The rest of the men watched from beyond: cloaked, helmed, silent. They knew this was not yet the storm, but the moment the anchor breaks.

I stopped a pace from the prince. I didn't bow.

"She wants to speak," I said.

"No," he said.

"She proposed a champion's duel."

He turned his head slightly — not in surprise, but interest. "Between whom?"

"She didn't say. She expects you'll offer yourself."

A slow smile worked its way across his mouth, warped by the bend in his lip.

"No," he said. "There's no time for theatre."

"She said she'd surrender if it was granted."

"She lies."

I said nothing. The rain tapped on the boards.

"What else?" he asked.

"She's waiting."

Illarion's gaze flicked past me, toward the slope. Toward the open gate, and the flickering fire behind it. He drew a breath, long and slow, and spat it into the sea.

"Let her wait."

Over his shoulder, Illarion said, "Bogdan."

The prophet stepped close.

"Kill them," the prince said. "As they stand."

Bogdan moved at once. Not with speed, but with that fluid certainty — as if the bones beneath his skin had been waiting for this moment to arrange themselves.

He raised one hand — crooked finger lifted like a conductor calling breath before song.

"Archers," Bogdan said. "Form."

And the line began to move.

Ten men stepped forward with pitch and flame — broad-shouldered, oil-streaked, carrying fire like it was weight rather than heat. Bundled arrows in one hand, stoppered pots in the other. Smoke coiled from the mouths of the clay flasks. Fire in waiting.

Behind them: twenty shieldmen. The wall.

Their shields were round, black-painted, rimmed in bronze, glinting dully in the wet. No one spoke. No one looked up.

Then twenty archers — cloaks thrown back, bows unwrapped, strings taut. Fire arrows at the hip, fingers already sticky with pitch.

Behind them came the rest.

Twenty-five men: the prince's guard, remnants from the *Cross* and the *Hand*, Urek with his barbed spear riding easy across his shoulders, and me.

I did not speak. I did not draw steel.

I only counted.

Where Markov should've stood — empty.

Good for him.

The gate still hung open. Salava still stood just past it. She did not call out. Did not move.

Then she did. One step back. Then two. She turned without flourish, without grace. No salute. No final cry. Only retreat. Her men followed — slowly at first, then quickening. The last ducked in just as the gate began to shut. It didn't slam. It closed steady, heavy — like the lid of a tomb being sealed.

A pause.

Then came the first arrow — sharp, fast, ill-aimed. It struck short.

Another followed. Then a handful more. Most fell before our front line. A few hit shields — thudded, stuck, slid down with wet wooden knocks.

"They're low on bowmen," someone said behind me.

Bogdan raised his staff.

"Fire."

Ten archers stepped forward. Dipped their arrows in flame. Drew.

The bows creaked once — then loosed.

The fire flew.

It struck the gate first — a scattered rain of light in the mist. Then the wall. Then the air beyond.

Flames stuck and curled. One arrow caught on a banner scrap near the hinge. Another lit straw at the base of the planks.

Inside, the defenders scrambled. Buckets. Rags. Cloaks. They beat at fire. Slopped water. One man used his helm.

Then the second volley came.

More arrows. More fire.

The wood began to darken.

The third volley came faster.

The smoke thickened.

And the gate began to burn.

It was not yet full night — but that thick, smothering hour when fire outshines the sun. Smoke rose in coils through the gate's upper seams. Shadows flickered behind the wall, red-lit and restless. The stone above was streaked black. Sparks clung to the wet like flies to meat.

The gate was burning.

Not fast — not clean. Wet wood fights its own undoing. But the flame had taken hold. It ate along the iron bolts. Curled up beneath the bars. Choked upward into the bracing.

The air turned thick.

The order came in a voice like iron dropped on stone: "Shields."

The front line lifted as one.

The air above stirred — a hiss, then a howl. Arrows. Rocks. Bottles. A rusted axehead. They came down like bones from a cursed sky.

One man went down at once — arrow to the throat, no cry. Another cursed, gripping his forearm. A rock glanced off a helm and spun into the mist.

"Forward!"

We moved.

Shields up. Feet steady. The noise behind us dimmed. Only breath. Only boots on wet stone.

The fire lit the path ahead — dirty red, like meat left too long in the sun.

Then the gate was before us.

Still standing — blackened, blistered, streaked with pitch and soot. But upright. Held by will or iron, or both. Its surface steamed where the rain struck heat. The top still bristled with spikes — pine logs hewn flat on one side, sharpened on the other, banded in rusted iron, bolts thick as a thumb.

Another volley fell.

Closer now. Arrows whickered past, low and fast — not fired in hope but in bloodlust. One took a man in the thigh. Another caught a jaw — bone cracked, teeth scattered like broken shell, and he dropped backward without a sound.

The front ranks did not pause.

Neither did I.

We struck the gate like tide on rock.

We fell back.

Half a dozen steps. No order — just the sense of it. The way wolves know when to spring, when to pull.

"Together!" someone called. I don't know who.

We ran.

The mud sucked at our boots. The ground slicked with blood, churned and pooled where the wounded had dropped. A dying man rolled beneath my foot — I stepped over him, didn't look down. Couldn't.

Crash.

We hit the gate again, this time with more than weight — speed behind it, rage behind it. It shook hard now. The hinges howled. A bar inside cracked. I felt it. Through the boards, through the pain in my shoulder.

"Back!" came the cry. "Again!"

We staggered. Stumbled. Found footing. A volley rained down from above — sharp, screaming. Arrows struck shields. One took a man in the neck beside me — a wet, glottal sound — he went down gurgling, arms flailing like a hooked fish. His body slid underfoot.

Another man slipped on him. Fell to one knee. Was up again.

"Run!"

We charged again.

Crash.

The bottom of the gate buckled. A spar tore loose. One beam bent forward. The air stank of pitch and heat and marrow. The ground was black with it — blood, ash, trampled muck. A broken spearhead lodged in the meat of my calf-guard. I kicked it loose.

Again.

Each time, a man fell. Each time, the line re-formed. We didn't scream. Screaming wasted breath.

Crash.

The last run hit hardest. The gate jolted wide at one edge. A gap — narrow, not yet enough — opened between boards. I saw shadow beyond. A figure moved — then pulled back. A spear stabbed out through the crack, caught a man in the gut. He screamed. Tried to fall back. Was pulled away.

"Break it!"

Crash.

"Break it!"

The last push was a roar of hate and prayer and dying.

Two more men pressed in. Another rushed past — blade drawn, breath ragged.

I followed.

The gate cracked again.

A scream. A clash. Smoke. Steel. Heat.

And then—

The gate broke—shattered inward like a rotten ribcage—and Stormhold opened its mouth.

There were no ranks now, no formation, no clear line of advance. Only smoke and screaming and the blur of shapes in the firelit dark. We didn't fight men at first. We fought heat and panic and motion—a force without mind, like trying to strike a wave.

My shield caught a face; it folded like wet bark. Steel scraped my ribs—glancing, jarring. I turned, glimpsed hair, teeth, metal, and struck. Not clean. Enough. A spear thrust past my jaw. I knocked it wide, shoved forward. The man behind it fell before he could try again. Arrows came down in panicked flurries—high, wild, unaimed. One thudded into a boy's back five paces ahead. He pitched forward, his scream swallowed by the press.

Another shaft hissed past my cheek. One struck a cloak, stuck fast; the man it hit didn't slow, just screamed and stabbed again. A broken shaft snapped under my boot. I slipped, caught myself on a shoulder—I didn't know whose—and drove on. Something slammed my shield; I staggered. Steel came again. I blocked, countered. The man shrieked and fell back, blood pouring through his fingers.

There was no line, no side. Just killing. Smoke thickened. The street reeked of pitch and blood. The sound of feet on wet stone merged with the animal groans of men dying in heaps.

Through the blur of shapes and shouting, I glimpsed him.

Illarion — black plate, silver-etched and soaked with blood not his own. The gorget caught the firelight. The claws on his gauntlets dripped. Broad as three men, taller than the rest, a white-hand crest half-torn from his back. He moved like a man twice his weight and none of the drag.

He didn't fight clean. He didn't need to.

Where the rest of us shoved or cut, he carved — blades spinning, arms wheeling wide, not with finesse but with fury. His left sword caught a man through the hip. The right split another from shoulder to sternum. A halberd came at him broadside — the prince took the haft across his ribs, stumbled, then answered with both blades. The head came off. The body stayed upright a moment longer.

But he did not fight alone.

Four men flanked him — his guard, white-hand tabards streaked with soot and gore. They didn't match his speed or strength. They didn't need to. They kept his feet beneath him. Covered his flanks. Pulled him upright when he overreached. One took a spear to the gut in silence and dragged the man down with him. Another caught an axe-blow meant for the prince's leg — and did not rise.

They died so he could keep killing.

His armour turned him into a judgement the city could not answer. Every strike broke bone. Every block crushed wrists. A boy ran — Illarion caught him by the cloak, flung him sideways into a firepot. The boy didn't rise.

The defenders scattered before him — not because they broke, but because they couldn't reach. No axe cut deep enough. No blade found seam. Their steel caught on etching. Their hands slipped on blackened mail. He killed like a tale told in war-feast songs — and like all such tales, it left the nameless dead behind it.

Someone cried out a name. I heard it break halfway. A boy rushed me with a hatchet. I crushed his hand with the rim of my shield; he dropped the blade. I had no room to swing. I drove the boss into his throat and stepped past as he fell.

The street narrowed. Fire crackled somewhere to the left—a roof catching. The rain was gone. The heat stayed. Faces blurred. A stone struck my helm; my ear rang. My shoulder burned. I didn't look—cut or bruise, it didn't matter now. A man screamed beside me, blade raised. I struck low—knee, then throat. He dropped in silence.

Urek passed me like a blaze unloosed. Laughing — not for joy, but because his body had outstripped his mind, and laughter was what remained. One eye swollen shut. Blood down his chest. His hair matted, mouth red. He dragged his spear behind him like a man dragging his own death, then hefted it overhead and howled — not a word, but a sound older than language.

He vanished into the smoke. A moment later — shrieking. The kind of sound men make when they're not sure if they're dying or being born again through pain.

I glimpsed him once more through the haze — standing atop a broken cart, shirtless, back lit by flame, hurling a torch through a second-storey window while someone screamed inside.

Not rage.

Not duty.

A man who did not fear fire, because he was fire.

He didn't fight for anything. He fought because he could not stop — and what else could such a man do, but burn the world around him to match what already lived inside?

We fought by inches, by instinct.

My world had narrowed to the weight of my shield, the burn in my arms, the step ahead. Nothing else held.

A child darted across an alley, barefoot, unarmed. I didn't move. The man behind me did. He called once. Then struck. The child dropped. Not clean. We pressed on.

To the left, a courtyard opened. Four defenders waited — axes gripped, faces raw. One lacked a helm. His mouth moved. A prayer, perhaps. Or breath. He hurled something — a rock. It clanged off a shield. Then they charged.

They didn't reach us.

The archers loosed without warning. One man took a shaft in the eye and dropped backward like a tree felled. Another twitched as a bolt struck his throat. The last two crumpled in silence. Their legs kicked in death long after we had stepped past them.

The fight was not long, but it was loud—iron against stone, bone against stone, cries swallowed by fire. Someone shouted, "Saint Mikula!"—plea or curse, I could not tell.

Through the smoke came a woman—axe raised, teeth bared, helmet dented. She struck high. I blocked. Stepped in. The shield rim caught her shoulder. She staggered but didn't fall. Another blow, low and fast—clever. It glanced off my mail. I answered with the edge of the shield under her jaw. She fell to one knee, still clawing for her weapon.

Illarion passed me.

His blades were already drawn. He didn't speak. Didn't pause. One stroke low, one high—crossing. She arched back, struck. He kicked her chest, brought both blades down. She folded without a sound. For a moment he stood over her, shoulders heaving. Then he turned and moved on.

They didn't have enough defenders. They were fathers. Brothers. Boys. Men too old, or too young, or simply not ready. Some threw stones. Some didn't fight at all. They died anyway—screaming or silent. It made no difference.

An archer fell from a rooftop. Landed wrong. Both legs snapped like twigs. He reached for his bow. One of ours crushed his throat beneath a boot.

My shield was cracked. My sword, notched. I remembered few of the cuts I made. I remembered the smells—burning hair, tar, sour bread blackened by heat.

A bell rang once, warped by the fire. The tone stuttered, choked, then failed. There was no signal left. Only pursuit.

We pushed through alleys, open doors, ruined halls where saints once hung painted in niches. One shrine burned. The icon cracked in the heat. A little girl tried to carry it away. She didn't get far. I do not remember striking her. Only that I didn't stop it.

At the heart of the city stood a well. Three women knelt beside it, pots at their knees. They didn't run. They didn't lift their eyes. One began to sing.

I passed them. Behind me, someone called for rope. Another retched into the gutter.

The defenders were gone. But the killing did not stop.

When the grainhouse caught, it was finished. Not declared. Not claimed. Just finished.

The city was broken.

Fires smouldered in the alleys. Blood ran into the gutters. Screams had thinned to weeping. Steel no longer rang — only boots, breath, the hiss of cooling pitch.

They were gathered in the square.

Not fighters. Not anymore. Just those who had survived. Women pressed their hands to children's heads. Old men clutched charms as if they might still mean something. Boys not yet grown — some bleeding, some barefoot — watched with wide, hollow eyes. A few held knives, but none raised them. They knelt. Not in reverence, but in surrender. Not bowed, but bent. Waiting. For mercy. For judgement. For death.

I saw a boy near the front. Thirteen, perhaps. Bruised. Dirt-caked. Shaking. But not crying.

His eyes met mine — dark, blank, familiar.

I had been that boy once. In another town, under another banner. My knees on broken stone, my brother and uncle dead, waiting for Mstislav's judgement. I had looked up. He had looked down. Long and silent. He spared me. Accepted my oath.

I did not know if Illarion would spare any of them.

He stood just beyond the line of captives.

The battle was over, but the armour had not let him go. His breastplate steamed in the cold. The pauldrons hung crooked on his shoulders, twisted where someone had grabbed or struck or tried to drag him down. He reached up — slowly, like a man drowning — and unbuckled the helm. It came free with a hiss of sweat and blood. He held it a moment. Then let it fall.

It struck the stones and rolled. A prince's helm. Silver-edged. Blood-marked. Abandoned.

Beneath it, his face was pale and hollow. The left eye blinked slower than the right. His jaw hung slightly askew, mouth open, chest heaving. Sweat traced lines through soot on his cheeks. His lips moved, but no sound came.

The crest on his cloak had slipped halfway down his arm. One gauntlet dangled, unlatched. His blades were still drawn, but the points sagged toward the ground.

He twitched — not like a man poised, but like one trying not to fall.

Still, he did not speak.

He paced. Once. Then again. His boots dragged.

Then, at last, he turned toward the kneeling crowd.

"Where is she?" he asked.

No one answered.

He stepped forward and pointed — a man, bald, bloodied, missing two fingers.

"You. Speak."

The man opened his mouth, but nothing came. Not plea. Not lie. Not breath.

Illarion cut him down. Not clean — the blade tore across the collarbone and into the throat. There was no cry. Just the thick, wet crack of gristle splitting and the dull thump of bone on stone.

The children wailed.

"Next," he said.

He pointed again. A girl this time — seventeen, perhaps. Mud-streaked. Hands clasped. Her lips parted, but before she could speak, another voice whispered behind her: "She's gone."

Illarion froze.

"Who said that?" he asked. His voice was soft. Almost calm.

No one answered. The captives stared at the stones. At the blood spreading cold between their knees. At the man whose body still twitched when the wind moved his cloak.

"Who said that?" he asked again, slower now, turning in a half-circle, his gaze unfocused.

Still no answer.

He raised one sword as if to strike — but his arm faltered. The blade hung for a breath. Then dropped. Not cast aside. Just lowered, like it had grown too heavy to lift.

His mouth worked, but no sound came.

Then, almost gently: "I want her. I want her head."

He stood there, shaking. Looking through them, not at them. The black plate still gleamed — but it hung heavy now. His shoulders drooped beneath it. His legs shook with every step. The claws on his gauntlets no longer struck — they trembled. Sweat streamed down his jaw, carving tracks through the soot. His breath rasped behind his teeth, shallow and quick.

He did not fall. But he leaned — first on one heel, then the other. As if the weight of glory was breaking him faster than the wound.

I said nothing. Only watched and thought how easy it is to burn a city.

And how long the burning lingers after the flames go out.

CHAPTER XL: THE RECKONING

The wind had shifted by morning. It no longer carried screams — only smoke. It rolled eastward, across the river mouth and out to sea, where no saint would smell it. But the stench still clung to the city. To the stones, to the scorched lintels, to the skin and cloth of the living. Even the bandages wrapped tight over wounds could not keep it out. Pitch, blood, and meat — not the smell of battle, but of burning men.

I sat in what had once been a shrine-house. The walls were blackened from the inside, the roof patched with tar-cloth and hope. The niche where Saint Kosma's image once stood had collapsed. Only a scorched chain and a thumb-sized fragment of icon remained, still nailed to the soot-dark wall. The floor was turf, soaked through now — not with rain, but with the discharge of bodies — blood, piss, and bile.

Low moans drifted like tide-surge between the prayers. A bone-doctor worked near the wall, bent over a boy whose ribs showed beneath the gauze. Two midwives from the lower quarter — women with faces like old bark and fingers worn to cords — moved from cot to cot, whispering to the nearly gone. A priest from the Sea-Fort muttered his verses, voice hoarse, eyes glassed. I saw another priest crouched behind a cracked shelf, rocking slightly, mouthing words he did not speak aloud. Their hands moved through the rites, but their faces told a different truth. They had the look of men who'd seen God turn his face away.

We had gone in with sixty-five. A lean line of steel and oath. Now we were thirty.

Ten could still stand. Still grip their axes, if called — though not one of them unblooded. Ten more bled slow through their wrappings, wounds too deep for binding alone. And ten danced at the edge, their eyes dim, breath shallow, hands twitching at nothing. Not yet dead, but too near. As if someone else were already calling their names, and they had begun to listen.

Stormgrave had paid worse.

A hundred and twenty-five of their fighters were in the sea — broken boats, shattered bows, ribs split like planks. Another hundred and thirty dead behind the walls, if the count was honest. Thirty were men of age and strength. The rest were not. The fires had not chosen who to take. The blood had dried on blades, but the heat had not left men's mouths. When there was no one left to fight, the women had paid. Again. That part never changed.

No one had tallied clean. No one ever did. But someone — a boy perhaps — had taken a stick and written numbers in the ash beside the gate. Just lines, slashed and crossed, like carving wounds into soot. As if that could make it mean less.

Pyres were built, fed with pitch and salted cloth, lit without rite or word. The people had asked — quiet, respectful. A bent woman at the edge of the square, her palms black with ash.

"Let the sea take them," she'd said. "They were Gvazdari."

Illarion had said no.

"They chose flame," he answered, loud enough for all to hear. "Now let it finish them."

There'd been no protest. But no prayer, either. Only the crack of bone and timber. Only the wind carrying smoke where no saint would breathe it.

Illarion had sent his wounded hobbling through the alleys. Every house searched. Every cellar. The boyarina's banner torn from the gatepost and pissed on. But she was gone. Her hall stood empty. The hearth cold. Her mastiff lay at the door with its throat opened like a purse. Rooms stripped. Chests wrenched apart. One cup left behind — copper, dented, overturned beside a hearthstone that had cracked from the heat.

I had taken wounds of my own. Shallow cuts on shoulder, thigh, flank — half a dozen. But one was worse. A deep cleave behind the ankle, where a dying man had swung wild and caught me just above the boot. I bled down the inside of the foot, and every step since felt like walking on a split bone. So I sat.

Urek was among the dying.

They'd found him in a pile of corpses near Stormhold's keep — his own spear shattered. Two arrows in his back, one in the lung. They thought him gone, and maybe he had been, but when they lifted him, he groaned. Now he lay on a cot near the corner, covered in a salt-stiffened cloak, breath rattling like a caught bell. His skin was waxen. Sweat pooled at his temples. One hand curled near his ribs, still half-clutching the shape of a haft. He hadn't spoken. Might never.

The priest said sleep was a mercy. But he said it softly. Said it like a man trying to convince himself that silence was a form of prayer.

Markov stood over him.

He hadn't moved in some time. He just stood there, eyes fixed, as if watching for a sign from Urek's breath. His blade was still belted at his hip — still stained, still unsheathed from the day before. I wondered if he even remembered it was there.

I watched him until he noticed.

He looked up. His face was slack — not pale, not wild — just emptied out. Like a man past the edge of weeping.

"I know I'm a coward," he said.

No shame. No excuse. Just flat. Like a truth finally named.

He looked down at Urek again.

"I hid in the hold." His mouth tightened. "You all charged into battle, but I couldn't breathe. I pissed myself in the dark. Sat there with a knife in my hand and shook like a drunk."

I said nothing. There was nothing cruel to say. And nothing kind that would've helped.

He went on.

"I'm not like you, Yaroslav. I want to live."

He took a breath. Shook his head.

His hand hovered over Urek's shoulder — then drew back, half ashamed of the gesture.

"I had a dream. Me and Vesha. Remember her? Hard and cruel — my queen of thieves. She don't love me, not really. But she pretends. She lies well enough I can forget. And when I'm with her, I feel like the world could be soft again. A bed with feathers. A place that doesn't stink of blood and rot. A woman who holds me like I matter. Even if it's false. I pay her, and she leaves. But for a moment, it's something."

He looked up again.

"I wanted that more than I wanted to be brave."

I nodded once.

"That's a good thing," I said. And I meant it.

Not all men are shaped to hold the line. Some are meant to survive. Some are meant to tell the tale. Some are meant to find joy and hold it a while, even if it costs. I hoped Markov found that feather bed. And the queen who pretended to love him. And the breath that came easy.

I hoped that for each man — whatever his measure.

Outside, I heard the call for another count. Heard the scrape of cartwheels as they dragged the next set of dead to the pyre pit. Heard a voice break in the street. One sharp, half-choked sob. Then silence.

There was no triumph in Stormhold. Only ash. Only loss measured in limbs and names. Only the reckoning.

CHAPTER XLI: SHADOWS IN THE FIRE

The prince settled in at Stormhold keep.

Not for rest, though the wounded needed it. Not for honour, though we buried our dead in the burnt square. We stayed because the only ship fit to sail was The Grey Hand, and no command to leave. *The Sea's Teeth* was still gone, and Illarion had no interest in returning to the capital with half a fleet and a cracked army. Stormward was his now. The sea would carry the word.

The sailors moved into the empty houses. The peasants made no protest. Their banners had changed before, and would again. Princes bled each other over saints and oaths and glory. The people only wanted to till land, raise children, and not be flayed for sport. A cruel lord was feared. A just one was prayed for. But even a hungry one could be borne, if his hunger had a pattern.

Illarion had no pattern, but he was not mad. Not yet.

He did not force their sons. He invited them — if the word meant anything when a starving boy was told he'd eat only if he fought. "Train with us," he said. "Eat like soldiers. Fail, and you go home." There were no uniforms. No ceremony. Just a line in the mud, and the knowledge that stepping across it meant bruises, blood, and the chance to live another day with meat in your belly.

Many knelt. More than I expected.

He trained them hard. Too hard. He culled them like animals, picked out the strong, broke the weak. Some he marked with bands of cloth. Others he left where they fell. One boy lost an eye by the third day and still limped out for drills. Illarion gave him nothing — not even a name.

He did not ask about their fields. He did not answer complaints. He took what food he needed and let the rest manage.

He took women, too — not by order, but by presence. And his men followed suit. There were no rapes that I knew of. But there were no refusals, either. Only fear. Hunger. Submission. He punished no man for bedding a woman — so long as she was not broken in the process.

But he did not kill the children. Did not sack the granaries. Did not burn for sport. And so they called him a fair master. Or at least, not a monstrous one. That was enough. That was always enough.

I walked on the seventh day. Limping. The bone-doctor had bound my leg tight and muttered that I might never walk clean again. He didn't say I was too old, too cracked, too thick with scars to be a warrior much longer. But I heard it all the same.

I went to find Bogdan.

He had taken Salava's house — a thick-walled stone thing with a timber upper floor and shuttered windows. The town's only real manor, if it could be called that. A burnt Stormhold banner still clung to the post above the door, half-peeled by rain.

I stepped to the threshold, let my hand rest on the wood. My shadow touched the hearthstone just inside.

"Bogdan," I called.

There was no answer.

No answer. Then boards creaked above. A scuffle. A half-choked gasp.

I stepped back.

A girl came down the stairs. Barefoot. Young — perhaps sixteen. Hair tangled, shift wrinkled. Her eyes widened when she saw me. Not in recognition. In fear. Her hands tightened on the rail. She looked ready to run.

Then he appeared. Bogdan descended behind her, slow and smiling, his mantle unfastened, tunic loose at the collar. Around his neck hung a collar of bone — finger-length pieces bound on rawhide, clacking softly as he moved. His chest was bare beneath the open tunic: lean, pale, hairless, marked by small burn-scars and the faded ink of old rites.

He did not hide it. He did not explain.

"Come in, brother," he said. "There is drink."

I crossed the threshold. The hearth still smoked faintly, though no fire had been laid that day. The air smelled of scorched herbs and burnt hair. On the mantel, bones had been set in deliberate shapes — tied with red thread and interwoven with wax, salt, and scraps of parchment marked in ink. Nestled among them were saintly icons — Saint Vira with her key, Saint Danilo with his dented helm — their faces soot-streaked, their edges crusted with wax. One bore a bone charm nailed over its heart. The shutters were drawn though it was noon, cloaking the space in a thick, root-coloured gloom. Salt lines crossed the lintel and were smeared with ash; another encircled the hearth like a ward. Above the door, dried thistles and elder bark hung in a bundled knot, daubed with a dark resin that clung to the wood like congealed blood. In the corner stood an altar of sorts — half shrine, half relic-pile — where icons leaned beside antlers, thorn-wrapped stones, and old tools whose purpose was long lost.

A clay jug stood open on the table, beside two cups.

Bogdan poured.

"I thought we were done bleeding," I said. "But I see you've taken spoils."

"She chose to stay," he said, tone flat. "And if she chooses to leave, she may."

We drank. It burned — not whitefire, but close. Thick, fermented. Bitter.

I set the cup down.

"We're not finished," I said. "You spoke of justice. Of vengeance. But after the fire, you said there'd be truth."

"I said God may show it. Not that He would."

I stared at him. His eyes were red-rimmed, but not unfocused. If he was drunk, it was only halfway.

"Dragomir told me there's a monastic order west of here," I said. "Saint Dobroslav the Sower. They keep records. Rites. Old maps. I'll go."

Bogdan poured again. Then again. He filled both cups to the lip.

"Drink," he said. "Then we ask."

He raised his own, muttered something low — a prayer or a rite — and struck a flint beneath the cup. A sudden flare of blue danced across the surface. I smelled oil. Pitch. The rim blackened.

He drank. Fire and all. The skin around his mouth sizzled faintly.

I raised mine. It trembled in my hand. My knuckles white on the clay. The heat licked my beard. I drank. Pain met me like a hammer. But I did not drop it.

When I looked again, Bogdan was kneeling. "Here," he said.

I lowered myself — slowly, stiffly — onto the floorboards across from him.

His knees touched the coals scattered before the hearth.

His eyes rolled back. "Saint Vira," he whispered. "Saint Danilo. Saint Kosma. Let the flame descend. Let the sinner be burned clean."

His arms raised.

I heard nothing but my breath.

The candle had gone out.

"Your fire," he whispered. "Your light. Blind us, so we may see."

My heart pounded. Heat rose in my chest — not from drink, but from something deeper. The world tipped. The air thickened. The silence rang. Images came. Not clearly. Not fully. But like dream-paintings left in ash: A black stone — not carved, not marked. Square like a box, or a coffin, hunched and half-submerged. Water — waves peaking, breaking. No — Fire. Or...something else. I saw like through fog.

No relic.

No light.

Just the weight of something waiting.

"Speak," Bogdan said, his voice echoing strangely. "What do you see?"

I opened my mouth. Nothing came.

He leaned forward. "Where is it? Look harder."

"I don't—" I swallowed. "There's nothing. Just water. A stone. Fire-water. I don't know."

He snapped upright.

The room snapped back with him — sound, breath, smoke, cold. He spat into the hearth.

"You are weak," he said. "Your faith is too thin. The Lord looks away from the sinner."

He turned from me.

I stayed on my knees. Not from shame. Not from prayer. I simply had no will to rise.

Magic was not for men like me.

Captain Soroka came just after midday. No horn, no summons. Just her boots in the ash-path mud, cloak soaked to the seams, and her voice at the doorframe.

"The prince wants you."

I followed without a word. The sky hung low and grey, pressing down like wet cloth. We passed where the pyres had burned, now nothing but slick charcoal and bone-sunk earth. Smoke still clung to the walls of Stormhold like a curse not yet lifted. The townsfolk kept clear.

"What does he want?" I asked.

"I'm not the prince's mother," Soroka muttered. "He didn't see fit to explain."

She marched fast despite the wind. Her seal-hide boots found the driest stones, her cloak snapped like a sail. She smelled of salt and steel. I liked her for it.

"I'd rather be out again," she said, half to herself. "These halls stink of pitch and prince's moods."

We came to the Sea Fort.

Stormhold keep was no palace. Just a black-stone wedge built into the cliffside, shaped more by erosion than architecture. Its sea-facing wall bore the gouges of centuries: wind, wave, and blade. Newer structures had been lashed on over time: a hall, a stair, a lean-to—until the whole thing looked like a shipwreck propped against a rock. The doors were bone-ribbed timber. The hinges screamed when they opened.

The great hall was cold, tall, and smoke-dark. Stone flagged the floor, wet in the seams. Sealskin banners hung limp from the rafters. A fire roared in the long hearth — by the prince's order, no doubt — but the warmth refused to leave the stone. It licked the air without touching the walls. The damp had settled long before him and would outlast his rage.

Illarion sat at the high table, legs spread wide, a half-eaten joint in one hand, the other resting on a silver cup. Markov was beside him, hunched and quiet. Food covered the table: bread torn open and left to dry, oily fish, a bowl of cloudberry stew already greying at the edges. Servants came and went, heads low. The prince didn't look up at first. He tore a strip of meat from the bone with slow, grinding teeth. Chewed. Swallowed. His fingers left grease on the silver cup. Another bite — tendons snapped between his molars. He set the joint down too gently. Then looked up. His eyes were blue, bloodshot, rimmed in shadow — and hungry in the wrong way.

"So."

I said nothing.

"Sit," he said.

I didn't.

He snorted. "Of course. The orders of a prince mean nothing to you. Or is it that you're too dull to recognise one when it's given?"

Markov shifted. I saw guilt in his face before I knew what it meant. The way he wouldn't meet my eyes. The way his hands stayed under the table.

Illarion drank deep.

"You know," he said, wiping his mouth with the back of his hand, "it's a curious thing. A man hears a tale in passing. A tale about relics. About a mission. About his name not even being whispered in the planning of it."

I looked down at the table. There was a grease-smear on the wood, where he'd set his meat. Men don't shout when they feel small. Not at first. They circle it, wait for the shape to form in someone else's mouth.

He reached down and tore a hunk of meat from the platter — not cut, not served, just seized — and bit deep, tearing gristle from bone like he meant to silence it. Then he rose. He didn't drop the meat. He held it low in one hand, blood and grease running down his knuckles.

"St. Ilyin's bones. A voyage to save the king. All planned. All sworn. And somehow, no one thought to mention it to me. Curious, isn't it? Almost like I don't matter."

For a second he stood looking at nothing. Then, without warning, he flung the meat. It struck the wall with a slick, meaty slap — left a red smear trailing down the stone.

No one moved. A girl near the door blinked too fast. Another drew breath. One flinched.

That was enough.

With a roar, Illarion drove his knee into the edge of the table. The whole thing tipped — platters and trenchers crashing, broth flung wide like blood from a wound. Iron cups rang against the stone. Bone shards flew.

"Out!" he bellowed, voice cracked with drink and fury. "All of you!"

The servants scattered — not bowed, not excused, just gone. Like gulls before a wave. One slipped in the grease and scrambled after the rest.

He stood there breathing hard, fists clenched, stew dripping from his boots.

Then he turned on me.

"You," he hissed. "Ugly bastard. You think your face is worth something just because it made a few cowards piss themselves? You think a flattened nose and a stare make you a leader?"

I said nothing.

"You can't read. You grunt like a dying ox. You've got no pride, no mind, no spine. Just a leash round your neck, and Dragomir who tugs when he wants a dog to bite."

He stepped closer.

"You're not a knight. Not a noble. You grew up on a fishman's rock. You'll die there, or in the mud. And the world won't even blink."

Then he struck. A sharp blow to the jaw — hard, fast. He'd fought before. Not like I had. But enough to land it clean.

I staggered. Didn't fall. That made it worse.

He hit me again — a backhand, open and furious. Rings split skin. I tasted blood. Then both fists, wild now, hammering my chest, my shoulder, the side of my head.

I didn't strike back. I raised an arm, turned my shoulder, caught what I could. But I didn't return the blows. Didn't speak. Just stood there and let him spend his rage.

It hurt.

His breath turned ragged. His mouth twisted into something too wide for words. Then he screamed — a raw, broken sound — and tore his blades free.

Markov leapt between us.

"No! Illarion, stop. God's sake, stop."

The prince shoved him hard. Markov stumbled. "Traitor," Illarion spat. "Lying rat."

Markov raised his hands. "Yes. I lied. He asked. I said I'd heard nothing. I thought... I thought he'd get over it."

I took a step back, hand to Greyfang's hilt. "You don't want this," I said.

Illarion raised both blades.

Bogdan's voice cut the air like cold iron.

"Put them away."

He stepped through the doorway, pale as bone, his mantle whispering like teeth shaken in a grave.

Illarion stared. "You knew too. Didn't you. Dragomir gave *him* the mission. This — this nothing. This pile of half-rotted scars."

Bogdan's voice was calm. "Yes. I knew."

It had been the queen, not Dragomir. But I didn't correct him.

"So I'm the only one who didn't?" Illarion shouted. "The whole damned court knew?"

"No," I said. "Just us."

He laughed. Bitter. Hurt.

"So you were going to sneak off. Find these relics. Save the kingdom. And let the prince rot?"

Markov opened his mouth, then closed it.

"Where are they? These relics."

"We don't know," I said.

"Of course you don't."

He stood heaving, blades drawn, face flushed and slick with spit and sweat. No answer came. No challenge. Just me — breathing slow, jaw bloodied, one arm still raised to guard. And then something turned in him. Not snapped — not rage. Not quite shame either. Just the weight of knowing. That he'd shouted, struck, drawn steel… and still hadn't been heard.

He sagged. Like a cord cut. Like breath let out. Sat heavy on the nearest chair, the only one still upright, and pressed both hands to his face. Palms grinding into his eyes like he could scrape the shame out.

"Clean this up," he said to Markov. "Get the servants."

Markov glanced at me. Then obeyed.

He stayed slumped, elbows on knees, breath still ragged.

Then he turned — slow, deliberate — and fixed his gaze on Bogdan.

"Tell me," he said.

So, we did.

Bogdan spoke first — his voice low and smooth, like smoke curling through a cracked wall. He spoke of flame, of visions, of Saint Ilyin's bones. Of a fire meant to burn the rot from the king's blood, if only the relics could be found. If only the path were righteous enough.

I gave what I had: a name pulled from Dragomir's records. Saint Dobroslav the Sower. A monastery, once — west coast, high in the mountains. No maps. No pilgrims in a generation. Maybe a ruin. Maybe a start.

Illarion didn't look at me. His eyes stayed on Bogdan.

"Can't you see them?" Illarion asked. "The relics. Scry them. Burn something. Speak a rite. Isn't that what you're for?"

Bogdan didn't flinch. Just lifted his cup, drained what remained, and set it down like an offering.

"I lit the flame," he said. "I prayed. The saints answered."

Illarion's jaw clenched. "Answered *what*?"

Bogdan looked at the hearth. His voice was softer now, but colder.

"They showed what was given. Doubt has no altar. I felt its presence. But the vision was not for me."

His eyes slid to me.

I didn't speak. My mouth still tasted of blood. The memory of fire still burned behind my ribs. He wasn't wrong.

"The failure was human," Bogdan said. "Something in the vessel was cracked."

The silence stretched. Then Illarion turned to me, slow and sure, like a knife being drawn.

"Of course it was," he said. "Why wouldn't it be?"

He stood again — slow, smiling, cruel.

"A man without faith. Without pride. Without purpose. And *that's* who Dragomir sends to chase saints and save kings." He barked a laugh. "It's a joke. A broken brute with empty hands and no light in his eyes."

Then he turned away. Looked at the fire. Quiet. Almost to himself he said, "It should have been me."

"We told you what we knew," I said, voice hoarse.

Silence again.

Then: "West, you said?" Illarion asked.

I nodded.

"Who knows?"

I counted it. "You. Me. Markov. Urek. Bogdan. Dragomir."

I paused. He might not like it, but there was no point in lying.

"And the queen."

He flinched. "Of course. *Her.*"

The word curled in his mouth like it tasted of iron.

He looked back to the hearth — not to see it, but to turn his eyes from them. The wound went deep.

"She gave *you* the charge," he said. "Not me. Her son. Her heir. Not even a whisper."

I didn't answer. He wasn't asking.

"I bleed in her name. I sail through death for her crown. And she sends *you* to save *my* father."

His voice dropped. "She sends the Volkodlak to carry her hope. While I rot in fog and storm."

The fire cracked. A spark leapt from the hearth — red, hissing — and landed on the stone between us. The prince crushed it under his boot.

"I'm taking it," he said. "Her charge. Her quest. The relics. The flame. All of it."

His jaw clenched.

"If she wants saving, I'll save him. If she wants glory, she can choke on it."

"And what of Stormhold?" Markov asked.

He waved a hand like brushing aside smoke. "Give it to someone else. I don't care."

Markov cleared his throat. "What about old Verdan? He's got the look of a lord, if not the mind."

Illarion didn't even blink. "Sure. Him. Call him in."

Illarion stared into the cold hearth. No fire now. Just the ash and what hadn't burned clean.

"Find a guide," he said at last. "We leave soon."

I stepped forward. "This cannot get out."

He turned, brow raised. "For whose sake?"

"For the kingdom," I said.

That stilled him. A flicker of calculation passed behind the anger.

He stood straighter now. Already somewhere else — already riding west in his mind.

I watched him a moment longer.

And felt the sea begin to shift beneath us.

We met in the sea-hall beneath the Sea Fort, where the tide still whispered between the stones. Wind slid through the vent-slits — thin as knives — and left salt crusted on the walls like frost. The place stank of damp wool, ash, and old fish. It was not a hall made for councils. It was a place built to survive storms.

The guide was a wiry man called Radek the Lowlander — sun-browned, goat-stinking, bent at the shoulders like a man who'd hauled nets uphill too many years. A belt of toggles and bone tools swung at his waist. He scratched his jaw as if the answer might be hiding in the grit.

Illarion stood before him, arms folded. "You've heard of the Order of Saint Dobroslav the Sower?"

"Aye," said Radek. "Mountain cloister, up past Zelezovka. Just above the cliffs. Order's long gone. No monks now. Not in years."

"You're certain?"

"Near enough. Last I passed that way, the shrine still stood. But no bells. No light. Just wind."

Illarion turned to Captain Soroka. "You know it?"

She nodded, jaw tight. "I know Zelezovka. West coast. Barely a harbour. Sits inside the fringe of the Kladovek."

I frowned. She saw it.

"The fishermen call it that. Last edge of the world. Means 'the broken cupboard.' Too many reefs. No shelter. Tides curl like thrown rope. Past that, nothing but endless sea and ghosts"

"Can we get there? How far?" Illarion asked.

"Through the Trozubye Gory? Three leagues," said Radek. "There's a goat-path in the pass. Steep, but walkable."

"Could we ride it?" Markov asked. He was crouched beside a fallen pillar, rubbing his jaw.

"Not on a proper horse. But the hillfolk use donkeys. Sure-footed. Ugly bastards. Might cut a day, depending."

Markov grinned. "Then we ride. Mountain donkeys, dried fish, stout sticks. Might be a pleasant little climb."

I said, "No."

He looked up. "No?"

"We sail around."

Radek blinked. "A day's sail, with a strong ship and good winds. Two, if the wind fouls. But—"

"Even if it takes ten days," I said. "Even if the shore's teeth bite, and the waves climb like towers. Even if the wind tears the sail and the rain turns to knives. We go around."

Illarion's eyes slid toward me. Cold. Curious.

"This is the end of the world," I said. "Things out here lie. And whatever waits in the cliffs above Zelezovka—trust me. We don't want to meet it."

I let the words hang. "I've walked roads like that. With Markov. Roads where nothing answers when you pray."

No one spoke.

All eyes turned to Markov. The memory lived behind his eyes.

That was enough.

Illarion broke the quiet. "Soroka. Ready *The Grey Hand*."

The captain nodded. "Aye, my prince."

Urek lived.

Not well — not whole — but alive.

The infirmary was largely empty now. Men had healed or died. The room stank of boiled herbs, blood-pads, and sweat. Not the blood of war. The blood that seeps slow and stubborn from deep places, days after the battle is over. The blood that smells like rot, not glory.

He lay on a cot too small for his frame, half-propped by wadded cloth, bare-chested, ribs bandaged thick. One arm lay slack, the other draped lazily across his stomach. His hair was matted, blood-caked, but his eyes were open — and watching the midwife as if she were a storm worth sailing into.

"Careful, witch," he croaked, voice rough as rope. "You feed me like that again, I might try to kiss you. Fair warning."

She didn't smile, but she didn't move away either. She was young, sun-browned, strong-handed — too clean for this place. Too clean for him.

Markov stood at the foot of the cot, arms folded, boots muddy, face unreadable.

"I thought you were dead," he said.

"I was," Urek rasped, and coughed. "Didn't like it."

"They pulled you out of a corpse pile."

Urek grinned. Or tried. One side of his face twisted up. "You mourn me proper?"

"We pissed on your spear," Markov said. "Said a prayer. Yarik cried."

I didn't bother to answer.

Urek looked at me then. Really looked.

"You didn't come to cry, did you?"

"No."

"To kill me if I turned wyrd? Saint-cursed? Possessed by sea-devils?"

"If needed."

He grinned wider. A dry chuckle came — then turned into a racking cough. Blood flecked his lips. The girl moved in fast, blotting with a cloth. Urek waved her off, wheezing. "Don't fuss, girl. If I die mid-laugh, it's a good death."

"You're not dying," I said.

"No?" he said. "Damn shame. Thought I might skip the worst part — watching you lot fumble toward glory without me."

Markov snorted. "Don't worry. We'll find your relic. Get blessed. Burned alive. All the good parts."

"I was meant to get burned first," Urek muttered. "That was the whole point."

"Next time," I said.

Urek tilted his head toward the midwife. "You hear that, witch? Next time. You save me up."

She shook her head. But she stayed. Still holding the bowl.

He closed his eyes for a breath, then opened one. "Where to now?"

"Zelezovka," I said. "An old cloister. Saint Dobroslav. It's probably just stones and wind, but we'll take a look. We've got nothing else."

"I hear there's good cliffs at the edge of the world," he said, voice slurring just slightly. "Winds like hammers. Good place to die."

"Stay," I said. "Heal."

He didn't answer right away. Just stared at the beams above, where smoke-black streaked the old roofline.

Then: "You'll need someone to make you laugh when the saints turn their faces."

"We've got Markov," I said.

Urek wheezed. "That rat-faced little bastard? He's a walking dirge."

Markov gave him a theatrical bow. "My lord."

Urek tried to raise a hand to flip him off. Couldn't manage it.

I stepped forward. Laid a hand on his good shoulder.

"We'll send word," I said. "If we find anything."

He looked at me again. Not grinning now.

"Just come back."

His hand found mine. Rough grip. Weak, but there.

Then Markov leaned in.

"She's only feeding you 'cause she feels bad your spear's broken," he muttered.

Urek didn't miss a beat. "Still got one that works."

Markov grinned. "Mad bastard."

He coughed, then waved us off.

I turned.

The girl moved back into place before the door had fully closed.

Behind us, I heard a cough. Then a chuckle. Then silence.

We left at dawn.

Not with banners. Not with horn or rite. Just the creak of lines, the slap of sail, the last boot thudding hollow on the gangplank. The harbour mouth gaped wide, and *The Grey Hand* slipped through it like a knife pulled from bone.

Stormhold shrank behind us. Smoke still curled from its gatehouse, but most of the fires had died. Men with ash on their boots now hauled stone instead of bodies. A ladder stood propped against the wall where the prince's charge had breached it — already patched with raw lime and new slate. The gate hung straighter. The square had been raked. The people moved slower now, but they moved.

Old Verdan stood at the quay — his one good boot planted, the other stuffed with rags. He raised a hand as we passed. A dozen others watched beside him. Not friends. Not farewells. Just eyes that marked who left, and who stayed.

Illarion had named him steward. Lord Verdan of Stormward, God help the place. Fifteen of our warriors remained. A few locals had joined the muster — boys too hungry to say no. *The Pilgrim's Cross* stayed behind as well, half-gutted and tar-sealed along her seams. If she held, she'd make for Velgrad, bearing word and weight and whatever taxes Illarion deemed due.

The rest of us — ten sailors from the old voyage, still loyal to Soroka, or the prince, or something older — kept to their knots and orders. Twenty warriors from the fleet manned the middeck and held the rails. The rest: Markov, Soroka, Bogdan, Illarion, Radek, and I — each alone in our own corners.

Captain Soroka stood at the tiller, one hand on the brace. She set a course and asked no more questions. But she knew more than she said. I watched the set of her shoulders, the easy balance of her stance, the salt-sheen in her braid. She had the sea in her bones. There was a steadiness in her — like a ship trimmed true, wind-bitten and unshaken.

Bogdan came to the centredeck as we cleared the headland. The sun had barely breached the cliffs. He said nothing, and yet the men fell silent. He wore his mantle loose, the bone charms at his collar clicking like teeth. In one hand he held Saint Vira's icon. The other held nothing at all.

He did not shout.

"You do not speak of this," he said, eyes on no one and everyone. "Not to your wives. Not to your sons. Not to priests. Not to your gods."

A breeze caught the sail. No one moved.

"This voyage is not yours to name. The queen does not claim it. The saints do not answer for it. It will be erased from records, rites, and prayer. You were chosen because you can hold your tongues."

His eyes flashed — not white, but pale enough to catch the morning like frost.

"Or because if you cannot — the fire will take them."

One man crossed himself. Another stepped back. No one laughed.

Bogdan raised the icon. "Swear it."

They did. One by one. Hand to hilt, or chest, or heart. Even the ones who didn't believe. Even Markov, though he did it with a flourish.

"Secrecy," he muttered. "The Isles are built on it. That, and bad ale."

Bogdan turned.

Markov grinned wider. "Sworn on the saints. And if they don't count, on my last unpaid debt."

Bogdan said nothing. Just turned back and walked to the prow.

Illarion watched all of it with that wild gleam in his eye. Not madness, not yet — but something kindled. He looked west like he saw a crown in the fog.

I stood beside the rail, one hand on the worn rawhide. The sea slapped the hull like a warning. Ahead, the coast curved away — rough, sharp, broken. Winds like hammers. Waves like towers. Waters that pulled men sideways into wolves' teeth. We sailed to find a cloister no one remembered, to search for relics that might not exist. With a prince who hated me. A dark prophet who spoke to flame. A rogue who could not stay quiet.

And the sea — always the sea — waiting to kill us.

CHAPTER XLIII: THE CLOISTER OF SAINT DOBROSLAV

The Grey Hand did not dock.

There was no pier, no cove, no proper harbour to speak of. Just a dark smear of houses on a wind-bitten rise, a crooked line of shingle below, and the wet teeth of the Kladovek grinding beneath the waves.

Three days it had taken.

Not straight sailing, not clean. Soroka had worked the ship like a midwife with a breached child — slow, silent, braced for blood. She took them around the southwestern rim of Stormgrave Isle, where the cliffs dropped sheer into black water, where gulls wheeled and vanished in fog.

The Kladovek Passage had no lanes. No charts. The waters there shifted like lies — cruel wind above, hidden stone below. They called it *the cupboard* because it slammed shut when you weren't watching. Soroka wouldn't sail in fog. Not there. Twice she stopped and dropped lines to take soundings. Once she changed course without explanation. When Illarion ordered speed, she ignored him. When he ordered again, she walked away.

The ship took little damage. A sail torn along one seam. A gash near the bow that bled slow and needed pitch. The wheel ropes frayed once and had to be rethreaded by lantern. But the ship held. And they arrived.

The coast here rose hard and bare — granite ribs jutting from the sea like something once buried trying to claw back out. No soil to speak of. Just stone split by frost, slick with lichen, streaked salt-white by wind and age. The moss grew low. Tough. Threaded with grit. Some grass clung in the cracks, more grey than green. Shrubs twisted inland like they'd tried to flee and failed. A few stunted trees clung to the gullies — bent eastward, bark flayed by years of salt and hunger. Behind it all, the mountains rose — sheer and sudden, black-faced, bone-thin. No softness in the slope. No welcome. Just height. Just stone. Just the end of the world laid bare.

Nothing here was made for comfort.

Everything soft had been stripped away.

The Grey Hand dropped anchor half a mile offshore — no closer. The swell near the shoals broke sideways.

The boat rode low. Heavy-built, tar-dark, thirty-hand length — made for hauling cargo or corpses, not for grace. It could have carried more. But it strained under what it had. Nine aboard: Illarion, Markov, Bogdan, our guide, Radek, four sailors on the oars, and me. The oars groaned with every pull. The sea caught the hull at angles, slapping broadside — not playful. Testing. The kind of slap that marked a man before dragging him under. The swell pushed hard from the north. Each stroke fought it. The prow skidded once on the cross-surge and had to be corrected — slow, wide, like dragging a wheel through gravel.

The shore rose slow — not a welcome, not a warning. Just there. Sloped and grey. Barnacled. A finger of shingle curling inward like a lip pulled back in contempt.

Markov watched it in silence, one hand on the rim of the boat.

"Three days," he said at last. "For this."

Bogdan murmured something I didn't catch. His mantle was pulled close, his eyes on the shrine above the beach.

Illarion said nothing. His hands were on his knees, gauntlets off, cloak hooded. He looked forward, but I don't think he saw the land. Just the thing waiting past it.

The keel scraped stone.

Not hard. Just once. Enough to say: *no further*.

The sailors leapt down fast, boots in the shallows, backs bent to keep the boat from drifting broadside. One unhitched the mooring line. Another slung the coil toward a half-rotted post lashed with eelhide. It caught.

We stepped off.

The dock was no more than four planks bolted to bone-grey timbers, cross-braced with wrecked oars. Salt had eaten every nailhead. Something dead lay tangled beneath — fish, or seal, or worse.

The oarsmen climbed back aboard. One nodded to me — a quick gesture, no salute.

"We'll check the line morning and dusk," he said. "If there's smoke, we come. If there's none…"

"Twice a day," I said.

He nodded again. Then pushed off.

The rowboat curved wide in the surf. Oars dipped, rose, dipped again — and soon it was gone, lost behind the teeth of the shoal.

Zelezovka lay crooked against the rise. No walls. No paths. Just a few houses crouched above the surf, thick-walled, turf-roofed, patched in hide and saltstone. Nets hung from every post. Goats wandered without rope or bell. Smoke rose from one chimney — thin, white, afraid of the wind. A shrine stood near the path — driftwood lashed into a cross, dark with offerings: fishbones, broken combs, the skull of a seabird with nails driven through its eyes. The place reeked of peat-smoke, drying cod, and a weariness older than famine.

A door opened.

A child stepped out. Barefoot, ash-streaked, eyes too wide for her face. She stared. Then her mother seized her by the collar and yanked her back. The door slammed.

A moment later, another door opened and a man stepped into its threshold.

No call. No greeting.

Just a presence.

He held a hammer. Not raised. Not hidden. Just held. He watched us the way a shipwright watches a storm roll in from the wrong direction — not surprised, not afraid, just *tired of what comes next.*

Bogdan muttered a blessing. Illarion said nothing.

I felt their eyes from every crack, every shadowed lintel.

These were the true Gvazdari. Wind-bitten. Stone-rooted. Unbroken by king or coin.

Dragomir had taught me the signs: no crest over the doors, no charm hung for show, no colour in the thread. These were not Mstislav's folk. Not anyone's.

Markov, as ever, moved first.

He straightened his collar, flashed the ghost of a grin, and strode toward the man with the hammer.

"Good day," he called. "We're—"

The man didn't move.

Markov kept going.

"Just looking for—"

The hammer shifted. Not up. Just forward. A weight turned.

Markov slowed.

Illarion spoke, his voice carrying over the crash of the surf. "We are here on the queen's business," he said.

A second figure appeared beside the first. Woman. Older. Sea-marked. Her face lined like knotted rope. She said one word.

"*Outsiders.*"

That was all.

Illarion bristled. Took a step forward.

I stepped past him.

Dropped my hood. Unbuckled my cloak. Let the wind see the scars.

Then I bowed.

Not deep. Not courtly. Just a man folding at the waist, slow, even, unarmed.

"Yaroslav Krovin," I said.

No title. No status. Just the name.

"I've come to ask for your memory."

That stilled them.

The hammer lowered half an inch. The woman squinted.

"Stormgrave's ashes still blow east," she said. "What's left to ask?"

I answered the way Dragomir taught.

"Not what's left," I said. "What still stands."

She studied me.

Then turned and walked inside.

The hammer-man waited.

Then nodded. Once. No smile.

We climbed the path.

If you could call it that. There was a trail, but it lied. Zigzagged, yes — but every turn stole breath, not eased it. And the slope never gave back. It only took. Loose shale underfoot, wind in the face, cliff-edge pressing the spine. Ten feet to the drop, then five, then less. One slip meant death. Not a clean fall. A break-and-bounce down rock-knife teeth until the surf swallowed you.

The villagers had pointed the way. A rough slope west of the barley plots, past a salt-spring where no birds drank. The cloister lay beyond, they said — up through the folds of the mountain, where even goats turned back. They spoke of it like a place half-remembered. No one had climbed there in years. *Too steep. Too far. Too old.* One woman claimed a hermit still lived there — a former monk, maybe, or just a man too stubborn to come down. "Saw him once, last harvest," she said. "Or the one before. Can't be sure." That was the most anyone could say. A shadow at distance. A light seen once in fog. Maybe he was there still. Maybe not.

Radek the Lowlander moved like a goat in boots. Never touched the cliff face. Just bent his knees and kept going, muttering under breath like he knew every stone by name.

The rest of us fared worse.

Illarion had traded his plate for hardened leather — easier to move in, though he cursed it now. The mail shifted wrong on the slope. His boots slipped. His bad hand clawed for grip that wouldn't come. More than once, he spat a curse and slammed his good fist against stone.

Bogdan struggled. His breath came sharp. His staff trembled with every step. The bones in his mantle clicked together like a dying man's teeth. Still he climbed — not fast, but sure, like something other than flesh was pushing him up the mountain.

Markov made a show of the heights.

"Go on," he called to me, grinning back from a turn. "Isn't this what brave men do?"

I didn't answer.

The wound from Stormhold pulled with every step. A dragging fire behind the ankle — not sharp, but deep — the kind that made the rest of the body lean wrong to carry it. I didn't limp, not if I could help it. But the slope made me choose: pain, or pride.

My legs were steady enough. My balance sure. But I wanted to crawl. To grip the rock like a beast, not a man. The drop pulled at the edge of my vision. The sea far below had no shape — just motion, and hunger. The trail narrowed again. My fingers brushed the stone wall. I kept my eyes forward.

We didn't speak much after that.

Just climbed. Breath by breath. Boot by boot. The wind had teeth. The cliffs had no mercy. The sun moved behind us like it was afraid to watch.

Then — a landing.

Not a true one. Just a patch of grass no goat had eaten, cupped in stone like a hand holding breath.

Illarion reached it first. He stood near the edge, pulling back his hood, drawing deep lungfuls of salt and sky. Markov joined him, grinning, hands on hips, hair blown wild by the wind.

Bogdan dropped to one knee. Head down. Shoulders heaving. His fingers dug into the turf like he meant to pray, or anchor himself to the world.

I stayed back.

Tried not to look.

But I did.

The sea found my eyes anyway.

Below lay the hamlet — Zelezovka — no bigger than a child's toy now, crouched against the rock. Then the Kladovek Passage, writhing like a thing in pain. Waves rising, crashing, vanishing, rising again — no pattern, no rhythm. Just fury.

And westward, anchored at the edge of vision, The Grey Hand. Small now. Steady. Holding like a lone nail in a rotted beam.

Beyond her, the Kladovek Isles.

Like the bones of a sea-beast butchered and left to drown — jagged, black, scattered in a line that never led home. No sails. No gulls. Just stone and silence.

And past even that—

Water.

Nothing but water.

Endless, grey-blue, curling to the edge of the world. No ship. No smoke. No shore. Just that great breathless wideness that unmade thought.

I stared.

And thought of Mstislav.

They said he sailed and charted and conquered all the world. Claimed every isle that bore fire or grain. Planted banners in ice, swamp, and sand.

All but one. That far mass to the southeast — the dark continent men call the Shadow's Heart. Even Mstislav did not take it. Men tried. They built settlements, sent priests, soldiers, ploughs, and bells. They planted banners, raised timber, lit fires against the dusk. But always, it ended the same. Silence. Word stopped coming. Ships ceased returning. And when they looked, the outpost was gone. No ruin. No grave. Just barren rock and watching trees where men had once stood. As if the land had swallowed them. Some say beasts took them. Others speak of spirit-men on the shore, of voices in the mist, of flame that does not burn. In the end, it did not matter. All that mattered was this: the land rejected them. It could not be tamed. It was not a place for men.

But here — here there was no land at all. Just water.

What lies at the end of it?

Does it go on forever?

They say that at the beginning of time, the world was soft. All hills, forests, rivers, fields. And the sea came, slow and certain, and washed it away. Piece by piece. Until only what could not break remained. These spines of stone. These cliffs. These scraps.

Even now, the sea keeps coming. Wearing down. Grinding. And one day, even these last peaks will fall. The cliffs will crack. The shrines will rot. And the grey water will wash over what remains. There will be no shore then. No fire. No man left to carve his name in bark or stone. Only the sea — endless, cold, unanswering. And perhaps that is as it should be. Perhaps we were never meant to last. A mere flicker against the vastness of the sea. The sea does not hate us. It does not love us. It does not even remember. It only takes.

The trail narrowed as we climbed.

Not a road — not even a path, in truth. Just a smear of mud along the mountain's flank, scarcely wider than a boot-scrape, where feet had passed long ago and the stone had never quite forgotten. No markers. No signs. Only the bent grass of old burden, and the way Radek moved without doubt.

At times, the way hugged the edge, nothing beneath us but air and scree, the sea long since vanished behind the cloud-wracked heights. At others it pressed between gorge-walls so tight we walked single file, the cliff-face on either side slick with moss and bone-pale lichen. The light vanished there. So did the wind. It felt like the mountain had shut its jaws and drawn breath through its teeth.

We trudged through a world of water and stone — the slap of boots in muck, the suck of mud at the heel, the trickle of unseen streams somewhere beneath us. No birds. No sky. Just the hush of old things not yet rotted.

In one gorge, the silence changed. Not stillness — not rest — but a deeper quiet, as if something had once screamed here and the echo still curled in the stone. I slowed, without meaning to. Radek did not. He walked as though he belonged to it.

The track we followed had not been built, only worn. Bent under sacks of grain. Trodden by men who counted solitude as prayer.

Saint Dobroslav. The patron saint of survival — of farmers, planters, and those who endure the lean years with back bent but spirit unbroken. His rites are plain. No bells. No relics gilded in silver. Only earth turned with care, seed cast with hope, and food shared before self.

They say he was a poor farmer, plowing his fields above Stormhold. But stubborn in his hope. When the last barley sacks were gone and the village's children cried in their sleep, he took the final grain meant for bread and walked into the frozen soil. *"Better the seed die than we,"* he said. And he planted. His field alone took root. The stalks rose pale and strong, enough to keep the children breathing and the old ones upright. Enough that the village buried no more of its own that spring. The next year, the raiders came. Smoke from the south. Black sails. Hungry blades. Dobroslav stood for his field — no spear in hand, just the hoe he'd used to turn the earth. They cut him down in the furrow. His blood mixed with the soil that had fed them.

The Gvazdari took him for their own. They made no icons, only marked their ploughs with a carved hand scattering grain. They kept soil from his field in oiled pouches. Each spring, before planting, they scattered the first seed in his name and whispered the words he had said. Not as prayer, but promise.

The monks who came after bore his name. They built no grand cloister, only a keep of stone where they could farm the high slopes, sowing barley in hard ground. Their walls were not for defence, but silence. Their wealth was not coin, but yield. When the rains failed or the ground froze, pilgrims climbed to beg for hardy seed — and left offerings of bread, not gold.

Now, perhaps, no monks remain. But the name still carries weight. In Stormhold, they still say: *"Let the seed speak for us."*

And when the weather turns, they scatter a pinch of earth and whisper Dobroslav's name to the wind.

By dusk, the wind began to stir again. The clouds tore ragged at the edge, and a seam of cold light broke through. That's when we saw it. Not a ruin, not a chapel swallowed by moss. A keep — square-backed, stone-wrought, crouched on the far spur like a fist braced against the spine of the mountain. No banners. No gatehouse. Just shaped rock, wedged into the world like it meant to stay when the sky fell.

It looked close, hunched and waiting.

But mountains lie.

It was another hour's hard toil along cliff edges before we reached the cloister. But at last, we stood before it. It rose from the stone like a blade left behind — wedged atop a mountain spur that dropped sheer on two sides. No walls. No battlements. Just height and emptiness, and the roar of the wind carving through the gap behind.

We passed the field first. Or what had been a field. The soil was cracked, half-choked with thistle and wild grass, but grain still grew there — barley, thin-stalked and wind-bowed, and something like oats clinging low to the earth. But they grew. Perhaps that was the saint's doing. Or perhaps it was just the kind of land where things refused to die.

The cloister itself stood beyond — stone-built, three levels once, though the top had long since fallen. The ruin bore the look of fire from above. Not flame, but something brighter — a sky-bolt, perhaps, split down from the clouds in some forgotten storm. The tower's crown was jagged now, blackened at the edges, like a helm cracked open mid-blow. Wind keened through the hollow windows, and the slope below was littered with slabs of fallen stone, scattered like teeth from a broken jaw.

The sky was breaking toward evening. Light slanted low across the rock. It cast long shadows between the broken outbuildings — stark, sharp-edged things that looked more like scars than signs of life.

We searched the smaller structures first. Cells, maybe. Stone huts, black with soot, open to the wind. No doors. No signs of use. Rooms for prayer, or punishment. Maybe both. Maybe just places to die alone. I stepped into one — crouched, silent — and stepped out again. There was nothing left inside but cold.

Then we came to the keep. The main door leaned inward on one hinge, half-rotted and grey with time. Birchwood bound in iron, warped by wind. It groaned when we pulled it open, one long, splintered sound. The slab tilted sideways as it gave, like it was nodding — to us, or to the sea behind us, or to something else entirely.

We stepped into darkness.

The first floor opened wide — one large hall, roof-beams exposed, a hearth long cold, broken tables sagging in the dust. A scullery to the right, dark and choked with cobweb. A storeroom to the left. But it wasn't the rooms that stopped us.

It was the walls.

Every surface — stone, doorframe, lintel — was carved. Not just marked. *Covered.* Tight spirals. Wide sweeping lines. Etchings done deep and shallow, in places smooth and jagged. Not decoration. Something meant. A map, maybe. A record. Names.

"This is wrong," Markov muttered. "Looks like a fever dream."

"They're not random," Bogdan said. "Look at the spacing. The balance."

Then we heard it.

Scrape.

A pause.

Then again — *scrape* — slow and sure.

It came from above.

Markov's dagger appeared in his hand. Illarion reached for his sword. Radek the Lowlander had already taken two paces behind us and started muttering about old monks and curses best left sleeping.

But I stood still.

The sound didn't stop.

It was calm. Not frantic. Just steady. The rhythm of something who had never been interrupted — or had stopped caring if he was.

I took the stairs slow — stone steps, worn crooked by weather and time. The wind had clawed them smooth. They curled to the right, and the sound grew louder with each turn. I moved forward, slow. No steel drawn. No shield. No armour to protect me. The sweat along my ribs was cold now, clinging beneath the cloth.

Then came light. Weak, flickering. A brazier, burning low in the centre of the second floor.

The carvings thickened. Every wall bore them — no longer ornament, but intent. Meaning pressed into stone. Even the stairwell held tight-packed lines, scratched deep by hand or blade. Names, maybe. Deeds. Warnings. I couldn't read them

— not truly. Dragomir had tried, once, to teach me letters, but they never stayed. My eyes kept shape better than script.

Illarion came up behind me, squinting at the walls.

"Not one tongue," he said. "Layered. Old dialects. Some before the union. Some older still."

I stepped forward. Let my gaze drift.

Then I saw it.

Carved low on the far wall — half-hidden beneath a curling spiral — was a figure etched in stone. A rough shape of limbs lashed with wire. No face. No eyes. Just black grooves where fire had burned deepest. I knew that shape. I had seen it lashed to hull-beams, stuffed behind oil casks. I'd seen it scratched in pitch on driftwood and sunk beneath stones. Sailors didn't speak the name. They just spat and crossed themselves, and prayed it didn't follow them home.

The Burned One.

He was no saint. But he came in dreams before shipwreck. Before famine. His effigy was made from ash-timber and rusted hooks, lashed with wire, hidden deep. The priests called it heresy. But every man at sea knew better than to laugh at what the tide remembered.

And here — carved in the cloister's wall — he remained. Not hidden. Not buried. Marked.

The grooves were blackened, as if the flint had sparked when it struck.

I thought to turn back then.

But the stair turned. The light grew. The sound of the scraping flint echoed slow and steady from above.

At the end of the hall, a doorway stood open.

Light poured out — not warm. Just enough to show movement.

And there he was.

A figure crouched at the far wall. Sleeveless robes. Flint in hand. He moved with precision — not quick, not slow. Every stroke was measured. He blew the dust. Scratched again. He didn't look up.

I wanted to speak. To announce ourselves. But the air had gone thick. The chamber felt like something claimed — not cursed, not sacred — but *held*. As if we'd stepped into a space where speech didn't belong. My tongue caught against the roof of my mouth.

Then he spoke.

"Why have you come?"

His voice was clear. Not old. Not cracked. Just steady — the kind of voice that once gave orders, and no longer needed to raise itself to be heard.

A simple question.

But somehow, I had no answer.

My mouth stayed shut.

Illarion stepped forward.

The man turned.

His eyes were pale — clear as winter water. Skin scorched and wind-scoured, with that hard Brackfolk cast: high cheeks, strong jaw, a nose flattened by time or war. His hair was coarse and black, streaked with grey, tied back in a single cord. He didn't posture. He didn't pose. His expression held no welcome. No fear either.

A soldier, once. Or a healer. One who knew which roots saved, and which bled the poison faster. Someone who had stood in fire and chosen silence — not to retreat, but to remember, because no one else would.

The brazier's flame bent in the wind. Shadows shifted. For a moment, the carvings on the wall behind him seemed to move — not in form, but in meaning. As if they waited to be read by someone worthy.

Illarion stepped forward. "I am Prince Illarion—"

"I know who you are," the man said.

His voice didn't rise. But it cut through the stone like a chisel.

Illarion stopped. Not because he was struck — but because something in the man's tone refused motion. A wall, not of power, but of certainty. The kind a man doesn't fake.

"How—?" the prince began, but the rest of the question never took shape. His weight shifted, uncertain. I saw his jaw tighten, his stance falter half a step.

The man didn't move. He just looked at each of us in turn, not to challenge, not to flatter — just to see. Like a carpenter checking the grain. Like he already knew what we were made of.

"Your bodies show me," he said. "Each of you."

Then, still calm: "I ask again. Why have you come?"

"We are charged with a holy quest—" Bogdan began.

The man lifted one hand. Not high. Just palm out — a simple stop.

That was all.

But the effect was instant.

Illarion's breath caught mid-sentence. Bogdan's voice died like a taper in wind.

The silence that followed felt sealed — as if someone had shut the air inside the room without ever touching the door.

Bogdan cried out — a choked, cracking sound, half curse, half plea. His eyes wide, the whites rimmed in red.

"Saints shield us — the Devil is here!"

He raised his staff between them — not to strike, but to ward. A holy line in the air, trembling in both hands. His mantle flared as he stepped back. His voice broke into a litany — no order, no form, just names and fragments, torn loose by fear:

"Vira, Stepan, Kosma, by the blood, by the key — strike him — strike him —"

The words tangled in his throat. Spit flew from his lips. His knuckles whitened on the stave. He made the sign of the cross, then again, backward. The third time it failed.

Then the man moved.

Not with force. Not with wrath. Just sure — like the moment had already passed, and he was only walking through its shadow. Not like a soldier. Not like a priest. Not like anything I'd seen. He crossed the space in three steps. Before Bogdan's words formed shape, the staff was gone. Twisted from his hand, flung backward in a short arc.

He caught it mid-air.

Stepped behind Bogdan.

Planted the butt against his spine — not to strike, not to break. Just *to place*. A pressure that froze the breath in Bogdan's lungs.

Illarion roared.

Blades drawn, boots pounding — he lunged, twin swords flashing.

The staff lifted.

Turned.

And the end of it caught Illarion clean beneath the jaw — a sharp upward snap that stole all momentum. The prince dropped hard. Flat. His mouth open but empty. His blades clattered to the stone.

Markov reappeared like a shadow. He must have vanished a breath earlier. Now he lunged from the rear, knife low and rising fast.

But the man was no longer where he had been. He stepped aside like smoke. The staff gone from his hands. It clattered aside. He grabbed Markov's wrist as it passed. Then he turned — smooth, unhurried — and struck once with the heel of his hand. The sound was flat. Dull.

Markov dropped to his knees, clutching his throat, eyes wide with pain but not terror. The throat wasn't crushed. Only silenced. And because the man had chosen it be so.

I still hadn't drawn. There hadn't been time. It was like time slowed while the man moved.

I felt the stillness in my limbs. The sweat cold on my back.

I'd heard of men like him — long ago, in Mstislav's hall. The Brackfolk spoke of them in half-belief: warrior monks who trained their bodies past the limits of flesh, who fought without armour, without fear, without wasted motion. No charms. No flame. Just breath and bone honed sharp as any blade.

Not just warriors. Keepers.

Men who moved before the eye could follow. Who could silence an enemy with a touch, or turn a killing blow turned aside with the edge of a hand. I'd heard of it. Never seen it done.

Not until now.

In less than a breath, the hermit had dismantled three armed men.

Bogdan still stood, but shaking — his eyes wide, rimmed in white, his breath uneven. Markov knelt on the stone floor, gasping, fingers pressed to his throat. Illarion lay sprawled near the wall, blades fallen, blood at the corner of his mouth.

Now the man stood before me. Still. Not crouched. Not braced. Just still — and yet I felt it: the tension of something coiled. Like a bow drawn to the limit. Like a snake before the strike.

If I reached for my sword, I'd be next.

I lowered my hands. Took a slow breath. Tried to quiet the pulse behind my eyes.

"Peace," I said. It was the only word that came.

He watched me.

And then, for the third time, he asked — not louder, not softer, just again:

"Why have you come?"

I felt it then.

The question was not an act. It was a measure. A weighing. It wasn't meant to be answered quickly. Or falsely. So I answered what was true.

"Because I swore an oath."

He didn't move.

But his head tilted, just slightly. Not in disbelief — in thought.

"There is truth in that," he said at last. "But not all."

I swallowed.

"Because I love the king," I said. "Even now." The words were hard, but I said them anyway.

He bowed — not low, not formal, but just enough to mean: *heard.*

He stood unmoving, as though the violence had drained no breath from him at all. Not triumph, not pity. Just still. Then he looked to Illarion. No words, no gesture. Only the weight of regard — assessing for wounds, for breath, for will. Then to Markov, who crouched low by the hearthstone, pressing his knuckles to the floor.

The man's voice came soft, like wind through reeds.

"Slow breaths."

Markov obeyed.

I stepped forward. The ache in my side pulsed with every shift, but I held my posture. No shame in pain. Only in false pride.

"We seek the Order of Saint Dobroslav," I said. "In hope of a sign. Or guidance. Are you its last monk?"

He did not answer at once. He turned instead and fetched the iron-bellied brazier from the antechamber. Coals glowed red within it, flame curling low and steady. He bore it with bare hands and set it between us. Then he sat, cross-legged on the stone. Firelight played over the grey folds of his robe, over the lines of his face. There was no expression there. Only presence.

"Come," he said. "Sit."

I did. My limbs obeyed like old dogs — slow, loyal, heavy. It was not the climb that had worn me. Not the wind. The weight had come long before. And it came with me still.

Bogdan scuffled back. He bent to Illarion's side, whispered a prayer that caught in his throat like grit. He touched the floor, then prince's brow, marked him with a thumb of dust. Illarion roused, groaning. No fury in him now. Just pain, and the hollow grace of a man who knows he has been bested.

Markov eased closer, wary as a fox watching fire.

The man didn't speak. Neither did I. The silence felt earned.

When the hush grew too deep, Markov cleared his throat.

"This is Yaroslav. That's the prince, Illarion. Bogdan's our fire-keeper. I'm Markov. And the one behind the door's Radek — guide, mostly."

The man gave no greeting.

"I have no name," he said, at last. "If I had one, it was washed away."

"How did you fight like that?" Markov rubbed the side of his throat where a single blow had laid him flat. "You move like smoke." He winced. "If smoke kicked like a mule."

The man smiled. Not kindly, but cleanly.

"Practice. Patience. Endurance."

"But the Order of Dobroslav — I thought they were sworn to peace?"

"To turn a blade back on itself is not the same as drawing it."

I studied him. His limbs were lean, knotted with old strength. No ornament on his body. No steel. But his presence filled the room like cold wind through a broken roof.

"What happened to this place?" I asked.

He looked past me, toward the fire, or the wall, or a memory.

"Withered," he said. "Like all things. It endures. Until it will not."

Bogdan stayed by the far wall, lips tight. He would not sit.

But Illarion, to his credit, rose. Unsteady, jaw tight, he moved to the circle and paused. The man met his gaze and raised one palm — open, inviting.

Illarion lowered himself to the stone. No posturing now. No complaint. Only the slow, hard breath of a prince learning respect.

"Did the monks here teach you that style?" he asked.

"No," said the man. "I learned long before I heard the call. In the cold wastes of Mirefast, among the burrows. I maintain the form, as best I can. It hones the mind."

"I'd learn it," Markov said.

"You are fleet," the man replied. "But these forms take decades. They are learned as a child, when the body listens without question. Your body has already learned too much."

Markov sat back, disappointed. But not insulted.

Illarion leaned forward. His voice was lower now, almost gentle.

"Your Order is dead. Why stay? Come with us. I am prince of Velgrad. Of the Kingdom of the Broken Isles. Of all the world. I could see you live with honour — with students, and respect. You could train warriors in your hand-style. And when your time came, the whole kingdom would know your name."

The man did not laugh.

"No," he said. "That is not my path. Saint Dobroslav called to me. I have my task. I write what I know. I write it here, and I will die here. My work ends when my hand no longer rises. When the silence comes."

"You wrote all this?" I asked, glancing to the walls.

"Not all. Some before me. But I mark what I can."

Markov shook his head. "Why write, if no one will read it?"

The man's eyes reflected the flame. But his voice came steady.

"Life is not about being seen. Saint Dobroslav was not crowned. Not martyred. Not gifted with tongues of fire. He broke no kings, raised no cities. He took a wooden hoe and walked into frozen ground. That is all."

He reached into the brazier with one hand, turned a coal, unflinching.

"The world says: *gather, eat, and live*. But that is not the truth of things. The truth is toil. To endure. Saint Dobroslav gave no promise but this: *That to endure is to mean something*. Not to build. Not to be remembered. Just to plant a grain in the frozen earth and see it for what it is — a speck where life vies against the endless dark."

He looked at each of us in turn.

"That is the moment of truth."

Markov exhaled through his nose. "I'd rather not build my life on frozen dirt and misery."

Illarion's gaze sharpened. "A man alone dies forgotten. That's no life at all."

But the words stayed with me. They rang true.

"What happened to the others?" I asked. "The rest of the Order."

"There were never many. A dozen, at most. From all corners. We came because we heard the call. We lived. We planted. Pilgrims came sometimes. Those who endured the climb had often found their truth already. If not — we helped them."

He shifted his weight slightly, a slow, careful motion.

"But fewer come. Fewer remember. When I arrived, there were three left. One blind. One dying. One silent. I listened. I learned."

He glanced again at the walls. At the lines etched by hand and flint.

"Saint Dobroslav's name still reaches beyond these cliffs. But not this place. Not the brothers who sowed and served here. Their silence runs deeper. I was the last to answer. And after those brothers stilled, I came to understand that I would be the last."

He did not bow his head. He did not weep.

"I stayed. I wrote what they taught me. And my own part, when I earned it. I do not take it to the world. I leave it here. In stone. And perhaps — perhaps — it will feed some soul who comes after."

The brazier hissed as a wind moaned through the vent-shafts.

"But it does not matter. What matters is that I endure. And that I mark the memory."

He paused. Then spoke again, quieter.

"And when I am gone, there will be only silence."

I nodded once.

No oath crossed his lips, but I knew the shape of it. It would hold.

We spoke at last of the king — of his sickness, and the slow unravelling of mind and body. A kingdom held together by oaths and fear — fraying. The relic we sought, and the prophecy that had sent us west.

Darkness fell while we spoke. Cold crept up through the stone. Wind pressed hard against the cliff face, wormed through the shutterless vents, and made the old stones hum. Far below, the sea roiled against the rocks with a heavy, hungry sound. As if it listened too.

The man did not move. But something in the room had shifted. The silence deepened — not empty, but full. A pause at the edge of some unknown truth.

Even Bogdan drew near the brazier now. He kept his hand wrapped around his icon, but his shoulders no longer held their scorn. Just a tightness. A watching.

Radek fetched wood. It was wet and mossed, but the man showed him how to set it — bark peeled, ash raked, coals nested. Soon the fire licked higher. Its warmth reached only a few feet, but we sat within it like animals at the last hearth on earth.

We shared what food we had. Salt bread, hard cheese, bits of dried eel. Markov offered sausage he claimed was smoked hare, but Radek smelled it and said rat. We ate it anyway.

The man without a name brought out a flask of rainwater, caught from a copper chute and kept in a hollowed gourd. It tasted of iron and sky.

He asked questions.

Not idle ones. Not out of curiosity. Each question was slow, deliberate, as though setting a stone in mortar. He had lived so long in solitude that the world had slipped past him like a storm tide. He had not heard of Mstislav. Did not know the Mirefast had fallen, or that the Hornlands had broken into three warring sons. But he listened. Not with shock or sorrow — with the stillness of one adding weight to memory.

He did not speak of prophecy. When Bogdan spoke of the Fire-Saint, of judgement wrapped in flame, he gave no censure. He only said, "Some things are best left sundered."

He said no more than that.

But he did not say he would not help.

Illarion pressed. His voice was calm, but determined.

"Is there anything in your memory about Saint Ilyin?" he asked. "Anything that might point the way?"

The monk was quiet. His gaze drifted to the wall — not to any mark in particular, just to the stone.

"No saint of that name," he said at last. "None I have recorded. But there is a mark that I have studied. You'll find it on the stairwell. Carved before my time, but I know the history."

Illarion's eyes turned sharp. "Tell me."

The man's voice was soft. But it pulled the air tight.

"They called him the Burned One. Not a saint. Not a martyr. Only ruin."

He leaned forward slightly. His hands hovered over the fire.

"Histories tell of a time before the breaking of the Kladovek. When it was one land, rich and abundant. But then he came. They say he came from the sea in fire. That a ship arrived from the west, from the endless expanse o f the sea. A ship from the west — black-sailed, fire-scored, empty of oarsmen. Only him. Skin seared black, eyes red as coals. His jaw hung slack, as if the fire had cracked it open."

Radek made a sign with his fingers.

"Some records say he was a prophet. Others, a horror. A king of cinders. He spoke no words, but walked ashore and left scorched prints in the peat. The fields withered where he passed. Sheep miscarried. Children bled from the nose. Storms came and tore apart the land."

The wind shrieked at the shutters.

"Where he knelt, the earth turned black and broke. Men came to drive him off, and burned instead. One by one. Even their bones would not sink. They say they still wash up at the foot of the cliffs, white as driftwood."

No one spoke. Even Bogdan had grown pale.

Markov swallowed. "And people worship this?"

"Not openly. Not in the towns. But there are those who worship power, even when it is destructive. In the out-isles, they whisper of him as a judge. In the Holt, as a warning. But in the Kladovek—" he paused, and his voice thinned, "—there are those who call him a god."

He turned the coal in the brazier. It hissed.

Markov rubbed his jaw. "I'd guess the Church wouldn't be thrilled with that."

"It is heresy," Bogdan muttered. "Fire given without penance. No saint would sanction such things."

The monk did not disagree.

"Few dare speak of them," he said. "But the name is still known in dark corners. The Ash-Faith. Or the Order of the Burned One."

Illarion leaned forward. His face had lost all jest. "Where are they?"

The monk raised one arm — bony, slow — and pointed past the door. Past the cliff. Beyond even the wind.

"Out there. Where the sea splits, and the fog drinks light. In the westmost Kladovek. The place men call hollow."

He dropped his hand.

"But no ship will dock. It is cursed. And nothing lives there."

CHAPTER XLV: A KNIFE'S EDGE

We arrived at the last known settlement of men.

Tikhoyar.

We had slept that last night in the cloister's dark — no fire, just the brazier's coals and the carvings like ghosts pressed into stone. In the silence, even dreams felt watched. At dawn, we bid our host goodbye and descended the way we'd climbed — boots skidding on shale, wind hard in the teeth, each turn a test.

We lit the signal fire. The rowboat came. We boarded and turned west.

Now — this.

The land was sheer rock clawed out of the sea. The broken island chain they called the Kladovek. Beyond it — nothing. Just the line where sea met cloud and memory failed.

And yet three driftwood hovels clung to the cliffside edge like birds nesting in the crags. Smoke curled once. Then stopped.

We climbed slow.

These were not fishermen. Nor farmers. Nor even exiles in the way that word was usually meant.

These were wild men.

Folk whose blood still answered the wind. Dressed in sealhide and carved bone, half-covered in talons and feathers, their skin seamed with old frostbite and knife-bites both. Perhaps ten in all, men women and children. More a pack than a band. They stood before us on a narrow ledge of stone. The sea was at our backs, and no room to draw breath.

A flock of grey-beaked birds circled overhead — not scavengers. Trained. One let out a shriek. One of the women answered with a hiss through her teeth.

I stepped forward. Dropped my hood. Opened both palms in peace.

I bowed — as I had at Zelezovka.

The answer came in a sound between bark and howl.

Then a spit — wet and full — struck the stones at my feet.

I stepped back.

"They do not appear," I said, "to speak the common tongue."

Illarion turned. "Radek?"

Radek scratched behind his ear. "These are the Krutniki. I've heard of them. But not well. They're not like other men."

"Can you speak to them?"

"I do speak some Gvazdari. But this dialect's broken from even that. Crooked like old bone. And speech alone won't do."

"What then?"

Radek sighed. "They'll want gifts. It's customary."

"What kind of gifts?"

"As I said…" he gestured, resigned. "I don't know. But I'll ask. If you'd like."

"Do it," said Illarion.

Radek stepped forward — not too close — and called out in their broken tongue. Words shaped like wind on stone. The men laughed. Sharp, overlapping. One waved a knife lazily. Another mimed a fall from the cliff.

Radek returned.

"They said three things," he said. "First: a gift of food. Second: a gift that glints or sparkles. Third — victory with knives. Their knives. They won't speak to a man they don't respect."

"Victory," I said. "What does that mean?"

"I think…" Radek hesitated. "I think it's first blood. A cut. On the far arm. Might have been face."

"Might have been?" Markov asked.

"I think it matters," I said. "Let's get clarity."

"I would rather *not* get clarity," Markov muttered. "Or involved."

"You're doing it," Illarion said.

Markov folded his arms. "I'm a coward. We all know it."

"No," I said. "You're a knife. A thin one. You cut. You dodge. This is you."

"In the face!" Markov said.

"Hopefully not," I offered.

"Radek?" Illarion asked.

Radek called again. More laughter. One man pointed at his own face. Another pointed at his arm.

"Arm," Radek said. "Definitely arm."

"He pointed at his face!" Markov said.

I said, "Tell them yes."

"No," said Markov. "No, I draw the line at mysterious knife fights with bird-whistling cliff-witches."

"You'll do it," Illarion said. "You're the best of us."

Markov looked at me. "Yarik…"

"It's a cut," I said. "Not death. Don't get cut. That's what you do best."

Radek handed over the food — smoked eel and saltbread. Illarion added a pendant from his belt — silver, sun-stamped, polished clean. The men inspected both. One held the silver to the sun and made a noise like approval.

They grinned. Then they shouted. Birds cawed. Men clapped. A rope was uncoiled and thrown.

One of the wild men stepped forward, unfastened his hide tunic, and stripped to the waist. Scarred, lean, pale. He wore only a ragged loincloth and a smile without teeth.

"Really?" said Markov.

He stripped off his own cloak, then his shirt, revealing the thin wiry frame beneath — quick, shadow-built. He rolled his shoulders.

The knife was tossed to him.

Markov caught it.

The wild men shouted something again — not to him, but to each other.

The rope was brought forward.

"No," said Markov flatly. "No, no, no. What's that?"

Radek squinted. "Uh. Arms. Tied together. You share the same rope. Left to left."

"Tied," Markov said.

"Tied," Radek confirmed. "I think it's about closeness. No retreat."

"It's a spiritual test," Bogdan muttered. "A ritual. For bonding."

"Yes," Radek said. "I think he said bonded wolves. Or blood wolves. One or the other."

Rough hemp, coarse as bark, knotted at their wrists and looped three times around their forearms. Left hand to left hand. Close enough to feel the other's breath. Close enough that a stumble could break teeth. The knot pulsed with every twitch — too tight to forget, too loose to trust. The rope forced closeness. Each dodge became a stumble. Each strike dragged the other.

The Krutnik smiled — a wide, toothless grin split by old scars. Shirtless, barefoot, lean as a whip. His knife flashed once in the light, short and chipped, more tool than weapon.

Markov held his lower. Afraid. But mind quick and calculating.

The crowd shifted— the other Krutniki crouching low on stones and driftwood, murmuring in their animal tongue. The birds above circled tighter, cawing as if they too understood the rite. One called out. A man answered with a hiss and a sharp click of the tongue.

Then — motion.

The Krutnik lunged.

The rope snapped taut between them, jerking Markov half a step forward. He pivoted, just barely keeping his feet. The man's knife came high — too high — and Markov ducked beneath it, his own blade slashing low toward the gut. The rope caught again, this time yanking the angle wrong. His blade glanced off skin and caught only air.

They spun.

The Krutnik pulled back hard, and the rope twisted between them like a gutstring pulled tight. Their arms locked for half a breath — both men off balance, bound at the wrist like fighters in some chained-dog rite. Sand and gravel ground beneath their heels.

Markov shifted left — the rope pulled.

He shifted right — too slow.

A flash — and the Krutnik's knife licked along Markov's hip. A shallow cut. Clean. But bright.

Markov hissed through his teeth.

The man laughed. High and hoarse. He snapped his teeth at the air like a dog denied meat. Blood from Markov's side dripped warm into the dust.

The crowd howled in approval.

Markov stepped back, then forward. The rope jerked again — a tug-of-war at the edge of flesh. Every breath narrowed. Every twitch mattered.

He let the Krutnik come. The man surged — arm high, knife cocked, eyes wide with the joy of the cut. Markov twisted left, ducked low — and at the last second, jerked the rope hard with his bound arm. The Krutnik's momentum carried him forward — overbalanced — and Markov pivoted, stepped behind the swing, and slammed his shoulder into the man's ribs.

They staggered.

The Krutnik stumbled. And that was enough.

Markov's right arm snapped across the arc — blade edge up — and scored a clean red line across the far shoulder. Just beneath the collarbone. A cut meant not to kill, but to mark. Deep enough to matter. Shallow enough to end it.

Blood welled.

Not a torrent. But honest. Proof.

The Krutnik froze.

Then exhaled. Laughed again — softer now. He dropped his knife. Opened his arms.

The rope was cut.

Markov stepped back, panting. His chest rose and fell, slick with sweat, skin marked by rope-burn and grit. The Krutnik grinned wider, then leaned forward and touched his own shoulder, then Markov's cheek, light as a child would.

The wild man raised both arms and shouted.

Radek translated.

"I think he said, 'Tooth and breath.'"

And just like that, the door opened.

One of the elders — hunched, bone charms knotted in her hair — spoke a word.

Radek murmured: "Scar-mate. Accepted."

Markov gave no bow, only stepped back and dropped the blade. It clattered once on stone and stayed there. That was enough.

Radek stepped forward. His accent thickened as he attempted to speak their tongue. He appeared to move like a man on rotten ice — careful, uncertain where the cracks might open.

"They ask what we seek," he said, glancing to me.

"Tell them we seek the Burned One's shrine," I said. "Do they know it?"

I heard the change in his tone — softer, more breath than voice. As if even naming it might stir some buried awake.

When the words passed his lips, the wild folk stilled.

The elder stepped close. Her eyes were river-stone grey — the kind worn smooth from watching water too long. She looked not at me, but through.

Radek whispered, "She says... it is cursed ground. That no man who steps there comes back whole."

I nodded. "We will not come back whole."

Radek hesitated, then gave them that line. It landed like a flint dropped into snow — no flame, but not lost.

The wild folk murmured again. A few laughed — dry, uneasy. One called the birds circling above. It came and landed on her wrist.

Then the man Markov had bested rose to his feet. He flexed his wrist, wiped blood from his shoulder, and said something sharp.

Radek blinked. "He says... the knife draws truth. He will guide."

I looked to him — this wiry, half-bent man with storm scars on his chest and a lip split long ago. He did not smile. Just nodded once, the kind of nod a man gives when the sea has taken the rest.

I returned it.

Then I said, "Tell him this. He need not like us. Only lead true."

Radek gave the words. The man touched his shoulder — the wound Markov gave him — then touched the ground.

That was the oath. No words. Just blood, earth, and breath.

There was no path. Just cuts in the stone where old water had run, and seams of gravel where a man might slide if his foot went wrong. My boots found holds out of habit, not trust. Every ledge gave a little. Every grip cut a little skin.

The sea fell away behind us. The mist did not.

Illarion cursed low when he slipped — once, twice — then said nothing more. Radek kept close behind me, breathing through his teeth. I could hear his knees crack on the steeper scrambles. No complaint. Just breath and climb.

Half an hour in, the wind came over the stone and found us. Cold. Knifing. It carried no birdsong, no scent of brine — only something dry, burnt, and bitter. Old fire sealed in the cracks.

The wild man never looked back. He climbed with a rope coiled over one shoulder, moving not as one who followed a path, but as one the stone itself remembered. Once he paused and crouched low by a cairn I hadn't seen. Just three stones stacked, smoke-marked, half-melted on one side. He touched them and said nothing. We waited, then continued.

The islet crested toward a ridge — not high, but sharp. The stone there was different: veined with red, split like it had once boiled from within. My fingers came away black. Not soot. Not dirt. Something older. Something that didn't wash.

By the time we reached the last rise, my side ached. The ankle tugged. I put my hand there once, then let it go. No sense in coddling a pain that never left.

At the top, the wild man stopped. He did not speak. Just pointed — three fingers, palm down, like casting a spell. And there, just off the far edge of the islet — a splinter of black rock rising from the chop — stood what remained of the shrine.

It was no shelter. No church. Just old stone, set in a ring once, now mostly fallen. Slab uprights like broken teeth. A few capstones still clung where wind had not yet taken them. The others lay half-submerged, blackened, sea-scoured, white with salt. But even broken, the shape remained.

A circle meant to bind. A circle meant to keep something in — or out.

The ground between us and it dropped sheer. Thirty feet of rough crag before it met the tide. But the land told a truer story than the sea.

I saw it at once.

The islet where we stood — and the shrine beyond — had once been one. The line was too clean. The rock split sharp as glass, black at the seam, not by weather or time but by something hotter. As if a blade of fire had come down from the sky and carved it free.

Like a sword. God's own, or something worse.

The wild man stood silent beside me. His face unreadable, but his hands curled tight at his sides.

Markov edged forward. "So… how do we get to it? Swim?"

He was trying to sound light. But I heard the hitch beneath it.

Then I saw the path.

There — below us, just past a jutting lip of stone — a line of quarried blocks. Laid flat. Old. Dark. Barely visible beneath the rush and retreat of the tide. A causeway, half-swallowed by the sea.

Each wave covered it, then fled. Revealed. Concealed. Like breath over a wound.

It led straight to the shrine. No rail, no rope, no promise. Just wet stone and depth on either side.

I said nothing.

Only watched the water take it again, as if the sea itself meant to hide the way.

As if it regretted letting any man find it.

The wild man said nothing. Just uncoiled the rope from his shoulder, walked to the cliff's edge, and cast it down.

It vanished fast — a hiss of hemp over stone, then silence. The wall below dropped sheer, near vertical, slick with sea-moss and spray. No footholds. No margin. Only the ledge below — narrow as a boot's breadth — where the causeway began.

He drove an iron piton into the rock. Tied it fast. Tugged twice. Then stepped back.

He did not speak but it was clear that he would go no closer.

Radek nodded and sat beside him.

We left our boots beside them and clambered over the edge.

The rope was wet from the mist and twice as heavy. It bit into my palms. The drop below wasn't long — thirty feet, maybe — but it felt like a fall into judgement. Toes searched for grip on stone slick as ice. I slid the last three feet and landed crouched on the ledge.

The others followed.

Bogdan cursed as he came over. His robes clung to him like seaweed. Markov laughed — once — then said nothing more.

Illarion lowered himself last. His feet landed on the ledge and stuck.

The causeway stretched ahead.

Four broad stones, old and quarried, linked in a straight line to the shrine island — twenty feet, no more. But each slab was half-swallowed, waves lashing over them in rhythm, never the same twice. Two iron hooks stood hammered into the stone beside us, and two more on the far side, half lost to salt and rust. Once, ropes might have run between them. Now there was nothing. No rail. No handhold. Just sea on either side — black, white-tipped, deep as judgement.

The waters didn't just move. They breathed. One wrong step and they would take you — crush you against stone, drag you down, break you on the hidden teeth of the deep.

Markov said it first. "That's impossible."

No one answered.

We'd come too far for that.

I turned to Bogdan. "Can you calm the waters?"

He didn't smile. Only knelt, bracing himself with his staff. "With the Lord's help, I will."

Then came the question no one wanted to ask.

Who would go?

"I will," said the prince.

Sharp. Certain.

Bogdan turned. "Illarion—"

"No," he snapped. "This quest should have been mine. It's my kingdom to save. Not his. And I won't watch while anyone else takes it."

Markov's voice cut between us. "Wait," he said again. "Drop the rope!"

I looked up. Radek heard. The rope was lowered.

Markov caught it. "Tie it to him. Then you. We lose him, we lose the Isles."

Illarion said nothing. Just tied the knot fast and clean. He removed and handed his sword belt to Markov. Then stepped to the ledge's edge.

The sea met him like a thrown fist.

It tossed him back, slammed him to the stone beneath us, dragged at his legs. He caught the edge and tried again — pushed forward — and again the waves hurled him off.

"It's not working," I said.

Markov's voice came again, sharper. "Your swords!"

"What?"

"Use your swords! There's a seam between each block — drive the steel into it!"

I looked. He was right.

Four stones. Three cracks between. Deep enough, maybe. If the point found true.

We hauled the prince back up.

He stood dripping, teeth bared. Snatched the sword belt. Buckled it.

I drew the Queen's Gift.

Held it out to him, hilt first.

He stared at it. His jaw clenched. Salt dripped from his brow into his eyes, but he didn't blink.

"This should never have been given to you," he said.

I met his gaze. Held it.

"Yes."

He waited. As if I might argue. As if I might defend what he could never forgive.

But I said nothing more.

Because he was right. I had never wanted the blade. Not truly. Not the weight of it, not the whispers that came with it. Not the look in men's eyes when they saw the hilt, or the memory of the hand who'd first worn it. What I wanted was Skelt. The cold wind. The sound of the tide and the peat smoke and no one needing me but the sea.

But peace was a selfish wish. And this man — for all his venom, all his drunken spite, and all the foulness that was slowly consuming him — was doing what princes must. Claiming the burden. Taking the first step into fire of his destiny.

It was hatred that drove him now — hatred of me, of the gift, of how he had been judged and found wanting his whole life. But maybe hatred was enough. If it brought him forward when fear might break him. If it carved a will where weakness used to be. If my presence, unwanted and unyielding, forced him to grow teeth — then perhaps I had done one thing right.

He took the sword.

And the tide surged.

We lowered him again.

Bogdan was already praying. Voice low. Steady. The wind caught at his robe, but his knees didn't shift.

Illarion waited. Watching the rhythm. Watching the pull. Then — in a blink — he surged forward.

The blade stabbed downward. Missed.

The sea took him, flung him back, nearly over the ledge. I hauled rope. He gasped, cursed.

Again.

This time Greyfang found the seam.

And the sea roared.

A wave higher than any before slammed the block. Foam blinded us. Salt filled my mouth. But the blade held — his hand locked to it.

Bogdan's chant rose louder.

Illarion drew his own blade with his free hand.

Waited. Judged. Drove it down.

It stuck.

The water heaved — then stilled, just for a breath.

He pressed forward.

One stone left.

The last seam.

He stabbed — disappeared.

Gone under. We shouted.

Then — he rose. Hand still on the hilt. Eyes wide. Water sheeting off him.

Bogdan stood.

Raised the staff.

Cried out a name I did not know.

The sea flinched.

The prince stood — stumbled — leapt.

The waves surged — then pulled back.

And he was there.

On the shrine island.

On his knees. On both palms. Gasping like a man born from the deep.

CHAPTER XLVI: THE BLACK ALTAR

The rope held. Just.

He tied it round the iron loop driven into the shrine-stone's far side. I tied off on the near end. The waves hissed between us, biting higher with every gust. Then I crossed — hand over hand, the soles of my bare feet slipping on the smoothed sunken stones, the wind clawing at my weight like it meant to throw me to the sea.

Bogdan did not follow. Whatever power he'd drawn on to steady Illarion's path — it had spent him. He stood hunched in his mantle, eyes hollow, lips white with salt.

Markov didn't stir from the rocks. "You know I'm not doing that madness," he called, voice thin in the wind.

Even with the rope's anchor, the sea nearly took me. The stone slicked beneath me, every foothold treacherous. The sea rose like something that remembered hunger. I could not believe the prince had made it across. Not without steel in his soul — and sorcery in his wake.

I reached Greyfang where he'd planted it in the first split. I gripped the hilt. Pulled.

It did not move.

Again. I set both feet. Strained.

Nothing. The rock had taken it. Like it meant to keep a piece of me.

Illarion was shouting something — but the wind stole it. His voice broke like foam on the breakers.

At last, I let go. Turned from the sword. Stepped down and crossed the last length.

His blades came free when I pulled them.

He took them without thanks, eyes not on me, but on the stones ahead.

"It wouldn't come," I said.

He nodded once.

"Come on."

The shrine-isle rose like a wound from the sea. No more than thirty feet wide, twice as long. A ring of weathered stones — standing, leaning, broken. And in the centre, the altar. A slab of black. Not stone I knew. Not basalt, not shale, not anything shaped by chisel. It drank the light. The red sun struck it, and did not return.

We stepped inside the ring. Around us, fog crept up from the sea's edge. A crown of white veils. Beneath our feet — nothing but cracked rock, bone-dry and salt-bleached. No moss, no weed, no bird-scratch. Just silence.

We searched. Hands over stone. Fingers scraped raw. The pillars bore no mark but sea's lashing. The wind carried no voice.

No revenant.

No flame.

No sign.

Only the prince's frustration and angry, growing ever more jagged, like broken glass.

When we had looked for half an hour, he stopped.

His hands shook, though whether it was from his sickness, rage, or grief, I could not tell.

He knelt. Leaned his head against a leaning pillar, rough with salt. For a moment I thought he was praying but then he lifted his head and screamed. A roar of pain and fury — raw, wordless, breaking. His shoulders shook. His mouth moved, but no words came — only a howling sound, too hoarse to name.

And then I heard him.

"Cursed!"

"Cursed by God!"

He sobbed once — a sound I'd never heard from him, never thought he could make.

Then he spoke again, cold now. Terribly calm.

"After all. This. An empty rock. Just like me. Cursed, lost, and a nothing."

I stood in the circle's edge, watching him break.

The wind turned colder.

The red light spread across the stones like spilled wax, seeping into every crack.

And then it came to me.

Not from the sea. Not from the wind.

From memory.

The vision Bogdan had forced on me — when I drank fire and shadow clawed at my throat. I had seen something then. I had not understood it.

Now I did.

A stone. Black. Unmarked. Square like a coffin. Half-submerged.

Water breaking. Light dying.

I turned to the altar. Reached out. I ran my hands along the top, then down the side.

There. A seam.

Just below the lip.

I called to him. For a moment, I thought he wouldn't answer. Then he came.

We braced. Pushed.

It did not move.

Again.

Stone ground on stone — the sound deep, old, full of pressure.

Again.

The lid shifted.

Once more — and the weight gave. The slab fell to the side with a shuddering thud that echoed out across the islet and into the sea.

Inside — a chest of ashwood, iron-bound, small enough to carry but heavy with more than weight. The wood was charred dark, its surface engraved with ward-signs cut deep into grain and band alike — saints' names, the spiral marks meant to hold back fire. The iron clasps were cold to the touch, but the chest itself was warm, as if heat lived within.

It burned my palms — not with fire, but with something deeper. Like a fevered curse.

We laid it on the stone.

Up on the cliff, Markov threw up his arms. Hugged Bogdan. Shouted something I could not hear.

The box hissed where it touched the ground. Steam rose.

Illarion knelt. His hands hovered over the latch. Then, slowly, reverently, he opened it.

The inside was lined with black stone. Smooth, polished, cold.

And in its centre — ash.

A thick, black bed of it, packed tight as grave-dirt, warm with something deeper than fire. It shifted faintly, as if it breathed.

Illarion hesitated. Then reached in.

His fingers moved through it slowly, searching — a prayer in the motion, or a challenge.

Then he stopped.

He brushed back the ash and lifted out a bone.

A forearm, perhaps. Burnt to cinder — yet whole.

And still burning.

The fire did not consume.

It endured.

Like judgement. Like memory. Like wrath that would not die.

CHAPTER XLVII: THE PRINCE OF FLAME

We had the relic — but the test was not done.

From the black altar we had crossed, we now had to cross again — back across the causeway, back across the slick stone and heaving sea, with the chest in our arms. And then the climb. Up the cliff where Radek and the wild man waited, wind-etched and watchful.

But the rope, our only line across, was still anchored on this side. It had to come with us. And that meant someone had to be last.

Illarion would not part from the chest. His fingers clutched the iron hasps as if they might vanish. His eyes — fevered, luminous — shone with something I did not like.

"I'll go last," he said. "You go first. I'll carry the chest to the rope. You'll pull me across."

"No," I said. "It's too heavy. Too awkward. One slip, one wrong wave, and it'll drag you off. Then it's gone — the relic, and likely you with it."

He met my gaze and held it. But he knew I had the right of it.

"Then what?" he asked.

"We carry the bones, not the box. Strap them to our person."

"The chest is needed," he said, voice taut. "It wards. It seals. The saints carved prayers into its lining. It holds the danger shut."

"Then we do it in two turns. Empty the chest, cross with it, return, fetch the bones, and seal them fast again before the ash cools."

We opened the box.

Inside — ash.

A dense black bed of it, packed tight as grave-dirt, still warm with something deeper than fire. It shifted faintly, as if breathing.

I stripped my shirt and laid it on the ground next to the altar.

The first bone lay just beneath the ash. A fragment of finger, charred to cinder but whole. When I touched it, it did not burn — but it was warm. Not with heat. With intent.

I thought of the old tales. Of Ilyin's fire not as grace, but as punishment. The hellfire that spared neither the guilty nor the innocent — only the faithful, and not even always them. As I lifted each fragment, I felt a pull. Not upward, but down — into the rock's dark belly, as if what was broken still longed for burial. I touched as little as I could. Lift. Place. Wipe the ash from my palms.

But Illarion lingered on them. His fingers curled round each piece like a hilt. Not reverent. Possessive. The way a man grips a sword he means to swing. His eyes never left the bones. He laid them out in order on the stretched shirt, careful, unblinking.

When the last shard was drawn from the ash, the arm was whole. A right hand and forearm, blackened to the marrow, each finger curled in slight repose. It looked wrong laid in the light — too complete, too deliberate, as if it had not burned but been made in fire. Illarion crouched beside it. His thumb traced the seam of wrist to elbow. No fear in him now. Only want.

I stepped back.

It looked ready to rise. To reach. To drag us under.

We sealed the box again. Latched it tight, said no word. One hand on the chest, one on the rope, we crossed. The sea had calmed with the coming dusk, but the swells still slapped high over the sunken stone. Twice I thought the weight would shift, that the chest would slip from our fingers and be lost. But we made it — salt-soaked, breathless, shivering — and passed the chest up the cliff to Bogdan and Markov above.

Then we returned.

Mstislav's sword still stood there. Driven into the stone like a spear of judgment, its hilt catching the dying light. I tried it again. So did Illarion. Neither of us could lift it. The shrine had claimed it — or the sea had. A toll paid, and not to be reclaimed.

We wrapped the bones in the shirt, tied the arms into knots, shaping a crude sack, and wound it tight with cord so not a finger could be lost. Illarion lifted the bundle and stepped to the causeway.

I watched him go.

The glow of the bones shone faint through the cloth, and the light touched his face, his arms, the black water around him — not with brightness, but with something else. It looked like fire. As if he passed not through water, but flame.

He did not flinch. Not once.

And I — I stood and watched. My gut was sick with a knowing I could not name. I thought of Mstislav, and the torc he'd worn that named him king of the Broken Isles. The madness it brought. The ruin.

And this was his son.

Illarion bore no torc of gold to mark him king. What he carried now was older, and worse.

Not empire — but bone.

Not tribute — but fire.

A fire that did not burn, because it had already burned. Because what it touched, it did not consume. It hollowed. It marked. It lingered.

He bore it like a birthright. And I saw then what he could not — that the price would not be rule, nor glory, nor even madness. Those were the wages of kingship.

This was something else.

The relic did not bind a realm. It judged it.

And Illarion had taken it into his hands as if it were meant for him. Perhaps it had been.

The saints might have turned their faces. The sea had quieted not from peace, but in warning.

What he carried now was no kingdom's weight. It was a reckoning. And it would come due.

We stood once more on the sea-worn ledge. The wind had turned — coming now from the west, sharper than before, as if the sea itself exhaled with cold intent. Dusk slid down the cliffs like water through a cracked stone bowl. The light thinned. The world narrowed.

Above, the cliff loomed — sheer, watching. Radek waited at the top, one hand shielding his brow. Beside him stood the wildman, still and dark against the sky, seal-hide wrapped round his shoulders, his eyes pale as drift-ice.

I took the rope in hand.

It was stiff with brine, clotted in spots with ash and black grit. My palms stuck slightly as I coiled it. Each loop pulled a small weight from the world and into my grasp. When I judged the length, I threw.

The rope slipped wide and fell.

Markov made no move to help. He leaned against the stone with arms crossed, one boot resting flat to the rock, the picture of ease — but I saw the tension in his throat.

He watched Illarion.

"Well," he said, loud enough to carry but not quite enough to mock. "Glory, then. And song. If the bards are in the mood for hymns about ash and rot."

Illarion did not look up.

He knelt beside the reliquary, bare hands blackened at the knuckles, sleeves damp and clinging. One by one, he returned the relics to their bed of ash. Not quickly. Not perfunctorily. With something between reverence and claim. When he lifted the final fragment — the finger, charred and curved in slight repose — he held it a breath longer than the others. He exhaled — as if the thing had found its breath inside him. Then he laid it down. Shut the lid. Fastened the iron hasp. His hands lingered a moment on the wood.

"Praise be to God," Bogdan said behind him.

His voice was low, shaped more by awe than triumph. He stepped forward and made the sign of the cross — not slow, but deliberate, as if each line cut through smoke.

"For sparing us," he said. "For not splitting the sea beneath our feet."

He turned to Illarion. Did not blink.

"But mark this, Prince. You do not carry a relic only. You carry a flame that once burned the flesh from a holy man and left only judgment behind. This is no honor. It is your burden. And you must not let it consume you."

I threw the rope again. This time it struck the edge and tangled. A shape above moved — Radek, I thought — catching it. A moment passed. Then a whistle, sharp and short. The line tugged twice in signal.

Secure.

Bogdan's voice had not softened.

"This fire was not meant for kingship," he said. "It tests the soul, not the throne. And what you bear now is not the weight of rule. It is the weight of reckoning. On you. And through you — on all of us."

Illarion rose.

He looked different in the dusk. Thinner. Edged.

"It is mine," he said.

Not defiant. Not humble. Just… claimed.

The wind stirred his cloak. The relic sat sealed at his feet.

I pulled the rope taut. Felt the knot cinch. It held.

Above us waited a cliff, and cold stone, and another climb. But below — and behind — the fire had not gone out. It had only changed hands.

We made it back to the houses of the Krutniki just as night settled in. Three huts, driftwood-bound and bone-stitched, crouched low in the wind like beasts waiting for the dark to pass. Smoke rose again from one — faint, cautious.

They came slow from their homes. Eyes hard from wind and wariness, yet what they saw gave them pause. The box was still sealed. Illarion held it cradled in both arms, as one might carry an ember in a cradle of stone. No words were exchanged at first. Only eyes.

Then the one who had fought Markov — who had led us up the shale paths, tied the rope, watched from the cliff — stepped forward and spoke. His voice had the rasp of gull-bone scraped on rock, sea-worn and broken in rhythm.

Radek, crouched beside the fire, lifted his head. His ear tilted, bird-like, toward the sound.

"They're pleased," he said slowly. "Not grateful — but… glad. Or maybe… unburdened."

I looked from face to face. No joy there. No awe. But a kind of relief so sharp it bordered on sorrow. Eyes turned from us to the sea, as if to confirm it. The birds overhead cried out, wheeling wider.

The man kept speaking — sharper now, more gesture than grammar. His hands cut shapes in the air: downward strokes, then a closed fist over the heart.

Radek reported, "He says we've taken the black fire. The heart. That their shore is clean now. The sea can breathe."

I did not answer. Could not.

Because he was right.

We had taken it. Dragged that cinder-heart from a shrine split from the land by godlight or hellfire. Lifted the box while the waves screamed around us. Unearthed and opened something that was never meant to be found. And now — it was ours.

Their eyes met mine. Not with worship. But something I understood better.

Pity.

I bowed my head.

When we explained we wished to hide it, they did not argue. One of them stepped into the smokehouse and returned with a bundle of sealhide, thick and dark, still smelling of brine and salt-rot. It was lashed with kelp-cord, cured stiff against damp and time. They gave it freely. The hide was warm where it had been held. It smelled of salt and tallow and something older — whale-oil, perhaps. The kind that stays in your hands no matter how long you wash.

I watched how they looked at each of us at we stood by the shore.

Bogdan they would not touch. Would not approach. When he stepped near, they stepped back — not in fear, but in something deeper. Recognition, perhaps. Of power unbound. Of judgment worn like a second skin.

Me, they watched the way you watch a shifting tide — warily, but without haste. A thing to navigate, not challenge. Something that might flood a valley or vanish in silence, and neither one a gift.

Illarion… they looked at with respect — and pity. As if they saw in him a man already claimed by something darker. Crowned not with glory, but ruin. A man marked. Not yet broken, but lashed to an anchor stone.

And Markov. Somehow — with no shared tongue, no clear signal — he found the right smile, the right shrug, the right joke with no edge. One of the Krutniki slapped his shoulder. Another passed him a clay bowl of fishfat stew. By the time the fire was lit, he'd become everyone's favorite cousin — the one you never trusted, but always fed.

We took our leave and rowed for *The Grey Hand*. They made no sign of farewell. No rites. No chant. Only watched. Watched as we bound the relic in the skin of the sea. Watched as we turned toward the boat that would carry us not to safety, but into deeper waters — toward a fate that would take more than it ever offered back.

In the morning, the ship lifted anchor and we began to move. She threaded through the Kladovek The sea was black beneath a low sky, thick as tar and flecked with fog. The shoals here rose like knives — some visible, others waiting just beneath the skin, grey-lipped and sharp.

Soroka stood at the tiller, one hand firm on the wood, the other wrapped round her tin. She muttered to no one. Eyes forward. Eyes that seemed made for this — cut to see through fog, sharpened for passage. *The Grey Hand* moved with her, like a thing she'd whispered into obedience.

She hadn't asked what we'd brought aboard.

But she knew.

You couldn't shift a sack of flour on her ship without her hearing it settle. Couldn't piss off the lee rail without her knowing which man, what he'd eaten, and how long it had been since his last drink.

She knew. And she let it pass.

That silence unsettled me more than questions would have.

We'd brought the chest aboard the night before, under wind and dark, when the crew were too sodden with cold and sleep to look close. It was swaddled in sealcloth. Lashed with wet rope. Lashed again. We moved it like any other crate — bonewood tools, saint-books, salted meat bound for Velgrad. Just another box.

Down we went — past the hold, the slop barrels, the spare sailcloth. Illarion had cleared space in the aftcastle — his quarter, claimed and kept. That's where we buried it. Beneath crates, burlap, bundles of dryweed. Low and hidden. The place smelled of mildew and oilskin. Still air. Still wood. But deeper than that, something else. A waiting.

It lay there now. Beneath us. Lurking in the dark.

When we turned to leave, she was already at the ladder.

Not blocking us. Not speaking.

Just sipping from her tin. Watching.

She sniffed once. Then turned away, back to the stars, back to her tiller — as if to say: *I see what you carry. I will not name it. But I will not forget it, either.*

Now, above, the ship groaned in its joints — deep, uneasy sounds that rose from the ribs and died in the rigging. I felt them underfoot as I stepped back into wind. *The Grey Hand* did not like what we'd brought.

I glanced again at Soroka.

"How long through the Passage?" I asked.

She didn't look at me.

"Depends how badly you want to live."

Illarion hadn't left the cabin since we stored the thing. The sickness clung to him. I saw it in the tremble of his hands as he drank broth. In the pale rash blooming under his left eye. In the greying scar that ran along his shoulder like a dying river. The same rot that had hollowed his father — rage in the marrow, fever in the blood. But now I wondered if it was only that, or if something else had entered him. Something worse.

My thoughts turned — not to the Queen's command, but to the other oath. The one Illarion forced from me in the Sea-Fort's belly, his hands shaking, eyes lit with fever and pride. If the rot takes me — truly takes me — you'll kill me. No warning. No chains. No robes. Just the end.

Back then, I thought it would be madness. The same unraveling that hollowed his father — not weakness, but a sickness of blood and judgment. Rage sharpened to cruelty. Memory turned poison.

Now I wasn't sure.

Now I wondered if he had made a bargain — not just with me, but with whatever fate had been watching. As if some part of him had known what was coming. That fire would find him. That it might crown him or consume him. And that one day, I might have to protect him from it. With his death.

Markov found me on the quarterdeck, gnawing a dried plum, face lit like a man who'd survived by luck and meant to brag about it. "So," he said, speaking around the fruit, "we did it. Dead saints. Mad priests. One flaming handbone. And not a single one of us eaten by a sea-devil."

He grinned. "I'm getting knighted. Or cursed. Maybe both. Hopefully paid."

"That was one relic," I said.

He blinked. "Right. One. Which means four to go. That's, what, twenty percent? A fine start."

"The worst start."

"Exactly. Law of stories. Worst one's first. The next'll be buried under a cider orchard. Guarded by bees."

He leaned beside me, shoulder brushing mine as we watched Soroka thread the rocks with one gloved hand.

"We'll get fat in Velgrad," he said. "Make plans. Maybe buy a boat."

He nudged me. "You and me — Salt-Bastards & Sons. Charters, relic-hunting, wedding speeches. Just think."

He was watching my face, too closely to be joking. I almost smiled. Almost.

A moment later, Illarion's voice came up the stairwell. No page. No ceremony. Just command.

"Yaroslav. Markov. Bogdan."

Illarion's cabin was narrow, the beams low. The walls were black with pitch. A single lantern swung from its hook, casting slow arcs of flame across the planks.

Illarion wasn't seated. He stood behind the table, both hands braced on the wood. His face was drawn, but his eyes were sharp — awake in a way that unsettled. Not with clarity, but with pressure. As if something inside him burned too fast to be hidden. The fever was still there — but shaped now, not scattered. As if the fire that once shook him had found a spine to climb.

"We're not returning to the Queen."

No one spoke.

"She cast me out. Left me to rot in shadow. That was her choice."

"And now?" I asked.

"Now I make mine," he said, and there was something too bright in the way he said it — not heat, but friction.

Markov gestured toward the chest. "We've got a box of burning bones. That seems like plenty. Why not wave it over Mstislav's throne and see if the old bastard stops rotting?"

"Because it's not enough," Bogdan said — and something in him broke, not in anger but in yearning.

And then I saw it. He didn't know. Not truly. For all his rites and riddles, for all the weight he carried like armor — he too was reaching. He needed the fire to speak. To mean something. Judgment, perhaps. Or mercy. Even ruin, so long as it was clear. Beneath the prophet's calm, he was groping in the dark like the rest of us.

"Partial fire is partial judgment," he said. "And that will burn us first."

Illarion raised a hand. The room fell silent.

"We find them," Illarion said. "All of them."

He looked to me.

"How many more?"

I didn't soften it.

"Dragomir said there were five chests. Four scattered to the ends of the earth. One unknown."

Illarion stood a moment in stillness. Then crossed to the wall. Took down a map — stained hide, corners worn soft — and unrolled it across the table.

"So where are the ends of the earth?"

Markov leaned in. "Can't get more west than this," he said. "So I'm assuming this is the end of the earth west. If the scatterers wanted to make our life easy… which may not be the case… we'd look in the East, South, and North. East — Fanghold. North — Grey Isle. South — Mirefast. That gives us a cross. Velgrad at the centre."

"And the fifth chest?" Illarion asked.

He turned to Bogdan.

"Where is it?"

Bogdan's brow creased. "I can ask again. But the fire may not answer me."

He looked at Illarion a moment longer. Then said, very quietly: "You ask for revelation. But when it comes, you already know the shape it must take."

A silence settled.

Markov tried one last time. "We go back. Just to see. Just to—"

"No."

Illarion's voice was not loud. Not heated. But final.

"We sail for Blackreef Isle," he said. "We find the next relic. Then the next. And when we hold them all…"

He placed his hand on the chest.

"I will decide what must be done."

He turned away from us then. We were clearly dismissed, and took our leave.

Markov hesitated. I took his shoulder. "Before he burns something we can't unburn," he muttered. We turned to go.

At the stairwell, Illarion spoke again.

"Bogdan. Stay."

A pause.

"We will pray," he said.

Bogdan bowed his head. But he did not close his eyes.

The sea flattened after midnight. No wind. No wave. Just drift — as if the world itself had gone still to listen.

The others slept, or pretended to. I did not.

I stood by the rail, near the prow, where the timbers curved like a blade cleaving dark from darker. My beard held the salt like frost. The boards were slick beneath my boots. Overhead, stars hung like ash caught in frozen breath. Beneath the deck, the chest lay sealed in the hold — iron-latched, ashwood-bound, wrapped in silence.

I watched the sea. I did not pray. Not aloud. Not to saints who burn and weep and hide their faces from men like me. But I stayed.

I thought of the seals carved into the lid. A sun flaring through ribs. A sword held by no hand. A flame with no source. Each mark a warning. Each mark a sentence. The box did not hum now. It waited. Like a soldier between battles. Like a wound between scarrings. Like judgment gathering breath.

A memory rose, slow and sharp.

Illarion's birth.

We had been in the Hornlands then — hacking through bramble and bone, fighting the Voryani in their red-inked warpaint, cleaving through stone-hewn fortresses and guttural prayers. Mstislav called it conquest. We called it surviving. While we bled in the east, another battle was being fought in Velgrad — Vezhena's war of the body, to bear the king a son.

When we returned, the city wore its grief like mourning cloth. The child had not sat right. The labor was long, the blood too much. The midwives were white with fear. They said the babe barely breathed, that the mother hovered near death, and the king — when word reached him on the field — was struck low by some wound no blade had dealt.

But the priests prayed. The whole country prayed. And God, they said, answered. Vezhena lived. So did the child — though twisted in limb and pale as wax. The queen would never bear again. That one bloody night had broken her. And the boy she bore lived, but not untouched. Not wholly.

I remember the baptism. The crowd packed tight as grain sacks. The air smelled of sweat and incense and old stone. Mstislav held the child aloft, high above his head, and the people cheered. They called it a blessing.

But I saw the queen's face as she watched from her bed of furs and ruin. And I saw the boy's eyes — not vacant, not afraid. Just wide. Too wide.

As he grew, so did his hunger. And his brokenness. The people who once praised him grew wary. Vezhena turned from him. He was not respectful. Not trustworthy. Not steady. And Mstislav — always busy with new wars — spoke of his son only when required. Even then, he did not linger.

That infant, born into suffering and prayer, had become this prince. Still twisted. Still broken. Still marked. And now he grasped after a power that was not of God.

What is it in men that draws them to power? They claim it is for justice, for peace, for righteousness. But it is never that. Power does not make. It only unmakes. It corrodes the hand that holds it and burns everything it touches.

What will Illarion destroy before this ends? Will it be the throne? His mother's legacy? His father's name?

And what of me, dragged in his wake? Loyal still to a king who wastes away in silence. Bound to a queen who set me on this path. And now yoked to a prince chasing ash.

Perhaps it was always this way. Like currents beneath deep water — I can steer, for a time, but never truly control. All I can do is try not to drown. Try to carry the fire without letting it consume what remains of my soul.

I would carry this. The prince. The fire. Even into judgment.

Once, I followed a king. Now, I follow fire. And I knew — it had always been fire that chose me.

Footsteps creaked behind me. Markov. He came to stand beside me, not too near. The night gave us space. He smelled of salt and apples and sleep disturbed too soon.

"Brooding?" he asked.

"Thinking."

"So brooding, then."

He leaned on the rail beside me. Looked out, not at me. "You really trust him?"

I didn't answer. The sea offered no reflection — only darkness where the stars refused to fall.

"No," I said.

Markov nodded. "Didn't think so."

"But I'll follow," I said. "Until I can't."

He turned partway. Just enough to catch me in the edge of his eye. "I never thought I'd follow a man for nothing."

"It's not nothing," I said. "It's everything."

He nodded again. Slower this time. Like it cost him. Then he went below.

I stayed. The prow creaked. The water held its breath. And somewhere in the dark, the fire waited.

APPENDIXES:

Maps

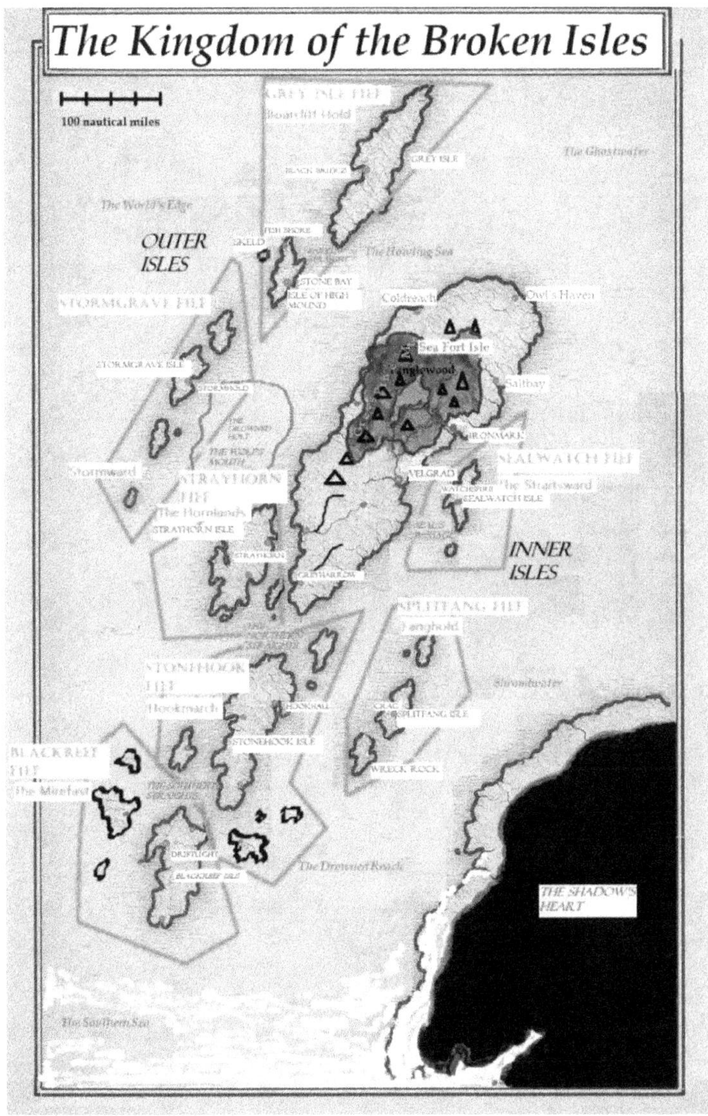

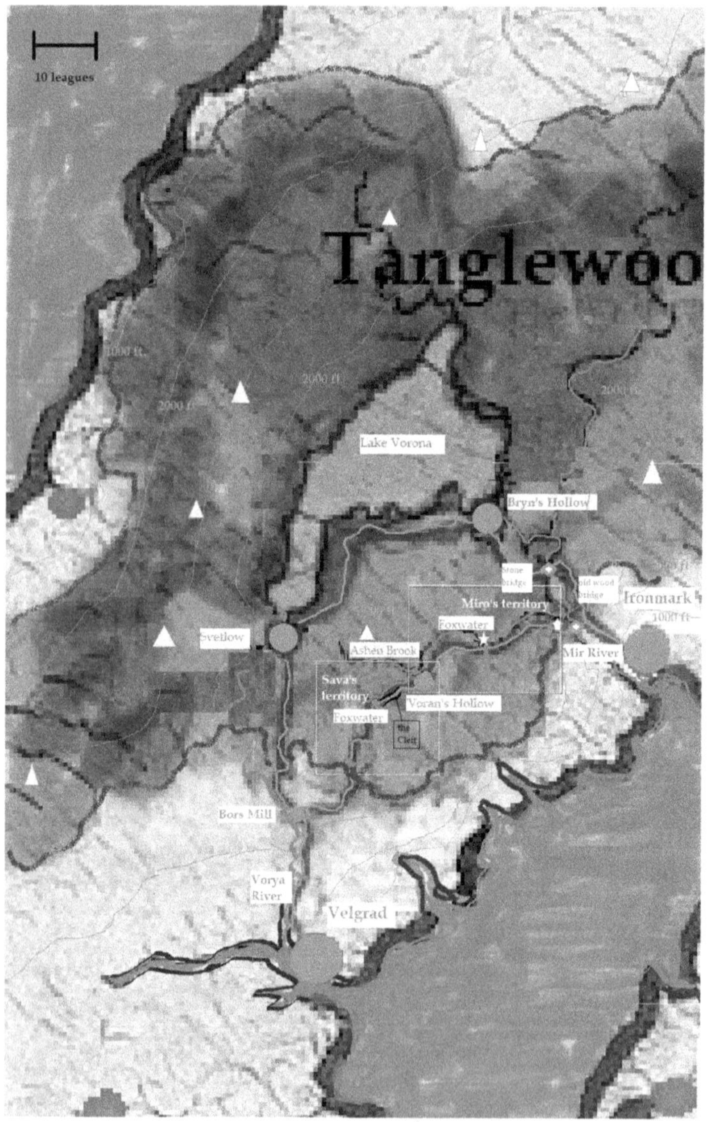

10 leagues
Tanglewoo
1000 ft
2000 ft
2000 ft
2000 ft
Lake Vorona
Bryn's Hollow
Stone bridge
old wood bridge
Ironmark
Miro's territory
1000 ft
Foxwater
Svetlow
Ashen Brook
Mir River
Sava's territory
Voran's Hollow
Foxwater
The Cleft
Bors Mill
Vorya River
Velgrad

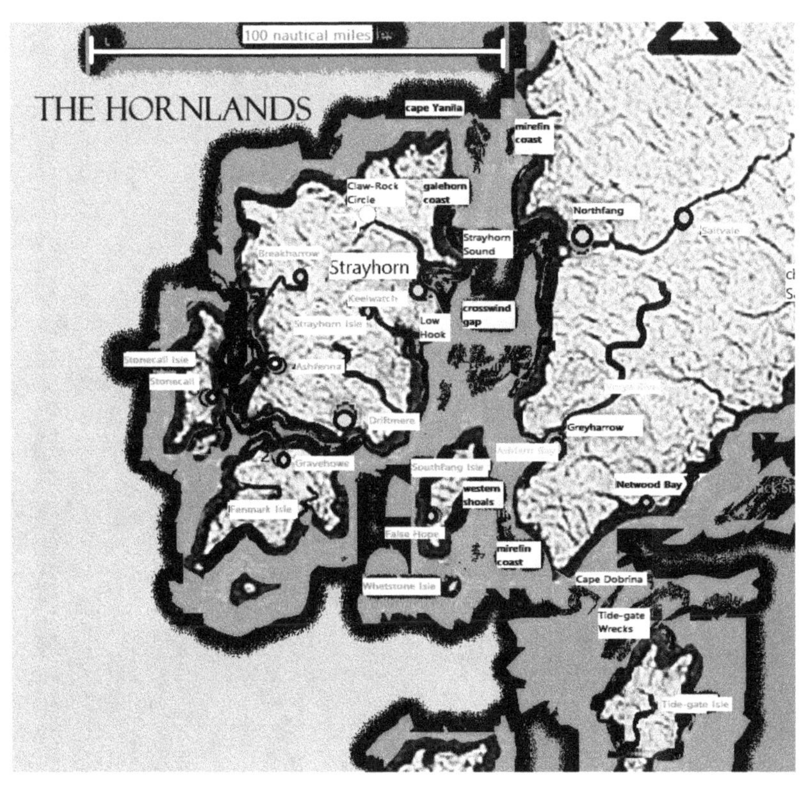
100 nautical miles
THE HORNLANDS
cape Yanila
mirefin coast
Claw-Rock Circle
galehorn coast
Northfang
Saltvale
Breakharrow
Strayhorn
Strayhorn Sound
Keelwatch
Strayhorn Isle
Low Hook
crosswind gap
Stonecall Isle
Ashfenna
Stonecall
Driftmere
Greyharrow
Gravehowe
Southfang Isle
Ashfenn Bay
Netwood Bay
western shoals
Fenmark Isle
False Hope
mirefin coast
Whetstone Isle
Cape Dobrina
Tide-gate Wrecks
Tide-gate Isle

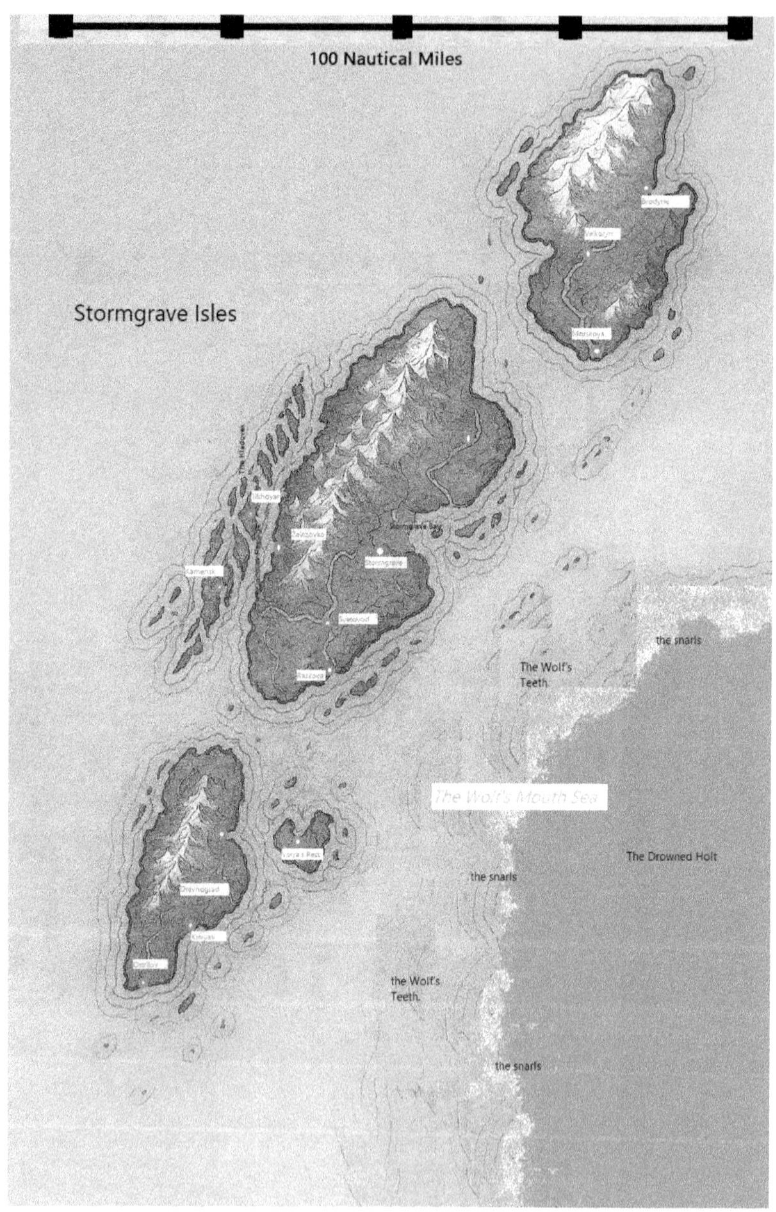

100 Nautical Miles
Stormgrave Isles
Brodyne
Vekseym
Medskoya
The Hidden
Tikhoyar
Ravizovka
Kamensk
Stormgrave
Stormgrave Bay
Svetolvod
Razlovka
Dreynograd
Krovost
Vorga's Rest
Dorinov
The Wolf's Teeth
the snarls
The Wolf's Mouth Sea
The Drowned Holt
the snarls
the Wolf's Teeth
the snarls

Common Saints

Saint Name	Patron of	Symbol	Expanded Lore & Symbolism
Danilo	Warriors, brave deaths	Dented helm	Once a boy-soldier who fell defending a retreat, Danilo was raised to sainthood by the survivors he saved. His helm, caved in by a war-hammer, is preserved in Velgrad's crypt. Warriors invoke him not for victory, but for a worthy death — no shame, no surrender. His rites are grave and spare: a thumb pressed to the brow, a name spoken only once.
Dobrina	Healing, birth, practical mercy	Crossroads	Midwife and wanderer, Dobrina carried herbs in a bone cup and walked barefoot between plague villages. Her death came nursing strangers. Crossroads are marked with her sign — a woven thread or a jar of fennel seeds — where choices must be made. She is called upon in childbirth, pestilence, and grief's wake.

			During the seven-year famine, Dobroslav refused to eat until every child in his village had been fed. His fields alone bore fruit — a miracle or curse, no one knows. Raiders slew him planting spring barley. Each spring, the first seed is cast in his name. His cult remains strongest along the western isles, where soil is poor and hunger constant.
Dobroslav	Farming, rural endurance	A hand scattering grain	During the seven-year famine, Dobroslav refused to eat until every child in his village had been fed. His fields alone bore fruit — a miracle or curse, no one knows. Raiders slew him planting spring barley. Each spring, the first seed is cast in his name. His cult remains strongest along the western isles, where soil is poor and hunger constant.
Ilyin	Fire, judgement, martyrdom	Teeth, bones	Burned alive beneath the old cathedral, Ilyin was said to rise again in flame, screaming warnings that came true. His relics blacken wood but do not burn. Fire-walkers and fanatics claim his blessing. Others call him the Burned One — no longer martyr, but omen. His symbol is feared on storm-prayers, carved with blood into shipbeams.
Kosma	Justice, lawful vengeance, judgement	Chain, fetters	Judge and penitent, Kosma was chained to the altar until he named every man he'd wronged — and forgave each name aloud.

			Salt lines are laid in his name to ward deceit; night vigils kept with iron and silence. His cult is strict and somber: no candles, no indulgence. Only truth, weight, and waiting.
Mikula	Oaths	Cairn	When called to raise arms against kin, Mikula laid down his sword, knelt upon the threshold, and was slain by his own cousin. They say he died smiling, bound to his vow. His cairn is kept by those who swear hard oaths — stones laid in silence, blood or salt between them. To break such a vow is to call his curse.
Olexa	War	Red-marked weapons	Banner-bearer of the last stand at Narven Gate, Olexa bled from five wounds but did not fall. Her banner, red with blood, rallied the broken host. Her symbol is daubed in red ash on spear-points before battle. Warriors say her ghost walks behind those who hold the line.

			Never a leader — always the one who stayed.
Stepan	Endurance, long suffering	Blood	Stepan was dragged behind an oxcart through the tidepools of Dunlev before he spoke a single complaint. His blood marked each hollow in the stone. In his name, penitents walk barefoot through salt shallows, bearing no burden but pain. He is not prayed to, only endured. His grace lies in silence.
Vira	Hearth, widows, home	Key	Vira was a widow who gave her door's key to every refugee who passed, until nothing remained. They found her starved but smiling, holding a child she'd hidden from raiders. Her image stands at thresholds — carved from bone or wood, tucked into lintels. In her name, salt and ash are placed at windows when the sea winds rise.

Yarila	Drowned, exile, fog	Driftwood, black shells	Some say Yarila was never a man, only a name murmured by those lost at sea. Others claim she was a mother whose child was taken by the tide — and she followed. Lanterns are lit in her name when ships depart, placed in hollowed driftwood and set adrift. She answers not prayers, but grief. Her voice is the foghorn no one hears until too late.
Yevstafiy	Drowned, sailors	Driftwood cross	A sailor who bound himself to his mast as the storm claimed his ship, Yevstafiy was found days later — dead, but unbroken. In his name, driftwood crosses are set afloat with candles when a ship is lost. His blessing is endurance, not rescue. Sailors say he walks the deeps, dragging drowned men home.

AUTHOR'S NOTE

The Oathbearer began with a decision to write a novel purely for myself. After several books written for market, I felt worn down. So I resolved not to write toward any shelf or readership, but simply to tell the story I most wanted to read.

The voice came first. I have always loved telling stories in the first person—it feels closer to how I speak in life, when memory and reflection mix with what is said aloud. I am not a young man, and so the voice that arrived was not youthful either. Yaroslav Krovin speaks with grey in his beard and weight in his silences. He is weathered, often grim, but thoughtful in ways only time and loss can teach. His voice owes something to Tolstoy, whose gravity and clarity have long stayed with me.

What followed was *the Prophecy of Flame*—because since Tolkien I have loved the sweep of epic journey and ordeal. Yet I wanted a quest that felt harsher, grittier, more rooted in the soil and salt of history. Much fantasy is written for younger readers or simpler tastes. There is nothing wrong with that, but I sought something else: prose with weight, thought, and a mythology that felt new yet ancient. For that, I turned east. Slavic myth and folklore—with their resonance, cruelty, and beauty—gave me saints who burned, wars that built kingdoms, and oaths that bound tighter than iron. In that soil I planted Yaroslav's confession, and from it grew the tale you now hold: not a prophecy of comfort, but of flame.

This book is the first step of a longer journey. If it finds readers, I am grateful. If it stands only as the book I needed to write, it has already served its purpose.

Should you wish to share your thoughts on The Oathbearer, please stop by www.harwoodjones.com. I'd love to hear from you.

—Troy

9 781069 698513